A World of His Own
In the Land of the Créoles

To John;

I hope you enjoy reading my book as
much as I enjoyed writing it.

Sincerely

Arlette Gaffrey

Arlette Gaffrey

Outskirts Press, Inc.
Denver, Colorado

A World of His Own
In the Land of the Creoles
All Rights Reserved
Copyright © 2007 Arlette Gaffrey
vr 8.0

Outskirts Press
http://www.outskirtspress.com

ISBN-10: 0-9788891-0-X
ISBN-13: 978-0-9788891-0-4

Library of Congress Control Number: 2006933928

Outskirts Press and the "OP" logo are trademarks belonging to
Outskirts Press, Inc.

This book is dedicated to Lee for all
his support.

Special thanks to Jack and Jo. Jack for his help
with my computer, and Jo for her patience
while he helped me.

Also special thanks to my cousin Willie.
She was such a great help also.
Couldn't have done it without her.

Courtyard photograph courtesy of Stanley Beck
www.neworleansphotographs.com

Prologue

The year was 1809, and at twenty-two years of age, André Raphael de Javon was starting out on a new life.

Someone had spotted land. Hearing the call, André rushed up the ladder to the open deck. He hurried to the railing, and shading his eyes, he peered across the span of water. Yes, there it was, the outline of the city.

André leaned against the railing and, taking a deep breath, filled his lungs with the sweet, fresh air. With his eyes closed, he turned his face to the sky. The warm sun was like a soft caress. The pleasant breeze ruffled his hair. Hair that was thick, wavy, and dark brown, highlighted with a tint of auburn.

When he opened his eyes, he could see the city more clearly defined. His gray-green eyes held a look of excitement and a hint of apprehension.

Suddenly, he felt a hand on his shoulder. He turned to find his new friend Charles du Fray standing next to him.

"Well, there she is, André," Charles said. "New Orleans, the most beautiful and exciting city this side of the ocean." He too gazed at the shoreline as it grew closer. "I am so pleased that you have agreed to settle in New Orleans. I know you will not be sorry."

"Well, since I know nothing much about this new country of America, and even less about your city, I feel I should settle where I know at least one person--you."

The two young men had become friends during the long voyage. When they found they were compatible, their friendship grew. During the course of the trip, Charles explained that he was returning home to New Orleans after spending six years in Europe.

"My parents sent me to France to complete my education, and at the end of my schooling, I took the Grande Tour."

He paused with a chuckle. "This is something most young men of means do once they reach sixteen. Our parents think it smoothes out the rough edges."

André nodded. "*Oui*, they do the same in France."

Another day, while they strolled the open deck, André explained a little about his life before and during the French Revolution and the Reign of Terror."

"Even children as young as two were sent to Madame Guillotine. So my little sister and I were smuggled out of France and sent to England. But she died and when I grew up, I didn't know what to do with myself. All that I held dear was gone."

André stopped talking, and seemed to be lost in thought. Then he spoke again. "I've been feeling so restless these past few years that I decided I needed to start a new life; and where better to start anew than in a new country."

Charles smiled at his friend. "I'm happy you made that decision. My parents will be delighted to meet you especially when I tell them how kind you were to me when I became seasick on the voyage."

André stepped away from the railing. "We'd best get below deck and gather our things before the ship docks."

The two friends laughed and joked when they thought about trying to move around in their small cabins.

"I feel like I've been living in a *petite armoire*," Charles said as they parted each to his own quarters to collect his things.

Charles sent a crew member to fetch his servant. As was the custom, the slave had accompanied his young master to Europe. But the servant was so seasick during much of the trip that he was of little use to Charles.

When they reached the open deck, they found the black man waiting for them. "Well, Samuel, you fared no better than I on the ocean," Charles said as he greeted his servant. Are you feeling better now that we are home?"

The young Negro's face broke into a wide smile. "*Oui, Maître*, me not like ship. Glad to be home, *oui*."

"Very well then, go and see about my trunks and those of Monsieur de Javon. And see that they are brought to the house as soon as we dock."

The servant nodded and hurried off. The ship was docking, and the gangplank was being lowered. André looked down at the wharf. All the color and activity amazed him. Black men, their upper bodies bare, muscles rippling and glistening in the hot sun, were loading large containers aboard a ship.

"Those are hogsheads of sugar," Charles explained. "Each hogshead holds 63 gallons of sugar."

Other blacks were rolling large barrels of molasses while still others carried bales of cotton up the gang planks of the ships that were anchored at the dock.

Strange-looking white men mingled about. They wore red shirts and rough-looking trousers, some made of leather. Their faces were covered with hair that made them appear wild. They yelled and spoke in a language Andre' had never heard before.

Other dark-skinned men wearing feathers in their hair and little else sat or stood around.

"Those are Indians," Charles said to André's questioning look. "They won't hurt anyone; they come to the market to sell and trade their wares. Those others are Americans. They come from Kentucky and Tennessee. They sail the barges and keelboats down the river. They're called 'mountain men.' Their English is so abominable one can hardly understand a word they say—an uncouth and savage bunch to say the least. Why, our slaves are more civilized than they are."

Many sights and sounds assaulted André's eyes and ears. His nose was filled with unusual scents of spices from the Orient, of fruit from far-off islands, and of the pungent smell of molasses.

Several carriages with ladies dressed in fine gowns lined up to meet the ship. The gentlemen were standing on the dock. Charles searched the crowd for his parents.

"There they are," he shouted over all the noise. "See that carriage to the right? That's my mother, and there," he indicated an older man making his way through the crowd, "that's my father."

André saw a stately gentleman dressed in the style of the day approaching the ship.

Charles was the first one down the gangplank. He threw his arms around his father, and the two stood for a moment embracing. Smiling, Charles turned to André who stood nearby. "André, I would like you to meet my father, Antoine Delano du Fray. *Pappa*, this is *mon ami,* André Raphael de Javon."

In no time, André had met both of Charles' parents and found himself in a carriage heading for the du Fray home.

Charles spent much of the time telling his parents about the trip and how helpful André had been to him when he was seasick. André, meanwhile, spent the time thinking about his future.

"You will stay with us, won't you, Monsieur de Javon?" Charles' mother asked, breaking into his thoughts.

"*Merci*, Madame. I should be honored to spend a short time with you until I find a place of my own—that is, if you are certain I won't be an imposition."

Monsieur du Fray smiled. "*Non,* Monsieur de Javon. We have a large home, and we would be delighted to have you as our guest."

That settled, Charles went on to relate all that had happened while he was abroad, and André was once again lost in thought. He wondered what his future would be in this strange and extraordinary city.

ANDRÉ
1809–1810

Chapter *1*

New Orleans 1809

"I think it was rude of Charles not to call on you immediately upon his return," Gabrielle Ste. Claire said as she climbed into the open carriage and took her place next to her sister. Fluffing up the lace around the neckline of her gown, she glanced over at Francesca, who remained silent.

Gabrielle continued. "Well, don't you think it was rude of him? After all, you are engaged to him, although he hasn't given you a ring yet."

Francesca shrugged. "I don't think Charles knows we are back in the city. Besides, a gentleman from France returned with him and is staying with the du Frays. At least that is what *Pappa* said this morning at breakfast."

"He did?" Gabrielle's eyes grew wide with interest. "Oh, why didn't I come down to breakfast instead of having mine in my room!" Once again, she waited for her sister to give her more information. "Well, did you learn anything more about the gentleman from France?"

Francesca shook her head. "*Non, Pappa* said nothing more and I didn't ask. And on the subject of Charles' not giving me a ring, how could he, when he's been in France for the past six years?"

Gabrielle gave her sister a look of impatience.

"Really, Francesca, you are so dumb! If I had been downstairs this morning, I certainly would have learnt as much as possible about Charles and his gentleman friend."

Francesca smiled. "Gaby, *chère,* that's the difference between you and me. You're nosy."

"I am *not* nosy!" Gabrielle snapped. "I'm simply interested. There is a difference."

"Oh, let's not quarrel. It's too pretty a morning to be unpleasant. Shall we stop at that little lace shop on *Rue Royale*? I promised *Maman* I'd pick up some lace for her while we're here in the city."

"Oh, I don't care," Gabrielle grumbled, twirling her parasol in annoyance.

The two girls rode in silence as the carriage rolled down the streets of *la Vieux Carré*. Gabrielle, who was two years younger than Francesca, continued to look at her sister with annoyance. Sometimes Francesca could drive her to distraction. The sisters were as diametrically opposite as humanly possible in looks and temperament.

Gabrielle had a head of rich black curls. The color set off her beautiful violet eyes framed with long, thick lashes. Her sister's hair was the color of warm honey, and her eyes were a soft velvety brown. Both were beautiful. Francesca had a quiet, sweet nature, much like their mother's, while Gabrielle was far more volatile, like their father.

The carriage drew up to the shop Francesca had mentioned, and the coachman jumped down to help the sisters alight. They spent several minutes in the store while Francesca selected the lace her mother had requested, and Gabrielle tapped her foot impatiently. Ever since Francesca had mentioned the gentleman from France who had returned with Charles, Gabrielle's only thought was to hurry home and quiz her father thoroughly on the subject.

When the sisters stepped from the shop onto the *banquette,* two young men were coming toward them, and one accidentally bumped into Francesca.

"*Pardonnez-moi, Mademoiselle,*" the man said as he bowed and tipped his hat. Then, suddenly, he stopped and stared. "Francesca? Is it you? Francesca Ste. Claire?" Francesca blushed and looked confused. Both men were now staring at her, and she wasn't sure what to do.

Gabrielle watched while her sister stood tongue-tied and blushing, and she brazenly took hold of the situation.

"*Oui,* this is my sister, Francesca Ste. Claire. But who, Monsieur, are you?"

"Francesca, it's me, Charles...Charles du Fray." Then turning, Charles bowed to Gabrielle. "I'm delighted to see you, Gaby. My, you're all grown up now."

Suddenly, Francesca found her tongue and her eyes grew wide with astonishment. "Charles? Is it really you?"

Charles laughed. *"Oui,* it's me—back from France after all this time. Have I changed so much you didn't know me?"

Charles had indeed changed, and Francesca wouldn't have known him. Gone was the awkward boy of sixteen who never knew what to do with his hands...whose hair always seemed unruly, whose nose was too large for his face, and whose feet were much too big for the rest of him.

Instead, there stood before her a handsome, polished young man with a continental flair. His dark hair now lay in soft, smooth waves. His nose looked perfect in his face, and his six-foot frame had caught up with his feet.

Francesca smiled. "I'm certain we've all changed to some extent in the past six years.

"Ma chère, Francesca, the only way you have changed is to grow more beautiful."

Charles continued to smile at her. Then, clearing his throat, he said, "You must excuse me for not calling on you. First, I had no idea you were back from the country so early. I know the fall season hasn't started yet. And second, I've been involved with my guest. Today, we hope to find him a place of his own on *Rue Barracks."*

The guest Charles referred to had been standing by quietly during the interchange.

"Francesca, Gabrielle, I should like to present *mon ami,* André Raphael de Javon. André, these are the Mademoiselles Francesca and Gabrielle Ste. Claire."

André bowed and tipped his hat. *"Bonjour,* Mademoiselle Gabrielle." Then turning to Francesca, he repeated the gesture. "I'm very happy to meet you both."

"And I am very happy to meet you, Monsieur." Gabrielle lowered her eyes, then lifted them back to André. "Tel me, Monsieur, will you be staying in New Orleans long?"

"Oui, Mademoiselle, I plan to make New Orleans my home." Andre' gave Gabrielle a devastating smile, and she felt her heart begin to race.

"Oh, how delightful, I do hope we will see more of you in the future." Gabrielle dimpled up at the handsome Frenchman, then turned to the other. "Charles, you must bring Monsieur de Javon for a visit

5

tonight." Turning her eyes back to André, she added, "I want to hear all about this nice young gentleman and how he came to choose New Orleans for his new home."

Lowering her eyes again, she looked up at André through her lashes and purred, "You will come for a visit tonight, won't you, Monsieur?"

"Oh really, Gaby," Francesca gave her sister a sharp look. Gabrielle was much too forward. Both *Maman* and *Pappa* had spoken to her about this more than once, but with Gabrielle, talking did little good if she preferred not to listen. "Gaby, *chère,* we must be on our way. I want to stop at the French Market and buy some pralines."

Charles caught Francesca's hand. "I'm so happy I ran into you today. I should like very much to call on you this evening, if I may."

Francesca smiled. "I'd be delighted to have you call, Charles. I look forward to hearing all about your stay in France."

Charles helped both girls into the carriage. But just as she was stepping in, Gabrielle stopped and looked over her shoulder at André. "Charles, you will bring Monsieur de Javon with you this evening, won't you?"

Charles glanced at André, who nodded. "*Oui,* Gaby, I'll bring André, I promise."

As the carriage drove away, Gabrielle looked back at the two men. "Mmmm, that Monsieur de Javon certainly is the most handsome man *I've* ever seen. Don't you agree, Francesca?" When Francesca didn't reply, Gabrielle poked her in the ribs with her elbow. Francesca didn't respond.

"Francesca, what's wrong with you?"

"Nothing is wrong with me. I was just thinking about Charles. He has changed so much and has become very handsome."

Gabrielle gave a rather unladylike snort. "Oh, Charles is nice enough looking, but Monsieur de Javon is *really* handsome. I can hardly wait until tonight when Charles brings him to the house. He is the handsomest man I've ever seen, and I shall make it my business to get to know him better. In fact, I think I shall marry him."

Francesca looked at her sister as if she'd taken leave of her senses, but made no reply. What was the use? Gabrielle would only start another argument if she told her she was crazy to be thinking such thoughts. And it really was too nice a day to quarrel.

Chapter 2

"Well, what do you think of the Mademoiselles Ste. Claire?" Charles asked, as they continued on their way.

"They both seem charming," André said, as they strolled down *Rue Royale*. "But, I wonder that you didn't contact your betrothed as soon as we arrived in the city."

"André, you are my guest. And, as such, my first responsibility was to you; to make certain you felt comfortable and at home. Besides, I knew I would be seeing Francesca in a short while. It would have been the height of ill manners to neglect you."

André smiled. "That was very kind of you."

"I do wish you would stay with us a little longer. There is more than enough room, and my parents enjoy having you."

"I know, Charles, and I do appreciate all the help you and your family have given me. You have been very generous; but now I really must move on."

When they reached the house, André hurried to the bedroom he had occupied, and gathered his things, as he did so he thought back on how it was when he first arrived in the city.

It was true Charles and his parents had opened their hearts and home to him, doing all they could to make him feel like one of the family. But he wasn't; and try as they might, André still felt like an outsider. It was a feeling he'd had most of his life, ever since he'd been taken from his parents during the French Revolution.

Now he wanted more than anything to feel as if he belonged somewhere. To prove to himself that, at twenty-two, he was a man capable of building his own world where he would truly belong.

Today, he and Charles had decided to go on foot.

"If we walk through *la Vieux Carré,* I can show you some places of interest, and we can stop at a coffee shop where you can sample some of our fare."

As they made their way, André saw that not all the streets had *banquettes*; and so, at times, they were forced to walk in the mud. No streets were paved; and when it rained, which it often did, they became almost impassable.

It was as the two strolled down *Rue Royale* that they had run into Francesca and Gabrielle Ste. Claire.

"I am so glad we didn't take the carriage or ride our horses," Charles said with a wide grin. "If we had, I probably wouldn't have seen Francesca. And since I thought they were still in the country, look at what I would have missed."

"How long have you known Francesca?" André asked.

"All my life our families have been close friends for years. In fact, it was our parents who decided we should marry."

"Did either of you have any objections?"

"I can't speak for Francesca; but I certainly didn't. I fell in love with her when I was a little boy. She was so beautiful and sweet," Charles paused and added, "totally unlike her sister. Gabrielle is also beautiful, but she can be very difficult."

They continued down *Rue Royale* until they turned onto *Rue Barracks.* "*Pappa* suggested I take you to *Tante* Suzanne's boarding house. It is the best in the city, and Suzanne keeps the place spotless and serves excellent meals. Ah, here we are."

When they entered the establishment, a beautiful woman, who looked to be in her early thirties, met them. Tall and slender, she had almost blue-black hair, beautiful dark eyes, and a lovely golden tone to her skin. She wore a plain frock but with a grace and air that made it seem more like an expensive ball gown. On her head, she wore a brightly colored kerchief called a *tignon.* It was wrapped around her head like a turban with the ends pointing straight up. Little curls escaped from beneath the *tignon,* and golden earrings shaped like hoops hung from her earlobes. Her features were soft and delicate, and André thought her one of the most beautiful women he'd ever seen.

Once André saw the suite of rooms, he knew he would take them and told Suzanne he would be moving in that day.

The suite consisted of a small sitting room with a fireplace and plenty of light. There was a sofa, a table with four chairs, another large chair, and one smaller table. A comfortable bedroom came next. It too had a fireplace and was well furnished with a bed, dresser, nightstand, and armchair. A smaller bedroom with a single bed, dresser, nightstand, and chair completed the suite.

"The large bedroom is yours, M'sieur; the smaller for your manservant," Suzanne said while André looked around.

After André paid her for the rooms, he and Charles headed for the street. Suddenly, Charles stopped and, turning back, said to Suzanne, "Monsieur's manservant will be here soon with his master's trunks."

When they were back on the street, André said, "Charles, I have no manservant and have no idea where to find one on such short notice."

Charles slapped him on the back. " Don't worry. It has all been taken care of. Just last week, my father bought a young slave. He has decided to give him to you in appreciation for the care you gave me when I was so ill on the ship."

"Give him to me?" André asked in surprise.

"*Oui,* as a gift. You will not have to buy him."

"But, Charles, I have never owned another human being!"

"Oh, *mon ami,* if you plan to live in New Orleans, or anywhere else in the south, sooner or later, you will have to own slaves. There is no way a gentleman can manage here without them. Here, it is a way of life."

André listened to his friend and knew that Charles was right. He was used to servants—had them all his life. But, in his heart, he felt uncomfortable at the thought of owning another person. However, being young, he put the problem out of his mind.

Later that evening, Charles stopped by. "I'm on my way to visit Francesca, and I know if I don't bring you with me, Gabrielle will give me no peace."

André laughed at his friend's expression. "Well, I said I'd go with you; so let's go."

When the two young men reached the Ste. Claire home, the butler ushered them into the parlor where Monsieur Ste. Claire was waiting to receive them. He greeted them both warmly. I'm pleased to meet you,

Monsieur de Javon. And Charles, I'm delighted that you've finally returned. "And he added with a chuckle, "it would seem my daughters are also quite happy."

Within minutes, the sisters appeared. Gabrielle had spent a great deal of time preparing herself for the evening. She wore a gown of midnight blue velvet. Besides being beautiful, Gabrielle was very vain and always dressed in gowns that showed off her slender neck, soft white shoulders, and violet eyes. Most of her gowns for evening also had a rather low *décolletage* that showed off her lovely bosom.

Francesca looked equally fetching in a gown of russet moiré. But, unlike her sister, she preferred a more sedate look.

"Where is Madame Ste. Claire?" Charles asked once the greetings were exchanged. "I hope she hasn't taken ill."

Monsieur Ste. Claire smiled. "Madame Ste. Claire is quite well, thank you. However, she is still in the country. I had to come to the city on business. Gabrielle is never happy when she is away from the city for very long. She badgered me into letting her come also." He gave his youngest daughter an indulgent smile.

"Her mother and I finally agreed but we insisted that Francesca come also."

Charles looked lovingly at Francesca. "I'm certainly happy you are here."

Gabrielle listened to this exchange and became annoyed. Who cared if Charles was happy to see Francesca? He had been in love with her for years.

It was André she was interested in. She jumped into the conversation and managed to change the subject by giving André her most fetching smile. "Do tell us about your decision to settle in New Orleans, Monsieur de Javon. And tell us how you came to meet Charles."

André explained about meeting Charles on the ship. "We seemed to have a lot in common and soon became friends."

Charles picked up the story. "Poor André, I'm not so certain he was all that pleased to meet me. When I became seasick, he spent much of his time nursing me. The rolling of the ship didn't seem to bother him at all. But my poor stomach rebelled most of the way."

Monsieur Ste. Claire asked about Charles' servant.

Charles smiled and shook his head. "Poor Samuel was even sicker than I. He was of no use."

Gabrielle turned back to André. "Pray tell us why you decided to come to Louisiana, Monsieur de Javon."

"There's not much to tell. My little sister and I were smuggled out of France during the Reign of Terror. I was six; she was four at the time. We were sent to live with distant relatives in England."

"Is your sister still in England?" Francesca asked.

"*Non*, my sister is dead. She died shortly after we arrived in England."

"Oh, how tragic," Francesca said. "How did she die?"

"She caught a chill when we crossed the Channel. It went into pneumonia, and she died within three days of our arrival in London."

There was a short moment of silence while each considered this sad news; then once again, Gabrielle brought the subject back to how André came to be in New Orleans.

"There was nothing for me in England once I was grown. I went back to France, but my parents and relatives had all met up with Madame Guillotine, and there was nothing left." He paused. "I've been restless for a long time, and decided I needed a change—thus the voyage across the ocean."

"But what made you choose New Orleans?" Gabrielle insisted.

"Charles convinced me. I had no other plans; so I saw no reason not to take him up on his offer. Besides, from what I understand, this is the nearest to France I will find in this country."

"I'm *sooo* happy you did," Gabrielle cooed.

André raised an eyebrow and smiled. "Mademoiselle, now that I have met you, I am also happy about my decision."

This remark caused Gabrielle's heart to beat even faster. And in that moment, she convinced herself that André was falling in love with her. It would be just a matter of weeks before she would have him proposing marriage, she was certain of it.

"Will you remain in the city long?" Charles asked Monsieur Ste. Clair as he and André prepared to leave.

"*Non,*" his host replied. "We will return to the country this week to finish out the summer. But we should be back sometime in late September or early October."

Gabrielle held her hand out to André, looked at him through her long lashes, and purred, "I'm looking forward to seeing you again when we return to New Orleans, Monsieur." Bowing and kissing her hand, André gave her a knowing look. "I shall be looking forward to seeing more of you, also, Mademoiselle."

Chapter 3

Once Monsieur Ste. Claire and his daughters had returned to the country, Charles introduced André to many of the Créole gentlemen of prominence in the city. The two made the rounds of the coffeehouses, gambling houses, and other amusements available to young men of means. André had been in New Orleans over two months, and now it was nearing the end of August.

"In about a month, Francesca and her family will return to New Orleans, and then the social season will really get underway," Charles said one evening as he and André sat in the courtyard of the du Fray home playing cards.

"I imagine you'll be happy to have Francesca back," André replied, as he swatted a mosquito that had landed on his neck.

"You're right about that. Every summer, the Ste. Claires go to the country, as do most families. They stay with relatives, since they no longer have their own plantation."

Charles shuffled the cards and started dealing. "Summer is always spent in the country, if possible,—not only to avoid the terrible heat of the city but also to escape *Bronze Jean*."

André wrinkled his brow. *"Bronze Jean*? What a strange name. Who is he?"

"It's not a he," Charles answered with a chuckle. *"Bronze Jean* is another name for the yellow fever. It's also called yellow jack. It breaks out almost every summer. Anyway, in the fall, the social season will be in full swing, and you will see why New Orleans is called the most exciting city in the country."

"Why is your family not in the country at this time?" André asked. He wondered if the du Fray family had a place to go to.

"Oh, they would have been, except for the fact that I was returning. Since they had already spent part of the summer out there, *Pappa* decided to return to the city and take care of some business. But you may be sure they will be there next summer. We have two plantations. One will be mine once Francesca and I are married."

A slight breeze blew off the river, and Henry, the butler, had lit the torches in the courtyard so they could see what they were doing. The air was filled with the scent of night-blooming jasmine and magnolia blossoms.

Time passed pleasantly while they continued to play. Both enjoyed a game of cards, and it was nice to sit back and relax after the hectic round of activities the past week.

On this particular night, Charles threw down his cards and pushed his chair back. "Ah, *mon ami,* I shall have to be very careful what stakes I put up when I play with you in the future."

Smiling, André picked up his winnings. "I'll give you a chance to win it back anytime you say."

Although André enjoyed the social activities and took those times to enlarge his acquaintances for future use, still, being of a more serious nature, he knew it was time to start thinking about his future.

Unlike Charles, he couldn't just play. He needed a way to build on the money that had been put into trust for him when he left France as a child. There were few opportunities open to a young man of his aristocratic background. And he spent many a night wondering what it was he should do.

He listened to conversations of men he admired when they spoke about business and making money. An idea began to take hold, and he hoped to speak to Charles about it before long. He knew he would need help and advice and felt his new friend could steer him to the right person or persons for that purpose.

* * *

Early one evening as André sat in his small parlor thinking on this matter, Charles came knocking at the door.

"André," he said as Demetrius ushered him in, "you are in for a treat. With Francesca away, this is the perfect time to introduce you to the Quadroon ball. Do you think you can be ready in about two hours?"

André looked up from his musing *"Oui.* But, Charles, what's a Quadroon Ball?"

"I'll tell you all about it later when I return."

André turned to his servant. "Well, Demetrius, I guess I'm going to a ball. Will you please lay out my evening clothes, while I bathe?"

* * *

Sixteen-year-old Marie Doricour sat cross-legged in the middle of her bed and watched her mother, Yvette, put the finishing touches on the gown she had made. "Oh, *Maman,* it is so beautiful."

"Oui, it is, *chérie.* And it will be even more so when you are wearing it tonight at the ball."

Yvette held up the gown and looked it over carefully. It was lovely and was made of silk muslin in a delicate shade of rose. A silver thread was woven through the fabric. The *décolletage* was cut deep. The sleeves were short and puffed, and a wide silver sash encircled the high waistline.

Marie's honey-colored eyes shone as she reached out and touched the gown. This would be her third Quadroon ball and once again Yvette was determined that her daughter would be the most gorgeous girl there, which would not be difficult.

"Now," Yvette said, as she laid the gown on the bed, "you must soak in a warm bath, and I shall put crushed rose petals in the water so your skin will smell of roses."

Together, she and Marie filled the tub and while Marie soaked, Yvette busied herself getting her own clothes ready for the ball. As she did so, she thought back on when she was Marie's age...

* * *

Yvette had been a house slave on Monsieur Doricour's plantation. She was the daughter of a black mother and a white master of a plantation in the northern part of the territory. Yvette was a mulatto, half Negro and half white.

The master had fallen on hard times and was forced to sell some of his slaves. Yvette and her mother were brought to New Orleans to be sold at the slave market. Yvette was twelve at the time.

Monsieur Doricour bought both the child and her mother. Yvette remembered that he was not married at the time, and she recalled how his eyes followed her whenever she was near him.

Although she was young, she was not unaware of her master's interest in her; and when finally she reached sixteen, Monsieur Doricour made her an offer. He would give her, her freedom, set her up in a little house on the Ramparts in the city, with a servant of her own and a horse and carriage, if she would become his *placée*.

The young girl didn't know what to do; but when she told her mother of the offer, her mother said, "Go, Yvette, let Monsieur Doricour take care of you. You will be free, you'll live like a white woman, and any children you have will be free also. Go, and never look back."

And so, Yvette left the plantation and took up residence in a little house on the Ramparts. For three years, it was heavenly...

* * *

"*Maman*, the water's getting cold. I want to get out," Marie's voice broke into her mother's thoughts.

"All right, *chérie*."

Once Marie was dried and in her underclothes, Yvette fixed her hair, and it looked beautiful. It was caught up on top of Marie's head in a mass of curls. A wide silver band was wound around the curls, and a rose, the same color as her gown, was pinned in the back. Then Yvette helped her daughter into the gown.

Marie stood smiling at her mother then twirled around. "Do I look pretty, *Maman*?" Her eyes sparkled, and her cheeks were flushed.

"You look beautiful, Marie, and you will be the most sought-after girl at the ball." Yvette's eyes glowed with love and pride.

Marie waltzed over to the full-length mirror and stood looking at herself for a long moment. "Oh, *Maman* I *do* look pretty." She clapped her hands in sheer delight and whirled around again. "*Maman*, I hope I meet a wonderful, handsome, wealthy gentleman who will fall madly in love with me."

"Well, several gentlemen have shone a great deal of interest in you, Marie. Monsieur Laurent, for one. He has already approached me about becoming your protector."

Marie nodded. *"Oui,* I know *Maman* but I don't love him. I want to be in love with the man who becomes my protector."

Her mother looked at Marie with sad eyes, started to say something, then changed her mind.

* * *

On the corner of *Rue Condé* (later a part of *Rue Charters*) near *Rue St. Ann,* there stood a large barn like building. It was here the Quadroon Balls, or *Bals du Gordon Bleu,* as they were properly called, were held.

The ballroom was large. The ceiling high and the huge crystal chandeliers, with their thousands of candles, cast a bright glow on the golden skin of the beautiful young girls dressed in elegant gowns. The candles caught the sparkle of the jewels that adorned the arms, throats, ears, and hair of the girls.

The air was festive, and Marie was filled with excitement and wonder as she entered the room. The sight never failed to cause her heart to beat faster. The other girls looked so beautiful, and the men so handsome in their evening clothes.

From the first night that she had appeared at a ball, Yvette had prepared her daughter well. In fact, Marie's entire life had been in preparation for the balls.

"You must wait until one of the girls introduces you to her gentleman friend, who may in turn introduce you to some of his friends," Yvette said. "These men must never for a moment get the wrong idea and think of you as cheap."

Marie was by nature shy, and the scene before her never ceased to overwhelm her.

"Marie."

She looked around and saw her friend Cecile.

"Oh, Marie, I'm so happy you're here. I've so much to tell you."

Cecile was a few months older than Marie and had already attended several more balls. She took Marie's hand and led her to a corner of the room.

"Marie, Monsieur Moniere has asked to be my protector. He and *Maman* will be working out the arrangement this week. Oh, Marie, think of it. I shall have my very own home, a servant, a cook, and maybe even a horse and carriage!" Cecile's ebony eyes danced with excitement.

16

"I'm very happy for you, Cecile." Marie smiled as she looked around. "Where is Monsieur Moniere?"

"He's over there with that group of gentlemen," Cecile indicated with a nod. "Come let us go and speak to them."

Marie glanced around for her mother, but Yvette had already joined the other mothers. They sat at the side on a slightly raised platform, like so many brightly colored birds.

Each mother was dressed as fine as her daughter, in gowns equally as stunning. Around their necks were jeweled necklaces or pearl chokers. They looked like wealthy dowagers or *grandes dames* at an important ball. And it was an important ball for these mothers. It was important for their daughters and their futures.

These young girls were not cheap. All were virgins, and their chastity was guarded as carefully as any white girl's. They were also as well educated as any white girl of the times. Some had private tutors; others went to a private school run by a small group of Negro nuns. They learnt to read and write, to sew and sing. Most played the pianoforte, all took dancing lessons. They were taught grace and elegance to speak in a soft, pleasing voice; to have refined manners; and to always conduct themselves as ladies.

So the mothers watched. And Yvette watched as closely as the others. If any young girl looked unhappy or uncomfortable in the company of one of the men, one glance toward her mother would send the latter hurrying to her side, where the older woman would manage with skill and diplomacy to remove her daughter from the offending man's company.

Yvette saw several young men surround Marie. She observed her daughter being swept onto the dance floor by first one and then another of the gentlemen. The mothers also compared notes.

"Yvette," one mother whispered. "See who your Marie is dancing with? That is Monsieur Laurent's son. Remember Monsieur Laurent? He was Marguerite's protector at one time."

Yvette nodded. Marguerite was sitting a few chairs away, watching her own daughter.

Marguerite's protector had left her shortly after he married. He could no longer keep her. Yvette recalled how heartbroken her friend had been.

That was the way it was for the quadroon women. A *liaison* could last a lifetime or it could last a few months. And each mother made her daughter aware of this fact. It was better not to fall in love. Better to accept the protector with a feeling of fondness, but not love, *non* love only led to heartache.

Being a white man's *placée* had its advantages. A quadroon woman and her children were free. She had her own home and even servants. But one's heart could be broken in time. However, there was always hope that her *liaison* would last a lifetime.

Chapter *4*

Later, when Charles returned to André's home, he smiled and said, "Now we go to the Quadroon Ball."

Once André was settled in the carriage, he turned to Charles. "Now, please explain to me about this Quadroon Ball. And what exactly is a quadroon?"

"Quadroons are the children of a mulatto mother and a white father," Charles explained. "The women are said to be some of the most beautiful in the world."

"And the Ball?"

"The Ball is the place where the young quadroon girls can meet wealthy white gentlemen. And only the *crème de la crème* of New Orleans gentlemen are allowed into the balls."

"But why do they need a ball? Can't they meet the gentlemen other places?" André was having a difficult time understanding what this was all about. "Do they hope to marry any of these gentlemen?"

"*Non*, of course not. A person of color can't marry a white. It's against the law. But let me start at the beginning. You see, there was a time when the quadroon women went about the city dressed in their beautiful gowns, adorned with the jewels given to them by their white protectors. They flaunted themselves every chance they could.

The Créole women knew of the quadroons and many of them knew their husbands kept such a woman in a house on the ramparts. They hated the idea; and when they could, they forced their husbands to give the girl up. When they couldn't, they tried to ignore the situation—a fact that was difficult to do when the quadroons flaunted themselves so."

"So, what happened?"

"Well, the Créole women made such an outcry, that finally in 1778, the Spanish Governor Miro issued a proclamation called a *bando de buen gobierno*. It forbids the quadroon women to appear in public wearing their finery. Henceforth, they had to always dress in plain, simple gowns. No jewelry other than a pair of gold hoops may be worn in their ears, and their heads must be covered at all times with a handkerchief, called a *tignon*."

"That doesn't seem fair."

"Oh, well, they got around the rules. At the Balls, the mothers and daughters can adorn themselves with all the fine clothes and jewelry they possess, and they can fix their hair in elaborate styles. At the Balls, they do not have to wear the *tignon*. Many of the girls hope to become the *placée* of a white man."

"Well, you've told me about the women, but what about the men? Or don't these people have sons?"

"Of course, they have sons. Some of them are so fair you would never know they had a drop of Negro blood in their veins.

"If the son is extremely fair, he is often sent to France to be educated, and hopefully remain in France, and marry white. If his skin is too dark, he's given a piece of land on which to live."

"Do quadroons ever marry each other?"

"Some do, but mostly the women look to a wealthy white man to be their proctor, while many of the men become very successful with their own plantations and have their own slaves."

Charles paused. "*Tante* Suzanne at the boarding house is a quadroon. When her protector got married and had to give her up, he bought her the boarding house so she could support herself and their children."

Just then, the carriage came to a halt.

"Ah, here we are."

When he stepped out of the carriage, André heard the sound of music and laughter coming from within. After checking their hats and gloves in the vestibule, he and Charles entered the ballroom.

Standing there observing the scene before him, André saw it was just as Charles had said Young girls dressed in beautiful gowns twirled about the dance floor in the arms of handsomely dressed men.

As his eyes swept the ballroom, André saw her.   Several men surrounded her. She was a true beauty, and he watched her laugh and speak to the men. She looked up; and when she did, her eyes met his. Neither could look away. Just then, Charles touched his arm.

"Come, André, I want to introduce you to my friends."

André tore his eyes from hers and followed Charles to where some men were gathered. After the introductions and a little conversation, Charles turned and said, "Well, André, is there any young girl, in particular, you'd like to meet?"

"*Oui*, that beautiful girl in the rose-colored gown the one with the unusual eyes." André glanced toward Marie. "Do you by chance know her?"

Charles followed his gaze. "I certainly do. Her name is Marie Doricour. Come, I will introduce you."

Her beauty struck André the moment he laid eyes on her. She was tall and slender with hair a lovely shade of dark brown. The candles showed the rich auburn highlights in her curls. Her skin was a warm shade of gold, and her features were fine and delicate. Her catlike eyes were fascinating. They were an unusual color, almost golden brown, with dark flecks showing through them, and framed with thick, long, dark lashes.

When he asked her to dance, André found she was as graceful as she was beautiful. Her voice was soft and easy on the ears, low and slightly breathless. The fragrance surrounding her was the scent of roses.

"I have never seen you here at the Quadroon Ball before, Monsieur," Marie said as they glided across the floor.

"Mademoiselle, this is my first time. And you? Have you come to many balls?"

"This is my third ball, Monsieur."

André smiled. "Do you enjoy these balls, Mademoiselle?"

Marie nodded. "*Oui*, I love to dance, and I love to get all dressed up. And the balls are fun."

"Well, since this is the first time for me, I think we should have a glass of wine and drink a toast to our first meeting at my first Quadroon Ball."

When the music stopped, André took her hand, but before they got very far, a short, dark-haired man walked up to them.

"Marie, I believe this next dance is ours."

"I'm sorry, Gerard, but I have promised the next dance to this gentleman."

Marie paused, "Monsieur de Javon, this is Monsieur Gerard

21

Laurent." Once the two men had acknowledged each other, Marie said, "*Pardon*, Monsieur Laurent, Monsieur de Javon and I are stepping out to the courtyard."

"Very well, but do not stay too long; I will still claim a dance with you before the night ends." Gerard bowed, but from his expression, André knew he wasn't too happy about Marie's leaving.

Together, the two stepped outside and sat at a small table. There was one candle and a single rose in a delicate vase on the table. The courtyard had a fountain in the middle, and there were many flowers and several trees. The air was filled with the fragrance from the flowers; and the tinkle of the water in the fountain, plus the music wafting from within, made for a very romantic atmosphere.

André ordered the wine, and when it was served, he lifted his glass and smiled at Marie. "I should like to propose a toast to us, to our first meeting, and to you, Mademoiselle Doricour, for making my visit such a special one. I shall look forward to attending more balls in the future. Providing, of course, you are here also."

Marie gave him a lovely smile.

"Now, tell me all about yourself," André said as he took a sip of wine and leaned back in his chair.

"There really isn't much to tell, Monsieur. What would you like to know?"

"I would like to know all about you. For starters, where do you live?"

"I live with my mother on the *Rue des Ramparts. Maman* is a seamstress; she makes beautiful clothes for some of the wealthiest ladies in New Orleans."

André reached across the table and took her hand. "Now I know about *Maman*. But it's you I want to know about."

Marie's heart skipped a beat. "There really isn't much to tell, Monsieur. I am sixteen years old; I can read and write. I sing and play the pianoforte a little."

She took a sip of her wine, and said in her soft, husky voice, "You know all about me, Monsieur. But I know nothing about you. Won't you please tell me something about yourself?"

André told her everything including his decision to settle in New Orleans. "I must decide what I want to do with my future now that I'm here. I have an idea, but I must first speak to Charles concerning my interest before I can put it into action."

André cleared his throat and then said, "Tell me a little about this

Monsieur Laurent. He didn't seem to appreciate your leaving the ballroom with me."

"Monsieur Laurent has approached my mother about being my protector."

"And how do you feel about that?"

Marie raised her eyes to André. "I do not want him for my protector. I want to be in love with the man I accept. I want to be the *placée* of one who will love me also."

There was a long pause. André cleared his throat again and said, "I think we should return to the ballroom. The evening will be ending soon, and I should enjoy another dance with you."

They went back into the ballroom where they spent much of the time on the dance floor, although Gerard Laurent did manage to snag a few dances with Marie.

When the evening drew to a close, Marie looked up at André with hopeful eyes. "Will you come back to the next ball, Monsieur? There will be another one in three weeks."

"*Oui*, Mademoiselle. If it is at all possible, I'll come again; especially if you will be here also." André's eyes caressed Marie's face. She was so beautiful.

* * *

"So, did you enjoy the ball?" Charles asked, as the carriage headed to André's home.

"*Oui*, it was very pleasant."

"And Marie Doricour? Was she very pleasant also?"

André smiled. "Marie is a lovely young girl, and I enjoyed meeting and dancing with her very much." André seemed preoccupied.

"There will be another ball soon. Would you care to go again?"

Coming out of his deep thoughts, André nodded. "I told Marie I'd be there; so, *oui*, I'd like to go. But Charles, sometime soon, when you have a minute, I would like to talk to you about some thoughts I have concerning my future."

"Of course, André anything I can do to help, I'd be happy to do."

* * *

"Oh, *Maman*, he is *so* handsome and wonderful!" Marie exclaimed softly as her mother helped her get ready for bed. "He is such a gentleman, so sweet, and kind, and such an excellent dancer. *Maman*, do you think he will ask to be my protector?"

"I don't know, *chérie*. Only time will tell. But he did say he would attend the next ball, so I'm sure he is interested in you." There was a long pause, then Yvette said, "Monsieur Laurent once again asked about being your protector. He would take excellent care of you if you accept him."

"But, *Maman*, I don't love him, and I couldn't be happy as his *placée*. It is Monsieur de Javon who has captured my heart. And, I think he likes me very much. He danced with no other girl all evening. And several of the girls were hoping he would ask them." Marie gave a sigh and plopped down in her bed.

"You've had an exciting evening, *chérie*. Now it's time to sleep. We'll talk more about it in the morning." Yvette leaned down and kissed her daughter. "Sleep well, my love, and pleasant dreams." Blowing out the candle, she left the room.

Marie lay in the darkness and relived the entire evening. She knew in her heart André was the one for her. But would she be the one for him? Oh, how she hoped and prayed she was. And before she closed her eyes for sleep, she offered up a little prayer.

Marie had no way of knowing that, all too soon, Andre's life would change so that all thoughts of her and the Quadroon Ball would be completely swept from his mind. It would be a long time before she saw him again.

Chapter 5

A few days later, André told Charles what it was he hoped to do with his future. "I want to own land and lots of it," he said, his voice filled with excitement. "I want to build a house, a big, beautiful house. I want to be a planter and own the largest plantation in the entire territory someday."

He paused for a moment and ended by saying, "Ever since I was taken from France as a small child, I have felt displaced. Now, I want a place where I will feel I truly belong."

However, when Charles questioned him, André admitted he had no knowledge of the land, of planting, or of harvesting; and had yet to even see a plantation.

"Well, then, we must take matters in hand," Charles replied. "You must meet and speak with one of the most successful planters in the territory, Monsieur Jean-Claude Charlevoix. He has a large plantation, knows more about planting than most, and has been extremely successful. He is also a close friend of my family."

"How soon do you think we could meet with this Monsieur Charlevoix?" André asked, his excitement mounting. "Now that I've decided what I want to do, I don't want to waste any more time."

Charles laughed and shook his head. "Oh, *mon ami*, you certainly are in a hurry to give up all this fun and pleasure and get to work. I do admire that in you, however, you do not seem to have a great deal of patience. And in this climate, you will have to learn to relax. But, don't worry, I'll send off a note at once."

A note was sent, an invitation was extended, and now the two friends found themselves about an hour on the road having slowed their horses to a walk.

It was late August, an especially hot and humid morning. The road was dusty, but the surrounding countryside was lush and green with all form of vegetation.

On one side rose a high man-made levee that kept the Mississippi River from reclaiming the land, since most of New Orleans and the surrounding countryside was below sea level.

Flooding was always a problem, and the levees helped curb it. These levees were almost as high as a small foothill. One could not see the river from the road. Nor could you see the river from the front *galerie* of a house.

Huge oak trees, their great branches draped with gray-green Spanish moss, lined the opposite side and provided some shade for the travelers.

As Charles and André rode along, a carriage suddenly appeared from around a bend. It slowed down when it drew near, and André saw that it held a little girl and her Negro maid. A large black man in fancy livery was driving.

When the carriage drew abreast, Charles suddenly called out, "*Bonjour,* Joshua. It's me, Charles du Fray."

The coachman brought the carriage to a halt and smiled. "*Bonjour, Michie* du Fray, Ah sho' is happy to see you, *oui.*"

Charles then turned his attention to the child in the carriage. "*Bonjour,* Julie, *bonjour* 'Toinette."

The black woman greeted him, and the little girl smiled. "Oh, Charles is it really you? How good to see you. *Pappa* said you had returned from Europe and that we might run into you on the road today. It's been such a long time."

"Indeed it has been a long time, Julie. Why, the last time I saw you, you were a mere baby of five. And now look at you! At eleven years old, you have grown into a beautiful young lady."

"Do you really think so, Charles?" The child's face was aglow with the compliment.

"Why, indeed I do," Charles assured her. "When you make your debut in a few years, you will be the Belle of New Orleans."

While this exchange was taking place, André sat quietly studying Julie. She certainly was a little beauty. Her features were exquisite. She blushed slightly at Charles' compliment. Then her eyes slid over to André.

Charles caught the look. "Forgive my rudeness, Julie. I was so taken back by how you've grown, I quite forgot my manners."

Introductions were quickly made and Julie turned her face to André and gave him a dazzling smile. He saw that she possessed a row of perfect white teeth, and a tiny dimple appeared at each corner of her mouth.

André smiled and tipped his hat. "I'm honored to meet such a lovely young lady."

"*Merci*, Monsieur," Julie responded softly as her cheeks turned pink once more.

"Tell me, Julie, where are you going so early in the day?" Charles asked. "Why, it's barely nine o'clock."

Julie frowned and wrinkled her small nose. "Oh, *Pappa* is sending me back to the Convent. He wanted us to leave before it got too hot."

Charles looked surprised. "The Convent?"

Julie laughed, and her laughter was soft and sweet like the tinkling of tiny bells. "*Oui, Pappa* says they must have more time to tame me."

"And how do you like the Convent?"

Julie shrugged. "It's all right, I guess. The nuns are very strict." Then, with a smile and a nod of her head, she added, "But I am learning many interesting things. They've taught me to read and write and all sorts of things."

While they spoke, André continued to study Julie and smiled to himself. It was obvious she was trying to act quite grownup, and there was something endearing about her efforts.

She wore a gown of soft yellow, its bodice was sheered, and the neckline was trimmed in a delicate lace. In her small, gloved hand, she held a tiny parasol to shade her from the sun. Her hair, which flowed from beneath a bonnet, was a thick, rich mane of dark curls that caught the sunlight and threw back highlights of gold and copper.

But it was her beautiful eyes that held André captivated. They were almond-shaped and so dark the pupils were not visible. Her lashes were thick and long. Her perfect eyebrows were shaped like the tips of a bird's wings.

Sweet Mother in heaven, he thought, *if she is this beautiful at eleven, how many hearts will she break when she reaches sixteen?*

Charles was laughing at something Julie had said. "Well, *chérie*, we certainly must not keep the good sisters of the Ursuline waiting. They are probably standing at the door watching for the wild bird *Pappa* is sending them."

Julie frowned and sighed "I'd much rather go home and visit with you. But I guess it's not to be." She shrugged and smiled again, "*Au revoir,* Charles, *Au revoir,* Monsieur de Javon."

* * *

When the carriage had traveled a short distance, Julie turned to her maid, "Is he not the most handsome man you've ever seen, 'Toinette?"

The maid smiled and nodded her head, "*Oui,* Mam'selle Julie, *Michie* du Fray be one fine lookin' man, heem."

"Oh, 'Toinette, I don't mean Charles, although he too is very handsome. I mean Monsieur de Javon."

There was a long silence and then, almost to herself, Julie said, "Someday when I am grown, I shall marry Monsieur de Javon."

'Toinette looked over at her young mistress and the look was one of shock. "*Michie* de Javon, he be grown man. You be *petitè fille* you only eleven year old. You be too young fo' grown man."

Julie shook her head. "But 'Toinette, I will grow up. Then Monsieur de Javon won't think me a child." Throwing a look of determination the servant's way, she added, "And 'Toinette, I promise you someday I will marry him!"

Chapter 6

After the carriage moved on, Andre and Charles resumed their journey to *Château Charlevoix* as the plantation was named.

André was the first to speak. "If the mother is as beautiful as the child, Monsieur Charlevoix is indeed a fortunate man."

"The mother was as beautiful, and Monsieur Charlevoix was a most fortunate man," Charles replied.

André raised an eyebrow. "Was?"

Charles nodded. "*Oui*, Julie's mother died in childbirth when Julie was three years old. The baby was stillborn."

"How tragic," André said softly. "That must have been very difficult on the man."

"It was. I don't think he's ever completely recovered from her death." A short time later, Charles stopped his horse. "Well, here we are. This is *Château Charlevoix*."

They turned their horses onto a long drive of oak trees, which led to a very large house built high off the ground. When they drew near, André saw that the *galerie* (as the Créoles called their porches) ran the entire length of the front and extended to the sides. The second story also had a *galerie*, smaller in size, that extended across the front and around the sides.

The house was built of brick and wood from the cypress trees so common to the area. The roof, which slanted on all four sides, extended well beyond the exterior of the house.

"What a strange-looking roof," André said.

"It's made that way to afford shade and a breeze, if there is a breeze on the hot days of summer," Charles explained.

Tall, square brick columns rose up to support the house. Giant oak trees surrounded it, and beautiful flowers grew in abundance. Their heavy fragrance filled the air, and Andre could hear bees buzzing around them in the stillness.

As they rode along, André saw that on each side of the main house stood a smaller replica. "What are those two houses for?"

"Those are *garçonnières*," Charles replied. "Many *Creole* families are quite large, and so most planters build them to accommodate the bachelor sons or guests who come to visit."

A small boy suddenly appeared, and the stillness was broken as the child ran towards the house, shouting at the top of his lungs, "Company comin', company comin'!"

When they reached the front steps, a well-dressed man was waiting to greet them. He was of medium height and slender build. His hair was dark and curly, with touches of gray around his temples. His eyes were much like his daughter's; the same almond shape, same darkness, and the same thick lashes. He was an extremely handsome man.

The two riders dismounted and gave their horses to the stable boy who led them away.

"Charles, how good to see you." The man came down the steps to embrace his friend. "Let me look at you. My, you've grown into a fine young man these past six years." He patted Charles on the back. He then turned to André. "This must be the young man you wrote about."

"*Oui*, Monsieur Charlevoix. This is André de Javon. André, this is Monsieur Jean-Claude Charlevoix."

Once the introductions and greetings were exchanged, Monsieur Charlevoix invited his guests into the house.

The rooms were enormous with ceilings reaching sixteen feet in height; and from the ceiling of each room hung beautiful chandeliers of sterling silver and crystal. The floors were of the highest grade of wood and so richly polished that they seemed like dark mirrors. Exquisite furniture made from rosewood and mahogany graced each room. The home exuded good taste and wealth.

"You two must be hungry after your long ride. Come, we'll have a bite to eat." Their host led them into the dining room.

Entering the room, André saw a table large enough to seat twenty-five comfortably. Once they took their places, Monsieur Charlevoix asked, "Did you meet my Julie on your way out?"

Charles smiled, "*Oui*, Monsieur we did. I wouldn't have known her but for Joshua and 'Toinette. She certainly is a beautiful child and looks a lot like her mother."

Just then, the servants entered with dishes and trays of food. There were slices of ham; fresh eggs; grits; several meats cooked *a la grillades*; and warm, delicious *brioches* plus steaming cups of *café au lait*.

While they ate, a small black boy sat in the corner and pulled a cord that was attached to the *punkah*, a huge fan that hung from the ceiling and stretched across the middle of the table. It swung back and forth with each pull of the cord, creating a gentle breeze, making the room more comfortable.

When they finished the meal and were enjoying their *café au lait*, Monsieur Charlevoix turned to André. "So, young man, you want to become a planter."

"*Oui*, Monsieur Charlevoix."

"Well, tell me, have you ever done any planting?"

André shook his head. "Monsieur, I know nothing about planting."

Monsieur Charlevoix looked at him for a long moment. "You know nothing about planting?"

"*Non*, Monsieur. In fact, this is first plantation I have ever seen."

"And you want to be a planter." His host murmured, shook his head, then laughed. "Well, young man, you haven't seen this one yet so I think we had better get started so you can see what owning a plantation is all about. Once you see what is involved, you might change your mind."

The older man pushed back his chair, rose from the table, and ordered their horses to be brought around to the front.

For the better part of the day, the three men toured the vast plantation. As they rode to the back of the house, André was surprised at the many buildings.

"I had no idea all these buildings where here. I didn't see any of them from the front of the house."

Monsieur Charlevoix smiled and glanced over at his young guest. "You are not supposed to see them from the front. It would spoil the appearance of the house."

First, there was the huge kitchen with three large fireplaces and several brick ovens; and it was filled with activity. A dozen black women were busy preparing food.

"During harvest time, all meals for everyone on the place are cooked here," Monsieur explained. "That is why it's so busy."

To André's question, his host explained that the kitchen was built away from the house in case of fire. A whistle walk connected the kitchen to the main house. It helped shelter the servants from the rain when they brought food from the kitchen to the dining room.

Further away, André saw the plantation office. "Here is where my overseer and I go over the books," Monsieur Charlevoix explained. "And here are the stables, carriage house, and blacksmith shed. I have those three grouped together for obvious reasons." He also pointed out the leather and candle huts near by.

"The men who work on the leather make all of the bridles and such that we use. They also make shoes for the slaves. The candles are made for every house on the plantation, including the slave quarters. You see, Monsieur de Javon, when you own a plantation you must be totally self-sufficient: You can't go to the store and get something you need at the drop of a hat."

There were still more buildings; the smokehouse where meat was kept, the summerhouse that stored vegetables, and last, the storage bin for the zinc-lined box that held ice.

They came to another long building set apart from others.

"This is our infirmary where slaves with a serious illness or accident stay until they are well again. And way over there in the distance is my overseer's home."

Finally, they came to what Monsieur Charlevoix called the "village." And, indeed, it resembled a small village with row upon row of small cabins each with its own yard surrounded by a picket fence. In actuality, these were the slave quarters.

Off in the distance stood a giant two-story building made entirely of brick, its tall chimneys reaching to the sky. Smoke poured from the chimneys, and the sound of a grinding machine could be heard as the three approached.

"That's my sugar factory," Monsieur Charlevoix said. "Sugar cane is the real money maker in this region of the territory. Would you like to see the interior?"

André assured him he would; so the three men dismounted and went in. As they entered, they were hit with the pungent smell of molasses, which was overpowering. The place was extremely hot, and it was a beehive of activity. Black men, with sweat pouring from their bodies, were busy working. Two oxen hitched to a large wheel walked in an endless circle.

"They make the grinding machine work," his host explained.

For the next half hour, André walked around watching the men labor. He saw two large black men lift a huge vat of melted sugar cane and place it in a cooling bin.

Suddenly, there was a loud scream. It sounded like someone was in great pain.

"*Michie, Michie Charlevoix*, come quick," a voice cried out.

Monsieur Charlevoix rushed to where the voice came from, with Charles and André close on his heels.

André was shocked to see one of the slaves lying on the floor writhing in pain. The man's arm had been seriously scalded.

"Petie, he get burned by melted cane, *oui*," said one of the men who was kneeling by the injured worker.

"Well, we must get him to the infirmary at once," Monsieur Charlevoix said. "And someone go for *Tante* Aurea. Tell her to bring her special ointment."

The three white men mounted their horses and slowly followed the four black men who carried Petie to the infirmary and laid him on a cot.

In another minute, *Tante* Aurea entered carrying a large jar. She pulled a stool next to the cot, and singing softly, she gently spread the salve over the scalded flesh. Poor Petie whimpered and moaned, but the black woman continued to sing and make soothing sounds. In a few minutes, she had the burnt flesh wrapped in a clean white cloth, and in another minute, she gave the injured man something to drink. Turning to Monsieur Charlevoix she said, "Petie sleep now. He need lots of rest to heal. I stay with him."

Her master nodded. "*Oui, Tante* Aurea, I want you to stay with him as long as you feel you should. And I want you to call me if he has a fever or takes a turn for the worse."

When the three men stepped out of the building into the bright sunlight, André felt almost blinded by the light.

"That was a terrible accident," he said.

"*Oui*, it was, Monsieur de Javon. But that is one of the things you must always be prepared for, although we seldom have such accidents. I am very fortunate to have *Tante* Aurea. She can cure almost any ailment the slaves have."

"But where did she learn all of that?" André asked.

Charles stepped in. "André, these women learn it from childhood. Every plantation usually has at least one slave who can take care of the others. We have one on our plantations."

"Well, shall we continue with our tour? Or would you rather go to the house?" Monsieur Charlevoix asked his guests.

Both young men agreed they would like to continue.

"Besides," Charles said with a chuckle. "I'm learning as much as André. You know, Monsieur, as soon as Francesca and I are married, my father will give me one of our plantations."

"Do you know which one you will have?"

"*Pappa* said he would give me Oak Grove. But either one would be fine with me, since they are both very successful."

Monsieur Charlevoix led them out to the fields of sugar cane. As far as the eye could see, there were rows and rows of the tall green stalks.

And there were miles and miles of cotton fields that made the ground look like it was covered with snow, and André smiled to himself. *Snow in this heat*! he thought as sweat dripped from his brow into his eyes.

The last place Monsieur Charlevoix took them was to the swamp. Several slaves were chopping down trees. "It takes a great deal of wood to keep the fires in the sugar factory burning day and night," his host explained.

It was late in the day when they decided to return to the big house. But before that, Monsieur insisted on stopping to see how Petie was doing. André was impressed with the man's sincere compassion for his slave.

By the time they reached the house, all three were tired, hot, and hungry. Much to his relief, André found his host had two bedrooms ready for his guests.

"Beau will show you to your rooms," their host explained as he pulled a bell cord and a tall black butler appeared. "After you have bathed and rested, we will dine together."

In a few minutes, André found himself standing in a large bedchamber. The French windows and doors reached almost to the ceiling. On one side of the room stood a lofty four-posted bed with a canopy of rich satin gathered in the middle and held by a beautiful golden medallion. Across the room was an armoire that was as tall as the windows.

There was a marble-top dresser against one wall with a large china bowl and pitcher. The hardwood floor shone as brightly as the floors below, and part of it was covered with a thick, lush carpet.

Lace curtains and satin drapes hung at the windows and French doors. André noticed a screen standing in another corner of the room. He walked over and peeked around and found a large slipper-shaped tub.

"*Michie* would like to refresh hisself, take a bath, *oui*?"

André smiled and nodded. "*Oui*, Beau, I should like that."

Beau bowed, left the room, and in just a few minutes, he returned followed by two young slaves each carrying buckets of water. Several trips were made before the tub was filled to Beau's liking.

André stripped down and eased himself into the tub. It was a pleasure to soak in the cool water, wash the heat and dust from his body, and think about all he'd seen. There certainly was a lot to owning a plantation; far more than he realized.

Once he was through with his bath, Beau entered. "You take rest now, *Michie*," he said as he turned down the bed. "You get called in time for dinner."

Nodding, André lay down and stretched out. Suddenly, Beau pulled a cord. A thin, almost invisible net or "*baire*," as the *Créoles* called it dropped down around him. The startled look on his face caused Beau to chuckle.

"Not be worried, *Baire* keep mosquito from botherin' *Michie*."

André thought about all he had seen and heard today. Owning a plantation was certainly more than he had bargained for. Should he really embark on this adventure? But what else could he do? He wasn't prepared to spend the rest of his life working for someone else. And with his youth and this gentleman's help, perhaps he could learn all that was necessary and someday become a wealthy planter in his own right.

Chapter 7

Later, André and Charles joined their host for dinner. Once the meal was over, Monsieur Charlevoix rang for brandy. Then he turned his attention back to André. "Well, young man, by the way, may I call you André?"

André smiled, "Please do, Monsieur."

"So tell me, what do you think? Do you still want to be a planter?"

"*Oui*, Monsieur, more than ever. This has been one of the most interesting days of my life."

"You are not discouraged or overwhelmed?"

"I am overwhelmed, but not discouraged. I feel confident that if I study and learn all that I can, soon I will be able to have a plantation of my own."

"Well, then, I have a suggestion. It is much too late for the two of you to return to the city. Why don't you stay the night? We can continue our discussion in the morning. There is still much you should know."

Both young men were happy to accept the invitation.

The next morning after breakfast, Monsieur Charlevoix said, "André, I shall not be returning to New Orleans until the first of October. Would you like to stay here until then? I will help you learn more about planting and all the details of running a plantation. You can ride out to the fields with me, and I'll teach you as much as possible in the time we have here. And believe me, young man, there is much to learn."

"Monsieur Charlevoix, I should appreciate that more than you will ever know. I am eager to learn all that I can."

Charles chose to return to the city. "I'll send Demetrius out to you," he said. "I'll have him bring you some clothes."

"*Merci*, Charles. I don't dare pass up an opportunity like this."

* * *

That first morning after breakfast, his host said, "Well, André, shall we get started? Since we only have a month, you will have much to learn and retain."

André took a deep breath, nodded, and smiled. "*Oui*, Monsieur Charlevoix, I am ready." He quickly tucked a small writing tablet and pencil in his pocket.

"We will start your education with the sugar cane. Since it is our most profitable plant, you must know as much as possible concerning it."

When they reached the fields, the two dismounted and walked between the tall plants while Monsieur Charlevoix explained the way the stalks changed color as the time for cutting drew near.

"Sugar cane, especially, demands a great deal of attention. The more you plant, the more you will learn. Many times, you will find yourself in a race against nature; your judgment against the weather. And, if your judgment is wrong, you can lose an entire crop."

"What happens if you are wrong?" André asked. "I mean what happens if you lose an entire crop?"

"Then you must start all over again. And you must look to your other crops in hopes of not suffering too much financially."

André felt a strong feeling of apprehension building within him but forced himself not to dwell on it. He must stay focused. He often stopped long enough to make a few notes before remounting.

Next, they rode out to the cotton fields, dismounted, and walked between the rows of cotton as the planter explained what was happening at that moment.

"Cotton can exhaust the land, so it is important to rotate the crop often. Cotton is better grown in the northern part of this area but we still manage to make money on it if we are careful."

"Monsieur Charlevoix, would it be better for me to buy land further north? I mean—would it be more profitable?"

"Not necessarily. You can be very successful and make a good profit every year right in this area. But you have to be aware at all times of what you must do."

Most of that day was spent in the fields with Monsieur Charlevoix explaining many things and André making notes on all that he said.

The next morning, his host said, "Now we go to the sugar factory. You must understand the entire process before you leave here. That way, you will know things are being done correctly."

Several days were spent in the factory until André had the entire process down pat. But he never walked into the building that he didn't remember the poor man who was so terribly scalded.

On their first day at the factory, André mentioned his feelings about the injured man.

Monsieur Charlevoix nodded. "*Oui*, on our way back to the house, we will stop by the infirmary and see how Petie is doing."

When they reached the infirmary later in the day, they found Petie still weak and lying in bed; but his face broke out in a happy smile at the sight of his master.

"*Bonjour*, Petie, how are you feeling today?" Monsieur Charlevoix asked.

"Me feel better, *oui*, *Maître*," the injured man said in a shaky voice.

Monsieur Charlevoix turned to the black woman who had just entered the room. "How is Petie doing, *Tante* Aurea?"

"He be better, *Michie*, but he take long time to heal."

"Well, you just keep him here until he is strong enough to leave and then let him continue to heal at home."

When they left the building, André turned to his host. "That poor man, will he ever be able to work again?"

"Probably, but I shall lighten his load considerably. He will never work at the factory again."

Many evenings, Monsieur Charlevoix would take his young student to the plantation office and together they would pour over the books and ledgers. He also pulled out books from several years back.

"You can see how my crops have been showing a profit over a period of time. You will note that every expense has been entered, no matter how small."

He looked over at his pupil. "You must keep good records, André. Farming is always a risky business."

All of this made André's head reel. There was so much to learn, so much to remember. Could he do it? He had to!

Monsieur Charlevoix also introduced André to his overseer, Monsieur Schultz. The man came from the German Coast of Louisiana and had a great deal of knowledge concerning agriculture.

André found the man's accent so strong he had difficulty understanding him at first. But within a few days, his ears became attuned to the sounds.

"It is important to have a trustworthy overseer," Monsieur Charlevoix said, as they road towards the house, "one who knows the land and can get the work done and not cheat you. If I couldn't trust Monsieur Schultz, I wouldn't be able to go to the city in the winter or take a trip to the north for a few months."

André looked at him in surprise. "Why would you go north? Aren't the Americans nothing but barbarians and uncouth? I saw some of them at the wharf the day I arrived. They seemed like a bunch of rabble."

Monsieur Charlevoix smiled. "*Non*, the Americans I know in the north are not like those you saw on the wharf. They are intelligent and hard working. I go north to learn about their machinery. If they have something I can use here on the plantation, I buy it and bring it back.

"You see, André, all we have down here is land, crops, and slaves; we will need machinery if we are to be more successful. Most Créoles will have nothing to do with the Americans who are coming to New Orleans now that she is part of the United States. I have cultivated the friendships of some of them and find them delightful people."

He paused and said, "A word to the wise, I would encourage you to do likewise."

André was amazed at how many it took to run the plantation smoothly. First, there were the house servants. They were the lucky ones, chosen for how quickly they could learn. The men were trained as butlers and valets the women as ladies' maids, housekeepers, cooks, laundresses, and seamstresses. Some men were taught to play musical instruments.

There were the stable boys and blacksmith, and the slaves who knew how to work on leather, and others who made the candles.

Besides all of these, André learned that there were more than one hundred slaves (called "field hands") who worked in the fields and the sugar mill. And, of course, there was the white overseer, plus the black slave who held the title and job of foreman.

"I brought a music teacher out to teach the men with a natural talent to play musical instruments. This way, we could have music when we held balls and such in the past. My people take great pride in their ability to play," Monsieur Charlevoix explained. "If you like, this evening, I will have them play some music for us."

Later that night after dinner while the two men were enjoying a glass of brandy and listening to the slaves play their instruments, Monsieur said, "André, you should know that when you acquire slaves, you must follow the law. Your slaves must be housed and fed adequately. They cannot be made to work in the fields on Sunday, although many of them do. But then you must pay them."

This last remark surprised André. "I had no idea there were such laws."

"Oh, *oui*," Monsieur Charlevoix assured him. "There are many laws to protect the slaves. And if a planter ignores them and mistreats his slaves, he can be hauled before the magistrate and fined a great deal of money."

"This owning slaves, Monsieur…this is one thing I don't feel comfortable with," André said with a pained expression.

"I know, André. I felt the same way when I bought my first slaves. But this is the Deep South, and slavery is a way of life. There is little you can do to change things. Someday, I'm certain slavery will be abolished, but not in our lifetime."

"I wish I could simply hire men to work my land, when I have land."

"You would never be successful if you did that. You would go broke just paying their salary since everything is done by hand. There are no shortcuts. You can't buck the system, André. So, if you really want to be a planter and be successful, you must have slaves. Treat them kindly, care for them and about them, and most of them will repay you with hard work."

Another night while the two sat in the main parlor, his host said, "André, you will need a good banker, and you are in luck, because Monsieur du Fray is the best in New Orleans. And, you will also need two lawyers and a factor."

"Two lawyers?" André raised an eyebrow.

"*Oui*," answered his host. "I have two. One is an American, and the other is a Créole. I find it much easier that way. You see, André, if you do want to be successful, you must do business with both the Créoles and the Americans. But the Americans don't speak French, and the

Créoles refuse to learn English. The Americans have even given *la Vieux Carré* an English name."

"They have?"

"*Oui*, they call it the 'French Quarter.'" He shrugged. "The Créoles, however, will always call it 'The Old Square.' So to make things easier for myself, I have one of each."

André gave his host a puzzled look. "But, Monsieur, aren't the Créoles Americans also?"

"Of course, they are. But, they have lived under so many flags; sometimes they never knew just which country they belonged to. So in their minds, anyone who is not a Créole is an American."

"Another question, Monsieur, what is a factor?"

"Ah, your factor is the most important man for a planter. He does what you never have time to do. He's the one who serves as your business agent in the city. He works out the best price for your crops. Even if you don't go to the city for months, your factor will see that your crops are sold at the highest price possible."

"What will I have to pay him for this service?"

"He will retain a percentage of the sale," the older man explained. "Usually two and a half percent; and whatever amount remains will be credited to your account. It is also through your factor that you will order the supplies you will need until your next crop comes in."

Monsieur Charlevoix paused, then added, "Your factor will also charge a commission on the purchases he makes for you. I will be happy to introduce you to my factory. You may want to use him."

"I never realized there was so much involved in owning a plantation," André said thoughtfully.

"There is a great deal involved. Are you having second thoughts?"

"*Non*, Monsieur Charlevoix, I knew it would take work, and I am willing to make it work. I want this more than anything in the world." He paused, "I want to be as successful as you. I want *beaucoup d'argent.*"

Monsieur Charlevoix looked at André for a long time. "I am happy to hear you say that. Because what you want is quite a challenge, especially for one who has never farmed before. I only hope your ambition does not outweigh your common sense. You will have to invest every cent you have just to get started. Pray God you will succeed."

Chapter 8

It was the day before they were to leave for the city. André had spent a sleepless night wrestling with his decision to become a planter. Was he really up to the task? And what if he sank all his money into this venture and failed? Then what would he do? He tossed and turned. *Non*, he would not think of such a thing. He *would* succeed, he *must* succeed. Once he was washed and dressed, he went down to greet his generous mentor.

"*Bonjour*, André. I hope you slept well." Monsieur smiled and gestured for André to sit down.

"*Bonjour,* Monsieur Charlevoix. I slept well enough, considering I had a lot of things going on in my mind."

Monsieur nodded. "I can well imagine. I have tried to teach you as much as possible. I hope you will be able to retain all that you've learned; but now it is time for me to return to New Orleans."

André took a sip of *café au lait* and said, "Monsieur Charlevoix, you will never know how much I appreciate all you've done to help me. And someday, I hope to be successful so you will know your time was well spent."

"*Merci*, André. When we are finished with breakfast, we are going for a ride. I have something I want to show you."

André was filled with curiosity as they rode further out into the countryside. After about a half hour, his host turned his horse from the road onto a small path. Suddenly, they came to a large clearing where he stopped.

André looked around. The land he saw was wild virgin earth, untouched by man.

Monsieur Charlevoix looked over at his young friend.

"Well, what do you think of it?"

"It's beautiful," André said softly. The sun, glittering through the Spanish moss that hung from the giant oak trees, gave the entire place a feeling of serenity, much like being in church. In the distance, one could hear the mighty Mississippi flowing by.

"Does any one own this?"

Monsieur Charlevoix was staring off into the distance. Then bringing himself back to the present, he said, "I bought this land right before my first child was born. I bought it for my son. But when he died, I couldn't bring myself to come near it again. I kept it hoping that someday there would be another son; but after giving birth to Julie, my wife died. I knew I would never develop it. I've been hoping to sell it for some time."

"But what about Julie?" André asked. "Don't you want her to have it?"

Monsieur Charlevoix smiled and shook his head. "Julie will have *Château Charlevoix* someday, and she will marry a wealthy man with land of his own." He paused for a moment. "As I said, I've been wanting to sell it for sometime, but not to just anyone. I've always hoped to find the right person, and now I feel I've found him."

He gave André a piercing look. "There are eleven hundred acres of some of the best and richest soil in the area. If you are interested, we can discuss a fair price and have the papers drawn up when we reach New Orleans."

André was speechless. This kind man who had taken so much time already to help him was now offering to sell him his land. When finally he was able to speak, André said, "You have been so generous to me this past month. I can never repay you for all you've done. I'd be honored to buy this property. I just don't know how to begin to thank you."

Monsieur Charlevoix held up a hand. "The only thanks I want, André, is for you to love this land as much as I do and make it succeed. Someday, I would like to see you the most successful planter in the territory. Is it a deal?"

"It certainly is," André said as they shook hands.

Heading back to the house, André turned to his host. "Why, Monsieur Charlevoix, why are you doing so much for me? You hardly know me, and yet you've taken your own valuable time to help me learn as much as possible about planting, and now you offer to sell me all this land."

Monsieur Charlevoix smiled. "You remind me of myself when I was your age and first arrived in Louisiana."

"You are not a native?"

"*Non*, André, like you, I too came from France. But, unlike you, I was not of noble birth."

"What brought you here, Monsieur?"

"I was one of seven children. My father was a farmer not dirt poor, but certainly not rich. Life was a constant struggle. Since I was not the first son, I felt there was no future for me if I remained on our farm, so at ten and six, I sailed for this new land. Louisiana was still quite unsettled when I first arrived, and I felt there were many possibilities."

"Did you know anyone here?"

"*Oui*, upon arriving, I lived with a friend of our family who had come to Louisiana a few years earlier. He gave me room and board and in return, I worked on his farm with him and learned all I could. Much like you have been doing. However, within two years after my arrival, the man and his family died of yellow fever. Since he left no other relatives to claim his land, I was able to buy it with the little money my father had given me."

"You mean all this land was his?" André asked.

"Oh, *non*, only a small portion was his; the rest I've acquired over the years; years of hard work, work like you will have to do. But this is what you can have if you, too, are willing to strive for it."

Later that night when André lay in bed, he thought of all his host had told him. *If this gracious man could do so much with so much less than I have, then I must succeed no matter what. I owe him that.*

* * *

When Charles first returned to New Orleans without André, he had some explaining to do to Gabrielle. She had a fit when she realized the man she was infatuated with had not returned.

"I can't believe he would want to stay out there with the social season just beginning," she stormed.

"Gabrielle, there are more important things than the social season, and André had good reason for remaining in the country with Monsieur Charlevoix."

But nothing Charles said made any difference so finally he promised to tell her just as soon as André was back, anything to shut her up and keep the peace.

When finally André did return, he contacted Charles at once. He could hardly wait to tell his friend the wonderful news. He spent much of the afternoon relating all that Monsieur Charlevoix had taught him.

"I have a stack of notes, and he even lent me some books to go over now that I am back."

Charles smiled. "André, I certainly admire you for wanting to take on such a daunting task."

André grew serious. "*Oui*, it is a daunting task. And I would be less than honest if I didn't admit that over this past month, I did have second thoughts. But it is what I really want, and somehow I must make it work."

Then his mood changed and he beamed. "Monsieur Charlevoix is selling me some of his best land." He went on to explain what his mentor had said. "Charles, I can't begin to thank you for introducing me to such a kind and generous gentleman."

The two young men were relaxing in the du Fray courtyard. Each sipped a glass of wine while André continued telling Charles more.

"How soon will you sign the papers on your land?"

"Monsieur Charlevoix has much business to attend to now that he is back. He said he crammed so much knowledge into my poor brain that I should have time to relax and enjoy some of the season."

André grew serious. "He's right, of course. Once I do sign the papers, I will have my work cut out for me. I must buy equipment, and slaves, and start taming that wild untouched land so eventually I can start planting."

"Monsieur Charlevoix is correct. Now that you are back, you must have some fun. Tomorrow night I am going to the opera. Perhaps you would like to go with me?"

André smiled. "*Oui*, I would enjoy that. It's been a long time since I've been to the *théâtre*."

"Gabrielle will be thrilled to see you," Charles added with a smile. "She has about driven me crazy badgering me with how soon you'd be back and how soon she'd see you."

"Well, she will see me tomorrow night, that is if she and her family are in attendance.

"Oh, she will be, you may be certain of that; especially when she learns that we will be there also."

* * *

On the corner of *Rues Bourbon* and *Toulouse* stood the French Opera House. When Charles and André arrived, the theater was fast filling up. The two made their way through the crowd to the du Fray box, where Charles' parents greeted them.

"Well, André," Monsieur du Fray said, as he shook the young man's hand. "I understand you are buying some land from Monsieur Charlevoix."

André smiled. "*Oui*, Monsieur du Fray. Monsieur Charlevoix has been more than kind to me."

"Charles has told us all about your time spent in the country," Madame du Fray added. "I am so happy for you."

"I have already met with Monsieur Charlevoix," said the older man. "I am even now drawing up the papers for the two of you to sign. So, as soon as he is available, I shall send you a note."

The two young men had settled down, and now André took the time to look around the theater. He was impressed to see that the ladies wore gowns every bit as beautiful as any he had seen in the best theaters in both London and Paris. The men were equally elegant in their formal wear.

Suddenly, he felt Charles touch his arm. "André, look here come Francesca and her family," he motioned with his head to a box across from them.

André looked over in that direction. No sooner had the Ste. Claires taken their seats when the box quickly filled up with several gentlemen. Each bowed to the parents, then turned their attention to the young ladies.

"We'll wait until those friends of mine thin out before we go over," Charles said.

Once she was seated, Gabrielle let her eyes scan the other boxes. She knew André would be there; Charles had promised her. Then she saw him but before she could make eye contact, the men who had converged on her blocked her view. She did her best to hurry them along, and was thrilled when, as the last gentleman was leaving, Charles and André entered.

Once the greetings were made, she turned all of her charms on André. "I am *so* happy to see you again, Monsieur de Javon. You have been away from New Orleans for such a long time." She sighed and looked wistful.

"*Oui*, it has been a while," André said, as he bowed and kissed her hand. "However, it was all for a good purpose."

Monsieur Ste. Claire inquired as to how things had gone in the country, and André told him a little.

Madame Ste. Claire smiled up at André. "Monsieur de Javon, we are having a *petite soirée* at our home next week. We would be delighted if you would join us."

"*Merci*, Madame Ste. Claire, I should be happy to attend."

The house lights dimmed, and André and Charles hastened to their box just as the curtain was going up.

Once the opera began, André became completely engrossed with what was happening on stage, a fact that was not lost on Gabrielle. She couldn't believe he was not looking at her. Many of the other men in the audience spent much time doing their best to catch her eye.

When, finally, the first act ended and the house lights were brought up, Gabrielle naturally assumed that André would hurry to her box. But he didn't, and that fact filled her with rage. Fanning herself furiously, she shot angry glances towards the du Fray box. How dare André ignore her! Just who did he think he was?

During the entire intermission, Gabrielle watched as André sat talking to the du Frays. Not once did he look her way. Well, she certainly would let him know she was not used to this type of treatment! She determined that once the opera was ended, if she saw André when they were leaving, she would simply ignore him.

But that didn't work, because as they were leaving, Gabrielle saw several young ladies talking and smiling at the tall, handsome Frenchman. And the fact that André responded to their overtures, made her even angrier.

She watched as he gave each girl his undivided attention when she spoke to him. She saw him bow and kiss each hand that was extended to him, and saw the young ladies give him a smile over their shoulders as they left.

Those stupid girls! She wanted nothing more than to box their ears and tell them, in no uncertain terms, that she had set her cap for Monsieur de Javon, and they had better not get any ideas.

All the way home, she brooded and fumed. Once in her bedchamber, she plotted her next move. Her parents were having the *soirée*. In fact, the party had been her idea, and André would be there. Gabrielle turned over, hugged her pillow, and with a satisfied smile, felt with the utmost confidence that, before that night was over, she would have André right where she wanted him.

Chapter 9

The moment Gabrielle saw André and the du Frays enter her
father's home, she excused herself from a group of guests and
hurried over to him. "Monsieur de Javon, how happy I am to see you
again," she purred. "I'm so delighted you came." She gave André her
prettiest smile.

"I am happy to see you again, Mademoiselle." André bowed and
kissed her hand. He smiled with amusement as he wondered just what
would happen this evening with the enchanting Gabrielle Ste. Claire.

Gabrielle turned her attention on her future brother-in-law.
"*Bonsoir,* Charles. Francesca will be down in a moment." With a coy
smile, she asked, "You won't mind if I steal Monsieur de Javon away for
a while, will you?" With out waiting for an answer, she slipped her hand
into André's hand and led him away.

With a possessive air, Gabrielle took him around and introduced him
to the other guests. Her manner made it clear to the other girls that this
gentleman was someone very special, and they were not to get any ideas.

André continued to view her behavior with amusement. Gabrielle
certainly knew what she wanted, and it would seem that what she
wanted was *him*. He wondered what she would think if she knew he
wasn't certain he even liked her. For all her beauty, she was a bit too
forceful for his taste. However, he was a guest in her father's home, and
as such, he would be the perfect gentleman, even if she didn't exactly act

like the perfect lady. So he would just wait and see what evolved.

André noticed that, once again, Gabrielle had chosen a gown of blue. It seemed to be her favorite color. And she was right, of course, as it did wonders for her eyes. He was also aware that she was vain enough to know she had beautiful eyes.

The gown was of gossamer silk. The short sleeves and low décolletage were trimmed with a delicate lace edged in silver. The bottom of the skirt was also edged with the same silver; and on her feet, she wore slippers of blue satin. Her hair was caught up with a blue satin ribbon. She was lovely to look at, and no matter his true feelings towards her, André had to admit she was a true beauty.

The music began, and he bowed to her. "Mademoiselle, may I have the pleasure of this dance?"

Gabrielle made a graceful curtsy. "I should *love* to dance with you, Monsieur."

As they danced, Gabrielle said, "Charles tells us you are buying a plantation."

"*Oui*, Mademoiselle, I shall be signing the final papers by the end of this week. But it will take much work before it can be considered a plantation."

"You sound ambitious, Monsieur de Javon. I like that in a man. And I am certain you will be very successful."

"*Merci* for your vote of confidence, Mademoiselle. I shall do everything in my power not to disappoint you."

As the evening wore on, Gabrielle always found a way to stay close to André's side.

When next André danced with her, Gabrielle looked up at him and said in a soft voice, "Monsieur de Javon, would you be kind enough to escort me out to the courtyard. I feel the need for some fresh air."

André hesitated. Was this a wise thing to do? But before he knew what had happened, he found himself in the courtyard with Gabrielle. He leaned his shoulder against a tree trunk and with a twinkle in his eyes, said, "Are you not afraid of causing a *scandale*, Mademoiselle? Alone in the courtyard with a man you hardly know, and without a chaperon?" One of the things he had learned was that Créole parents guarded their daughters like hawks. Thus, the girls were always chaperoned.

"Oh, don't worry about that," Gabrielle said with a shrug. "And stop calling me Mademoiselle, it sounds so formal. You may call me Gaby;

everyone else does. And I shall call you André."

"Very well, Gaby, but I repeat. Are you not afraid of causing a *scandale*? I should not like to get myself killed in a duel just yet."

"Oh, the devil with that." Gabrielle lowered her head, then looked up at André through her long lashes and said in a soft husky voice, "Don't you find me pretty?"

"I find you beautiful. I can't imagine anyone not finding you so." It was true, she was beautiful, and she knew it.

André wanted to add, "*You are not only beautiful, but you are very conceited.*" He wanted to, but he didn't. To do so would have been the height of bad manners, and that *could* have gotten him involved in a duel.

While he was giving this some thought, Gabrielle stood on tiptoes, and he felt her warm breath on his neck. Suddenly, her lips were on his. They were soft and willing, and André found himself kissing her back with a passion he hadn't expected.

When the kiss ended, Gabrielle smiled up at him. "You liked kissing me, didn't you?"

"Of course. Any man in his right mind would enjoy kissing you. You are not only exquisite but also very desirable."

The moonlight filtering through the lacy trees gave a soft glow to her face and hair. Gabrielle stood on her toes once again; her lips close to his, her eyes closed.

"Kiss me again, André, kiss me again."

"*Non, ma chère,*" he answered softly. "I think there has been enough kissing for now. It's time we went in before your father comes looking for us and I find myself in a great deal of trouble."

His breathing was heavy, and it was all he could do to control himself. With determination, he took Gabrielle's arms from around his neck and, gently holding one of them, he led her back to the house.

It was a disturbing moment for the young man. His natural desires, having been subdued for many months, came rushing to the surface. He could have easily spent the next several minutes kissing Gabrielle in the moonlight. But his good sense told him not to.

Never before had he met a well-bred young lady who behaved like Gabrielle. And he certainly hadn't expected to be so attracted to her considering his initial feelings.

But the truth of the matter was she had stirred emotions within him that he was not ready to pursue.

Eighteen-year-old Gabrielle Ste. Claire was in a terrible mood the rest of the evening. She had danced with other young men but continued to keep her eyes on André. She watched as he moved about the room, meeting and speaking to the other guests, and her heart fluttered at the sight of him.

She noticed how well his wine velvet coat fit his broad shoulders. She admired the large ruby nestled in his white cravat, which was enhanced by the wine and deep blue waistcoat. His satin breeches of the same color and his white stockings fit his long legs to perfection. His black shoes with gold buckles were polished to a high sheen.

The sun from the days he spent at *Château Charlevoix* had lightened his brown hair even more. His face was tanned from the days spent in the country. And his hazel eyes, which seemed to always be twinkling, were fringed with thick lashes. The more Gabrielle watched André, the more her heart began to beat furiously. And he was tall, at least six feet two. She *loved* tall men.

She had been as charming and flattering to him as possible. She did everything she could think of to gain his attention and keep it; and for a while, it had worked.

But once they returned to the house, André had grown quite cool towards her. When she sat across from him at the late-night supper, he had paid her scant attention, although she had tried to engage him in conversation at every opportunity. He had been charming and witty to everyone around him, and she realized with a feeling of annoyance that the other girls were even more impressed with him.

But it was she he had kissed, and she knew he enjoyed it. He had even said so. She had stirred feelings within him, and she was determined to find a way to keep those feelings alive.

Gabrielle knew her family and friends would be shocked if they were aware of her behavior, but she didn't care! Also, the fact that André's attention had changed towards her once they were back indoors made little difference to her. Gabrielle knew what she wanted, and she wanted André. She always got what she wanted, and she would stop at nothing to get him!

Chapter 10

André signed the final papers on his property, and purchased the tools, machinery, oxen, and wagons needed to clear his land. Then, much to his dismay, he learned that the Federal Government had put an embargo on the importation of slaves from Africa.

Two days later, Charles stopped by for a short visit only to find his friend pacing the floor of his small parlor.

"Charles, why didn't anyone tell me about the embargo? Surely both you and Monsieur Charlevoix knew."

"André, don't work yourself into such a stew," Charles said when he heard what was causing his friend such worry. "Just relax and be patient."

At this remark, André paused and looked over at the other with an expression of sheer exasperation. "Relax, be patient? Charles, you don't seem to understand. Time is money, and I've already spent a great deal. Now I must get busy making that land pay off."

"You are quite right, André. But, *mon ami*, I promise you the problem will be solved. There is nothing you can do about it now. Come, we will stop by the bank and speak to my father. You will find that he is already working on a way to help you."

André knew Charles was right. There was nothing he could do at the moment, so with a nod he bid Demetrius good-bye and followed Charles out of the boarding house.

Later that day, while the two sat in the du Fray courtyard, André said, "Do you think Jean Lafitte will be able to help me?"

"Oh, I'm sure he will be. Monsieur Lafitte is always interested in making a profit. When you meet him, you will find he is not the terrible person some people would have you believe."

It had come as a surprise to André when he learned that Monsieur du Fray knew Jean Lafitte and handled Lafitte's accounts.

A couple of days later, Charles again stopped by André's place. "Good news, André, my father has arranged a meeting between you and Lafitte. It will be held at his home on the corner of *Rues Bourbon* and *St. Philip*. The meeting is to take place this evening, so I shall say *au revoir* and let you get ready." Charles smiled, "See, I told you everything would work out. Good luck."

A short while later, a note arrived from Jean Lafitte inviting André to his home at eight o'clock that evening.

While he dressed for the appointment, André found himself wondering just what sort of person Jean Lafitte was.

He had heard much about the man. Lafitte and his brother, Pierre, owned a shop on *Rue Royale* where they sold wines, fine laces, materials, and other items of worth.

Today, he learned that Lafitte and Pierre also sold slaves that they bought from Santo Domingo. Some in New Orleans called Lafitte and his brother pirates, while others said they were buccaneers. André had heard about them from Charles shortly after arriving in New Orleans. He had also seen Lafitte in a coffeehouse the day he and Charles found his new living quarters. André was struck by the man's appearance. Lafitte was tall, handsome, and well dressed. Not at all what one would expect of a pirate.

"The man speaks French, Spanish, Italian, and English flawlessly and has impeccable manners," Charles had informed him. And that, too, was not at all what one would expect from a pirate. So it was understandable that André wondered just how this meeting with the infamous Lafitte would go.

* * *

At the allotted hour, André found himself standing before a palatial mansion. When he knocked, a black butler wearing a fine uniform of deep scarlet opened the door.

André was led into a beautifully furnished and decorated parlor. Jean Lafitte was sitting on a sofa; four other men were also present.

When Lafitte rose to his feet, André saw that they were the same height. The man's features were classic, his dark hair thick and curly; but it was his eyes that held one's attention. Black and piercing, it was as though he could look right into your head and know what you were thinking. He certainly didn't look like a cutthroat. He was dressed fashionably in a coat of deep blue velvet with white satin breeches, a white ruffled shirt, and a brocade waistcoat.

"*Bonsoir*, Monsieur de Javon."

"*Bonsoir*, Monsieur Lafitte." André hoped his nervousness didn't show.

The two men shook hands, Lafitte ordered wine for his guest and then made the introductions.

First, there was Pierre Lafitte. Totally unlike his tall, handsome brother, Pierre was short and fat.

"Pierre is my right-hand man," Lafitte explained. "He has a keen mind and a shrewd business head."

Pierre Lafitte extended his hand. "*Bonsoir*, Monsieur de Javon. We have heard much about you from Monsieur du Fray."

After the two shook hands, André was introduced to Dominique You. "Dominique was once an artilleryman in Napoleon's army," Lafitte said. "He is my principle lieutenant."

Dominique You bowed and extended his hand. "I'm pleased to meet you, Monsieur de Javon." The man had black eyes that seemed to be laughing at the young visitor.

There were two other men in the room, and Lafitte quickly made the introductions. Once that was done, his host invited André to take a seat, and wine was served.

"So, you need slaves." Lafitte studied André closely.

"How much land did you buy?"

"Eleven hundred acres."

"And how many slaves will you need, Monsieur de Javon?"

"In the future I'll need a great many; but for now, I must have at least twenty-five."

"Twenty-five?" Lafitte cocked an eyebrow. "Surely you don't expect to cultivate eleven hundred acres with only twenty-five slaves?"

The other men in the room chuckled at this remark.

André looked Lafitte straight in the eye and, in a calm voice, said"*Non,* Monsieur Lafitte, I am not so foolish as to think I can do such a thing, but I have to start somewhere. And twenty-five men will give me a start. As my income increases, so will my purchase of slaves."

Lafitte studied André closely. "How soon do you need them?"

"As soon as I can get them."

His host stood, bowed, and excusing himself, motioned for his brother, Dominique You, and the other two to follow him.

André remained in his chair, sipped his wine, and waited.

Lafitte and the others were gone almost an hour, and André began to wonder if they would ever return. He continually checked his pocket watch. It was getting late, and he was becoming very uncomfortable just sitting there waiting. But he didn't dare leave; he needed Lafitte's help and would sit there all night, if necessary. Then he heard footsteps, and the five men reappeared.

Lafitte resumed his place on the sofa, refreshed his wine glass, took a sip, and said, "Monsieur de Javon, you are in luck. I have a shipment of slaves coming up from Santo Domingo any day now. They won't be brought into the city; instead they'll be sold along the river from as far south as Donaldsonville all the way up to Natchez."

He paused and sipped his wine. "However, because Monsieur du Fray sent you to me, you will be notified when the ship arrives and will be given first choice. This means you will have to go with me to *Grande Terre.* It is a full day's journey, and we must leave before or near daybreak. Can you be ready on short notice?"

"*Oui,* Monsieur Lafitte, I can be ready anytime."

"Very well, I shall send word when they arrive."

André thanked his host, finished his wine, and having no further business, rose and extended his hand. Lafitte shook it with a firm grip, and André departed.

With a sigh of relief, he stepped out onto the *banquette.* He was now onestep closer to his dream. There was much at stake; pray God things would go well.

* * *

A week later, André got word that he was to meet Jean Lafitte on the west bank of the Mississippi River.

It was still dark when André arrived at the designated place. The buccaneer greeted him warmly. "Ah, Monsieur de Javon, I hope sailing agrees with you, because we will be going by water to fetch your slaves."

"Monsieur Lafitte, I crossed the ocean with nary one day of illness; so I think my stomach can handle the river."

"I'm happy to hear that. We will go first by barge and then by *pirogue*. From the river, we will enter a channel that extends seventy miles south of New Orleans."

"Exactly where are we going, Monsieur Lafitte, if I may ask?"

"Of course, you may. We're headed for Barataria Bay. It lies between the river and Bayou *La Fourche.*"

After traveling a ways, the barge stopped.

"Now we shall take the *pirogue*," Lafitte said as he and André made the change. In answer to André's unasked question, Lafitte said, "The barge is too large to pass through the bayous, swamps, and small streams to come. But the *petit pirogue* can travel anywhere in these waters."

A black slave stood at the back of the little boat, and with a long pole, pushed it through the muddy waters of the bayou.

As the *pirogue* slowly made its way, André said, "I have a feeling that without a guide, one could get hopelessly lost in this maze of waterways."

Lafitte looked over and nodded. "You are correct. And the truth is, that many have gotten lost, never to be seen or heard from again."

The bayous and swamps held a fascination for André. He had never seen anything like them. It was now daybreak, and a strange, heavy mist hung over everything. André felt the cold, clammy mist on his face, and it made him shiver. Slowly, the sun began to break through the trees, and André turned to his host to inquire as to what type of trees they were.

"Those are cypress trees. They are plentiful throughout the bayous and swamps."

"They look so strange," André said. "Rising out of these still, black waters, they appear more like distorted giants, with their limbs hanging in grotesque poses."

Gray-green Spanish moss draped down from the branches giving the swamp the appearance of being covered with giant cobwebs.

As the morning heightened, a large form suddenly moved and slipped into the murky water.

Startled, André asked, "What on earth is that?"

"That is an alligator," Lafitte said. "They'll snap a man's leg off before he knows what hit him. They've been known to eat a man alive if they sank their teeth into him before he could escape."

"Looks more like a large, ugly log that swims," André said as he continued viewing the reptile with a healthy respect.

Lafitte laughed. "*Oui*, he is an ugly creature. Only another alligator would find him attractive."

The stillness of the bayous and swamps was so heavy one could almost feel it. When a beautiful bird suddenly took to the air, André asked about it.

"That is a red-winged blackbird," Lafitte said. "The bayou is filled with exotic birds. There blue herons, marsh wrens, laughing gulls, and woodcocks. These are only some of the birds one will see in the trees."

André watched with fascination when a brown pelican swooped to the water for fish, its wings flapping noisily as it took to the sky again.

Leaving the swamps and Bayou *La Fourche*, they boarded another barge and entered another channel. Although he had appreciated the beauty of the land he'd just left, André breathed a sigh of relief to be back in more familiar territory. He felt as if he'd just passed through a strange, dream-like world.

In a short while, Lafitte looked over and said, "Well, Monsieur de Javon, we have finally reached our distention, *Grande Terre*."

Chapter 11

W hile they disembarked, Lafitte said, "*Grande Terre* is a small island, three miles wide and six miles long. But it suits my purpose. It guards the entrance to Barataria Bay, and it's my home."

A crowd of the most ferocious-looking band of scoundrels André could have imagined met them as the two came ashore. They were noisy, dirty, drunk, and threatening.

"Enough!" Lafitte roared. "Is this any way to greet a guest of mine? Stand back and keep your mouths shut!"

André watched in amazement as, with one word from his host, the mob grew quiet and fell back.

He may look like a fine gentleman, but he has_obviously done something to command the respect of this unholy scum, André thought as he followed Lafitte.

While the two walked down the streets of *Grande Terre*, Lafitte said, "These thatched huts are for the men and their women." A little further, he said, "You will also note that there are cafes, bordellos, and gambling houses everything to keep this unruly mob of mine happy when they are not busy doing their job."

Walking through the streets, André could hear loud voices coming from the taverns and gambling houses. He felt a bit apprehensive when fistfights would erupt around them, but Lafitte paid no attention to them. He heard women laughing, screaming, and fighting; still Lafitte paid them no heed.

As though reading André's mind, his host said, "Don't let all that racket bother you, Monsieur de Javon. It's just the natives having a little fun."

Soon, they came to several large buildings.

"These warehouses were built to house the treasures brought in by my men. And that building is the *barrocoon*. I built it to house the slaves once I bring them back from Santo Domingo." Lafitte kept up a constant dialogue, pointing out other sights of interest.

André wondered what type of treasures where kept in the buildings. He didn't hear any noise from the *barrocoon* where the slaves were housed, and wondered about that. But he didn't feel comfortable asking questions just yet.

In the center of the island stood Lafitte's home, a beautiful mansion of stone and brick. André was surprised that the man could live in such splendor among so many men who appeared to be nothing but a bunch of cutthroats.

When they reached the *galerie* of the house, he observed that from this vantage point, Lafitte had a commanding view of any ships approaching the island.

"Well, here we are, home at last. Muzetta, bring us some wine."

A pretty young Negress, who had been waiting at the entrance, nodded and in a second, reappeared with the liquid. Lafitte invited André to sit down and enjoy the beverage.

Later, Lafitte showed his guest around his home. André noted that the house was filled with the finest furniture, dinnerware, linens, and crystal. Rich, thick carpets from Persia and Turkey covered the floors, which were made of the finest wood. Beautiful paintings graced the walls of almost every room. And André was impressed with how clean and spotless everything was.

The man certainly knows how to live. Would that some day I might live as well, he thought. Later, he was shown to a beautifully appointed, guest bedchamber where he bathed and changed before joining his host in the opulent dining room for the evening meal.

They were served an excellent dinner of *gumbo file*, pheasant, potatoes *a la Duchesse*, oysters on the half shell, and a dessert of *charlotte russe*. The meal was washed down with a fine wine and topped off with a cheroot and a glass of the smoothest brandy André had ever tasted.

When the meal was over and the two were sitting on the *galerie* looking at the stars, Lafitte leaned back in his chair. "So, you want to be a planter," he mused as he eyed André through a haze of smoke from his cheroot.

"*Oui*, Monsieur Lafitte. I have listened to other planters in New Orleans. Many of them have been very successful, and I had the pleasure of spending time with Monsieur Charlevoix, who is also very successful. He gave me a great deal of help, and sold me my land."

Lafitte nodded and silently smoked his cheroot. After a few moments, he said, "Tell me about yourself, Monsieur de Javon."

Lafitte's eyes bore into his guest while André related some of his life. He spoke of how he and his sister were smuggled out of France during the Reign of Terror and sent to England. "When I was grown, I knew I must do something. I never cared for England; but when I returned to France, there was nothing left of my family. So I decided to come here."

Lafitte continued to study André, and then he spoke in a soft voice. "Ah, *oui*, the Reign of Terror. That was a terrible time for France. I managed to escape that period also, although I was a bit older than you."

"How did you happen to come to Louisiana?" André asked, hoping to learn more about this strange man.

"Oh, I heard about it from others, and like you, there was nothing left in France for me or my brother."

"And Dominique You, how did you come to meet him?"

"You served under Napoleon for a while but grew tired of that life and managed to escape. We hooked up later." Lafitte chuckled. "Dominique is a good man."

André wanted to ask more questions. He wanted to know how Lafitte came to be the leader of such a horde of scum as was on this island.

He had heard stories about how the Lafitte brothers arrived in New Orleans and started a blacksmith business. He'd heard that one day Jean left his brother Pierre in charge of the business and disappeared from the city for a while. When he returned, it was said that he now headed up a gang of cutthroats on *Grande Terre*.

There were many stories of how Lafitte and his band of pirates plowed the seas and plundered the ships of other nations with little or no regard for life or property. Some wondered if Pierre was really his brother and if Dominique was also his brother. No one knew for certain if the stories were true. Lafitte never admitted or denied any of them, only adding to his mystic.

André hoped the man would fill in the details of his life, but suddenly Lafitte stubbed out his cheroot and stood up. Looking down at André, he said, "We must be up early in the morning, so I shall turn in for the night. Feel free to sit here as long as you wish. *Bonne nuit*, Monsieur de Javon."

André waited until the other had retired to his room before he too stubbed out his cheroot and returned to his bedchamber. As he walked to his room, he could still hear the men and women screaming and fighting. It amazed him that Lafitte didn't seem the least bit threatened by the mob living so near his home.

André woke the next morning to the smell of fresh coffee and the savory aroma of food cooking. Once bathed and shaved, he joined his host who was sitting on the *galerie* enjoying his coffee. The two greeted each other, André sat down, and in a short while, breakfast was served.

"I hope you had a peaceful sleep, Monsieur de Javon," Lafitte said, as he sipped his coffee. "Sometimes the natives get restless and make a great deal of noise."

André smiled over the rim of his cup. "*Oui*, I heard them, but the moment my head hit the pillow I went right to sleep. I thank you for your concern."

"And the bed, it was comfortable, *oui*?"

"It was like sleeping on a cloud."

Lafitte seemed satisfied with the answer, and when they had finished eating, said, "Come, let us go and see the 'black ivory.' "

The slaves or "black ivory" as Lafitte referred to them, were led from the *barrocoon* and lined up for André's inspection. Looking at these proud men and women, André felt extremely uncomfortable. The thought of buying another human being still lay heavy on his heart, but he had no choice. It was the way it was and if he didn't buy them, someone else would, someone who might not treat them kindly. He knew in his heart he could never mistreat any of these men. Still with mixed feelings, he set about selecting twenty-five large men who were unmarried, or so he thought.

Just as he and Lafitte were leaving, the largest and tallest of the men broke from the ranks and moved down the line. He reached out and took a woman's hand and walked with her back to André. He was the same height as the white man and walked erect with his head held high.

Looking André straight in the eye, he said, "Dis be mah wife. Ah not go widout mah wife, *non*."

André looked over at Lafitte, who nodded. "*Oui*, that's his wife. I didn't think you wanted any women just yet." He smiled. "Their former master named them Samson and Delilah: Samson, because he is as strong as an ox, and Delilah, because she is quite pretty. You're welcome to her if you wish."

"I can't separate a man from his wife. I'm sure he would be of little use to me if he were miserable without her. So, I'll take her also."

Early the next morning, before daybreak, the slaves were loaded aboard the barge and later onto several *pirogues* for the trip back to the river.

Before leaving for *Grande Terre*, André had Monsieur du Fray deposit the money for the slaves in Lafitte's account. He had also arranged for Charles to bring his wagons and other equipment and meet him at the river near his land.

When Charles saw the barge, he lifted the lantern and gave the signal. The barge pulled as close to shore as possible, and the slaves were off-loaded. André held out his hand. "Monsieur Lafitte, I want to thank you for all of your help and for your gracious hospitality."

Lafitte smiled and clasped André's hand. "*Au revoir*, Monsieur de Javon. I enjoyed your company at *Grande Terre*. And when you are in need of more 'black ivory,' I'll be happy to supply you."

It was near nightfall. All day, it had been gray, cold, and damp. With a feeling of frustration, André realized it was too late to do any work.

Charles was in excellent spirits and spent the better part of the ride filling the other in on all the social news of the city. André listened with half an ear, all the while thinking of the enormity of the job ahead of him. Charles went on to ask about Lafitte's home.

"*Grande Terre* is a city within itself," André said. "But I have never seen such a group of scum in all my life."

"What do you mean?"

"Lafitte lives in a beautiful, palatial home, yet he lives amongst the worst cutthroats you could ever imagine. But somehow he keeps a tight rein on them."

When they turned onto his property, André realized they would have to improvise some type of shelter for himself and his slaves. It was too damp and raw an evening, and he couldn't afford to have anyone fall ill.

Finally, they reached the path that led to the clearing, and André felt such a burst of pride he could hardly contain it. This was *his* land, and he would have to prove himself within the next year as to how good a planter he would be.

Reaching the clearing, he peered around. It was almost too dark to see; but it looked like a three-sided shed was standing on the edge of the area.

"Charles, I wonder what that is over there?" André dismounted, and still holding the reins of his horse, walked towards the strange-looking shed. "I know this wasn't here before."

"It's your new home," Charles said. "And, look over there, that's your slave's quarters." He pointed to another larger shed on the other side of the clearing.

"After you left with Lafitte, I brought some of my slaves over to build you a small cabin; but unfortunately it rained so much we couldn't get much done. This was all we could manage." He paused and said, "I had the earth in each shed covered with straw. The straw will be easier to sleep on and will keep all of you warm."

"Charles, I can't begin to thank you for your help. You have solved my most immediate and pressing problem."

"André, I would be less than honest if I didn't admit that I admire you greatly for taking on such a tremendous challenge. Turning this wild untamed land into a working plantation will not be easy."

He walked over to one of the wagons and called a couple of the slaves to lift out several large pots. "If you get a few of those boys to gather some wood and build a fire, you will find your dinner is ready. I've also got blankets. This is no weather to be sleeping without one."

Charles pulled a pile of blankets out and handed them to the black woman Delilah. "Now, I must get back to Oak Grove. I'll be returning to New Orleans tomorrow, but I'll ride out again soon to see how you're doing."

He mounted his horse to leave, then stopped. "Oh, by the way, André, Francesca and I have set the wedding date. We will be married the first week in February. I'd be honored if you would be my best man."

André smiled. "*Merci beaucoup*, Charles. The honor is mine, and I am more than happy to accept."

After Charles left, the food was heated and served. When all had eaten, André called them together.

"Tomorrow, we must set about building our cabins. I want you to know that I will be a fair master. I'll not mistreat you, but I expect you to work, to do your full share, and to do your best. As long as you do, we'll get along fine. Now get some sleep, we have a long day ahead of us."

Chapter *12*

When Julie woke that morning, she was delighted to find the rain had stopped. Her father had come to *Château Charlevoix* for the planting of the sugar cane, and she had begged to come with him. "I'll go back to the Convent in February, *Pappa*. Please, let me go with you until the end of January."

She had sat on her father's knee and kissed him and pleaded so successfully that he finally smiled and said, "You little minx, you certainly know how to get your way."

However, the first week at the *Château* had been ugly and rainy, and Julie found herself cooped up in the house. Now the rain had stopped, and all she could think of was getting out and riding over the plantation.

She had outgrown her pony, and her father told her she was now ready for a horse of her very own. When asked what type she wanted, Julie decided on a jet-black, thoroughbred filly, and her father ordered one from a planter he knew in Virginia.

The horse was to be delivered in time for her birthday; but since it hadn't arrived yet, she knew she would have to ride one of her father's horses. A new sidesaddle was also being fashioned for her by one of the slaves, but that too was not quite ready.

Julie slipped out of bed and quickly donned the boy's clothes she had found in the sewing room at the back of the house. It was in that room that the slave's clothes were mended and repaired after first being thoroughly cleaned and washed.

Once dressed, she surveyed herself in her full-length mirror. With her hair tucked up under the cap and the cap itself pulled down low, she felt certain that if anyone saw her riding, they'd think she was a boy, and she wouldn't cause a *scandale*. With great care, she hurried downstairs and slipped out of the house. She hadn't had breakfast yet, but that could wait. She ran to the stables and quickly found Simon, the head groom, working in one of the stalls. As she approached, he looked at her in surprise. "Mam'selle Julie, what you doin' heah so early? An' dressed like a boy!"

"I want to go riding, Simon. My horse hasn't arrived yet, and my saddle isn't ready so I'll just have to ride one of *Pappa's* horses." She gave the black man a dazzling smile.

"Now, Mam'selle Julie, days no hoss heah you can ride. Days all too big fo' *petite fille*. 'Toinette, she skin me 'live iffen Ah lets you ride one of dem big hosses." The groom shook his head. "And yo' *Pappa*, he kills me iffen anythin' happen to you."

"Oh, Simon, don't be such an old grouch. If you don't tattle on me, no one will know. Now, go and saddle Thunder."

Simon's eyes grew wide. "Mam'selle Julie, now Ah knows you wants to git me killed and skinned 'live. Dat der Thundah, he be too big, too wild. *"Non,* please, Mam'selle, please don't ride ol' Thunder."

Julie was getting impatient. She wasn't used to being told no, and least of all by a servant. She stamped her foot and said, "Simon don't argue with me, you do as you are told."

"*Oui,* Mam'selle." Simon shook his head and mumbled all the way to the horse's stall. When the poor, frightened man had saddled the huge stallion that stood sixteen hands high, Julie made him help her up on the animal's back. With much grumbling, Simon did as she ordered.

When she sat astride Thunder, Julie felt as if she could see for miles. She dug her heels into the horse's sides until she prodded him into a canter, and soon she had him at a full gallop. The cold, damp air felt good on her face, and with Thunder's long legs covering so much ground, she felt like she was flying.

She had ridden quite a distance when suddenly she heard a strange sound. She slowed the huge horse down and listened carefully. It sounded as if someone was chopping wood but who? This was *Pappa's* land, and *Pappa* never came out here.

Slowly, Julie steered the big horse toward the sound and stopped before she reached the clearing. She saw several large black men busy cutting wood and carrying it over to a strange-looking shed. Then she saw the white man whose back was to her.

Who was he, and what was he doing on her father's land? Slowly Julie nudged Thunder forward for a better look. Just then, one of the black men stopped chopping and looked straight at her. Her heart stopped. Who were these men? Would they harm her when they realized she was there?

She was poised and ready to gallop off when the white man noticed that the slave had stopped working and was staring at something turned and followed the black man's gaze. Then he too saw her. "Well, it seems we have a visitor."

Julie couldn't move she sat staring back at him. It was Monsieur de Javon! The gentleman she'd met on the road with Charles. He was coming toward her and she couldn't decide if she should turn and run or stay and hear his explanation of what he was doing on her father's property.

"Hello, young man. Whom have I the pleasure of addressing?" André looked up at the small figure on the giant horse.

"Before I tell you who I am, would you please tell me what you are doing on this land?" Julie asked, as she tried to lower her voice so she would sound more like a boy.

"Well, my young friend, I am building cabins so all of us will have a place to live while I cultivate my land."

"*Your* land? Since when is this *your* land?" Julie felt great indignation. "This land belongs to Monsieur Jean-Claude Charlevoix." Her voice was stern and a frown creased her brow.

"Ah, but Monsieur Charlevoix just recently sold this land to me. Allow me to introduce myself. I am André Raphael de Javon." André smiled at her and said, "Now, who may I ask are you?"

From the look on André's face, Julie realized he had no idea who she was, and it tickled her to think she had the advantage because she certainly knew who he was.

"Oh," she said trying to lower her voice even more. "I'm a friend of the family. I was riding by and heard the sound of wood being chopped. Monsieur Charlevoix hadn't mentioned anything to *me* about selling this land."

"And does Monsieur Charlevoix usually discuss his business transactions with you?" André asked with a chuckle, as he suddenly took

68

the reins and led Thunder out to the clearing. "Why don't you come down from your horse so we can get a good look at you? Come down, and I'll show you the cabin I've built for myself."

Not waiting for an answer, he lifted her from the saddle. "You're such a little thing to be riding such a big horse. Aren't your parents afraid you might not be able to handle him?"

"Well," Julie answered, with a toss of her head. "I've handled him without any problems so far."

"A little hot-headed, aren't you?" André said with a grin. He put his hand on her shoulder. "Come, I'll show you around my cabin. I've been working non-stop since dawn, and I could use a short break."

He showed her through the place, and Julie was surprised to see how big it was. There were four large rooms in all. A parlor, a dining room, a bedroom and a small room off of the bedroom that held a small slipper-shaped tub and other items of a personal nature. Even the furniture was more than she had expected.

"I bought the furniture in New Orleans just recently," André explained. "Since I have to be out here by myself, I decided to spare no expense in having a nice place."

He glanced down at his little visitor and smiled. "Well, now you've seen my home. Rather primitive, wouldn't you say? But it will have to do until I have the money to build a proper one."

As they stepped out on the *galerie*, André reached to close the door, and in doing so, his arm brushed Julie's cap, knocking it from her head. A mass of dark curls fell down around her shoulders. André stopped and stared at her. Julie knew he wasn't certain just who she was. She couldn't resist and gave him a lovely smile.

"Julie? Can it be you? The lovely young lady I met on the road last September?"

Julie nodded. "*Oui*, it's I."

"But what are you doing riding that huge horse? And dressed like a boy?"

When she explained, André threw back his head and laughed. "Well, you certainly had me fooled for a while. I thought you were a young boy, a very handsome young boy, to be sure."

Julie stayed around for several hours, following André about, chattering like a small magpie all the while he and his slaves worked.

She watched as he became frustrated when something went wrong. And when that happened, he threw down the tool he was working with, said a few swear words under his breath, and stalked off to give himself a moment to cool off.

The slaves looked worried when this happened; but since he didn't take his anger out on them, they simply continued working. Once he cooled down, he would return, glance at Julie with an embarrassed smile, and continue working.

It was easy to see he could use more help. Some of the slaves were busy building a small kitchen so Delilah would have a place to cook. A few were also working to clear a small patch of land for planting.

André came back from one such outburst and said, "I'm sorry Julie, I shouldn't lose my patience. It's just that there's so much to do I sometimes lie awake at night trying to figure out how the devil I'll ever get it all done. With only twenty-five men, it takes more time than I can afford. And, the rain we had this past week didn't help." Then with a sheepish grin, he added, "And I am not all that proficient with hammer and nails."

"But, you will do it," Julie answered nodding her head. "I know you will." Hoping to sound encouraging, she continued, "Why, you've done so much already! You just need more help."

"I know," André agreed, a grim expression on his face. "But, for now, I must hold on to the money I have. I can't afford more help just yet. That's why I work alongside my men, to take up the slack. Only, sometimes, I feel like I'm all thumbs."

When, finally, it was noon and Delilah rang the big bell André had given her to call everyone to lunch, he invited Julie to join him. She was quite hungry by now and more than happy to accept his invitation.

"For the first time since I left the city, I have been able to relax," he said, with a gentle smile. "I've enjoyed your company."

Julie's heart almost fell out of her chest with this compliment, as she blushed and thanked him for his kind remarks.

"And now that we have become friends, you must call me André."

Finally, Julie knew it was time to start for home. Because it was overcast and gray, it seemed much later, and André was reluctant to have her go alone. "Give me a few minutes, and I will be happy to escort you home," he said as he started to order one of the men to saddle his horse.

"Don't worry about me," Julie assured him with a sweet smile. "I'll be perfectly all right. I don't want to take you away from your work."

At first André insisted, but Julie was just as adamant.

"Please don't worry about me. I've been riding this land for years. I

70

shall be home in no time. *Bonsoir*, André."

André chuckled at the remark, "for years." He helped her onto the horse and watched as she started off. She turned around and waved, and soon had Thunder at a full gallop.

André was sorry to see her go and hoped she would come back and visit again. He watched the horse and rider fade in the distance and hoped she wouldn't be in trouble when she got home.

Chapter 13

J ulie was in a great deal of trouble when she finally reached home.
Her father, 'Toinette, and Simon were all waiting for her on the
front *galerie.*

"Julie, where have you been all day? You've had us worried sick!
You didn't tell anyone you were leaving, and you didn't even have
breakfast. I was about to send a search party out to look for you!" Her
father's eyes blazed, and his face was stern as he came down the stairs
and lifted her from the big horse.

"Mam'selle, you be worrin' yo' po' *pappa* neah to death. Look at
you ridin' 'round dressed in dem awful clothes! What da sistahs at da
Convent gonna say?" 'Toinette stood at the top of the stairs, her hands
on her hips and a scowl on her face.

"Lawd, Mam'selle Julie, Ah sho' is glad to see you. Ah sho' is glad
dat dah hoss Thundah didn't do you no harm!" Simon took the reins
from Monsieur Charlevoix and led the horse to the stables shaking his
head and mumbling all the way.

Filled with guilt for worrying everyone, Julie tried to explain,
"*Pappa*, I went for a ride around the plantation and I found Monsieur de
Javon. I didn't know you sold that land to him."

Before her father could say a word, she rushed on "Anyway, I
stayed and watched him work. *Pappa*, he has so much to do!"

She had a plan of how they could help André, and she was anxious to discuss it with her father; but 'Toinette reminded her that it was almost dinnertime and she must hurry and bathe and change.

Her father agreed. "When you come down for dinner, we'll talk." Glaring at her, he turned and went into the house.

Julie hurried to bathe and dress. She couldn't wait to speak to her father about André's need for help.

Her father was already seated when Julie entered the dining room. Once she was seated, the butler brought a steaming bowl of *gumbo file* made with freshwater shrimp. Her father bowed his head and waited for her to do the same then he said the blessing. But before she could say a word, he fixed her with a stern eye. "Julie, I am very upset with you. You should never have stayed away so long and without telling someone. You caused a great deal of worry. You shall have no dessert and after dinner you will go straight to your room and stay there for the rest of the evening."

Julie lowered her head. "*Oui, Pappa.* I'm sorry I caused you to worry but I do have something very important to tell you." With a look of proper repentance, she waited for her father to give her permission to speak. Jean-Claude nodded his head.

Julie took a deep breath and proceeded to tell him what André was doing. "*Pappa*, he has only twenty-five slaves. He's so worried he won't get the planting under way fast enough. Is there any way we can help him?"

Her father smiled in spite of himself. "In what way would you like to help Monsieur de Javon, *chérie*?"

"*Pappa*, could we lend him some of our slaves, just until he gets his cane planted? His men could finish building while ours do the planting. You know if he doesn't get started soon, it may be too late; and he could be ruined."

Jean-Claude listened quietly and knew she was right. Time was running out, and so much depended on the crop. If André didn't have a successful year, he wouldn't be able to pay back his loan. If that happened, they would both lose money.

"You have a good argument, Julie. Since much of our planting is well under way, I think we may be able to work something out. I'll discuss it with Monsieur Schultz after dinner."

When the meal ended and Monsieur Schultz arrived, Julie hoped she could stay and hear what her father and the overseer had to say. But when she hesitated, her father said, "Julie, I thought I told you to go to your room."

73

"Please, *Pappa,* please let me stay while you talk to Monsieur Schultz."

"Go to your room this minute, young lady. I've had enough trouble with you for one day."

"*Oui, Pappa,* I'm going but please come and tell me what you and Monsieur Schultz decide. I'll never be able to sleep until I know. Please?"

"I'll come and tell you, now go."

It was sheer torture waiting in her bedroom until her father came. Julie was certain he would make the slaves available but waiting to find out was so hard.

She had planned a surprise for her father tonight, and now it would have to wait. She wanted to show him how well she could play the harp her mother had once played. One of the nuns at the Convent had taught her.

* * *

When Julie first entered the Convent of the Ursulines, the nuns had their hands full. Although she was by nature a sweet child, she was also a spoilt and neglected child. She was allowed to do pretty much what she pleased. She didn't follow any rules and wasn't taught any form of restraint.

With the death of his wife, Monsieur Charlevoix plunged into a grief so deep it took several months for him to begin functioning again. Meanwhile, the little girl was left in the care of the servants. Her father, so preoccupied with his sorrow, gave her free rein of the plantation, and with each passing year, she became more unruly until no one could do anything with her.

As she grew older, her behavior and appearance became the concern of all who knew Monsieur Charlevoix. The mothers of her little friends were appalled. Finally, one lady, a close friend of her late mother, prevailed upon the father to consider how his child was growing up.

"Jean-Claude, you must do something about Julie," Madame Gauthier said. The good lady had brought her own daughter Marie-Annette to visit.

Madame Gauthier was shocked at Julie's appearance and behavior. The little girl was loud, her hair was a tangled mass of unrestrained curls, and she looked totally unkept.

"The child needs discipline. If you don't do something soon, she will be impossible to handle." A look of concern and dismay filled Madame Gauthier's face.

Jean-Claude listened, then asked, "What would you have me do with her, Claudine?"

"You should put her in the Convent. The nuns will straighten her out. They will make a lady out of her. It's for her own good."

Jean-Claude nodded. "I know you are right. I've not been much of a father to her these past few years. She is growing up and needs discipline and an education and someone to teach her the things a young lady should know."

"Then you'll put her in the Convent soon?"

"*Oui*, Claudine, I'll go and speak to the Mother Superior and enroll Julie as soon as they can take her."

Madame Gauthier left the Charlevoix residence knowing she had done a good deed for her dead friend's child.

Suddenly, Julie found herself in a school where she was forced to follow rules and regulations. She had to rise at a certain hour and spend at least an hour on her knees at chapel for Mass and saying her rosary. She was required to go to class and then spend a certain amount of time studying. There were hours to practice music and dancing, plus singing and sewing. All of this came as quite a shock to the little girl who, until then, had done exactly as she pleased. She fought the nuns every step of the way. It took all the patience the good sisters possessed to deal with her.

One of her first infractions was the day Sister Marie Louise found her sliding down the banisters. With her skirts hiked up and her legs sticking straight out, Julie came flying down to land in a heap at Sister Marie Louise's feet.

"And just what do you think you are doing, Mademoiselle?" the nun demanded, a scowl on her face.

"I'm late for chapel, and the banister is much faster than the stairs," Julie said. She seemed not the least bit concerned at the picture she made in her descent.

The next thing she knew she was standing before Mother Superior. "Do you realize how much money your father is spending in order for you to attend this prestigious school?" the nun asked, her face red with anger.

Julie shook her head.

"Well, it is a great deal." The nun continued with her tirade. "The reason you are here is to learn how to behave like a well-bred young lady. But I fear you are hopeless."

Julie took a deep breath and said, "I'm sorry, Mother Superior, but I was late for chapel. That's the reason all of this happened in the first place...and now, I'm going to be even later."

In sheer exasperation, Mother Superior threw up her hands. "Very well, go to chapel...but try to behave yourself!"

It was one disaster after another for a while, and Julie pleaded with her father to let her come home. She wanted to be at *Château Charlevoix*. But her father was firm.

"When you're older *ma petite*, you'll fall in love and want to get married. But in order to marry a proper young man, you must know the right things. The nuns will teach you what you must know. Someday, you'll thank me for sending you to the Convent."

Julie was certain her father was wrong. She didn't know anyone she wanted to marry someday. But that was before she met André de Javon. From the moment she saw him, she knew what her father meant.

She had met the man she hoped to marry. And even though she was only eleven years old, she knew he was the one she wanted to spend the rest of her life with. So when she returned to the Covent in September, the nuns found a very different child. Oh, she still had her moments, but at least she seemed headed in the right direction. And, after a while, the nuns felt they could finally breathe a sigh of relief.

Julie applied herself to her studies; she practiced her music for hours and became the dancing master's best pupil. She planned to learn all there was to know while she was at school; so when she was old enough, she could win André's heart.

She would also learn all she could about running the plantation. When she returned to *Château Charlevoix*, she asked lots of questions, and her father was more than happy to explain and answer them. Since he had no sons, he was delighted his daughter showed an interest in how the plantation operated. He had no idea what had brought about this change in her, but he was very pleased.

* * *

Julie was sitting up in bed trying to read a book to keep her mind occupied, when there was a knock on the door and her father entered.

"Everything is arranged. Monsieur Schultz will choose the men tonight, and we will leave at daybreak for Monsieur de Javon's place."

Julie flung her book aside, jumped up, and threw her arms around her father's neck. "Oh, *Pappa*, I love you so much, and I'm so sorry for today." She covered his face with kisses.

Her father chuckled. "*Ma petite minx*, you can hug and kiss me and sweet-talk me all you want. But I am still very upset with you and don't you forget it!"

Julie smiled. "I know, *Pappa*, I know." After another kiss, she asked, "Please, *Pappa*, may I go with you tomorrow?"

"*Chérie*, I think if anyone has a right to be there, you certainly do. You'll have to get to sleep now. We must make an early start." He kissed her good-night, and blew out the candle.

Chapter *14*

It was barely daybreak when Julie, Jean-Claude, and seventy-five slaves set off for André's place. Julie was once again wearing the boy's outfit and riding Thunder, much to 'Toinette's dismay.

Simon was equally upset when he heard he was to saddle the huge horse for her again. He shook his head and crossed himself as he helped Julie up to Thunder's back, but her father laughed. "Don't worry, Simon, Julie will be safe. I'll not let any harm come to her."

By the time they reached André's property, they found him and his slaves already hard at work. The sun was nowhere in sight, and it looked like it would be another gray day.

When they appeared, André threw down his tool and hurried to meet them. He was surprised to see Monsieur Charlevoix and the wagon of slaves. After the greeting, Jean-Claude explained the reason for their visit.

"Monsieur Charlevoix, you are most kind, but I don't want to take your men away from their work on your place," André said when the men jumped down from the wagons.

"Don't worry, André. Much of our planting is well under way and this will cause no hardship for me," Monsieur Charlevoix assured him. "My men will be paid for the work they do for you. Besides," he said smiling, "I had no choice. This young lady insisted we help you."

Her father lifted Julie down from Thunder. "When you get to know my daughter better, you will find that it is very difficult to say *non* to her. She is nothing if not persistent."

A tender smile filled André's face as he made a courtly bow. "Mademoiselle Julie, I am forever indebted to you. You are a very kind and sweet young lady to show such concern for me."

Julie felt her face grow warm and her heart flip-flop. *Oh, André,* she thought, *I love you so much I'd do anything for you.*

André set about showing Monsieur Charlevoix and the slaves where the cane was to be planted. The older man stayed around for a couple of hours discussing many subjects pertaining to the crop, and then said he must leave.

"*Pappa*, may I stay here with André for a while?"

"Julie, you should not be addressing Monsieur de Javon by his first name. That is very rude."

André smiled. "Do not worry, Monsieur. Julie and I have become good friends, and I told her to address me so."

"Well, André, if you have no objections, then neither do I." Turning to his daughter, he smiled, "I will not object if you stay, as long as you won't be in the way, and if André doesn't mind."

"Monsieur, Julie is a pleasure to have around. She is welcome here anytime."

After her father left, Julie did as she had done the day before: she watched André work; she kept him company with her chatter; she followed him about, making certain to stay out of his way. Once again, she shared the noon meal with him. While they ate, she told him about school and her friends and regaled him with some of the adventures and misadventures she'd had.

When she told him about flying down the banister, André threw his head back and roared with laughter.

"Oh, Julie, you are so funny and entertaining. It has been a long time since I've enjoyed anyone's company as much as yours."

This remark caused Julie to love him even more.

"What other stories can you tell me?"

Julie thought for a moment and then brightened. "Well, I guess I could tell you about the time the nuns thought they had misplaced me."

"Misplaced you?" André's eyebrows shot up. "What do you mean?"

"That's what Mother Superior said when I finally showed up in her office. She said she didn't know how she would ever tell my father that I had been misplaced, and no one knew where."

André strangled a laugh and said, "Julie, start from the beginning. This sounds too interesting to miss any of the details."

"It was late one Sunday afternoon, and I decided I wanted to go to Congo Square to see the voodoo dancers."

"Voodoo dancers?"

"*Oui*. You've never seen them at Congo Square?"

"*Non*, but go on with your story."

"Well, like you, I had never seen them either, but I'd heard about them, so, of course, I had to go."

Doing his best to keep a straight face, André nodded. "Of course."

"Oh, they were so exciting to watch, André. They danced and sang and shouted, and made all sorts of noise."

Julie paused and said, "Next time you are in New Orleans, you really must go and watch them."

André nodded. "I'll be sure to do that, but go on, what happened next?"

"As I neared the Convent, I heard a loud knocking on one of the windows, and there was Sister Marie Louise motioning me to hurry and get inside."

"Did she scold you?"

Julie shook her head. "*Non*, she didn't. All she did was turn red in the face and tell me that I was really in for it. She stretched her arm out and told me I was to go to Mother Superior's office. Then she bellowed, 'MARCH'!"

The expression on Julie's face sent André into another fit of laughter. "So, then what happened?"

"Mother Superior was sitting behind her desk, with her hands clasped on the top. She looked at me for a long moment, then said, 'Will you please explain to me just where you have been all this time?'"

"So I told her." Julie shrugged and seemed lost in thought.

"Don't keep me in suspense, then what happened?"

"That nun's face turned *so* pale, and she said, 'You did what?' So then, I was subjected to a long lecture. When she was through, she stared at me for a long moment and asked what was to become of me.

"I thought about that for a moment, wondering just what *was* to become of me. Then I thought to please her by suggesting I could take the veil."

André shook his head, laughed, and said, "Oh, *non*."

"That's exactly what Mother Superior said. She threw up her hands and said, 'Merciful heavens!' She actually said she feared the pope himself would leave the faith if I were to do such a thing."

Another pause, and Julie said, "Then I told her that I could open up a coffeehouse."

André rolled his eyes. "Oh, that should have *really* pleased her."

"It didn't. In fact, she turned so pale I really thought she might get the vapors. Then she asked me what in the world did I know about coffeehouses, so I told her I stopped in one on my way home. I'd never seen one of those either, you see."

"Did she faint at that remark?"

"*Non*, she got *really* upset and told me no decent woman ever goes into such a place; but I reminded her I was not a decent woman; I was only a child. Well, she finally gave up and told me to go to dinner. When I left, I heard her praying and begging the Lord for help."

This brought another burst of laughter from André, and then he turned serious. "But, Julie, *ma chère*, do you realize how dangerous that might have been? Out all alone at that time of day."

Julie gave him a reassuring smile. "Oh, nothing happened to me. In fact, no one noticed me."

"Well, I want you to promise me you will never do such a thing again. Your *pappa* would be very upset if he knew what you did...by the way, did he ever find out?"

Julie nodded, "*Oui*, and I got another lecture."

It took several seconds for André to stop laughing.

Later, he took a short break, and together he and Julie sat on the step of his cabin. He was surprised at the child's knowledge concerning running the plantation and all it entailed.

"How have you learned so much? You're so young."

"*Pappa* has been teaching me, and I ask a lot of questions. *Pappa* says I should have as much knowledge as possible since some day *Château Charlevoix* will be mine. He says it is wrong to treat grown women like children. He says I have a good brain and should use it."

She paused and sighed. "The only problem is most people don't agree with him. Most think it unseemly and unladylike for a woman to be too educated." She glanced over at André. "How do you feel about it?"

André gave her a reassuring smile. "I think your father is right. You are intelligent, and it would be a shame to let your wonderful brain go to waste. Besides I wouldn't worry too much about what others think."

"Oh, I'm so glad you said that." Julie lowered her head and said in a soft voice, "I wouldn't want you to think me unladylike."

André took her small hands in his. "I think you are one of the loveliest young ladies I've ever met."

Julie giggled. "I do wish the nuns at the Convent could hear you say that. I'm not sure they would agree."

She knew she was a child, and it upset her that she was so young and there was nothing she could do to change that fact. But she also knew André truly liked her and enjoyed her company, and that fact made her heart dance with joy.

It was getting late, and although she would have liked to stay longer, Julie knew she had to leave.

André told her she was welcome back any time. "I like having you here—you are fun to talk to, and I haven't laughed so much in a long, long time." He lifted her onto Thunder's back. "*Au revoir*, sweet Julie."

* * *

Julie returned every day. She watched as first the cabins were finished, and then the kitchen was completed. She rode out to the fields and watched André and his slaves join her father's slaves in planting the cane.

It was the happiest time of her young life.

Sometimes, she and André would race their horses to the fields, and often he would let her win. They would end up laughing so hard she would almost fall off Thunder's back.

One day when it started to rain, they sat in the little parlor of André's cabin where Julie sent him into fits of laughter with more stories of her misdeeds at the Convent. She told him about a girl in school who, as Julie put it, was a "real pain in the neck."

"Her name is Felicité, and she is so stuck up! Always lording it over us younger girls, ordering us around, and acting so stupid!" Julie said this with such a look on her face that André started laughing again. "But I fixed her."

"What did you do? Although, I'm almost afraid to ask."

Julie got a wicked gleam in her eyes. "Well, I couldn't resist. It was true, Felicité did have lovely hair, but she was so vain about it. And one morning, she was going on about her *beautiful* hair. Why, the way she carried on, one would have thought the rest of us were bald!"

With a deep sigh, Julie continued "Anyway, I got so sick and tired of listening to her that I poured a bowl of grits over her head. Then her hair didn't look so beautiful, and neither did she, with grits dripping down her face."

"So, what happened to you?" André asked between gasps for breath from laughing so hard. "What did Mother Superior do to you that time?"

"Oh, she gave me a penance. And, in truth, I do believe she thought she was punishing me; but as it turned out, it was the other way around."

André raised an eyebrow and tried to maintain a serious face. "What do you mean? Young lady, just what did you do?"

Julie heaved another big sigh. "Mother Superior decided I needed to learn humility. Well, this came as quite a shock to me. It was Felicité who needed humility. But when I tried to tell this to Mother Superior, it made her really angry. She grabbed me by the arm and hauled me up to the sewing room and told me to mend all the stockings that had holes in them." Once again, Julie's expression sent André into gales of laughter.

"Whose stockings were they?" he asked.

Julie's eyes grew wide. "They were the nun's stockings. Can you *believe* it? She wanted *me* to mend them."

"And did you?"

"Well, I tried."

"Don't keep me in suspense. What *did* you do?"

"Oh, I mended them. But when I was finished, the nuns couldn't get their feet in."

André choked on his coffee, and after gasping for breath, asked in a strangled laugh, "How in the world did you manage to sew them closed when all you had to do was mend the holes?"

"That is exactly what Mother Superior asked me."

Julie rolled her eyes, shook her head, and once again sent André into fits of laughter.

"But," Julie said with her head tilted to the side, "it was interesting to note that, for the next few days, none of the nuns had much time for us students. They were too busy un-sewing their stockings. They were all quite upset." With a pause, Julie sighed and said, "I don't think they like me very much."

This last remark brought another roar of laughter from André as he reached over and gave her a hug. "Oh, Julie, you are priceless."

André had never laughed so much and so hard in his life. By the time they left the cabin and he went back to work, his sides hurt, his eyes were running, and so was his nose.

When Julie wasn't regaling him with her wild stories, he would tell her about the house he hoped to build in the future, and how it would look. "But it will have to wait for awhile, as the next project is my sugar factory."

Julie loved when he shared his plans with her. She would close her eyes and picture the house in all its splendor. "There is so much to do, André, but you will."

"*Merci, chère*, you are so certain of my success; you help make me certain also." With a gentle smile, André said, "I shall miss you when you leave for school."

"I'll miss you also, André. But, I will see you at Charles' wedding, won't I?"

"You certainly will. I am to be best man."

All the way home, Julie thought about how wonderful the past days had been. She knew she would have to return to school in the near future; but the thought made her so sad, she put it out of her mind.

As André watched her ride away, he found himself still chuckling over her funny stories. She was such a delightful little girl. *Someday I hope to have a beautiful little daughter just like you, Julie.*

Chapter 15

I t was the week before Julie would return to New Orleans. It was also her twelfth birthday. When she woke that morning, she was pleased and surprised to learn her horse had finally arrived. Her father told her this just as they sat down for breakfast. Without touching her food, Julie jumped up. *"Pappa*, please let's go see her right now."

The horse was just what she wanted, a jet-black filly. "Oh, *Pappa*, she's beautiful. Her coat is as soft as velvet and so shiny and as black as *minuit*. I shall call her *Minuit*."

Jean-Claude smiled and gave her a hug. "I have another surprise for you, Julie. Your saddle is finished, and there are still two more gifts for you at the house."

When they had inspected the saddle and returned to the house, Julie found two new riding habits wrapped and waiting for her. One was made of deep blue velvet, the other of black broadcloth. Each had a little hat with a feather and gloves to match. Shiny new riding boots and a hand-tooled crop completed the outfit.

After breakfast, Julie hurried to her room to dress, calling 'Toinette to come and help her. Both riding habits were laid out on her bed. She chose the blue velvet in honor of her birthday. It fit close to her figure from her shoulders to her waist and billowed into a long skirt with a train that looped over her arm. The collar and under-sleeves were cream-colored Belgian lace.

When her toilette was completed, Julie looked at herself in the mirror. She was pleased with how well her new riding habit fit; how it emphasized her small waist and she thought how grown up it made her look.

With the velvet outfit, her hat, and gloves, she felt quite grown-up. She hurried downstairs to get her father's approval, then rushed out to where *Minuit* was saddled and waiting.

* * *

André almost didn't recognize Julie as she rode up. At first, he thought it was a young woman and was surprised when he realized it was, indeed, Julie. He was used to seeing her in boys' clothes, her long hair tucked up under the cap, and riding the giant horse. Now here was this lovely young lady in a velvet riding habit, her hair loose, curls dancing in the breeze, with an elegant little hat perched on the side of her head. A feather of lighter blue curved near her face, and the horse she rode was as beautiful and dainty as its mistress. "Why, Julie, how lovely you look." André lifted her down. "Well, turn around, let me look at you."

He stood back, as slowly Julie turned so he could see her in this new mode of dress.

With eyes glowing and cheeks flushed, Julie looked at him in expectation. "Do you like it, André? Do I look pretty?"

"You look more than pretty, fair lady. You look absolutely gorgeous!" It came as a shock to André when he realized that, in a short while, his little friend would leave childhood behind and become a beautiful young woman.

Julie gave him her most dazzling smile and twirled around once more. "Do I look very grown-up?"

"*Oui,* Mademoiselle Charlevoix, you look very grown-up, indeed."

"I'm so glad you think I look older, because I am, you know." Julie nodded and looked quite pleased with herself.

"Oh?" André arched an eyebrow and his eyes twinkled. "You mean to tell me you have suddenly aged right before my eyes?"

"Well, I have," Julie answered with a giggle. "Because you see, Monsieur, today is my birthday—I am now two and ten."

"Oh, Julie, you should have told me I would have given you a gift. Well, we'll have to plan something special in honor of this day."

86

André stood looking off in the distance, a slight frown on his brow. "Now, what would you like to do that would make this birthday special? I've been working so hard I think I need a break. So what shall we do, where shall we go?"

"I know what let's do. Let's have a picnic."

"Why Julie, that's a splendid idea. Is there any special place you'd like to have this picnic, *chère coeur*?"

"*Oui*, there is, and I'll show it to you. It's my very favorite place in the whole world."

"Very well. I'll tell Delilah to fix us something special for our picnic. Meanwhile, why don't you come and keep me company?" When the sun had risen high in the sky, André stopped working and told his men to do likewise. He put Samson, who had already been appointed foreman, in charge and went to get the picnic basket Delilah had prepared.

Once they were mounted on their horses, he turned to Julie. "Now, young lady, suppose you show me this spot that is your very favorite in the whole world."

With a smile on her face and the words, "follow me," flung over her shoulder, Julie turned her horse in the direction of her home and urged *Minuit* into a trot that quickly turned into a gentle canter.

They rode side by side in silence for a while. Then Julie turned her filly toward a clump of trees. André was amused at her secretive manner, for, while they rode, he asked several times where they were going. Julie would only smile and say "Just be patient; we'll be there soon."

As they pushed their horses through the heavy brush and plants, André wondered about this "special place." He seldom ventured far from his place of work, and there was much of this land he was unfamiliar with. Someday, he hoped to have the time to do some exploring on his own. There was much he had yet to see.

Now he found himself sitting on his horse in a beautiful glade. There were the ever-present oak trees with their thick moss, stretching their branches out to shade parts of the glade. The grass was thick, soft, and vivid green. Wildflowers were sprinkled everywhere. André noticed a little stream, its water clear and sparkling, unlike the muddy waters of the Mississippi or the black waters of the swamps and bayous.

"Well, what do you think of it?" Julie asked, turning to him with a happy smile.

"It's beautiful," André answered, looking around. "I had no idea such a spot as this was here."

"The best part about this glade is that it belongs to both of us. Part of it is on our land, and part of it is on yours."

She smiled and said, "Every morning, *Pappa* sends some slaves out here to kill any snakes that may be around. He knows this is one of my favorite places."

Andre smiled. "Your *pappa* is very wise. I certainly learned about snakes quickly once I was out here."

He dismounted and lifted Julie down from her horse.

"I was so afraid you'd find this before I got the chance to show it to you. This was my parents' favorite spot also. They came here often when they were first married and even after I was born. We used to have picnics here."

Julie reached into the basket and pulled out a large cloth and spread it on the ground as she spoke. Patting it, she said, "Come and sit down, André, and I'll see what Delilah has prepared."

André followed her instructions and stretched out, watching her as she began to unpack the basket. What was there about this child that made him feel so relaxed and happy? She was a child, and far too young for him, but still she was such a delightful person he enjoyed being around her more than he thought possible. He smiled as she continued to lay the food out.

"Ah, what have we here?" Julie glanced over at him with a mysterious grin on her face. "Why, there's fried chicken, cold roast beef, hominy *croquettes*, celery, biscuits, and strawberry jam, mmmmmmmmm."

She licked her lips and carefully laid each item out on the cloth. "But I'm not finished yet," she said with a look of surprise. "There's more. Look, we have cheese, cupcakes, and lemonade." She drew out two plates, two cups, and the flatware.

"That Delilah is a true jewel, André. You must always be kind to her. Serving women like Delilah are worth their weight in gold, *Pappa* always says."

André hadn't said a word but inwardly he chuckled. He enjoyed the way she made a big to do about each item in the basket. She was truly an enchanting little girl. She had a way of making even the simplest things seem important. Everything was nicer when this sweet little girl came to visit.

Julie served the food and poured the lemonade into the cups; but before she could take a sip, André stopped her. "*Non,* don't drink yet. This is a special occasion and it deserves a special toast."

He cleared his throat and held his cup up to her. "To the sweetest, dearest person I know, on her very special day. Julie, may you have many more lovely years and continue to bring joy and happiness to all who know you." Leaning forward, he gave her a gentle kiss on her cheek. "Now," he said, picking up a chicken leg with a flourish. "Let's eat I'm starved."

They dug into the food with relish. They laughed and talked and ate, and Julie knew that for the rest of her life, she would never have a birthday that would ever be as wonderful as this one.

When they'd finished eating and rinsed the dishes in the stream and repacked the hamper, Julie grew quiet. As André looked over at her, he became aware that her face was suddenly filled with sadness.

"Julie, *chère coeur,* what's wrong? Why do you look so sad?"

"*Pappa* says I must be leaving for New Orleans the first of next week." Julie lowered her head so he couldn't see the tears that welled up in her eyes.

"Oh, *chère,* I'm sorry, but you must go back to school." He took her hands in his. "Julie, you may come over as often as you like until it is time for you to leave."

"But I don't want to leave. I want to stay here with you."

André put his finger under her chin and tilted her face up. Her lovely dark eyes were filled with tears, and such a look of sadness was on her face it tore at his heart.

"Julie, there is no one in the world I would rather have with me than you, but you must return to the city. Besides, I'll be coming to New Orleans in just a short while for the wedding. We'll see each other then." He took out his handkerchief and tenderly dried her eyes, and Julie tried to smile.

"I tell you what," André said as he got to his feet and helped her up. "Let's ride back and give this basket to Delilah. I'll check on the men, and then I'll ride home with you. I need to speak with your father."

André was in need of an overseer, and Jean-Claude had told him of someone who might be interested in the job. Now André wanted to know how soon he could expect the man to arrive.

Jean-Claude was delighted to see his friend; and as they sat in the parlor sipping coffee, André asked if the man from the German coast would be arriving soon.

"*Oui*, André, I spoke to my overseer. His wife has a cousin who recently lost his wife in childbirth and now has no family left. I think he would be happy to move closer to his relatives. He should be here next week."

The day before Julie was to return to the city, she had to tell André she would be leaving in the morning.

"I'm going to miss you, *chère*. You've made this past month delightful. I owe you a debt of gratitude I can never begin to repay." André gave her a gentle smile and Julie fought back the tears that sat right behind her eyelids.

When it was time for her to return home, André said, "I'll ride back with you."

As they mounted their horses, Julie asked, "What are you going to name this place?"

André shrugged. "I don't know. I've been so busy, I haven't given it much thought."

"But you must name it something," Julie insisted. "Every plantation has a name."

"Well, little one, if it were yours, what would you name it?" Julie looked around for a moment. "The oaks remind me of royal sentries guarding the entrance to the castle." Her voice was soft. She thought for a moment, and then her face brightened. "You could name it 'Royal Oaks.' That has a nice sound to it."

André arched an eyebrow and repeated the name. "Royal Oaks, *oui*, I like the sound of it." Smiling over at her, he said, "Now little one, when you come to visit, you can be proud to know you have given Royal Oaks its name."

Chapter 16

Not long after Julie's departure, her father rode over with his overseer's cousin. The man's name was Karl Hoffman, and André was surprised to find Monsieur Hoffman was not much older than himself. The three sat down and talked for over an hour.

André showed Monsieur Hoffman around his land, explained what would be expected of him, and also showed him the small cabin that had been built for him.

"You must also know I do not abuse my slaves, and you must never abuse them either. If ever you have a problem, bring it to me, and together we will solve it, *n'est ce pas?*"

Although Monsieur Hoffman had a limited understanding of French, he understood enough to know what he had been told, and assured André he would abide by the rules.

Christmas and New Year's came and went, and still André worked on. Now it was February, and he prepared to leave his property in the hands of his new overseer and go to New Orleans.

* * *

André didn't know it, but he was now completely accepted by the Créole society. And this happened shortly before his return to the city.

Charles and his parents were having a late breakfast, when Henry entered carrying a small silver dish. On it sat a white envelope that he presented to his mistress.

"Ah, it is finally here," Madame du Fray said. "It is in answer to a letter I sent to France the same day you and André arrived from Europe."

"*Maman*, what are you talking about?"

"As soon as I met André, I was certain he was all he said. But just to be safe, I wrote a quick letter to a good friend of mine in Paris. I asked her to look into André's background and tell me if such a family named de Javon had existed."

"And?"

"Well, here is her answer. Everything André told us is true." She quickly read the message out loud.

When she finished she said, "You know, Charles, one can not be too careful. There are so many of those *gens de couleur libre* who go to France and try to pass themselves off as white, I simply wanted to assure myself that André wasn't one of them."

Madame du Fray, like all Créoles, was concerned that there not be one drop of Negro blood in the members of their society. Because there was much mingling of the races, between white master and black slave, over the years, there evolved a group of colored people in whom it would be almost impossible to detect their Negro bloodlines.

Because these people started calling themselves Créoles, (much to the horror of the true Créoles), it was of the utmost importance to know as much about a newcomer as possible.

The pure Créole was of the Caucasian race, being a mixture of French and Spanish. Thus, did Madame du Fray feel her concern in Andre's background justified.

No amount of money could buy one's way into the Créole society (as the Americans quickly learned). What made one acceptable was family and background.

"Since you are determined to have André for your best man, and I know several of the daughters of my friends have had their eyes on him since he first arrived, I felt it my duty to learn as much about him as possible. Now I can tell them they need have no worries. André has passed the test."

Charles, too, breathed a sigh of relief to know his friend was completely accepted by his family and friends, especially since his soon to be sister-in-law, Gabrielle, was so taken with André.

Charles had insisted that André spend a month in the city. "You've been working so hard, the rest will do you good."

* * *

André was excited as he prepared to leave for New Orleans. He'd worked side by side with his slaves from sunup to sundown. He'd chopped wood, built cabins, cleared land, and planted crops, and it amazed him that he had done it. Since he'd never worked before in his life, he couldn't believe all he'd accomplished.

Except for Julie's visits, he'd had no amusement or diversions. At twenty-two, André was still young enough to feel the pull of the city, to want to go out and play. He smiled to himself at the phrase, 'go out and play'—but it was true, to have fun, to forget for just a little while the tremendous job still facing him. The *théâtre*, the *soirées,* the balls, and parties would all be a welcomed relief from the months of hard work.

When Charles last visited Royal Oaks, he told André that Gabrielle sent her regards. "She certainly is looking forward to seeing you again. That's all she talks about." He grinned at his friend. "You had better watch out, André. Gaby is more than fond of you. I think she wants to marry you."

André gave the other a rueful smile and shook his head.

"Charles, that's foolish. She hardly knows me, and besides how could I marry her? How could I ask her to come out here and live in this primitive cabin for another year or more?" Again, he shook his head. "*Non*, a man must have a decent home for his bride."

"But, André, someday you'll have the home you want. If Gaby really loves you, where you live won't matter. The fact that you have someone who loves you, who can share your hopes and dreams with, that's what's important."

His grin widened. "Besides, Gabrielle will bring to her marriage a handsome dowry. Monsieur Ste. Claire may have fallen on hard times, but he had the good sense to put aside a large dowry for each of his daughters. You should think about it, André. Gaby is beautiful and comes from one of the best families in the city. She could be a great help to you, not only financially but in other ways as well."

* * *

André rode in a carriage Monsieur Charlevoix had lent him.

Demetrius sat next to the coachman. As he neared the city, André mulled over what Charles had said. Did Gabrielle really want to marry him? He had to admit he was lonely. It would be good to have someone by his side, to encourage him, someone to come home to in the evening.

Gabrielle *had* stirred feeling in him the last time he'd seen her. Feelings he's purposely subdued. He'd had to force himself to remain cool and indifferent towards her. And now, he wasn't sure how he really felt about her. He certainly hadn't wanted to be distracted from his plan by any woman. Now his plan had been put into action; so perhaps he should give it some thought. Charles' remark forced him to reexamine how he felt about many things.

He wondered if Gabrielle's father would allow her to marry a man who was just starting to build his empire. What if, God forbid, he failed? What then? But, she did have a handsome dowry. Charles had said so, and he ought to know. He was marrying her sister.

A large dowry could be a great help. While he prided himself on becoming successful on his own, still, with her dowry, he could buy so much more of what he needed. He shook his head. *Non, it is too soon to be thinking of marriage.* He forced himself to put all thoughts of failure and Gabrielle out of his mind.

* * *

When André finally reached the city, he went directly to the du Fray home. Henry, the butler let him in, and Charles hurried to greet him. "Well, André, you finally made it. Come into the parlor. Henry, bring us some wine."

Monsieur and Madame du Fray greeted him also. "We are so happy to have you stay with us," Madame du Fray said warmly.

"*Oui,*" her husband added. "But, *mon ami*, you look tired. Don't let Charles wear you out before you have a chance to rest."

Once his parents left the room, Charles gave André the itinerary of events. But, for the moment, what André wanted most was sleep. "Charles, it all sounds interesting. But your father is right. At the moment, I can't think of anything but taking a bath and getting some sleep."

"Of course, André. I'll have a tub brought to your room at once. Sleep as long as you like."

Demetrius and some other servants filled the tub, and André felt the hot water work its therapeutic magic on his tired, sore muscles. When he was through bathing, he lay down, Demetrius lowered the *baire*, and within minutes, André was sound asleep.

When he woke, he remembered Charles had quite a list of social events lined up, but he wasn't ready to take part in any of them just yet.

As he and Charles sat in the library, André said, "I'm sorry, Charles, I wish I could join you tonight. But the truth is, that I would really appreciate having at least one evening of doing absolutely nothing." He gave his friend a tired smile.

Charles looked shocked. "André, you've been out in the country by yourself these past months. Now you're here in the city, and all you want to do is stay home?"

André shrugged, and tried to explain. "I know it sounds crazy. But, tomorrow, I'm meeting with the man who will be building my sugar factory. Tonight, I'd like to go over the plans he sent me. I didn't have time to review them when I was at Royal Oaks."

Charles rose and went to a small table where a bottle of wine sat. He poured two glasses, and crossing the room, handed one to André. "I understand. But, you know, of course, Gabrielle will be disappointed when you aren't at the party tonight." His eyes held a teasing glint.

André took a sip of wine, and gave Charles a cynical smile. "I'm sorry to disappoint her, but first things first. I'm certain you will be able to make my excuses for me."

"I'll do my best, but it won't be easy. Gabrielle is spoilt and self-centered and does seem to think everyone is here for her pleasure. But I'm the one who will have to explain when you don't appear tonight."

"Sorry, Charles. I can't be of any help. Maybe you'd best tell her beforehand." He paused. "And speaking of hands, look at mine." He held them out, palms up, and Charles saw the heavy calluses.

"*Mon Dieu*, they look bad. I'll have one of the maids bring some salve to your room and treat them before you retire tonight."

"*Merci*, Charles. And tomorrow night, I'll be sure to wear my gloves most of the time."

* * *

Charles was correct. The one person who didn't appreciate André's need for rest was Gabrielle. She'd waited and looked forward anxiously to his return, and when she learned she wouldn't see him that night, she was furious. "What do you mean he won't be at the party?" she demanded.

"I told you, Gabrielle."

"Well, I don't see why he didn't go over his plans this afternoon. I can't believe he's come all this way, and now all he wants to do is study some stupid plans!" Gabrielle glared at Charles as though it was his fault.

As a result of André's absence, the evening was less than enjoyable for Gabrielle. Oh, she had enough young men dancing in attendance to her, but none of them could compare with André. It was he, and *only he,* she was interested in. But, she wouldn't let him know it. She'd show him when next she saw him!

The next night when André appeared at a pre-wedding party given for Charles and Francesca, Gabrielle couldn't take her eyes off of him. He looked so handsome in his formal attire. His shoulders had filled out more, as had his chest and arms. The sun had lightened his dark hair, and his face was tanner, which only enhanced his white teeth and hazel eyes. His six-foot-two inch frame towered over everyone else's. He was far more handsome than any other man present, and the other girls were all but swooning over him.

Gabrielle made sure André was aware of her presence. She was popular and always had a swarm of young men around her. She was on the dance floor every moment the music played, but André showed no sign of being jealous of her other admirers.

Indeed, he had more than his share of admirers also. Every girl present made some attempt to catch his eye and dance with him.

Gabrielle watched him laugh and speak with several of them. She observed him dancing with several others, and as she watched, her jealous nature took hold. *Oh, the fool!* she stormed to herself. *Doesn't he know I'm here? How dare he ignore me!*

André was very aware of Gabrielle. He could feel her eyes on him throughout the evening. But he was determined not to allow her to monopolize his every moment as she had done the night of her parents' *soirée.* Instead, he purposely ignored her. He would wait to see what she would do.

He watched Gabrielle make her way to where he stood. But, at first, she pretended not to see him. Then slowly she turned toward him. Giving him a look of happy surprise and smiling up at him as sweetly as possible, she cooed, "Why, Monsieur de Javon, what a pleasant surprise. I had no idea you were here. How nice to see you again. I hope you will be staying in the city for a while."

André's smile was one of amusement. Who did she think she was fooling? Slowly, he allowed his eyes to slide from her face down her curvaceous body to the hem of her gown and then back up. He watched as she grew flustered and her cheeks turned pink. She put her fan to her face to hide her confusion.

With his eyes twinkling, André bowed and kissed her hand. "I shall be staying until after your sister's wedding. Then I shall return to my home."

He wouldn't let her know it, but he suddenly realized he'd almost forgotten how truly beautiful she was. With her delicate features, heart-shaped face, hair as dark as midnight, and eyes a deep violet, she was the most beautiful young woman André had ever seen.

She wore a gown of deep violet that matched her eyes. It was made of water taffeta, with a neckline cut so low it allowed the top of her bosom to show. Her hair was caught up with violet ribbons, and diamond-headed pins. Diamonds encircled her neck and hung from her earlobes. Just then, the music started, and the next thing André knew, Gabrielle was in his arms.

As they glided across the floor, she looked up at him and asked, "How is your plantation coming along, André?"

He told her all he'd done in the past months. "I've recently hired an overseer, and next, I'm having my sugar factory built. While I'm here in New Orleans, I shall also order a carriage."

Gabrielle listened and held on to every word as though it was of the utmost importance. She flattered him and did everything she could think of to impress him, and André found himself enjoying her attentions.

It was nice to have someone to talk to who was interested in what he was doing on his land. Julie was always interested, and that was one reason he'd grown so fond of her. But Julie was a child. His male friends were also interested. But to have this beautiful young lady, who could have her pick of any man, to have her interested, to have her hanging on every word, flattered him more than he cared to admit.

Over the next week, he began to have a different opinion of Gabrielle. She was much sweeter than he remembered. She didn't seem so spoilt and self-centered. Perhaps he had misjudged her.

Gabrielle was also more passionate than André expected. He knew all too well the code of behavior expected of an unmarried Créole girl. And Gabrielle wasn't living by the code. At least, not where he was concerned.

André knew the ethics expected from a gentleman. And he knew if he overstepped those rules, he could easily find himself in a duel or a marriage.

In the Créole society of New Orleans in the early eighteen hundreds, it was assumed, that if a gentleman was seen paying undue attention to a young lady, a marriage would soon follow.

Knowing this, Gabrielle used it to her advantage. When her friends hinted that, "Monsieur de Javon seems to be getting serious about you, Gaby."

She made no effort to contradict them. She would smile and say, "Perhaps he is. We are very fond of each other." And the look she gave them implied much more.

She charmed André, flattering him and stroking his ego every chance she got. She found every opportunity to stir his emotions and passions while keeping him at arm's length. And it was working she knew it was. She could see it in his eyes. He wasn't paying attention to the other girls. He seldom danced with anyone but her. Gabrielle smiled to herself. If things went the way she had planned, he would be proposing marriage before he left the city of that she was certain.

Chapter 17

Every time André appeared at a social event, the conversation among the young girls was who would be lucky enough to capture this tall, handsome, cultured Adonis. But the truth of the matter was, although André was well thought of and completely accepted by the Créoles, still, he had a rather uncertain future.

Many a father vowed, "I'll never allow my daughter to marry a man who is just starting to rebuild his life. *Mon Dieu*, the man hardly has a penny to his name."

Other fathers agreed. "My daughter must have a husband with a solid future, a decent home, and money in the bank."

The mothers also had much to say. "*Ma chère*, I understand he actually works in the fields alongside his slaves! Can you imagine it? His hands are covered with calluses. I felt them when he took my hand to kiss it."

"Did you see how dark his skin is? That's from being out in the sun too long. Why it's positively indecent!" said another.

Still others, like Charles, admired André greatly.

"I think it is admiral," one gentleman said when André was being discussed at a coffeehouse. "The man is willing to work to achieve his goals. Someday, I'm sure he'll be a great success."

"Well, until he is a success, I'll not encourage his attentions on my daughter," another father added.

Gabrielle cared not a whit about what others thought of André, or his future. He was tall and handsome, and the most exciting man she'd ever met. For her, that was all that mattered.

It was at another pre-wedding party that she and André were dancing, and as usual, Gabrielle's thoughts were centered on how to make André fall in love with her. When the music stopped, she feigned a slight touch of faintness.

With a weak smile, she leaned against André, fluttered her fan, and sighed, "It's rather close in here; perhaps a stroll in the courtyard will help. Would you be kind enough to escort me?"

Nodding, André said, "Of course," and offered her his arm. Once outside, he lit a cheroot and leaned his shoulder against the trunk of a fig tree, as he lazily studied Gabrielle's face in the moonlight. Reaching out, he gently rubbed his knuckle against her cheek. "Feeling better, *chère*?"

At the sound of his voice, and his touch, Gabrielle melted into his arms. Tilting her head back, she whispered "I always feel better when I'm with you, André."

Tossing his cheroot aside, he slowly brought his lips down to hers and kissed her long and passionately.

André was not one to have his head turned easily by a pretty face, but he'd been living alone in the country too long and was much more susceptible to Gabrielle's charms than he cared to admit. She made him feel like the most important man in the world. She aroused feelings and passions he'd tried not to think about. As a result, she was having a profound effect on him.

Gabrielle responded, and the kiss deepened. "Oh, André, you do care for me," she whispered when the kiss ended.

Over the next few nights, they were thrown together at every event. And, often, Gabrielle managed to be alone with him more than was considered proper. Her forward behavior at times left André puzzled. When his kisses became too demanding, she would push him away and act indignant.

Other times, when they were alone, she would put her arms around his neck, press her body against his, and whisper, "André, darling, kiss me. Kiss me like you've never kissed me before."

She would respond to his kiss with a fervor that surprised him, only to once again push him away. In anger, he would lash out at her. "Good lord, Gabrielle, I'm only human. If you don't want me to kiss you, then stop throwing yourself at me!"

"I am *not* throwing myself at you. How can you say such a thing?" Gabrielle said in a huff.

"You are leading me on and it is the same thing. You seem to think you can toy with a man's emotions with no repercussions. I don't need this aggravation or your stupid games!" Glaring at her, he would turn on his heel and go back into the house.

After such an outburst, André would give her a cold shoulder, turning his attention to the other young ladies.

This, Gabrielle could not tolerate; and as soon as she could, she would immediately turn sweet and affectionate. "Oh, André, don't be angry with me. I don't mean to upset you. I care for you so much, honest I do. And I love when you kiss me it's just that I must think of my reputation." She would look up at him with her incredible eyes, a sweet smile, and a voice that would melt ice, and beg his forgiveness.

Often in his anger, André wanted to shake her and give her a good tongue-lashing. Just as often, he got angry with himself. Why did he put himself through this nonsense? But, he knew why. It was because he was lonely, and Gabrielle was lovely, and passionate, and he couldn't seem to resist her.

Eventually, Charles noticed the effect Gabrielle was having on his friend. "What is going on between you and that dear future sister-in law of mine?" he asked André one afternoon when they were relaxing in the du Fray courtyard.

André looked over with a wry smile. "I wish I knew. That dear future sister-in-law of yours is driving me crazy. One minute she is sweet and loving, and the next she is giving me trouble because I act affectionate. I never know where I stand with her or what to expect from one minute to the next."

"I told you Gabrielle can be difficult. There is no denying it. But I also told you she has set her cap for you. What Gaby wants, Gaby gets." He gave André an impish grin.

"I have it, on the best authority, that what she wants is *you*! And I might add, you couldn't do better. Her family thinks the world of you, and Gaby will bring to her marriage that healthy dowry I told you about. You should give it a great deal of consideration."

"I *have* given it some thought," André said, "and marriage to Gabrielle is very tempting." *And also very profitable—two can play this game*, he thought.

* * *

The wedding was in two days. Charles, along with André and a few other friends, sat out to have one last fling before Charles' marriage.

When asked what he would like to do that evening, André said, "This is your night, Charles. I'll do whatever you want."

"Oh, we'll do what I want but this is your first Créole wedding, so you get to have first choice."

"Well then, I would like to go to Congo Square. I've heard about it, but I've never seen it."

Charles slapped him on the back. "Excellent choice. Come on fellows, to Congo Square."

Congo Square was a large open lot between *Rue Rampart* and *Rue Orleans*. Already, a crowd had gathered to watch the slaves dance Congo.

"The slaves are allowed to come here and dance from four o'clock until six-thirty," Charles explained. "Their masters give them written permission to gather. It is a chance for them to relax and enjoy themselves."

"Are any of your slaves here?" André asked.

"*Oui*, if you look over there, you will see some of ours."

Andre looked at the group of black men and women and spotted a few from the du Fray household. Some of the slaves' children had also come to dance.

Charles explained that a few of the men got their master's cast-off finery to wear. The women wore bright calico dresses of vivid reds, yellows, and greens, and various other colors. Some women had their hair tied in the *tignon*, while others let their hair hang loose and flowing. Large loop earrings (the only jewelry they were allowed to wear) swung from their earlobes.

Ribbons and feathers had been attached to the children's nondescript clothes.

Suddenly, a huge Negro appeared carrying a couple of large animal bones. He rolled out what looked like a tall drum and began beating it.

"That is called a *bamboula*," Charles said.

Slowly, with the beating of the drum, the slaves, both men and women, began to move to the rhythm. As the tempo increased, the men stomped and leapt about, chanting and occasionally shouting. They had small pieces of metal tied around their ankles that made a tinkling sound as they stomped their feet and leapt in the air. In no time, their bodies were glistening with sweat as they moved to the tempo.

The women took up the chant and began to sway and move their bodies from head to toe.

They twirled and dipped, leapt in the air, shook their shoulders, and swished their full skirts so that their legs were exposed, their bodies moving faster and their voices getting louder as the tempo increased.

Even the children moved about to the rhythm.

The very air pulsated with the beat of the drum, and the earth shook from the stamping and leaping of the dancers.

"They are doing their favorite dance," Charles explained. "It is called the *Calinda*. The other is the Dance of the *Bamboula*. These are dances that they use in their voodoo ceremonies."

André was mesmerized by sight and sound. Every nerve in his body seemed to respond to the drumbeat. He could feel the energy all around him. Others seemed caught in the same trance. He was amazed at how graceful the women were. He'd never seen anyone move their body like these women did.

Besides the drumbeat, the chanting and shouting, there were also the vendors who plied their wears amongst the white folks.

"Lemonade, *Michie*?" a Negro asked as he came up to André.

André shook his head. Another man came up with a tray of small ginger cakes. "Try one, they are excellent," Charles said. "And you must have an extra one for *lagniappe*."

André raised an eyebrow, but it was too noisy to try to understand the word *lagniappe*, he'd ask about that later. He took the treats and paid the man. Another man came up with a tray of candy. "Those are pralines, and they are the best," Charles assured him. "You must have one of those."

André slowly ate the confectioneries as he continued watching the slaves dance. He had never seen anything to equal this.

The group stayed for a while, but then it was suggested they move on. Charles wanted to go to a coffeehouse for a game of cards.

They continued on to Charles' favorite coffeehouse, and finally, to a room on the second floor where some card games were in progress.

André was not a gambler and had he not drunk so much, he might have thought twice about risking much of what he had in a game of cards. But he chose to throw caution to the wind and try his luck at playing faro. There was always the chance that he might win.

At first, he and Charles played at the same table; but as André's luck improved, Charles' luck did not. Finally, Charles dropped out of the game and his place was taken by an older man.

Somewhere in the back of his mind, André knew he too should quit; but a feeling of recklessness took hold, so he continued to play. His luck wavered, one minute he was winning and the next he was losing. Still he couldn't seem to stop.

It was as though he had lost all common sense. Then, once again, his luck changed and he began to win. All the right cards kept coming up. Now that he had a change of fate, he played with more caution. He kept his eyes hooded, and played his hand close to his chest. He was in too deep to stop. He had to win!

But then, once again, his luck changed, and he found himself losing. What would he do if he lost? *Non*! He must win he couldn't afford to lose.

As the hours passed, André's luck continued to fluctuate. One minute he was up, and the next he was down. One by one, the other gentlemen who had been playing dropped out but remained standing around the table to see the outcome of the game.

Now it was between André and the older man who had taken Charles' place. One could feel the tension in the room. Sweat broke out on André's forehead, and he took out his handkerchief and wiped his brow. His heartbeat increased when he realized he had just one more hand to play. If he didn't win, what would he do?

But with his last play, the right cards came up and when they did, the other man threw down his cards and said, "Ah, *mon ami*, I fear tonight that my luck has failed me."

The game was over. André almost fell off his chair he was so relieved. Once again, he mopped his forehead and tried to calm his heart rate down. Much to his surprise, he found he had ended up with an IOU for fifty slaves, plus a check for one thousand dollars. When the game ended, one could feel the tension leave the room.

"Now, André, aren't you happy you came with us tonight?" Charles said as they drove home. It was obvious he had overindulged and was feeling no pain.

The long hours of card playing had sobered André. With a grim smile, he said, *"Oui,"* I guess so. I'm also happy things turned out the way they did." I can't imagine how I could have been so stupid! Watching that man lose all of that money and fifty slaves, knowing it could have been me, made me ill. And it also made me feel sorry for him."

Charles only laughed. "Ah, the wages of sin. You play the game, you have the pain."

The next morning, the two joined Monsieur du Fray at the breakfast table. "Well, Charles, did you bid farewell to your bachelorhood?" There was a twinkle in his father's eyes.

Charles, with the look of one who is suffering a terrible hangover, nodded. "*Oui, Pappa.* I think I bid farewell to everything including the lining of my stomach and the inside of my head. Thank heaven, I have a day to recover before the wedding." Both he and André spent the rest of the day nursing their hangovers.

* * *

The wedding day dawned gray and ugly and Francesca fretted that the day might be ruined by rain. But by midmorning when the ceremony took place, a feeble sun managed to push through the clouds.

The nuptials were held in the Saint Louis Cathedral that was directly across from the *Place d'Armes*, the square where first the French flag, then the Spanish flag, then the French flag again, and now the American flag flew.

Créole weddings were quite different from American weddings. At the start of the ceremony, Swiss Guardsmen dressed in colorful pink-and-gold uniforms preceded the wedding procession. After the Swiss Guards came Charles, escorting Madame St. Claire, followed by his parents, then Francesca escorted by her father, followed by André. There was no maid of honor or bridesmaids.

The marriage vows were followed by a high Mass, and in all, the ceremony and mass took well over an hour. A reception was held at the home of the bride's parents where there was an elaborate meal, dancing, and much champagne.

During the early part of the reception, André spotted Julie and her father across the room. He hurried over to greet them. A few minutes later, Monsieur Charlevoix was called away by some other men. "You look lovely Julie," André said, smiling at her.

She did indeed look lovely in a gown of soft pink moiré, her mass of curls tumbling about her shoulders.

"Oh, André, it is so good to see you again," Julie said, looking up at him. "Tell me every thing that has been happening at Royal Oaks."

André looked around for a place to sit and saw two empty chairs against the wall near the dance floor. "Come, let us go and sit down." Once seated, he told her what had been happening at Royal Oaks and about the card game.

When she heard this news, Julie's eyes grew wide. "Oh, André, think of all you can do with so much money and help."

André laughed. "*Oui*, but first I must build more cabins so they will have a place to live." He told her about the sugar factory and his new carriage, and Julie listened attentively.

As they sat together talking, Gabrielle, looking lovely in a gown of dark blue lampas, hurried up to them. "André," she purred. "I've been looking all over the place for you. Come, I have some friends I want you to meet." Without giving Julie a second glance, she started to steer André to the other side of the room.

Disengaging his arm from her grasp, André said, "*Excusez-moi*, Gabrielle." He then turned back to the little girl. "Julie, dear heart, please excuse me. I'll see you again before the evening is over."

Julie's eyes filled with pain when she tried to smile. "That's all right, André, I understand." But she didn't. She couldn't understand why André allowed Gabrielle to just come up and take him away.

Chapter 18

As the month of February drew to a close and André's stay in New Orleans was coming to an end, he found himself reluctant to leave Gabrielle.

It was another night at another ball when Gabrielle asked him to walk with her in the courtyard. As the music came to an end, André danced her over to the French doors, and together they slipped out. The night had turned cool, and Gabrielle gave a shiver.

"You don't mind if I snuggle up to you?" she asked as they walked to the far corner of the yard. She looked at him; and in the moonlight, she was so lovely and desirable, André could not resist her.

The moonlight filtering through the large tree that stood near the back gate, the scent of the many flowers that filled the courtyard, the soft sound of water trickling in the fountain, plus the perfume she wore, all added to feelings of intoxication that overcame the young man.

"Kiss me, André," she whispered.

His arms enveloped her, and he felt her soft curves pressed against him. His lips came down on hers, soft at first, then with a swift intensity that sent a tremor through her body. He'd kissed her before but never like this. His heart pounded and his hands shook. His kiss became more demanding, and suddenly she pushed him away. "André, what are you doing?"

It was as though a glass of cold water had been flung in his face.

André stopped and looked at her for a long moment. "I'm sorry, Gabrielle, I couldn't resist you."

Slowly, he put his arms around her again; and holding her more gently, whispered, "You are driving me crazy! I can't go on like this I want you, Gabrielle. I want you more than I've ever wanted anyone or anything in my life."

It was true. She was indeed driving him crazy. He'd been alone too long, and having Gabrielle here in his arms made him realize how lonesome life had been. With her as his wife, he would no longer feel that way. Her voice brought him back to the present. "You want me even more than your plantation?"

"More than anything."

Once again, his lips found hers. His kiss was soft at first, but as before, he felt her respond, and the kiss became more passionate. His hands caressed her body, and Gabrielle made no attempt to stop him. With each second, his fervor rose. Again, she pushed him away.

With an effort of control that was almost painful, André brushed his lips against her forehead. Gabrielle looked at him with a seductive smile. She moved closer to him and melted against him. "Darling, I want you also, but it has to be right. If you want to kiss me in such a passionate manner, then it must be under the proper circumstances." She put her hands on the back of his neck and whispered, "And I'm sure you know what circumstances I mean."

André's eyes burned with intensity as he said, "*Oui*, Gabrielle I want to marry you."

"Oh, André, that is what I've wanted to hear ever since I met you. I love you, too, my darling, and I want to marry you as soon as possible."

When finally they left the courtyard and returned to the house, André felt a deep sense of relief. He had taken the step. For better or worse, he'd made the commitment. He'd been toying with the idea of asking her to marry him ever since he'd returned to the city, and now it was a relief to know he'd finally done it. Suddenly, it was as though a great load had been lifted from his shoulders. He felt relieved and happy. He told himself he loved her, she was beautiful, desirable, and many other young men would be more than happy to have her for a wife. True, she could be difficult at times; this he knew for himself and also from what Charles had told him. But he convinced himself that once they were married, everything would be fine.

From that moment on, André purposely blinded himself to any faults

Gabrielle had. Yes, this was the right decision. She loved him; everyone seemed to expect them to marry so why not? And what other young lady of good breeding would have allowed him to take such liberties with her?

A few days later when they spoke again of marriage, Gabrielle insisted they should marry as soon as possible. André insisted they should wait at least a year. "I've given it much thought, Gaby; in a year I'll be better established."

He *had* given it much thought. He knew her dowry played a part in his decision to marry her, but he didn't want to think he was marrying her only for her money. He wanted to believe he sincerely *loved* her and would marry her even if there was no dowry.

Gabrielle was sitting on his lap in her family's courtyard as he tried to explain to her. "Gabrielle, *chérie*, I can't have you living in my small, primitive cabin. When we marry, I want you to have a big, lovely home in which you will be comfortable."

Gabrielle put her arms around his neck. "André, dearest, I love you. I don't care where I live as long as it's with you."

He tried to explain his other reasons for waiting. "Besides the cabin, I'll be spending all of my time in the fields with my slaves until the cane is ready for cutting and grinding. And once the factory is built, I'll spend much of my time there."

Gabrielle brushed every argument aside as she swore her undying love for him, her willingness to endure what ever was necessary to be with him. "André, you say you love me and want me with you; then why shouldn't we be married now?"

To André she looked adorable, and he found it difficult to explain his reasons. "I do love you, *ma chérie*. And it's true I can't bear not having you with me right now. But your family would expect us to be engaged at least a year. In that time, I'll work as hard as possible to have a successful crop so I can build you a fine house as a wedding present."

"But I don't want to wait a year! And I don't care about a fine house!" Jumping up, Gabrielle stamped her foot and pouted.

"If you really love me, you'll ask my father for my hand now, and we can be married soon."

Suddenly, she burst into tears. "You don't love me, you just say that so you can kiss me and get familiar with me. Oh, how can you treat me like this?"

"I *do* love you, Gabrielle. But..."

"Then do something, *now!*" She continued to cry and carry on.

Finally, in desperation, the week before he was to return to Royal Oaks, André formally asked her father for her hand.

Monsieur St. Claire had no objections to his daughter's marrying André, but he too was concerned about where they would live. He was also concerned about the future of André's plantation. The young man was asked to wait a few days for Monsieur St. Claire's answer.

Gabrielle's parents tried to convince her to wait at least a year before marrying. "Gabrielle, think of what will happen if it is a bad season, and André has a crop failure," her father said, trying his best to make her see how difficult that would be.

Gabrielle would have none of it. "I don't care about a crop failure. I don't care about a bad season. I only care about marrying André!"

She stormed, and cried, and carried on. "I'll kill myself if you don't let me marry him *now!*" she screamed. "I'll run off with the first man who comes along if you make me wait to marry André!"

When her threats didn't work and she didn't get her way, she went on a hunger strike, refusing to eat.

Her mother pleaded with her, "Gabrielle, *chérie*, you must eat something. You will make yourself ill if you don't."

Still, she refused to eat. When finally she became so hungry she had to eat, she showed her temper by tearing her bedroom apart and carrying on so that her father finally threw up his hands.

"*Mon Dieu*, I can't stand this any longer. You may marry André de Javon, if you are that determined. However, your marriage will not take place until the last part of August. You will be engaged for six months, which is better than nothing."

When André showed up in the afternoon, Monsieur Ste. Claire invited him into the library and explained about the engagement.

André smiled. "*Merci*, Monsieur Ste. Claire. And I quite agree with you concerning the length of our engagement. That will give me more time to work towards my goal." He paused and added, "I want you to know, Monsieur, that I will make every effort to be as successful as possible. And I shall also do all in my power to be a good husband and make Gabrielle happy."

Monsieur Ste. Claire nodded. "No one can ask for more than that, André. You are a fine young man, and I know I can trust my daughter to you."

Later that night when Gabrielle had gone to bed, her parents sat in

110

the parlor. Monsieur Ste. Claire lit his pipe and said, "I hope I did the right thing, giving them permission to marry so soon. But I simply couldn't put up with Gabrielle's temper any longer.

"Well, we have six months, and if André isn't successful there will be time to end the engagement," Monsieur Ste. Claire added.

Madame Ste. Claire sighed. "I hate to say this about my own daughter, but I fear Gabrielle is totally incapable of loving anyone but herself. To her, people are simply a means to an end, and André is no exception. Her faith in his ability to succeed has nothing to do with the man himself; it is more the fact that she wants it her way, and in her mind that is enough."

Chapter 19

With Francesca and Charles' wedding over, Julie returned to the convent where she remained until summer; but things were not the same. She had a difficult time concentrating on her studies her thoughts kept returning to the day of the wedding and André's attention to Gabrielle.

And Gabrielle! Julie thought of how possessive Gabrielle had been, how she had clung to André and managed to keep him from talking to her for the rest of the day. But as time passed, Julie's spirits rose when she thought of the long summer months ahead and the time she would spend with André at Royal Oaks.

In the summer when she returned to *Château Charlevoix*, Julie's first thought was to ride over to Royal Oaks but things were different there also. André, while happy to see her, had little time for her. She would find him in the cane fields, his face bronzed from the sun. He'd give her a wide grin and stop for a moment to greet her.

"*Ma chère*, how good it is to see you. I wish I had time to stop and visit, but there is too much work. You do understand, I hope?"

Julie would nod. She knew the importance of his urgency. It was too hot to sit in the sun; so after a while she would leave.

One day when she arrived, André invited her to lunch with him. "Much of my work here in the fields is done. So let's go to the house and have a bite to eat."

Julie was thrilled to be with him again now it was like the year before. Once again, she told him funny stories that set him laughing until his sides hurt.

They had just finished eating when a carriage turned onto his property. As the coach drew near, Julie saw André's face light up with a smile. He put down his fork and hurried out to meet the young lady who had driven up.

Julie watched him help Gabrielle out of the carriage. He took her in his arms and kissed her, then, with his arm around her waist, walked back to the cabin.

"Gaby, you remember Julie Marie Charlevoix. She's my neighbor and comes over to keep me company and give me advice on running this place."

Gabrielle gave Julie a tight little smile. *"Oui,* the *child* you were talking to at the wedding, *bonjour."* She gave Julie an indifferent nod.

Julie tried to smile. "I am pleased to see you, Mademoiselle Ste. Claire."

She dropped a curtsy but in her heart, she wasn't at all pleased. She hated Gabrielle, and wished with all her heart she could tell her so but held her tongue for André's sake. She would never embarrass him by being ill mannered while she was a guest in his home.

There was an uncomfortable silence between them. Julie could think of nothing more to say, and it was obvious Gabrielle had nothing to say to her.

After studying Julie for a moment longer, Gabrielle dismissed her with a cold look and turned to André. "I drove over today, because we must discuss our wedding plans. *Maman* had a fit when I told her I was coming to see you. She insisted I bring Millie along." She indicated the young black girl sitting on the coachman's bench. *"Pappa* wants us to be married at the Cathedral, but Francesca wants the wedding at Oak Grove."

Frowning, she said, "You know, André, you really haven't paid any attention to me since my parents and I arrived at Oak Grove; and we came out for the summer especially so you and I could spend time together."

Here she sighed and gave André a wistful look. "Instead, I hardly ever see you. You spend more time with your slaves than you do with me."

André smiled at her tenderly. "I know, sweetheart, but there is so much to do before our wedding. I want to get as much done now so I can spend more time with you once we're married."

Julie's heart lurched, and she felt ill. *Married? André is marrying Gabrielle Ste. Claire?* But he hadn't said a word about it to her, and Julie felt like she had been kicked in the stomach.

André caught the look of surprise on her face. "Oh, Julie, I'm sorry I thought I told you about my coming marriage; Gaby and I will be married the first week in September; and, of course, we want you and your father to attend."

Julie jumped up. "I must be going, André. Thank you for lunch. *Au revoir*, Mademoiselle Ste. Claire."

As she started for her horse, André excused himself from Gabrielle and hurried after her. "*Chère*, must you leave? Stay a while and visit with Gabrielle while I work. I'm sure she would enjoy your company."

Julie turned away from him, trying to hide her tears. "*Non*, André, I must leave. Besides, you and Mademoiselle Ste. Claire have much to discuss."

She felt his hands go around her waist. "Here, let me help you." He lifted her onto *Minuit's* back and smiled up at her. "You will come back and see me tomorrow, won't you?"

Julie gave him a weak smile. "I'll try."

Tears filled her eyes; and before André could say a word, Julie swung *Minuit* around and took off.

He's marrying Gabrielle Ste. Claire! Julie urged her horse on, tears streaming down her face. *Oh, how can he! Doesn't he know what she is really like?*

Francesca and Gabrielle had attended the Ursuline Convent several years before Julie. However, Julie had friends whose older sisters had known the Ste. Claire sisters at the Convent. And it was Gabrielle who was best remembered for her behavior. She had been a problem for the nuns, never learning to curb her temper or her tongue.

As soon as she reached home, Julie rushed to her room where she threw herself across her bed and cried heartbroken tears.

'Toinette hurried after her and seeing her young mistress in such a state, tried to comfort her.

"'Toinette, André's marrying Gabrielle Ste. Claire! Oh, how can he do such a thing? I love him so much! Why can't he wait for me to grow up?"

'Toinette tried to soothe her. "Mam'selle, you jes' be too young, you. You still little girl. *Michie* André, he be grown man. He need ah wife now. Someday you finds da right man, den you gets married too, *oui*."

"I'll never marry anyone but André! *Never, never, never!*" Julie cried. Finally, in exhaustion, she lay still, her eyes swollen, her nose red, and her body rigid with unshed tears.

'Toinette quietly left the room. She would let the little one rest until her *pappa* came home.

Julie, left alone with her thoughts, felt the tears gathering again. *I hate Gabrielle Ste. Claire! I hate her, I hate her, I HATE her!* She pounded her fists in her pillow, wishing the pillow was Gabrielle.

* * *

After Julie left, Gabrielle turned to Andre. "Does *that girl* spend much time here with you?"

"Julie?" Andre smiled and nodded. "*Oui*, she likes to come over, and I enjoy her company. Her knowledge of the land is quite astounding for one so young; why she knows..."

"Do you think it's proper to have her here so often?" Gabrielle pressed on. "I mean, what will people think? A girl like that hanging around a young man's cabin!"

André raised an eyebrow. "A girl like that? What are you talking about Gaby? Julie's a child and a lovely one at that."

He couldn't believe she would really object to Julie's visits. In a quiet voice, he added, "She and her father have been very kind to me. If it hadn't been for Julie, I wouldn't have nearly as much work accomplished."

He proceeded to tell Gabrielle all that Monsieur Charlevoix had recently done for him, but Gabrielle was not impressed. "Still, I feel it's wrong to encourage that girl to come around so often. I want you to promise me you will put a stop to her visits at once!"

André shook his head, looked annoyed, and his eyes seemed to grow darker. "I'll do no such thing, Gabrielle. Julie is my friend, and she's welcome to come here anytime she wants." He looked at Gabrielle for a long moment and added, "I don't want to fight with you over this; so, let's have no more talk of Julie. You were saying about our wedding?"

Gabrielle was not too happy to have the subject dismissed so quickly, but she had the good sense to let it go. Instead, they sat in the parlor and discussed where their marriage should be held.

They finally decided to have the wedding at Oak Grove as Francesca had suggested.

Once that agreement was made, André stood up. "Well, my sweet, I really must get back to work."

"I drove all this way, and now you plan to go back to work?" Gabrielle said, with a pout. "I thought we could spend the afternoon together."

"Gaby, I'd love to spend the afternoon with you, but the work won't get done if I don't help. Please try to understand. Why don't you stay? You can sit in your carriage and watch what we do. Then, later, perhaps we can spend time together."

"Sit in my carriage? I think not. I would die in this heat. I think you're hateful not to want to spend time with me now!" Gabrielle turned eyes filled with anger on him.

André's eyes were equally angry. "Gaby, I told you it would be like this. I told you in New Orleans that this place would demand most, if not all, of my time for a while. I warned you, and I'm sorry if you're upset; but for now Royal Oaks must come first." Once again, they had a fight. And, in a fit of temper, Gabrielle climbed into the carriage and headed back to Oak Grove. During the drive, she thought about Julie's visits. *I may not be able to do anything about those visits now. But as soon as we are married, I shall certainly put a stop to them*!

She also brooded over the fact that André had insisted on returning to work instead of spending time with her. Then she brooded more over Julie so that by the time she reached her destination, she was in a terrible temper. Immediately, she sought out her sister and proceeded to tell Francesca the problem.

"Really, Gaby, don't you think you're making too much of the situation? I mean, André's right, Julie is a child. What harm can there be in her visiting him while he works? She's much too young to be a threat to you." Francesca tried to mollify her.

But her sister's remarks only added to Gabrielle's rage. "How dare you side with André? How dare you not understand that this is a serious problem? Why, he hardly pays attention to me as it is. All he thinks of is his stupid land, and now I must put up with that girl over there spending time with him." Gabrielle's face was livid as she stormed about the room.

Finally, in view of her fit of anger, Francesca agreed with her, anything to shut her up and calm her down. "Then by all means, Gaby, put a stop to Julie's visits, and the sooner the better."

However, Francesca's agreeing with her did nothing to abate Gabrielle's fury, and for the rest of the day, the entire family was subjected to her outburst.

Julie didn't return to Royal Oaks, which pleased Gabrielle and saddened André.

While Julie stayed away, Gabrielle drove over to André's place several times and was pleased to see that "that girl," as she always referred to Julie, was not hanging around. Perhaps the problem had solved itself.

Gabrielle did her best to remain in a good mood when she arrived at Royal Oaks. But this was not easy for her and after a few days of remaining calm and sweet-tempered, she would return to her old ways and once again find fault with something.

She resented the fact that André worked in the fields with his slaves and told him as much. "It is demeaning to have my future husband working like a field hand," she said with a pout.

With a look of irritation, André said, "Gabrielle, I'm sorry you feel that way. I see nothing wrong with working on my land if it will help me to better understand the crops and how things are done. I'm proud of the fact that I've had as much a part of carving out my future with my bare hands as have my slaves.

"Besides, everyone knows I've been working out here I've not tried to hide that fact."

"I just don't want my friends to get the wrong idea," Gabrielle said in a whining voice.

"If your friends get the wrong idea because a man is willing to put in an honest day's work to improve his lot, well that's their problem!"

Exasperation filled André's voice, anger filled his eyes, and when Gabrielle heard the tone and saw the look, she knew she'd pushed him too far. They had another ugly fight. In a fury, Gabrielle climbed into her carriage and left.

Another day, she said in resentment, "It's not fair. Charles is never too busy to spend time with Francesca."

André raked her with cold eyes. "I'm sorry you refuse to understand, Gabrielle. I have not had the good fortune of having everything handed to me on a silver platter like Charles. You have chosen to throw your lot in with a man who has to earn it the hard way, THROUGH HARD WORK!"

Glaring at her, he added, "I'm sick of discussing this subject. If all you can do when you come here is complain and find fault, then don't come so often."

"Oh, darling, I'm sorry. Please forgive me." She reached up and tried to kiss him. But André wasn't in the mood for kissing. Instead, he took her hands from his neck and turned away.

"I think you had best leave, Gabrielle. I have work to do, and I can't stand around arguing with you all day."

Uneasy feelings were building up in André. But there was nothing he could do. They were engaged, it had been announced, and there was no way he could get out of the marriage without losing honor and much more. *Non*, there was too much at stake.

Chapter 20

Julie missed André terribly. It had been more than a month since she'd seen him. One day, she was out riding and decided to pay a call to Royal Oaks. If Gabrielle's carriage was anywhere in sight, she would keep riding. But there was no carriage; so she rode up the path to André's cabin.

Julie found André in the swamp. He was busy and at first didn't notice her, but when he turned around and saw her and *Minuit*, he smiled and came over to her.

"Julie, I'm so happy to see you. I've missed you."

Julie's heart skipped a beat. He'd missed her. He was happy to see her. It was impossible to carry on a conversation; so she sat on her horse happily watching as he spoke to the men.

After a while, he and the overseer told the slaves to stop for lunch. "We'll continue in an hour," André said, as he turned back to Julie. "Come and have lunch with me, *ma petite*."

Riding back to the cabin, André said, "We must get the wood chopped now so it will be ready when the sugar factory is built."

"How soon will that be?" Julie asked.

"The contractor is coming out next month. I've had some of the slaves making the bricks for the building while others are working in the swamp."

Julie nodded. "*Oui, Pappa* says it takes a great deal of wood to keep the furnaces going during the grinding season."

Once at the cabin, they sat opposite each other while Delilah served them fried chicken, biscuits, gravy, and green beans.

After the food was served, and grace said, André looked at Julie for a long moment. "I've missed your funny stories, Julie. What mischief have you gotten into at school this past year?" His eyes twinkled and he waited for her answer.

"I haven't gotten into any mischief lately. I've been so good, I'm boring!"

André chuckled at this remark. "Boring is the last thing I would ever imagine of you, young lady." He reached over and with his finger and gently tapped the tip of her nose. "Everyone here at Royal Oaks has missed you. Why have you stayed away so long?"

His eyes were so tender that they made Julie's heart ache. Putting her head down, she could feel the tears right behind her eyelids. How could she tell him how she felt, how heartbroken she was? Had he no idea how much she loved him? Did he not realize that even at her young age, she could love him so deeply? Now he was to be married; so what could she say?

André reached across the table, cupped her small chin in his hand, tilted her face up, and saw the tears. "Ah, *chérie*, what's wrong? Please tell me…what makes you so unhappy?"

"You're marrying Gabrielle Ste. Claire instead of me!" Julie gasped, her face turned red, and her hand flew up to her lips. "Oh, Andre, I'm sorry. I shouldn't have said that."

Before André could say anything, she rushed on, unable to keep her feelings a secret any longer. "Oh, André, I love you, I've loved you from the moment I saw you on the road with Charles. I've prayed so hard for you to wait for me. I've tried to grow up faster, but now you're marrying Gabrielle, and I want to die!"

Now the tears were flowing unchecked. Her small body shook with her sobs as she poured her heart out to him. Despair and grief filled her face.

André was so startled by this outburst from the little girl, he almost smiled; but he didn't. He had no idea the child held such feelings for him. Although her declaration of love amused him, he knew it was very real to her.

His heart went out to her in her distress. He got up from his chair, gathered her in his arms and sat down and held her.

"Julie, I had no idea you felt this way. But, *chère coeur*, I'm much too old for you. Why, someday when you are grown-up, you will meet a young man, fall in love, and marry."

His attempt to make light of Julie's feelings upset her so he continued to console her. "Julie, you've become such a precious little friend. You've given me encouragement when I felt like quitting and so much good advice in the past. I could never have accomplished so much without your help, and now I've hurt you. But, dear heart, even though I'm marrying Gabrielle, my feelings for you will never change. You'll always be special to me, and I'll always care a great deal for you."

"But once you're married, things will change. It won't be the same." Julie had her face buried in his chest as she continued to sob.

"That's true," André replied as he gently stroked her hair. "Things will change in that Gabrielle will be here but that doesn't mean you can't come to visit. You know you're always welcome. Besides, I want my two best girls to become friends."

"But I'm not welcome, at least not by Gabrielle. I doubt if she would ever want to become friends with me. And she would hate it if she heard you call me your best girl."

"Oh, Julie, I'm sure you're mistaken. Gabrielle has no reason to dislike you." André refused to think that what Julie said was true. Although he knew in his heart that it was. "I've told Gabrielle how I feel about you, and I've told her you may come and visit anytime you want."

Julie shook her head. "Gabrielle would hate it if I came to visit. She doesn't like me she hates me, and I hate her!"

André sighed and brushed a stray curl from her forehead. "I think you judge Gabrielle too harshly, Julie. I'm sure when you get to know her, you'll see how wrong you were."

Julie looked at him through her tears and suddenly jumped off his lap. "I HATE her, do you hear me? I HATE HER, and I HATE you too! I hate you for marrying her, and I'll NEVER come back to Royal Oaks as long as I live!"

Her small fists were doubled; her face was filled with rage; and stamping her foot, she turned and ran from the room. "I HATE YOU BOTH!" she cried over her shoulder. "AND I'LL NEVER COME BACK!"

André was so startled by her behavior, he couldn't move. In all the time he'd known Julie, he'd never seen her act this way, and it left him stunned.

Gabrielle's carriage was driving toward Royal Oaks when a small figure on a black horse galloped by sending up a cloud of dust. Gabrielle looked over and saw Julie stick her tongue out at her and heard the words, "I HATE YOU, Gabrielle Ste. Claire, I HATE YOU! I HATE YOU!" flung at her.

Gabrielle coughed and sneezed and held her handkerchief to her nose as she whipped out her fan in outrage.

Jake, the coachman, looked back over his shoulder. "You all right, Mam'selle Gabrielle?"

"*Oui*, I'm all right; but that horrible creature certainly stirred up the road!" She was furious.

"*Oui,* Mam'selle. Dat dah creature be Mam'selle Julie Charlevoix."

"I *know* who she is! She's a miserable, uncivilized *BRAT*! Someone should teach her manners," Gabrielle retorted with a snort, still coughing and fanning the air.

The carriage stopped before André's cabin, and Jake helped her out. Gabrielle hurried to the door and knocked. There was no answer; so she knocked again...still no response. With an air of impatience, she opened the door and saw André sitting with his head in his hands.

"André, didn't you hear me knock?" she demanded. "That miserable Julie Charlevoix rode by me on the road and kicked up so much dust she nearly choked me to death. And the brat had the nerve to stick her tongue out and yell at me!"

Still, André said nothing nor did he move. Gabrielle stamped her foot. "*André*! *Did* you hear me?"

Slowly, he looked at her, his face filled with such sadness it puzzled her. "Good heavens, André, what on earth is wrong with you? You look like you just lost your best friend."

He stared at her for a long moment, then shrugged and said in a soft voice, "*Oui*, Gabrielle, I think I have."

GABRIELLE
1810–1814

Chapter 21

With the summer coming to a close and September drawing nearer, Gabrielle did a complete about-face. She didn't visit Royal Oaks as often; but when she did, she was sweet tempered and congenial. There were no more complaints, no more fights. Instead, she would arrive at lunchtime, eat with André and leave with a sweet smile when he had to return to work.

At first, André was suspicious of this change in her behavior. He wondered how long it would last but she remained sweet all through August and into September. He felt such relief, he could hardly believe it. And with the relief, he also felt much better about his coming marriage.

* * *

When Francesca was first promised to Charles, she was little more than a baby. But the two families were close and the decision was made long before Charles left for France. She wasn't certain how she felt about Charles. So, while he was away, she put all thoughts of marriage out of her mind. But when he returned and she saw how he had grown and changed, she was more than happy to marry him. As it turned out, theirs was a true love match.

Francesca was not by nature a cruel person; but all too often she had been subjected to Gabrielle's bullying, temper-tantrums, and rages, and she often wondered if she would ever have a chance to give her strong-willed, spoilt younger sister a little payback. Then the occasion arrived, and she relished the thought of what she would do.

* * *

It was the day before her wedding. Gabrielle was in her bedchamber at Oak Grove where the wedding would take place. She was in a fever to find out something that had been on her mind for some time now.

Créole girls were kept in total ignorance concerning the facts of life. Even on the plantations, they were never allowed to see the animals mate or give birth. Still, they sensed that something happened on their wedding night. Nothing was said. But they often heard hints, saw sly smiles and winks.

As her wedding drew nearer, she tried to find a way to learn why Francesca, with a strange smile on her face, hinted that there was something she should know but refused to tell her what it was. Gabrielle caught the hint, saw the smile, and brooded about it until she couldn't stand it any longer.

Now that she and her sister were alone, she was determined to force Francesca to tell her what she meant. But when she asked, her sister wouldn't give her an answer. She was obviously embarrassed. "Oh, please, Gaby, I don't know how to tell you."

"Tell me *what*?"

"Well, it is when you go to bed that it happens."

"When *what* happens?" Gabrielle's eyes were wide with concern. "Tell me, *please*."

Francesca bit her lip, and her face turned a bright shade of pink. "Well he does something to you."

By now, Gabrielle's face had lost all of its color, and she was visibly shaken. "You have got to tell me!" She was almost screaming.

Francesca shrugged and rose to leave. Let Gaby stew in her own worry. She wouldn't tell her anything. But that didn't work, because Gabrielle followed her and carried on so that she finally gave in.

Francesca thought for a long moment and remembered a conversation she had overheard one night at a party. *Oui, I'll tell my dear sister what I heard—that should keep her up all night.* This was totally unlike her, but one could tolerate Gabrielle's demanding ways just so long.

She took a deep breath. "Gabrielle, men have this animal lust that they must release, and as their wives, it is our duty to submit to it." That said, Francesca once again rose to leave.

But Gabrielle reached out and grabbed her arm. "Well, tell me this, did it hurt?"

"*Oui*, it hurt...the first time."

"The *FIRST TIME*? How many times does it happen?"

Francesca enjoyed her husband's lovemaking but she was not about to tell her sister that or anything else. Instead, she looked down and said, "Really, Gaby, don't you think you are getting a little *too* personal?"

"Francesca, you can't leave me like this. You've got to answer my question."

But the subject was closed, and nothing she said or did could force Francesca to say another word. For the rest of the day, Gabrielle worried herself sick.

* * *

The next day, the wedding took place. The rooms had been decorated with fresh flowers and ribbons. Ivy and grapevine were draped around the banisters that led to the second floor. Roses, camellias, gardenias, and magnolias were intertwined with the greens and tied with ribbons.

The guests sat in the two large parlors in chairs lined up like pews in a church. The slaves gathered around the front *galerie*. Excitement filled the air.

A priest drove out to conduct the ceremony and say Mass. André's slaves, along with his overseer, were also in attendance. Everyone was in a festive mood.

Tables were set up around the yard where there was an abundance of food such as ham, beef, pheasant, chicken, and fish. Fresh fruits and vegetables, potatoes, and rice were also on the menu. Champagne, wine, the best liquor, plus a large punch bowl filled one table.

The slaves had their own party out by the cabins. Later, there would be dancing in the house for the white folks and, later still, a supper. The slaves, too, would have food, dancing, and supper.

Gabrielle looked like an angel in her wedding gown of pale blue. Everyone thought André looked more handsome than ever.

Francesca was delighted to be hosting the wedding and party, because this one would go on for days. Several families who were attending would stay as guests for a while; so there would be much to do.

As the week wore on, the men would ride, hunt, and fish during the day, while the ladies would take light excursions on the waters of the bayou. In the evening, there would be dinners and more dancing.

It was a lovely day for a wedding. The sun shone brightly, and just the hint of a gentle breeze from the river made it more comfortable.

Everyone enjoyed the celebration immensely, everyone but Julie. She stayed in the background as much as possible. However, she was far too beautiful to be ignored, and several young boys near her age attempted to speak to her.

"Mademoiselle Julie, may I fetch you a cup of punch?" asked one young boy who looked to be about sixteen.

Julie smiled and shook her head. *"Merci*, Gerard, but I'm not thirsty."

Other young men offered to get her a plate of food; still others tried to engage her in conversation. Julie was polite to each but to all of their questions and efforts, the answer was *non*. From where she stood, she could see André and his bride. Gabrielle clung to André's arm and looked up with adoring eyes at her tall, handsome husband; and every time André smiled down at Gabrielle, Julie's heart would ache.

As the evening wore on, Julie, along with the other children who lived nearby, was making ready to return home with her servant. She was upstairs in the house when she heard the music start. As she descended the stairs, she could see the ballroom glittering with the beautiful gowns of the ladies and the sparkling jewels that adorned them. It was a wonderful night, and Julie would have been thrilled to be a part of it had it not been André's wedding day.

When she reached the middle of the stairs, she caught sight of him. He was standing near the doorway to the ballroom surrounded by some of his friends. They were all laughing, slapping him on the back and congratulating him.

André threw back his head and laughed and as he did so, he caught sight of Julie. He excused himself from his friends and crossed to the foot of the stairs. Looking up at her, he gave her a tender smile.

"Julie, how beautiful you look. Come down and let me give you a hug. I'm so happy you've been a part of my wedding day."

Slowly, Julie descended the stairs. Even though he was married, he still thought she was pretty and was happy to see her. His remarks made her heart sing. When she reached him, André gave her a gentle hug and stood back smiling.

"I can see that in just a few years, you'll be the belle of New Orleans." He gave her such a loving look that Julie thought her heart would fall out of her chest.

She was as happy as she could be under the circumstances but when she started to say something to him, Gabrielle suddenly appeared at his side.

"André, darling," she cooed as she slipped her hand in his. "How dare you go off and leave me on our wedding day. You know I want your undivided attention. Besides, the music has started and I want to dance." With that, she pulled him away, never giving Julie a second glance.

André laughed and looked over his shoulder at Julie with a look that said, "What can I do? My bride calls."

Julie slowly made her way out to the carriage. André would never know she'd left. He was too happy. Being young was so difficult.

Créole brides didn't throw their bouquet. Instead, it was taken to the convent where they had been educated. So after much dancing, and once the cake was cut and more toasts were made, the bridal couple retired to one of the *garçonnières* Charles had made available to them.

Gabrielle was not at all happy to be ushered away by her mother and Millie, her personal maid. "But I don't want to leave the reception, *Maman!*" she cried. "The dancing will continue for hours, and then there will be the supper. I don't want to leave all the fun!"

Madame Ste. Claire looked apprehensive. Was her daughter going to throw a fit in front of all the guests on her wedding night? "Gabrielle, *chérie*, you must leave. Tradition decrees that the bride and groom leave early. Please, *chérie*, please don't make a scene and disgrace the family."

André had been watching this display of temper. He stepped forward and, taking Gabrielle's arm in a firm grip, said softly. "Gaby, it's time to leave. Don't embarrass your parents or me."

In truth, Gabrielle had spent the entire day convincing herself that whatever had happened to Francesca on her wedding night would not happen to her. She simply wouldn't allow it and would let André know in no uncertain terms that she would not be subjected to any such thing that would cause her pain. So once she had her mind made up on the matter, she relaxed and enjoyed herself tremendously. But now that was all about to end.

It did no good for her to try to protest. As much as she hated to admit it, refusing to leave would cause a scene so with an angry look at her husband, she flounced out of the house.

Créoles didn't go on honeymoons. Since they felt that New Orleans and its surrounding countryside was the most beautiful and exciting place to be, they saw no reason to leave and go elsewhere.

When they entered the *garçonnière*, Millie and Gabrielle's mother accompanied her upstairs to the bedchamber while André settled down with a glass of brandy.

Madame Ste. Claire and Millie helped her undress and get into her nightgown, with Gabrielle fussing all the while. Madame Ste. Claire knew she should tell her daughter something about what to expect on her wedding night; but she didn't know what to say. Gabrielle always made her nervous. And she, being a shy, quiet person, didn't know how to even approach the subject. So as soon as she had her daughter dressed for the night, she gave her a quick kiss and hurried from the room.

Millie stayed to brush her mistress's hair until it hung in soft waves and curls down her back. Then she too left.

André finished his brandy and went up stairs. Gabrielle was sitting on the edge of the bed. She looked breathtakingly lovely in a white silk nightgown trimmed with delicate lace and soft ribbons. He stood for a moment looking at her. Then, without a word, he closed the door and in two strides was beside her on the bed. He took her in his arms and felt a burning passion as he kissed her.

Burying his face in her soft hair, he whispered, "Gabrielle, you're so beautiful, and I love you so much." He continued kissing her as slowly he pressed her down onto the bed, his hands caressing her body.

He felt Gabrielle stiffen. Her eyes were closed and her lips were moving rapidly. André watched her for a moment. "Gabrielle, what are you doing?"

Her eyes flew open. "I'm praying."

"Are you saying your prayers?" he whispered nuzzling her ear.

"*Non*, I'm praying to the Blessed Mother and all the saints in heaven that I will survive what will happen to me when you fulfill your animal lust." Her body was rigid and she wouldn't meet his eyes.

"Fulfill my animal lust?" André drew back in shock. "Is that what you think it is animal lust? If it were just that, Gabrielle I wouldn't have married you. I'd have gone to a bordello in New Orleans to fulfill my *lust!*"

"But Francesca said..." Gabrielle couldn't go on. Her face felt flushed, and she turned her head away from him.

"What did Francesca say?" André's voice was soft as was his touch.

Gabrielle said nothing. All she could do now was lie there and pray that he would go away and leave her alone.

André sat up and looked down at her. She hadn't moved an inch. "Gaby, I know it's not your fault. I know you're frightened and you don't know what to expect. I love you darling. Don't be afraid of me. I'll be as gentle as possible."

He leaned down and kissed her, but there was no response. Each time he touched her, he felt her shudder and withdraw. He kissed her and spoke tender endearments. But still she lay there, her head turned away from him, her lips moving in silent prayer.

Finally, in total frustration, he got up, left the room, and went out into the night. He could hear the guests in the house as the party continued. Pushing his hands in his pockets, he walked around the garden. After a while, he stopped, leaned against a tree, and pulled out a cheroot. Lighting it, he inhaled deeply and then blew a puff of smoke into the air.

Looking up at the heavens, he thought of Gabrielle lying on the bed, frightened and praying. Damn! He didn't want to frighten her. He didn't want to take her by force. But she was his wife, and he had dreamt of this night for months. She had always led him to believe that once they were married, her passion would match his. Now, she wanted no part of him, and he wondered how long she'd feel this way. Taking one last drag on the cheroot, he tossed it aside and returned to the *garçonnière*. The candle in the bedchamber was still burning, and Gabrielle was under the covers.

André undressed, blew out the candle, and slipped into the bed. He reached over and drew her to him. Kissing her gently, he explained to her what to expect. He covered her face and throat with light little kisses as slowly he began to caress her body, whispering to her all the time— telling her how he loved her, how beautiful and desirable she was, how he had longed for this night.

Slowly, his passion mounted. His kisses became more demanding, his hands and lips roamed her body, delighting in every curve. With each kiss, each touch, Gabrielle tried to pull away.

André continued to make love to her, trying to be as gentle as possible. Gabrielle felt pain and cried out but André muffled her cry with a kiss. He had waited too long for this moment. When his passion was spent, he held her and whispered words of love.

Gabrielle was furious! "How dare you do such things to me!" she cried, her eyes blazing and her body shaking with the rage and the indignation she felt. "How dare you! It is disgusting! If I had known what to expect, I certainly would have thought twice about marrying you!"

She stormed and cried for what seemed like hours, until she finally fell into an exhausted sleep.

André lay staring at the ceiling during her outburst. He felt sick to his stomach. He should have waited until she was used to the idea of what would happen. But he had waited so long, and she had promised so much. He had allowed his passion to overrule his common sense. Now he wondered if, because of his impatience, he would live to regret it.

Chapter 22

All that week of the wedding, there was hunting, fishing, boating, picnics, and parties for the guests who remained at Oak Grove. And much to everyone's shock, André and his bride were in the center of the activity.

Gabrielle flaunted the Créole custom that decreed the newlyweds must be alone for five days neither seeing nor speaking to anyone else. A special servant would tend to their needs. She also refused to follow another custom that said a Créole bride should not be seen publicly for at least two weeks after her marriage.

Although André was perfectly happy to go along with this custom, Gabrielle had other ideas. "Stay cooped up in this *garçonnière* when everyone else is dancing and boating and having fun?" she cried. "Why, the very idea. I *won't* do it!" She threw a fit.

Her mother was greatly distressed. "But, Gabrielle, *chérie*, you must," she insisted. "What will people think if you show your face so soon after your wedding? It's indecent!"

"I don't care what people think," her daughter retorted. "It is a stupid custom anyway. After all, this is 1810, *Maman*, not the dark ages!" She became even angrier at the thought of being cooped up in the *garçonnière* with André pawing her every chance he got. She simply wouldn't tolerate such a thing! She continued to pout and cry and carry on until finally both her mother and André gave in.

"What does it matter?" he said, hoping that by giving in to her, she would be more receptive to his nightly lovemaking. "We'll be alone once we return to Royal Oaks."

While in the public eye, Gabrielle continued to cling to André, looking at him with adoring eyes, making sure he never spent much time with anyone else. However, when they were alone, she turned cool and indifferent.

One evening while she was putting the finishing touches to her toilette, André came up behind her and, slipping his arms around her waist, kissed her nape and whispered, "I love you, sweetheart. Let's not stay too long at the party. Let's come back early."

Gabrielle became annoyed and pushed him away. "Oh, André, don't do that. You'll mess up my hair, and Millie spent hours fixing it."

He smiled and whispered in her ear. "I don't care how messed up your hair gets you're beautiful and I love you."

Gabrielle shrugged him off. "Oh, leave me alone."

André felt frustrated and angry as he turned and left the room. Once again, he found himself making excuses for her. She was a new bride, and there was so much going on.

He would have preferred remaining with her in the *garçonnière* for a while, and said so one day. "Gabrielle, let's stay here for a few days. It will give us a chance to get more comfortable with each other. Perhaps, it will help you to relax so you're not so frightened during our lovemaking."

"I don't want to be locked up in here," she answered angrily. "I want to be with the others. I want to have fun." She went into a pout and then became even colder.

André forced himself to stay patient, hoping things would get better once they were alone at Royal Oaks.

The one thing Gabrielle found that helped her to relax and handle the nightly lovemaking was wine. Until she turned eighteen, she never had much wine. Now, she was served wine with her meals along with everyone else. Wine and champagne were often served. The champagne made her happy and a little giddy; the wine made her feel warm and relaxed. She managed to have some extra glasses of both each night before the evening ended.

Lovemaking was the one thing about marriage she had no use for but since she had to put up with it, she felt justified in using spirits to help her withstand the assault, as she viewed it.

André was unaware it was the alcohol that was finally making his wife less frigid. He only knew she seemed more relaxed lately, and for that he was grateful.

As the week came to an end, the guests who had been staying at Oak Grove departed, each to their own plantation in preparation for their return to New Orleans for the winter social season.

The newlyweds also prepared to depart but Gabrielle became outraged when she learned they would not be going to the city. Instead, they would go to Royal Oaks. She and André had a terrible fight their last day at Oak Grove.

"Everyone will be in New Orleans!" she cried. "There will be parties and the *théâtre* and dances and balls, and I want to be a part of it." She stamped her foot and glared at her husband.

André tried staying calm. "We will go to the city for Christmas and New Year's. But, for now, we will return to Royal Oaks. I must see that everything is going well with the building of my sugar factory and, also, the cutting of the cane, which must be done before the frost sets in."

"Well, why can't Monsieur Hoffman take care of all of that? That's what you have an overseer for, isn't it?"

"Gabrielle, be reasonable, this is my first crop of sugar cane. And it is costing me a fortune to build my factory. I can't leave two such important jobs solely to my overseer. Maybe in a year or two when things are more stable then we'll be able to spend more time in the city..."

"A YEAR or TWO!"

"Yes, a year or two! But, for now, we're going back to Royal Oaks so you might as well accept it!" His anger was almost beyond control as André turned and slammed out of the room.

* * *

Gabrielle rode in stony silence beside her husband as the carriage rolled away from Oak Grove with Charles, Francesca, and her parents waving good-bye. He tried to make conversation as they rode along; but Gabrielle would only nod or grunt in answer.

André had turned the path that led to his cabin into a wide drive paved with crushed shells. The large oaks that had once reminded Julie of sentries, lined either side of the drive. Now, as the carriage turned onto the avenue of oaks, the slaves slowly began to appear from the back. "Look, Gabrielle, the servants are coming to greet us."

Gabrielle gave a disinterested glance out the window. "Oh, who cares about a bunch of slaves?" she growled.

Although she had been a frequent visitor to Royal Oaks, Gabrielle had made no attempt to get to know any the people who lived on plantation.

When the carriage stopped, André got out and helped Gabrielle alight. All of his slaves were now smiling and calling greetings and clapping their hands. André responded by telling them how happy he was to be home. He then introduced all to his wife who was not the least bit interested in meeting any of them, although each came by to give her a personal greeting.

After their trunks were unloaded, the slaves returned to their work and André carried Gabrielle over the threshold. He then ordered his horse to be brought around.

"I hope you'll excuse me, darling, but I must take a quick ride about the place and check on the factory and cane. I won't be long, and then we'll spend the entire evening together." He bent to give her a kiss, but Gabrielle turned her face away.

She was left standing alone in the parlor. Looking around, she slowly made her way through the rest of the cabin. She had been in the place many times before, but never really saw it.

Until now, she always pretended it wasn't here. She had convinced herself that as soon as they were married, a big lovely house would magically appear. She had refused to face reality. Now, reality hit her right between the eyes.

This is no house! *This wretched, primitive cabin is no better than the slave quarters at Oak Grove*! In a rage, she rushed into the bedroom and threw herself across the bed, crying and beating her fists into the pillow.

She conveniently forgot that both her parents and André tried to convince her to wait to get married. She refused to remember how stubborn and headstrong she had been. Instead, she placed the blame on André. "It's all his fault! He made me fall in love with him. He should have warned me that I really *would* have to live in this miserable hovel for heaven knows how long. Oh, it just isn't fair." She continued to cry and carry on.

When André returned to the cabin a little later, he was greeted by a crying, hysterical wife who hurled angry words and accusations at him. "You tricked me into marrying you! And now you bring me to this terrible place!"

André couldn't believe his eyes or ears. Gabrielle was completely out of control. Screaming at him, she demanded he let her return to New Orleans to her parents' home at once!

"How can you expect me to stay in this place? How could you trick me like this?" she shrieked.

"Gabrielle, I never at any time tricked you. I told you what it would be like at first. But you insisted that where you lived was *unimportant!*"

"Well, where I live *IS IMPORTANT!* And, right now, I want to *LIVE* in New Orleans!" Her face was contorted with rage. "I won't be stuck out here in this godforsaken shack, in this miserable hovel you call a home! This dump is no better than the slave quarters at Oak Grove."

She continued to scream at André. "I can't entertain in this horrible place. My friends would laugh if they saw the way you expect me to live! You're a terrible, hateful brute. I HATE you! Do you hear? I HATE you!"

She turned and rushed back into the bedroom, slamming the door, throwing her self across the bed where she cried and screamed.

André listened to her for just so long then crossing to the bedroom, he opened the door and with cold rage said, "You married me for better or worse, and since you are married to me, your place is with me. This hovel, as you call it, is our home like it or not!"

He stormed from the cabin. He could hardly contain his anger. He had to get away from her before he *really* lost his temper.

He was sick at heart. He wanted a nice comfortable home as much as she did. Did she think he enjoyed living in the cabin? But it would take time. He had to see how his crops did this year before he could even begin to think of building a house.

Angry and heartsick, André urged his horse into a gallop and headed out to the factory and the cane fields, anything to get his mind off of Gabrielle, anything to get as far away from her as possible!

He was pleased to see the progress on the factory and when he left there, he headed to the swamp. More trees had been cut down, and now they were being chopped up. They would be transferred to the shed he'd built to store the logs. They would need time to dry out before they could be used in the furnaces.

Once she calmed down, Gabrielle sat in the parlor, a sullen look on her face as she watched Millie unpack her trunks and put her things away. She looked around and asked, "Is there any wine or champagne here in the cabin?"

Delilah who was also in the cabin, said, "Day be wine and brandy, *Maîtresse*, but day *non* be champagne."

Gabrielle had never tried brandy. "Well, fetch the bottle of brandy, and pour me a glass."

Later, when André returned to the cabin, Gabrielle flung herself into his arms, begging his forgiveness.

André was still so upset he had a difficult time letting go of his anger but he wanted peace, so he said little. When he sat down in a chair, Gabrielle curled up on his lap and kissed him and ran her fingers through his hair and told him how much she loved him.

When she brought her lips to his, the scent of brandy filled Andre's nostrils. Raising an eyebrow, he looked at her with suspicion. "Have you been drinking, Gabrielle?"

"Only a little brandy," she answered, an innocent expression on her face. "I was so tense, and Delilah said you had wine and brandy in the cabin. I'd never tried brandy but I only had a little, just one glass. Please don't be angry with me."

André felt apprehensive but said nothing. They had already fought enough for one day. But the smell of brandy was so strong that he couldn't help but wonder just how much she *had* drank. Hopefully, this would not become a habit with her.

* * *

The cane had been cut and would be taken to *Château Charlevoix* for the grinding until such time as André's factory was completed. Monsieur Charlevoix had made this arrangement with André earlier.

André now spent all day with the contractor at the factory. He also rode out to the fields where the slaves were readying the soil for the next planting.

His overseer had graciously offered to share his cabin with the contractor while he was at Royal Oaks. André had a bed sent out from the city for the man.

Gabrielle continued to be unhappy and bored, and sought comfort in the bottle of brandy. She liked the taste; it relaxed her and made her lightheaded. For a while, she could forget her miseries. Still, the brandy couldn't block out all her feelings.

Some mornings, it was difficult for her to get up. Her head hurt, and her stomach was upset. She had no idea it was her drinking that was causing her this problem even so, she did her best to hide the fact from André.

One morning when the two sat down to breakfast, Gabrielle took a sip of coffee and said, "I don't see why you have to spend so much time at that building and in the fields."

André tried to make her understand the importance of a successful crop. "Why don't you ride out to the factory with me? It's almost completed." he said with a smile. "Let me show you what's happening. Perhaps if you understand, you'll be less unhappy."

"Oh, really André, I have no desire to go in that stupid place. I couldn't care less what goes on there. Besides it's too hot to be riding around."

Just then, Delilah set a plate of food before her mistress. There were sliced oranges, boiled grits, broiled chicken, and several other savory dishes but Gabrielle had little appetite. When André saw that she wasn't eating much, he commented on it.

"I'm not hungry, because I'm so miserable," she snapped.

André took a deep breath. "Gabrielle, I've done everything I can think of to make this cabin more pleasant for you. I've sent for some books for you to read..."

"I don't like to read it bores me. There's nothing fun or exciting in just sitting around reading a dumb book."

She took another sip of coffee but before André could say anything, she continued, "And I'm not interested in that pianoforte either. I don't like playing the pianoforte any more than I like reading." She paused and added, "As for that horse, I don't care how beautiful it is I don't enjoy riding, and besides, I'm afraid of horses." She glared at her husband.

André threw up his hands. Taking one last sip of coffee, he matched her glare with one of his own and then turned and left the cabin.

* * *

Since Charles and Francesca hadn't left for the city yet, Gabrielle took to spending as much time with them as possible at Oak Grove. She sat and watched the servants pack the things her sister would take to the city and felt deep resentment.

"It isn't fair!" she said one day when she and Francesca were sitting in the parlor. "Your marriage was arranged, and you didn't even love Charles. And here you are with a big country home and a lovely townhouse. It just isn't fair!"

Francesca tried to placate her sister. "But Gaby, you'll have a big home too. André promised you one as soon as he can afford it. You just have to be patient."

"I'm tired of being patient," Gabrielle glared at Francesca who threw her hands up and tried to ignore her.

As the time drew near when her family would return to the city, Gabrielle spent more time at Oak Grove. "I won't be seeing you all for a while; so I want to spend as much time with you as possible," she said to her parents and sister.

"I don't approve of your being away from André so much," her father said on one of these occasions.

"Oh, he doesn't care," Gabrielle assured him. "Besides, he spends most of the day at his sugar factory, and there's nothing for me to do. Half the time, he doesn't even know I'm gone."

In truth, she and André had had several ugly fights on the subject of her being gone so much. Nothing he had said made a difference and in the end, he found it easier to let her go. It took too much energy to fight with her constantly, and he needed his energy for the work ahead.

When the sugar factory was finally completed, and all the equipment was installed, André finally convinced Gabrielle to go with him to the building. He was excited and wanted to show her around. In his heart, he hoped she, too, would catch the excitement and become more interested in what he was doing.

"Now that the building is done, I can start grinding my own cane," he said with pride as they road side by side. "I still have some that I kept back for just that purpose."

But the moment Gabrielle entered the factory, she started complaining. The smell of the sweet cane, mingled with the sweat from the Negros bodies made her sick, and the noise made her head hurt.

"Really, André, I am not the least bit interested in standing in this noisy, smelly building just to watch a bunch of darkies work. How can you possibly think this could interest me?" Flinging him an angry look, she turned and headed for the door.

"I'm leaving, and I hope you never expect me to come into this horrible place again."

Anger and frustration boiled up in André as he watched her storm off. Later that evening when he reached the cabin feeling like he was at his wits end in trying to please her, and knowing he'd had about all he could stand, Gabrielle met him at the door and flung herself into his arms and once again begged forgiveness.

* * *

The day before Charles, Francesca, and her parents were to leave for New Orleans, Charles rode over to Royal Oaks to visit. "We'll be leaving for the city tomorrow," he said as he dismounted his horse and greeted André.

"So I've heard." There was a slight edge to André's voice.

Once they entered the cabin, André turned to Charles. "I wish Gabrielle and I could join you and Francesca in the city next week; but as I've told Gaby, I simply can't leave yet."

Charles nodded. "I understand. Every time I come here, I am amazed at all you've accomplished. Do you realize that just a year ago you were visiting Jean-Claude Charlevoix? Now you have a factory and cane and cotton fields." He shook his head. "I don't know how you've done so much in such a short period of time."

"Hard work, Charles, nothing but hard work." André gazed out the window, then with a sigh, added, "But I can't work all the time so Gabrielle and I will be in the city for Christmas. I told her we could stay for a couple of weeks, and then I must return."

Charles looked at André for a long moment. "You look tired *mon ami*. And I know living with my sister-in-law can't be easy."

André shrugged. "Let's not talk about her for now."

Instead, they spent the next hour talking, laughing, and reminiscing about their trip across the ocean while they shared lunch. André realized how tense he'd been lately, how long it'd been since he'd really felt relaxed. He was also happy that Gabrielle was spending the day at Oak Grove.

Later, when Charles took his leave and André went back to work, thoughts of the coming trip to New Orleans kept invading his mind. He had an uneasy feeling about the fact that often when he returned to the cabin, he smelt brandy on Gabrielle's breath. It upset him but every time he spoke to her about it, she turned hateful.

"Well, it helps me relax," she would grouse. "After all I'm stuck here in this horrible dump you call a home." She'd give a snort. "You won't let me go to New Orleans. I can't have any fun so a little brandy makes me feel better."

Although in his heart, he knew better, André refused to believe that his wife could be developing a serious drinking problem. And he had no idea what to do about it if indeed such was the case. As far as he knew, such a thing was unheard of among *Créole* ladies of good breeding.

Chapter *23*

T he month of December was the happiest month of their marriage. André couldn't believe the change in Gabrielle. She was sweet tempered and loving. She tried to show an interest in all he was doing on the plantation.

She rode out to the fields with him and listened while he explained what was happening with the crops. She even went back to the sugar factory and walked around and listened as he explained the entire process to her. Their nights were spent in lovemaking and that too was a little better than before.

André was more relaxed and happier than he'd been since their wedding, and he hadn't smelt the brandy on her breath as often lately. He was reluctant to say anything about her drinking for fear of ruining her good mood, better to leave the subject alone for now. They'd had enough fights to last him a lifetime.

He was in excellent spirits for another reason. One day, after being out in the fields and sugar factory, he came into the cabin all smiles. He swept Gabrielle up in his arms and twirled her around.

Gabrielle squealed with delight. "André, darling, what are you so happy about?" she asked when he finally set her down again.

"Oh, sweetheart, I've had such a good season. It has far exceeded my expectations." He plopped down in his favorite chair and pulled his wife down on his lap. "It is the end of the year, and Royal Oaks has yielded six hundred and thirty hogsheads of sugar, ten barrels of molasses, and one hundred and fifty bales of cotton." He kissed Gabrielle and said, "Isn't that wonderful?"

"*Oui*, darling, it is wonderful. Does that mean we are rich now?"

André laughed. "Well, not as rich as we will be in the future, but it certainly is an excellent start. I understand from my factor that the price of sugar has risen, and the molasses alone will enable me to pay all of my plantation expenses. I will also be able to pay off my first year loan to Monsieur Charlevoix and have a thirty percent profit. A couple of more years like this and I will be almost clear of debt."

He paused for a long moment, and spoke almost to himself as he said, "With my profits, I will order more equipment, more oxen, and more cottonseed. I will also grow more corn and other vegetables. I shall increase my order of livestock, cows, chickens, and hogs. And as soon as we reach New Orleans, I will contact Jean Lafitte and tell him I need to buy more slaves."

Gabrielle had no interest in all of this. She was just ecstatic to be going to the city. She sang, played the pianoforte, and chattered on endlessly about all the fun they would have in New Orleans. She kissed André and ruffled his hair as she moved about the cabin. Her mood was contagious, and Andre felt his hopes building. Everything had been going so well lately. With their trip to the city, perhaps things would continue to get even better when they returned to Royal Oaks.

To keep her in this good mood, André promised that if it was at all possible, he would start building their home next year. "I'll order some furniture from France while we are in the city. And I'll contact an architect and at least speak to him."

The day before they were to leave, André returned to the cabin to find Gabrielle waltzing around the parlor. Her eyes were closed, and she was humming a little tune.

As he stepped into the room, André stopped, leaned against the door jamb, folded his arms, and with a smile on his face, watched Gabrielle glide about the room. Suddenly, as though she felt his presence, she opened her eyes. With a happy little cry, she flew into his arms laughing. He swept her into a waltz as they both hummed the tune.

After a few minutes, André dropped into his favorite chair, pulled her down on his lap, and kissed her. His eyes caressed her face as he whispered, "Gabrielle, I'm so happy." Kissing her again, he murmured, "I love you so much."

She cuddled closer to him. "I love you also, my darling, and I too am very happy." She looked at him seriously for a moment, then her eyes began to sparkle as she sang, "We're going to New Orleans, we're going to New Orleans."

* * *

Francesca and Charles were thrilled to see them.

"We're so delighted you are here," Francesca exclaimed, as they all enjoyed some *café au lait*.

"Tonight, my parents are giving a Christmas dinner in honor of the two of you," Charles said.

This remark pleased Gabrielle greatly.

Later, the couple retired to the guest room to freshen up and prepare for the evening's festivities.

The sisters, in a good-natured sense of sibling rivalry, were each trying to outdo the other in what they would wear and how they would look.

Gabrielle chose a gown of crimson velvet with a deep *décolletage* and long sleeves. A lace made of silver threads encircled the neckline and framed her face. A long satin sash tied at one side of the high waistline. Around her neck, she wore a diamond and ruby necklace with earrings and bracelet to match. On her feet were soft crimson slippers, and Millie pulled her thick dark hair into a cluster of curls held by the diamond-headed pins.

Francesca wore a lovely gown of deep green moiré trimmed with lace. She, too, wore diamonds at her neck, ears, and wrist.

When the time for departure arrived, the two young couples met in the parlor.

"Well, aren't we a feast for the eyes?" Charles said good naturedly. "You both look beautiful," he added as he turned his eyes on his wife and sister-in-law.

He was correct. It would have been difficult to choose which of the two young women was more beautiful that night.

"Well, you and André are equally handsome in your evening clothes," Francesca answered as she made a graceful bow.

However, when they arrived at the du Fray house and all the guests were assembled, it was easy to see that André was without a doubt the most handsome man there. And although he was extremely masculine, his natural grace made his every move a pleasure to watch. And Gabrielle was well aware that every woman in the room delighted in watching her husband.

There was champagne before dinner with many toasts to the young couple, and wine with the meal and more toasts, and dancing until dawn.

André remembered Charles' telling him that Créoles enjoyed their liqueurs, but to overindulge was considered the height of bad manners. "A gentleman may enjoy his drink," Charles explained. "And a touch of light-headedness from the drink is perfectly acceptable. But a gentleman of good breeding will never get drunk, especially in mixed company. To do so would bring disgrace to the family name." He paused and added, "Only the American *Yanquies* and the barbaric mountain men from Kentucky and Tennessee drink to excess!"

"And the ladies?" André asked with trepidation, his mind going to his wife.

"Ah, the ladies well!" Charles rolled his eyes. "The thought of a lady ever getting tipsy is simply unthinkable! A lady may enjoy a glass of wine with dinner or champagne on special occasions, but that is the extent of it. I can assure you."

Of course, Charles didn't know it, but there were always exceptions to every rule; and his sister-in-law was on her way to becoming the exception. And that night, she managed somehow to have more than her share of both champagne and wine.

The first hour was spent sipping champagne and visiting with friends and family; and Gabrielle's glass was always full. Dinner was announced just in time to keep her from drinking too much.

Upon entering the dining room, the guests found the table set with an elegant lace tablecloth. Beautiful silver candelabras holding tall candles and a huge crystal chandelier cast a bright glow on the *epergne* filled with fresh flowers. From the *epergne*, silver ribbon streamers flowed to each lady's place. A tiny bouquet of red tea roses and baby's breath lay at the top of their plates. Fine china, gleaming silverware, and crystal goblets completed the picture.

The meal was started with a toast to the newlyweds, and Gabrielle was delighted to have her goblet filled once more.

Everyone enjoyed the magnificent dinner fit for royalty. There were seven courses; and throughout the meal, Gabrielle managed to have her wine glass filled several times. With so much talking, laughing, and gaiety going on, André and the others seemed unaware of just how much she was drinking. And because she preferred the wine to the food, she began to feel a little light-headed.

When the meal was ended, Madame du Fray laid aside her napkin. "We ladies shell retire to the main parlor while the gentlemen remain to enjoy their port and cheroots," she said.

Gabrielle felt sleepy, but she managed to walk to the parlor without too much trouble. However, it became difficult to follow the ladies' conversations. She excused herself and carefully made her way upstairs to find a bedroom where she could lie down and think. What was wrong with her? Suddenly, she could hardly keep her eyes open, and her head felt so strange. She lay down on the bed and closed her eyes. She had no idea how long she lay there, but suddenly she felt someone gently shaking her; and looking up she saw her sister.

"Gabrielle, what's wrong?"

"I don't know I just started feeling so strange." Gabrielle tried to sit up, but her head felt so heavy, she quickly lay down again.

"I'll call André. You wait here and don't move." Francesca started for the door.

"*Non*! Francesca, don't do that. He'll just get upset with me for disturbing him and ruining his evening."

"Don't be ridiculous. If you're ill, he should know. I hardly think he'd get upset with you. He can take you home if you're not well."

"But I don't want to go home. I want to dance. Listen, Francesca, the music has started. I'll be all right, honest I will, just don't tell André."

She got up and walked slowly to the door. She still felt strange as she and her sister made their way downstairs; but for the remainder of the evening, Gabrielle made a concerted effort to walk steadily and act like nothing was wrong.

However happy and carefree she may have appeared, once she returned to the parlor, she kept a sharp eye on her husband. She noticed which ladies he danced with and which ones he spoke to. If he lingered too long with any one of them, she made haste to steer him away as quickly as possible.

André was in a wonderful mood. He had a successful year under his belt, and every man there came up at some time during the evening to congratulate him on his success. Not being of a jealous nature, he wasn't bothered when his wife indulged in some innocent flirtation. She was happy and in a good mood, and that was all that mattered.

At dawn, as was the Créole custom, everyone was served another bowl of gumbo and *café noire*, then each departed for their homes.

On the carriage ride back to the house, Gabrielle thanked the Blessed Mother and all the saints in heaven that she had somehow gotten through the evening; but when she lay down in bed, the room began to spin, and she quickly passed out cold.

André had hoped for a night of lovemaking; but much to his dismay, Gabrielle could barely make it to bed before she fell asleep, or so he thought. As he leaned close to her, he could smell the heavy scent of wine on her breath, and it left him feeling anxious. This was something he wasn't sure how to handle.

* * *

André was up early the next morning. He had things to do.

Gabrielle slept late; but when Millie came in to wake her, she found her mistress suffering from a terrible hangover.

Without saying much, Millie disappeared and returned with a foul-tasting brew that she assured her mistress would make her feel better. Even though it was difficult to swallow, Millie insisted it would take the bad feeling away.

Whatever was in the cup, worked, because, in just a short while, Gabrielle was feeling well enough to dress and join her sister for lunch.

Later that night, when they were alone in their bedroom, André decided to bring up the subject of her drinking. It had bothered him so much he found it difficult to concentrate when he was speaking with his factor. Now, he decided to get the subject out in the open and face it head on.

"Gabrielle, last night when you went to bed, you fairly reeked of wine. I had no idea you drank enough to incapacitate yourself."

Gabrielle gave him a sheepish look. "Oh, darling, I didn't drink *that* much. I only had a few glasses during the evening."

André shook his head. "You had more than a few glasses. I would say you had *quite* a few glasses, and I want it to stop."

"Are you telling me how I must act when we're out?"

"*Oui*," André replied, his eyes dark with anger. "I will not have my wife making a spectacle of herself in public, and I give you fair warning: This drinking *will* stop."

Gabrielle's first impulse was to lash out at him, but something in his expression warned her not to. Instead, she lowered her eyes and looked contrite. "You're right, darling. I did have a little too much wine last night, and I'm sorry. It was the excitement of being here in the city again. I guess I lost my head; but I promise it won't happen again."

Gabrielle put her arms around André's neck and gave him a seductive smile. "Am I forgiven?"

André nodded. Perhaps he was worrying unnecessarily. Perhaps it was all the excitement of being back in the city. It was only natural that she should want to celebrate being back in the social whirl. And even though she had smelt of wine, she had not acted in any way to cause eyebrows to lift.

She looked so lovely at this moment that it was easy to forgive her. "*Oui*," he said softly as his lips brushed against hers. "You're forgiven."

Without another word, he swept her up in his arms and carried her to bed.

Chapter 24

Throughout their stay in New Orleans, André and Gabrielle continued to enjoy the social activities. Many times, Monsieur Charlevoix was at the same function, and André always found pleasure in talking to him about Royal Oaks.

"How long will you remain here in New Orleans?" André asked.

"I'll be leaving for *Château Charlevoix* right after the New Year, and Julie will spend the month of January with me as she has in the past."

"I'm delighted to hear that, Monsieur. And I invite both you and Julie to visit me at Royal Oaks. I should like to show you both how well things are going."

"I shall be happy to accept," Monsieur Charlevoix assured him. "And I'm sure Julie would enjoy visiting Royal Oaks also. I feel we three have a vested interested in your land." They both laughed at this remark.

Things were indeed going well: Gabrielle looked forward to the parties and was in a good mood most of the time. Parties meant she could have champagne and wine. Although she tried to limit the amount she drank, she didn't always succeed. But when she felt bad in the morning, Millie would give her a cup of the nasty-tasting brew and everything would be fine.

Even André's lovemaking was less distasteful after a few glasses of wine. She did, however resent whatever time he spent talking or dancing with the other ladies, whether young or old, and they had some serious fights on the issue.

150

Because of her drinking, sometimes Gabrielle had difficultly keeping her emotions in check. Others were beginning to notice, and this caused André to worry. He *must* put a stop to her drinking.

The first time they fought was one night after Gabrielle had more than her share of wine. She became increasingly angry as she saw André spending what she considered an inordinate amount of time speaking to Monique Valletta. The more she thought of it, the angrier she became.

Later that night when André entered their bedroom, Gabrielle who was sitting at the dressing table, turned to him in a fury. "Well, you certainly spent enough time with Monique Valletta this evening."

"Gabrielle, what are you talking about?"

"You know very well what I'm talking about. I saw the way Monique looked at you with those big cow eyes of hers. And you, standing there, acting so gallant and interested in what she had to say!" She picked up her brush and began brushing her hair vigorously. "And this isn't the first time I've seen you flirting with some woman. You're making a fool of me, and I will not stand for it, do you hear me?"

This change in her behavior was such a shock to André that at first he couldn't believe what he was hearing. But then his eyes grew cold and hard. "Madame, I think you should concern yourself with your behavior before you worry about mine."

"And just what is that supposed to mean?"

"I mean, my dear Gaby, that you spend a little too much time drinking wine. I told you before I won't put up with this. From now on, you will limit yourself to one glass of wine for the evening. If you don't, *you* will probably end up making a fool of yourself without any help from me." Abruptly, André turned and headed for the door.

"Are you accusing me of drinking too much?"

His eyes were scathing as he looked back at her. "I am, and it's becoming obvious to others. The next time we're out, you *will* limit yourself to one glass of wine, or I'll see that you're taken home at once!" With that, he left the room.

Gabrielle was angry and frightened. Was he right? Had she been drinking too much? Had anyone else thought so, or noticed? She studied herself in the mirror. She didn't look any different. The wine just made her feel better. Surely, there couldn't be anything wrong with that. Was André saying that to ease his own conscience?

André went down to the parlor. The room was dark and empty, and for that, he was grateful. He didn't want to see or speak to anyone just now.

A fire still burned in the hearth, and with a deep sigh, André pulled a chair close and sat down. Stretching out his long legs, he put his elbows on the chair arms and pressed his fingertips together. For a long moment, he stared into the flames and thought about Gabrielle. And doing so left him depressed and angry.

He sat for about a half hour and then realized that he was tired and must get some sleep. He had a meeting with Jean Lafitte in the morning. Slowly, he climbed the stairs to their bedroom. As he did so, he thought of their marriage vows. *For better or worse* So far it had been worse rather than better. *For richer or poorer* Well, until now, he'd been poorer rather than richer. *In sickness and in_health* They were both in excellent health. *Until death do us_part* He would be twenty-four soon, Gabrielle would be twenty shortly thereafter.

We could have a great many more years together. If we must spend them together, please, Mon Dieu, let them be better than what we have had so far.

The rest of the stay in New Orleans was less than pleasant. What had started out to be a lovely, lazy vacation for the two of them was turning sour.

André found himself watching Gabrielle more closely. She, in turn, resented the fact that after her first glass of wine he made certain it was her last. They fought constantly.

"You never let me have any fun!" she cried one night when André put a stop to her drinking. "You're worse than my parents."

"Oh, behave yourself and stop acting like a spoiled brat, Gabrielle. I'm sick of it!"

Then, when he was about ready to strangle her, Gabrielle would pull her usual trick and turn sweet and loving again. The drinking would stop, and she would make a real effort to get along with him. The constant upheaval was beginning to wear André out.

When it came time to return to Royal Oaks, Gabrielle informed her husband she wanted to stay with her sister and brother-in-law for a while. "I have no wish to go back to Royal Oaks yet," she announced. "Charles and Francesca said I could stay here with them a while longer."

"Gabrielle, I must return, and you know it," André answered with a feeling of apprehension. Was she going to give him trouble? Would it start up again? "We've already stayed longer than I intended, and now it's time to leave."

"Well, just because you have to leave, doesn't mean I do too." she snapped. "I have a right to stay and enjoy myself if I wish."

"And I have a right to expect my wife to accompany me back to our home!" André's voice was filled with blistering rage.

Once again, the fights started. Finally, in sheer exasperation, André gave in. The thought of having Gabrielle at the plantation always in a bad mood, throwing it up to him that he had dragged her away from her family, friends and parties, was more than he cared to deal with. She was so unpredictable one minute acting like a spoiled, miserable, selfish brat and the next being so sweet and loving it made his head spin. Maybe it would be better to let her stay for a while. Then when she did return home, hopefully, she'd be easier to live with.

He did, however, remind her that if she drank and disgraced herself, she would be sorry. There was no hug or kiss instead, he simply walked out of the bedroom one morning and Gabrielle didn't see him again.

* * *

Riding home, André recalled the excitement he'd felt when, during the day, he had gone to the wharf with his factor. Together, they had watched while his goods were loaded aboard the ships and boats that would carry the cargo to other parts of the country and the world.

He saw the Negroes who worked on the wharf carry the huge bales of cotton aboard the ships. Others rolled the barrels of molasses and the hogsheads of sugar up the gangplanks to the decks of ships and boats. The air was filled with excitement, and André was caught up in all of it.

Yes, that part of the trip had been wonderful, and he smiled as he rode along.

When he turned onto the drive leading to his cabin, he heard the familiar cry "*Maître* comin'." As he reached the cabin, everyone came running out to meet him. They were genuinely happy to see him. He, in turn, was just as happy to see them and very pleased to find that Karl Hoffman had taken such excellent care of his people and his plantation in his absence.

"Tomorrow will be a holiday," he said in good humor. "You will all have the day to relax and enjoy yourselves."

Two days later, Monsieur Charlevoix rode over for a visit.

"André, I'm very impressed with all you've done in such a short period of time." The older man smiled warmly.

"*Merci,* Monsieur." André felt pride in his mentor's praise. "I'm sorry Julie didn't come with you," he added.

"I asked her to come, but she said she didn't feel up to riding today."

"She isn't ill, is she?"

"*Non,* I think she just wanted to be by herself. She has days like that." Monsieur Charlevoix smiled. "My daughter is growing up, becoming a young woman, and changes are taking place: so I think it is having an affect on her. But it is nothing to worry about."

André was disappointed that Julie hadn't accompanied her father. It made him sad that she didn't want to come back to Royal Oaks and visit as she'd done in the past. But he remembered her remarks about Gabrielle and realized how right she had been. Perhaps when she knew that Gabrielle had remained in the city, she would change her mind.

* * *

Julie didn't change her mind. She was happy to hear how well André was doing. Her father told her all that was happening at Royal Oaks.

"He'll be building his new home sometime soon," Monsieur Charlevoix said during dinner that evening. "His wife chose to remain in New Orleans a while longer." He paused, and added, "He asked about you and was sorry you weren't with me."

It broke Julie's heart to think of André alone at Royal Oaks while his wife was in the city. She wanted to see him but what was the use? As young as she was, she knew being around André under the circumstances would only cause her pain. *Non,* she would not go to Royal Oaks, at least not now.

The next week, the rains came, which prevented Julie from going anywhere. But her mind kept going to Royal Oaks. How was André doing, all alone with no one to talk to, no one to keep him company? Perhaps, when the rains stopped, she would ride over and see how things were. But all too soon, something happened that prevented her from visiting.

* * *

It was evening; André was sitting at his *secrétarie* working on his ledgers with Monsieur Hoffman when there came a pounding on the door. Opening it, he found Samson and two other slaves.

"*Maître*, slaves comin' down da road say dey kill all white folks!"

André looked at the black man in surprise, and it took him several seconds to realize what Samson was telling him.

The slaves had a way of communicating with each other across the vast plantations. It was called the "grapevine." One slave would sing a song, say one word differently; hold a note a little longer. Another slave would pick it up and repeat it, and in no time, all the slaves on all the plantations for miles around would know what was going on.

Samson had gotten word that the rebellious slaves were marching down the River Road toward New Orleans.

"*Michie* Jean-Francois Trepagnier, he be killed by his own slaves, *oui*," Samson added, visibly shaken.

This remark didn't surprise André. Everyone knew that Jean-Francois Trepagnier was a cruel master and that there was great unrest on his plantation. He had been cited for his treatment of his slaves more than once, and it would appear that things hadn't changed after all.

"I must get to the city at once and see what I can do," André said. He ordered his horse and asked his overseer if he wished to accompany him. "Samson, you'll be in charge until we return. I know I can trust and count on you to keep everything under control. We'll be back as soon as possible."

The two men headed down the road; but as they neared *Château Charlevoix*, André turned to his overseer, "I must stop here for a moment. You keep riding to the city and report to the Militia. I'll catch up with you as soon as I can." He turned his horse onto the avenue that led to the house. As he drew near, Monsieur Charlevoix came out to meet him. Like André, he too, had heard the news from his slaves.

"André, I'd appreciate it if you'd take Julie to the city. I must stay here long enough to make sure my home is not destroyed. I understand they've tried to burn down several plantations up the river, but Julie must be taken to safety."

From where they stood on the *galerie,* the two men could see carriages choking the road. The white families, learning of the approaching slaves, were now heading for town. It was mostly women and children. The men stayed behind to protect their homes. There was genuine mass hysteria throughout the countryside. Many remembered

155

the terrible slave uprising in Santo Domingo that took place in 1790. Then, whole families of whites men, women, and children had been slaughtered.

André followed Monsieur Charlevoix into the house, and 'Toinette was sent to fetch Julie. "I will ride in over the fields and take a short cut just as soon as I know this place is in no danger," Monsieur Charlevoix explained as Julie hurried down the stairs. When she learned what was happening, Julie begged her father to let her stay with him. But her father was firm, *"Non, ma chérie,* I can't let you stay. You must go to New Orleans with André. There, you will be safe with Madame Gauthier. I'll come for you just as soon as I can." He gave her a kiss and told her she must hurry and leave. André picked her up, ran down the stairs, swung her up on the saddle, and in a second, was on the saddle with her, urging his horse to a gallop.

Once they were on the road, it was difficult to maintain the same speed. There were just too many carriages and carts. But André managed to weave his way through the throng, and soon he was able to urge the horse to a quicker pace..

It was the first time they had seen each other since his wedding. Julie had changed, not much…a little taller and even more beautiful than André remembered.

He held her tightly with one hand, and the reins with the other. Julie leaned against him, her head nestled beneath his chin, and he caught the faint fragrance of jasmine she always wore. Except for a brief greeting, not one word had been spoken between them. His first concern was getting her to safety.

Now riding with her cradled in his arms, he suddenly realized how much Julie meant to him. She was still so young, but he thought of how sweet she was, all the funny stories she told him, and how much fun they had had together.

He remembered how encouraging she had been, how patiently she had waited while he worked in the fields or the sugar factory until it was time for lunch.

In reflecting on Julie's attributes, Andre couldn't help but compare Gabrielle to this dear, sweet, young girl.

Sadly, he realized that except for her beauty, Gabrielle had few attributes. Her sweet nature was never as apparent as her hateful one. When he thought of the years ahead and his life with her, his heart grew heavy. He'd married her, and he knew there was no changing what had been done.

Divorce was absolutely unheard of among the Catholic Créoles of New Orleans. A divorced man or woman would never be accepted in their society. Not only would the man or woman be unacceptable, but any children from that union or any future union would also be ostracized. It was far too high a price to pay, and the thought of divorce never crossed André's mind.

Now, as he rode along, his thoughts jumped to what lay ahead. Rumor had it that there were over a thousand slaves heading for the city. Rumor also had it that many white families already lay dead in their homes. It was all rumor; but since no one knew the facts, the rumors took on a life of their own.

André had to admit he wasn't looking forward to the coming confrontation. He had never killed a man, and the thought of doing so now filled him with apprehension. But he knew that if it came down to "kill or be killed," he could pull the trigger on his pistol with no hesitation.

Suddenly, he thought he heard Julie's voice. He bent his head down. "Did you say something, little one?"

"I said, do you think they will come and kill us?"

Julie's voice was shaking and he could feel her body tremble. She turned eyes, large with fear, up to him, and it tore his heart to think that one so young had to fear such a horrible fate. Instinctively, his arm tightened around her body as though to shield her from the terrible thought.

"Non, chère coeur, they'll not harm you. I promise. Besides, they will have to face the entire Louisiana Militia before they ever reach the city. You'll be safe, I would never let any harm come to you." He hoped his gentle smile, and reassuring tone, and his strong arms would help calm Julie's fears.

When they reached the city, André steered his horse to Madame Claudine Gauthier's home. This kind lady had been best friend to Julie's mother, and it was the Gauthier family that Julie stayed with when her father was in the north on business in the months she was not in school.

They saw André's overseer, along with the Louisiana Militia, riding out to meet the rebellious slaves. André explained his mission. "I'll catch up with you directly," he said.

Madame Gauthier met them at the door. She, too, had heard the slaves were headed for the city; and after she welcomed Julie, she questioned André. "Do you think you'll be able to stop them? Where should we go if they attack?" Her face was ashen and her voice shook.

"I doubt they'll reach the city," André reassured her. "Already, there is a large contingent of men heading out to meet them and keep them from getting any closer. Just stay inside and bolt all your doors and windows."

He turned to Julie. "Don't worry, *ma petite*, you'll be safe. Your *pappa* will come and fetch you as soon as possible." Giving her a quick hug and a light kiss on her forehead, André galloped off to join the Militia.

The two factions met on the road about four miles from the city. It could not be called an even match by any means. The slaves had marched down the road with drums beating and flares lit. They had gathered what tools they could from their masters' plantations to use as weapons: machetes, pitchforks, axes, clubs, and sticks.

The white militia marched in great numbers, with swords and guns ready. There were about five hundred slaves, and they were well outnumbered.

Revenge was swift, although there were some casualties among the white men. André saw one large black man with a pitchfork lunge at a white man. The pitchfork entered the man's body; and with a scream of delight, the slave pulled the bloody fork from the body and looked around for another victim. However, his victory was short-lived as a bullet from André's pistol cut him down, and in a second, he lay dead. For a moment, André stood stunned. He'd shot and killed a man! But too much was happening. There was no time to think or worry about it. His own life could be snuffed out if he did.

Sweat poured down his face and dripped into his eyes, causing them to burn. It was the cold sweat of fear and nerves. Never had he imagined he'd find himself in such a situation. From the corner of his eye, André saw a glint of metal as a slave with a machete swung at him. André's pistol discharged once again, but not before the machete grazed his arm. The slave fell dead, and André watched as blood slowly oozed from the fabric of his coat. It didn't seem to be a deep cut, and there was too much going on. He didn't have time to think about pain. The night was filled with the screams of the injured, the smell of blood and death, and it sickened him.

Many slaves were shot on the spot and then hurled into the river.

Others were hanged by the neck on hastily built scaffolds. Still others were taken to the *Calaboose* in New Orleans, where they were later tried and decapitated.

The white men who were injured were taken to their homes to be tended by their families and doctors. The dead were buried as soon as possible.

It was the worst rebellion in the history of Louisiana, and one that would be spoken of for years.

Chapter 25

When the nightmare was over, André and his overseer headed back to Royal Oaks, but not before Charles asked André if he cared to spend the night at his townhouse, especially since it was obvious he'd been injured. "You really should come home with me and let us take care of that wound. You don't want to get an infection."

"*Merci*, Charles, but I must get back to Royal Oaks. Besides, it's just a flesh wound, and I'm sure Delilah can take care of it. She seems to have a cure for almost every ailment."

He paused and added, "Besides, I have no idea if my slaves joined the rebellion. In the melee that has taken place, it was difficult to tell. I didn't see any familiar faces, and I pray that none of them were here in this horrible carnage; but I won't know until I'm home."

"Of course, I understand. But you make certain that Delilah tends your wound."

"Charles, aren't you concerned that some of your slaves may have been involved in this nightmare?"

Charles shook his head. "*Non*, André. My slaves have been a part of our family all of my life. I have faith that they stayed loyal to us."

After inquiring about Gabrielle and being assured that she was fine, André saw no reason to remain.

As he and his overseer reached *Château Charlevoix*, André was relieved to see the house and all the other buildings still standing. He stopped long enough to assure 'Toinette that both Monsieur Charlevoix and Julie were safe and would return home shortly.

When they reached Royal Oaks, André and Hoffman found the place deserted but unharmed. There was no sign of life anywhere, and André wondered if all of his slaves had run away. He knew it would be difficult for them if they had, because of their numbers. They would be caught and it would mean certain death, people assuming that they were part of the uprising. It was pitch-black. The moon, as though in mourning for the lost lives, had hidden behind the clouds.

André and his overseer rode out to the cabins that were also dark and empty. They continued riding out to the farthest fields. The night was too dark to see anything, and the air was heavy with the stillness.

Then suddenly, they heard a noise. The hair on the back of André's neck stood up. Were his slaves in hiding? Would they suddenly appear and kill him and Karl Hoffman as the others had killed their masters?

But, André reasoned, he had never mistreated them. He'd never allowed any of them to be whipped. He'd never made a promise he couldn't keep. He'd always treated them with respect and kindness. Surely, they wouldn't repay him with violence. These thoughts were going through his mind as his hand reached for his gun.

"Please, *Mon Dieu*, don't let me have to kill any of my people." Until that night, André had never killed another human being. Now, the thought of having to kill any of his slaves, even if it was in self-defense, was even more repugnant to his nature.

He heard the sound again, and in the intense darkness, he thought he saw a form moving in the distance. Yes, it was a form, and it was moving towards him.

André squinted, trying to pierce the blackness. Just then, the moon slipped partway from behind the clouds and threw its feeble light across the area. He saw the form, and behind it was a mass of forms moving slowly and cautiously. His hand remained on his pistol, and he held his breath waiting to see what would happen next.

The mass of human bodies started running towards him, with Samson in the lead. André and Hoffman both tensed up. What would happen when the slaves reached them? They kept their horses quiet, their hands on their pistols, and waited.

"Samson, is that you?" André called out. "If it is, you may come out, everything is all right."

Relief flooded André's senses as Samson answered.

"*Maître, Maître*, you all right? You be *non* hurt?" Samson called as he ran towards André. Now they were all running and yelling. When they reached André and they had quieted down, Samson in, his Gumbo French, explained. "We hide in swamp. We *non* want to be wid bad slaves. Iffen we do dat, we be killed. We *non* leave our families."

He went on to say, "We be 'fraid *Maître* be killed. Iffen dat happen, we be sold to *maître* who *non* treat us kind. Maybe sell us families apart. We hide, feared of what might happen if *Maître non* come back." He paused and his face broke into a wide smile. "But *Maître* come back, everythin' fine, we all be alive, *oui*."

André knew that although not one of them wanted to be a slave, they would not join any rebellion. They appreciated the fact that he was kind and caring.

André valued their loyalty so with a broad smile of his own, he declared the next day a holiday. He rewarded them by letting them have a party. There was lots of food, some punch, and much dancing. *Oui*, life at Royal Oaks was good.

* * *

When Charles returned to his townhouse that night, he found Francesca and Gabrielle waiting up for him. They were eager to hear about what had happened. He told them everything; but when he mentioned to his sister-in-law about André's riding into New Orleans with Julie and then returning to Royal Oaks without stopping by, Gabrielle flew into a rage.

"You mean he rode through the city with that girl on his horse and didn't even want to come here to make certain I was all right?"

"Gabrielle, he was only taking Julie to Madame Gauthier's home where she would be safe. And I told him you were fine."

Charles tried to reason with her, but Gabrielle would have none of it. She ranted and raved and vented her spleen on him. She went on about Julie and stormed around the room. "André doesn't care anything about me! He didn't even care if I was in danger or not."

"But you weren't in any danger, Gaby," Charles said in exasperation. "And André knew it, and he had to get back to Royal Oaks to see if everything was all right."

"Oh, Royal Oaks, Royal Oaks, that's all I ever hear about. That's all he cares about! Well, I hate the place. I wish I'd never set eye on that horrible place!"

Gabrielle was too angry to be reasoned with. Finally, in her fit of temper, she picked up a beautiful porcelain vase and threw it across the room where it hit the wall and shattered into a hundred pieces.

Francesca stood in shock. "Gabrielle," she cried, "how could you? That was my very favorite vase! It was so beautiful." When she saw the pieces scattered all over the floor, she burst into tears.

"Oh, it's just a stupid vase," her sister said with indifference. "You can always get another one. But, I'm married to a man who doesn't care anything about me."

Before he knew what was happening, Charles found himself in the middle of a verbal battle between the two.

When they had each exhausted their energy, Francesca ran crying to her bedchamber and Gabrielle stormed off to hers slamming the door as hard as she could.

Charles decided he'd had enough. Gabrielle would go back to Royal Oaks as soon as possible. He was tired of her behavior. She'd always been difficult but now she was getting out of hand. He must speak to André about her when he stopped by Royal Oaks.

He certainly didn't want Francesca upset. He'd just found out a few days earlier that she was expecting a baby in August. She had kept it a secret as long as possible, knowing that once the fact became known, her social life would come to an end, at least until the baby's birth. Now, her gowns were getting too tight, and her condition could no longer be concealed.

Charles was pleased by the news; and although Francesca was happy at the prospect of becoming a mother, she had suffered morning sickness and feared how dangerous giving birth could be.

Francesca and her sister had gotten into several heated arguments lately. Now Charles felt that sending Gabrielle back to André would be in his wife's best interest. Of course, he would have to be careful how he explained it all. He certainly didn't want to offend his brother-in-law. Nor did he want to insult Gabrielle. That could cause far more problems. *Non*, he would simply explain to André that Francesca was not feeling very well lately, and it would be better if Gabrielle returned home.

* * *

Upon reaching his plantation, Oak Grove, the next day, Charles found that his slaves had stayed loyal to him. He thanked each for their faithfulness, and like André, declared the next day a holiday with a party for everyone.

He stayed at Oak Grove for two days and then headed for Royal Oaks. He found André in the sugar factory when he arrived. Later, as they rode back to the cabin for lunch, André said, "Charles, I never thought I would ever be involved in such a horrible nightmare. What on earth could have set off such a terrible uprising?"

"It's a long story one that has been around for some time," Charles said. "The wonder is that it hadn't happened before now."

They reached the cabin, and the two dismounted and entered the house. Once Delilah served the food and left the room, Charles picked up the story.

"Years ago," he said, "Monsieur Trepagnier bought a little black slave. The child was a bright and charming boy, and Monsieur Trepagnier and his wife treated him like a little pet. They dressed in him fancy livery and gave him more freedom and liberties than any of the other slaves." He paused to take a bite of food, and then continued.

"This of course caused some resentment among the other slaves. Finally, when the boy reached ten and five, he went to his master and asked if someday soon he could have his freedom. Monsieur Trepagnier told him he could when he learned to read."

"But, I have been told it is against the law to teach a slave to read," André said.

"It is but Trepagnier told the boy he could take any book from the library, and if he could teach himself to read, he would have his freedom."

After a sip of coffee, Charles said, "Well it took a few years, but eventually the boy did teach himself. Once again, he asked to be free. But again, his master gave him new challenge. He was told he would have to read every book in the library, and it was quite an extensive library. By now, the young slave was in his twenties, but he accepted the challenge and over a ten-year period, he mastered every book. Now, when he asked for his freedom, Monsieur Trepagnier laughed and told the man he would never be free. He was born a slave and would die a slave. But at least he could read."

André shook his head. "What a terrible thing to do."

Charles agreed. "*Oui*, it was, and Monsieur Trepagnier paid the ultimate price. Such resentment and rage built up in the slave that it was easy to get the others riled up. And so, Monsieur Trepagnier and his entire family were killed as were many other families."

They discussed the topic a little longer then Charles changed the subject. He went back to his reason for his visit and explained the problem between his wife and her sister.

"Francesca is not herself lately. She and Gaby seem to irritate each other constantly. I'm certain once Francesca is feeling better, they will get along again."

He paused for the other to say something, but when André remained silent, Charles continued. "For now, I feel it would be best if Gabrielle came back home. Besides, we, too, will be returning to Oak Grove in the near future."

Finally, André spoke and assured his brother-in-law that he understood the problem. "Gabrielle has been away long enough," he said as he took a bite of food. "It's time she came home and began behaving like a wife should."

He couldn't help wondering if Francesca's condition was the only reason Charles wanted to send Gabrielle home but was afraid to ask.

Chapter 26

Three days later, André went to fetch Gabrielle. She wasn't at all happy to be leaving the city, but she had no choice. Throughout the trip to Royal Oaks, she sat beside him pouting and with a scowl on her face. André felt equally angry and frustrated. "Gabrielle, are we to spend the rest of our lives like this? Will you never be content? What in heavens name is wrong with you? Is there no pleasing you?"

Gabrielle merely shot him an angry look.

Later that evening when they'd finished dinner and the servants had left, André tried talking to her. "Gabrielle, the architect will be coming out soon so we can refine the plans for the house. Tell me, how would you like it furnished?" He waited a minute and then said, "What ideas have you concerning how the interior should look?"

Gabrielle shrugged. "I don't know." With indifference, she sipped her wine. "I can't think about anything except getting out of this miserable dump as soon as possible."

André drew a deep breath and tried again. "Well, we will be out of this dump, as you call it, as soon as our house is built. It will be your home, too. I thought you might have some ideas as to color scheme or how you want the rooms to look."

Gabrielle sighed with irritation. "I don't know what I want. Except to get out of this horrible place!"

André looked at her for a long moment, his hazel eyes filled with vexation. "Gabrielle, why are you so hard to get along with? All you've done is complain about this place, and now that I am ready to build the house you've always wanted, you won't tell me how you would like it to look."

Once again, she shot him an irate glance.

In anger, André jumped up from the table, knocking over his chair. Not bothering to pick it up and without a word to his wife, he slammed out of the cabin. He got his horse and went for a ride, hoping to cool off. He never should have married her! But he *was* married to her, and damn it, he wanted his marriage to work.

He was pleased when he realized he was now able to afford the home they both wanted. Between the money he had left from his family, his profits from his crops, and Gabrielle's dowry, he felt comfortable in hiring an architect who would be coming to Royal Oaks to discuss the plans. But, as usual, his wife was not making any of it easy.

A couple of days later, Gabrielle surprised him when they sat down to dinner. "I have decided it is time we did discuss what I want in my new home." André remained silent.

"I want a beautiful ballroom, with a musician's *galerie,*" she said, her eyes shining. "I want a large formal dining room with the very best furniture. I want a huge bedroom with my own dressing room, and I want...." She went on and on about what *she* wanted.

"It would be nice if, for once, you would ask me what *I* want," André muttered. But Gabrielle didn't hear him; she was too absorbed with her own wants.

While they'd been in New Orleans, André had ordered some of the furniture, and rented a large storeroom where it could be kept until such time as the house was completed. Since Gabrielle had no interest in the subject, he felt free to choose what *he* wanted.

He'd ordered the very best his money could buy marble fireplaces from Italy, huge crystal chandeliers from France, furniture of rosewood and mahogany, massive sideboards, tall armoires, and great four-poster beds. Carpets from Europe and rugs from Persia were to cover the floors.

When the architect arrived, he and André spent hours pouring over the plans, and Gabrielle sat in on their talks. André tried to explain the plans to her, but she became impatient.

"Oh, don't clutter my mind with all those details; I don't understand a thing you're talking about. Just tell me how soon the house will be completed so I can start entertaining."

Her voice was strident and the room was heavy with tension. The architect glanced at her and then at André, who looked embarrassed but said nothing.

* * *

In March, the foundation was laid, and the slaves who could be spared from the fields were sent to the swamp to cut down the huge cypresses that would be used for the house. Other slaves set about making bricks. The work continued, sometimes going slowly because of the rain that came and stayed for days.

After the rain came the steaming heat, and still the work went on. Finally, by late June, the house was almost completed.

André and Gabrielle were at peace with each other. Gabrielle tried to show an interest in all that was going on; but it wasn't in her nature to get involved with things that took too long. So she often lost patience. It was hot and stuffy in the cabin and it was at these times, that she sought comfort in the brandy.

Then she became upset over another matter. "It's my twentieth birthday and we can't celebrate in the manner I want," she cried. She and André were getting ready to go to Oak Grove for the evening.

"Gabrielle, Charles, and Francesca are kind enough to invite us over so that we can celebrate your birthday with them."

"I know—but the only people who will be there will be my parents." She shot André an angry look. "If Francesca wasn't enceinte, she could have invited other guests and we could have had a real party." The evening was less than successful. When she and André arrived, her family greeted Gabrielle warmly, each with a kiss and a happy birthday wish. She responded with cool indifference and hardly said a word to any of them. Dinner was even more unpleasant. Gabrielle pouted, picked at her food, refused to speak, and had her wine glass filled often, much to André's concern.

When finally they left, she didn't even bother to thank her sister and brother-in-law for their efforts.

Not a word was spoken on the drive home. Although André thought about giving her a good tongue-lashing, he decided against it. What was the use? They would only end up having another fight, and he was sick to death of the fights. They retired to bed in total silence.

168

* * *

André spent much of his time with the builder, checking every detail. The house was built of cypress, cedar, and brick. It rose twelve feet above the ground to prevent the interior from being damaged in case of floods.

Each day, André stood out in the blazing sun to watch as the house began to take shape. He saw the thick brick columns that had been whitewashed put in place. These columns supported the *galerie* and arches. He watched when the roof was put on. Like all Créole plantation homes, this roof slanted out on all four sides.

Double exterior stairs, gracefully curved, led to the long *galerie* that extended across the front of the house and wrapped around the sides. The ground floor was built of brick and would be used for storage. The upper floors were of cedar and cypress.

Both exterior and interior staircase banisters were fashioned from imported teakwood that was less apt to warp in the Louisiana dampness.

Once the house was completed, André walked through the rooms and admire their beauty. Within the house, the ceilings reached sixteen feet on the first floor and twelve feet on the second floor, with doors and windows to scale.

The exquisite molding around the ceilings of each room only added to the grandeur. The huge crystal chandeliers that hung from the ceilings reposed in the middle of beautiful medallions. The foyer was large, and it, too, had a double staircase that gracefully curved to the upper floor.

The main floor (which was really the second floor) consisted of a large parlor, a banquet room, ballroom, music room, small library, a *petit* salon, and a butler's pantry.

The furniture André had ordered for these rooms fit perfectly. The fabrics were of the very best quality and taste. The drapes and curtains were also of the finest material, and the objects d'art complemented each room.

On the next floor were six bedrooms, each with a small dressing room. The master bedroom was the largest and had two small dressing rooms: one for André and the other for Gabrielle. André had added a small room next to the master bedroom. Hopefully, someday, it would hold a sleeping child.

In the rear of the house were the servants' staircase and four small bedrooms for the servants who would sleep in the main house.

A large, new kitchen stood in the backyard, and a small *garçonnière* was built on either side of the house.

Amid all this activity, Francesca gave birth to a son. Charles was delighted and was the epitome of the proud father, telling anyone who would listen all the details of the baby's every move. "When your house is completed, you and Gabrielle should have a *bébé*. It's been wonderful for Francesca and me," he told André one day.

André only nodded, wondering what kind of mother Gabrielle would make.

The baby was christened Antoine after Charles' father, and André and Gabrielle were his godparents. His little godson fascinated André. He'd never before been around a new baby. He would hold the infant and play with him whenever he visited Oak Grove. It delighted him when the baby responded to him with a smile or held tightly to his finger.

He noticed that Gabrielle, on the other hand, showed little interest in the child; and one day after visiting Charles and Francesca, he remarked on it. "Gaby, you don't seem to care for our little godson. You never hold him, and you give him scant attention."

"Oh, I don't see what's so wonderful about that *bébé*. He cries all the time and gets on my nerves. And the one time I did hold him, he wet on me! It was disgusting!"

"He doesn't cry all the time," André answered softly. "He's a delightful little fellow. Why, he smiles and grabs my finger, and tries to make noises. I think he wants to talk."

Gabrielle gave him a wry look. "Oh, really, André. That's positively the most ridiculous thing I've ever heard."

André worried about her attitude but hoped it would be different if and when they had children of their own. He wanted a child and hoped that, once they were settled in their new home, Gabrielle would conceive.

However, when he tried to discuss the subject with her, Gabrielle informed him there was no way she wanted a baby for a long time. "I have no desire to lose my figure, get fat and ugly, and be miserable like Francesca was for nine months. I want to enjoy my new house and all the parties I plan to give. So don't get any ideas about my having a *bébé* anytime soon."

She had no idea as to how to prevent this from happening, she only knew she didn't want it to happen, and in her selfish mind, figured that was enough.

* * *

Before the house was completed, André made several trips to *Grande Terre* with Jean Lafitte to buy more slaves.

Even before the house was built, a music teacher, along with several musical instruments, had been brought out from New Orleans to teach the men with natural talent to play so that there would be music at the parties Gabrielle was determined to have.

André would smile when he heard his slaves learning how to play a horn or the violin, or some other instrument. For a while, the sound was painful but in due time, it turned sweet, and André once again felt pride at how well and how quickly the men were learning.

* * *

They moved into the house in July, and Gabrielle was in her glory, as she wasted no time planning her first party.

"I shall invite all my friends and neighbors. I will even invite the girls who said mean things about me before we were married," she said, as she made out the guest list.

"I hope you will consider inviting some of my friends also," André said dryly.

"Of course, darling, don't be silly. Most of my friends are your friends, too." Gabrielle's mood was such that nothing made her angry. "Oh, how I will love to show off my gorgeous home. Let those mean girls see how beautifully my house is furnished and how many servants I have." She put great emphasis on the words *my* and *I*, and laughed softly, as she continued writing.

André listened with half an ear. Everything was "I," "me," or "my"; never "we" or "ours"—whenever she discussed anything that had to do with their life together.

* * *

What a bevy of activity took place the week of the party. Servants scurried about polishing the hardwood floors until they could see their faces in them, and polishing the teakwood banisters to bring out the beautiful grains of the wood. The crystal chandeliers were filled with hundreds of candles. Ivy, grapevine, and fresh flowers were brought into the house and twined into the curved banisters and then tied with ribbons. Fresh flowers in crystal vases filled every room. The silverware was polished until it gleamed, and the crystal was washed until it sparkled.

André sent his slaves out to fish, while he himself went to hunt the game they would serve at the party. And they were all successful. In the kitchen, wonderful delicacies were being prepared for the occasion.

Wild turkey, duck, pheasant, geese, venison, and pigs were brought in. Several chickens lost their lives. Fresh river shrimp, trout, crab, oyster, and red snapper were caught in the waters of the bayous and other streams. Vegetables fresh from the gardens, berries, fruits, and pecans from the trees were on the menu. And the desserts...they were heavenly! The best brandies, wines, and liqueurs were brought from New Orleans.

* * *

On the night of the party, the house was ablaze in candlelight, and what a beautiful sight as carriages drew up before the entrance. Friends and neighbors alighted and ascended the curved staircases and stepped into the large foyer.

Gabrielle was a vision in a gown of silvery blue tissue. She stood next to André and delighted in greeting her guests and watching their reaction to the beauty of her home.

And the guests! There were at least a hundred. Some came by carriage, others by boat, docking at Royal Oaks' private wharf where André's carriage met them and drove them up the long avenue of oaks to the house.

And the music! The musicians had learned to play their instruments well and took great pride in their accomplishment.

Gabrielle was in her element. She was warm, charming, and gracious, and went out of her way to make certain everyone felt welcomed.

André was pleased to see how nice she could be when she put her mind to it. And he had to admit that he was proud of her. She had really outdone herself to make this first ball a great success.

"Oh, *ma chérie,* Gabrielle," Madeline Duval gushed. "I simply can't tell you how thrilled I am to be here. Your home is truly beautiful, and you, *ma chère*, you look absolutely exquisite."

"*Merci*, Madeline," Gabrielle said sweetly. "I'm happy you like my beautiful home, and I'm delighted to have you and Jules as my guests for the evening."

Gabrielle felt like a queen. Everyone told her how beautiful her home was, how gorgeous she was, how thrilled they were to be in attendance. She danced and flirted and kept her drinking under control.

From force of habit, André found himself watching how much she drank. He didn't want a scene. He hoped that she would behave herself and keep her drinking to a minimum, and it appeared she succeeded.

All the guests congratulated André on all he had accomplished in such a short period of time. And with Gabrielle behaving herself and acting so sweet to everyone, he found it easy to erase from his mind all of the ugly scenes that had taken place in previous months.

Now that they had a beautiful home, Gabrielle would be able to entertain. Now, she would have no reason to complain. And now, hopefully, they would have a happy, peaceful marriage (well, at least peaceful). André doubted if anything could make Gabrielle truly happy. She was too wrapped up in herself.

Chapter 27

Summer passed in relative serenity. Gabrielle was happier than she'd been since her wedding day. She was sweet and loving to André, joining him at breakfast, and looking beautiful and fresh when they sat down again for lunch and dinner. She was not drinking, and this made a great difference in her behavior and attitude. As a result, André too was more relaxed.

Gabrielle filled the house with guests giving dinner parties, *soirées,* and balls. She was so busy planning her social activities she hardly noticed the time André spent at his job of running the plantation. Yes, having the large house made all the difference in the world. Now they laughed and talked together, and enjoyed each other's company.

The season was winding down, and soon it would be time to pack for the city at least that was Gabrielle's hope. But, once again, she was disappointed.

"I'm sorry, Gabrielle, but it will be closer to Christmas before we can go to New Orleans," André informed her.

At first, Gabrielle tried to get her way by being sweet and loving. She sat on his lap, ran her fingers through his hair, and kissed him.

But André remained firm. "Gabrielle, I'd love to go, but I can't. Now that we have this large house, it is more important than ever for me to remain here and make sure all goes well, at least until the holidays.

"In case you don't realize it, this house cost me a fortune to build and furnish. I'm sure by next year we'll be able to spend more time in New Orleans."

"Next year!" Gabrielle wailed. "Next year, I could be dead! I want to go now!" Jumping up from André's lap, she screamed, "You're being mean and impossible again, and I hate it and you!" In a fury, she ran from the room in tears.

When Gabrielle realized no amount of sweet talk would change André's mind, she became more upset. Once again, the fights started; and once again, she nursed her anger and frustration with a bottle of brandy. It was her refuge; her only relief when things became intolerable and she couldn't have her way.

In the morning when the sun danced into the bedroom making little patterns through the lace curtains, André would look over at his sleeping wife and feel heartsick. He could smell the brandy from the night before and see the lines and dark circles under her eyes as a result of her drinking. With a heavy heart, he would rise and go about his business and try to put the disquieting thoughts of her drinking from his mind.

Gabrielle would stay in bed long after André left. When finally she did rise, she ordered Millie to bring her a decanter of brandy. Sitting in her favorite chair, she stared out of the window and brooded as she drank. *Everyone is in the city, going to parties and balls, and having fun—everyone but me! Oh, that hateful man!* The more she thought about her plight, the more she drank.

Often, when André returned for lunch, Gabrielle was in no condition to join him. He, however, had too much on his mind to worry about her. The cane had been cut and now the grinding began. The cotton had been picked and was being readied for shipment. Hogsheads and barrels were being readied for the sugar and molasses, and he prayed his crops would be as successful as the previous year; and from all appearances, they would be.

At first, the brew Millie brought her to drink always worked when Gabrielle woke in the morning with a hangover and nausea. Now, suddenly, it seemed to have no effect at all. Now, the upset stomach was there in the morning and stayed with her much of the day. Not only was her stomach in turmoil, she could keep nothing down. Every morning, she would throw up what little food she ate.

After a couple of weeks of this, Millie became alarmed and told Delilah of her concern.

"There be somethin' wrong wid Mam'selle Gabrielle," she said, her eyes wide with concern. She went on to tell Delilah what was happening to her mistress.

Delilah smiled and put her fears to rest when she said, "There be nothin' wrong wid da *Maîtresse*. She gonna' have ah *bébé*. You watch soon her clothes get too tight."

Millie felt relief knowing what the problem was, but it didn't make life any easier for her. Gabrielle too began to realize what was causing her such misery. Her sister had told her all the details of having a baby, and this knowledge, plus the morning sickness, put her in a terrible mood, and she took it out on the Millie and everyone else in the house.

One morning, André returned to the bedroom before she was up. As he entered the room, he found her throwing up in a bowl Millie held. "Gabrielle, what's wrong? Are you ill?"

Gabrielle looked up at him. Her face was devoid of color. "*Oui*, I'm ill thanks to you!" She spat the words out.

"Thanks to me? What have I done?"

"Oh, you, you and your, your...stupid lovemaking!" She glared at him and fell back on her pillows.

Millie left the room and returned with a bowl of fresh water and a cloth. She dipped the cloth into the water, wrung it out, and placed it on her mistress's forehead.

André turned to her. "*Merci*, Millie, that will be all for now." The young girl nodded and left the room.

Reaching over, André took Gabrielle's hand. Softly, he asked, "Gaby, are you telling me you're *enceinte*?"

She turned her head away from him, nodding, and he heard her sob. Gently, he sat on the edge of the bed and gathered her in his arms. "Darling, that's wonderful news. It's nothing to cry about. It's what I've wanted ever since our marriage."

Gabrielle was crying harder now. "What *you've* wanted? What about what *I* want?"

André continued to hold her, his hands caressing her tousled hair soothingly, gently, his voice soft and filled with love. "Oh, Gaby, dearest, I know you're not feeling well, and with this heat it must be very uncomfortable. But think of it, darling, we'll have a little one like Antoine. I've hoped we'd have a child for so long. Dearest, it's wonderful news."

Gabrielle wrenched herself from his embrace. "Oh, it's wonderful, is it?" Her blue eyes blazed with fury. "Well, it may be wonderful for

176

you, but you're not the one with morning sickness. *You* don't throw up every day. *You're* not the one who will get fat and ugly and will have to stay indoors and miss all the fun for months and months." She took a deep breath. "And, *you're* not the one having this *bébé*. *I'm* the one, and I'm scared to death!" With that, she fell back crying and beating her fist on her pillow.

Once again, André reached out to gather her in his arms. "I know you're frightened darling, but you'll have the very best doctor in New Orleans."

Gabrielle pushed him away. "What good will a doctor do? I still have to *have* the *bébé*, and Francesca said giving birth is terrible. She said the pain is unbelievable!"

"I'm sure it is very painful; but Francesca herself said Antoine was worth it. She adores that child and says she hopes to have more children."

"Well, *I'm* not Francesca, and I don't want *this* brat, much less *more*!" Gabrielle lifted her swollen tear-streaked face and gave Andre a venomous look. "I don't want to be *enceinte*, do you hear me? I don't want it!"

André recoiled from the look on her face. He stood up and looked down at her with total revulsion. "Gabrielle, this child is as much a part of me as you. I *do* want this *bébé*, and God help you if you do anything to endanger its life."

He left the room sick at heart. What should have been one of the happiest moments of his life had turned into a nightmare. She didn't want the child! His rage was almost unbearable at the thought of Gabrielle doing anything to harm his unborn child. He rode out to the fields, but his mind wasn't on what was happening around him, his thoughts were on his unborn child. What kind of a person was this woman he'd married?

* * *

September remained as hot as July and August. The sun hung over the land like a giant lump of red-hot coal. Gabrielle found little relief. Her clothes stuck to her body and the morning sickness continued.

With October, there was little change in the weather except for the rain that did nothing to improve the climate or Gabrielle's disposition. The thought of being pregnant until the following spring made her far more miserable than her actual condition.

Each day, she would check her figure in the mirror. You couldn't tell at first glance; but, yes, she could see her waist thickening. As she looked at herself, the frustration of her condition overwhelmed her; she stamped her foot and burst into tears. Throwing herself across the bed, she lay there crying and thinking of how it would be for her at Christmastime in the city.

"I've got to find a way to get rid of this *bébé*," she cried. "I simply *will not* remain in this horrible condition throughout Christmas and the rest of the social season." The tears and temper tantrum continued.

One day, André came home and found her in this condition and was filled with concern. Was it healthy for her to be this upset? Trying to soothe and comfort her, he took her in his arms.

"Gaby, please don't act this way. It can't be good for you or the *bébé*."

"Oh, the *bébé*, the *bébé*! That's all I hear from you! Do you realize that by the time we go to the city, I won't be able to wear any of my pretty dresses and beautiful ball gowns?

"I will be fat and ugly and won't be able to go anywhere except to the *théâtre*, and then I'll have to sit behind the *loges grilles*. No one will see me or even know I'm there so what fun will that be? Oh, how could you do this to me?" She sent up another loud wail.

Nothing André said made a difference. Gabrielle carried on until, in sheer frustration, he got up and left the room. Once he was gone, she continued to indulge her self-pity.

Now, with the morning sickness, even the brandy offered little relief. Sometimes, it made her so ill she would spend much of the day throwing up, but still she continued to drink whenever she could. Drinking was one of the few pleasures she had left, and this brat was not going to deprive her of that. She resented the baby and continued to think of how to rid herself of it.

Since nothing André did pleased her, he stopped trying. He concentrated instead on the unborn child. Now, he must be even more successful.

He hoped once the child was born and Gabrielle held it in her arms and nursed it at her breast, she would be happy she'd had it. Why shouldn't she be happy? Lord knows, she had everything she wanted! And he'd worn himself out giving all of it to her!

Chapter 28

I t was the first week in November and Gabrielle was lying in bed bemoaning her plight. She was finally over the hateful morning sickness, but she was bored and miserable.

I need to do something, she thought. *I don't want this brat. I must think of some way to rid myself of it.* Suddenly, a thought came to her. She left her bed, crossed to the armoire, and took out her riding habit. She hadn't worn it but twice since she'd married. Now it was tight, hot, and uncomfortable, but she managed to struggle into it. Another few weeks and she wouldn't be able to get into it at all.

Once dressed, she hurried downstairs, found one of the young house servants, and ordered the boy to run to the stable and have her horse saddled. "And hurry," she said with a look of urgency on her face.

The boy took off, and Gabrielle went into the parlor. She stood by one of the windows to watch for the horse. Suddenly, she heard footsteps behind her. She whirled around to find Delilah watching her. "Well, what the devil are you staring at?"

Delilah lowered her eyes. "Madame dressed in her ridin' clothes," she said softly. "Madame not be ridin' in her condition."

"Well, that's for me to decide," Gabrielle snapped. "What I do is none of your business. I'm sick of sitting in this house. I'm bored to death. A ride might do me good." Gabrielle felt uncomfortable. She would never admit it, but she had always been afraid of Delilah. The woman's quiet serenity, the way she would suddenly appear, and the way she looked at her mistress always unnerved Gabrielle.

"*Non,* Madame." Delilah shook her head and looked Gabrielle straight in the eye. "A ride might do you harm, maybe harm da *bébé, oui.*"

Just then, Gabrielle saw the stable boy bringing her horse around to the front. Without another word, she swept out of the house and down the stairs, and with the help of the young boy, mounted the animal.

Delilah hurried to the back of the house, found one of the yard boys and called out, "You, boy, hurry and find da *Maître* tell 'em Madame go ridin' on her hoss. Tell 'em come quick. Now hurry!"

The boy set off at a run. Finding André at the sugar factory, he related Delilah's message; and before he could finish, André was on his horse and headed for the house.

When he reached there, Delilah was standing on the gallery. Without a word, she pointed in the direction Gabrielle had ridden, and with a nod, André urged his horse on.

Gabrielle started out walking her horse, not being sure of how well she could handle the animal. Soon, she urged it into a trot. Like all ladies of her day, she rode sidesaddle; but since she was such a poor rider, she was jarred with each step the horse took. She silently hoped the jarring would cause her to lose the baby without doing any real harm to herself.

Suddenly, she heard the faint sound of hoofbeats behind her. Looking over her shoulder, she saw a rider bearing down on her and knew at once it was André. She became frightened at the thought of facing him, and in a panic, laid her riding crop across the horse's flank. The poor animal, so startled by the sudden slap, jumped and took off at a gallop.

The horse seemed to sense the uncertainty of the rider, and Gabrielle knew she'd lost control. Terrified, she hung on any way she could. She saw the fence looming up before her. In panic and fear, she pulled the reins, jerking them, and pulling them with all her might. Crying and screaming at the horse to stop, she sawed its mouth with the bit until it drew blood. The horse had been spooked by her behavior, but just as it reached the fence, it did stop, hurling Gabrielle to the ground where she lay in a heap.

When André reached her, she was unconscious but alive. He looked over his shoulder to see Demetrius coming toward him in the carriage.

Together, they lifted Gabrielle into the coach; then turning to his valet, André said, "Take my horse and ride to the city. Fetch Doctor la Poyntz—tell him it's an emergency and to please come as quickly as possible."

André laid Gabrielle on the seat tied her horse to the back of the carriage and slowly headed for home. Even going slowly, it was a bumpy ride; and several times, he heard Gabrielle moan.

All the house servants were waiting by the front door when Andre reached the house.

Millie watched wide-eyed as André carried Gabrielle up the front stairs. "Is my *maîtresse* dead?" she asked in a hushed voice

André shook his head. "*Non*, but I've sent for the doctor. Now I need both you and Delilah to come up to her bedchamber and care for her until he arrives."

Once André had carried Gabrielle to her bedroom, he went to wait for the doctor who seemed to take forever to arrive. When finally he did make his appearance and was apprised of what happened, the physician went directly to Gabrielle's room.

André sat in the parlor, his heart filled with fear and rage, rage at Gabrielle for doing such a stupid thing and fear that she or the baby or both might die. He got up and paced the floor like a caged lion. Demetrius brought him brandy to calm and steady his nerves. It seemed like hours before the weary doctor finally appeared at the parlor door.

André stopped his pacing. "How is she?" he asked in a tired voice, his face pale and drawn as he poured the doctor a glass of brandy.

Thanking him for the drink, the doctor took a sip, and then drew a deep breath. "Monsieur de Javon, I'm happy to tell you your wife will recover. She's badly shaken, of course, has some nasty bruises but no broken bones, thank God."

"And the *bébé*?" André searched the doctor's face. "What about the *bébé*?"

Doctor la Poyntz sighed and sat down heavily. "I wish I didn't have to tell you this, but she lost the *bébé*. She was about four months along. She took a nasty spill. I would have been surprised if she hadn't miscarried. She never should have been riding in her condition in the first place."

André's face was drained of all color. She'd gotten her wish. She'd lost their child.

"It was hard on her." The doctor's voice broke into his thoughts.

"She's lost a great deal of blood, and she's very weak. She must remain in bed for several weeks. But she's a strong, healthy young woman, and once she gets her strength back and regains her health, she'll be able to give you more children."

Long after the doctor left, André sat in the parlor staring into space. Delilah brought him a tray of food; an hour later, she took it away cold and untouched. Demetrius brought him a cup of coffee; that too, was taken away cold and untouched. Only the brandy seemed to dull the pain and rage.

For several days, André wandered about the house, unshaven and uncaring about what was happening around him.

Delilah became concerned. "*Maître*," she said quietly, "*Maître*, you gots to eat somethin'. Be *non* good not to eat."

Demetrius tried to lift André's spirits or perk his interest. "*Maître*, you should see how that *petite* filly doin'. She growin' fine, *oui*."

When nothing the two did or said made a difference, Delilah finally sent a boy over to *Château Charlevoix*. Perhaps *Michie* Charlevoix or the *petite* Mam'selle could come over and help. But the boy returned alone, telling her *Michie* Charlevoix was still in the city, and Mam'selle Julie was back at the convent.

Delilah knew the family was not at Oak Grove either. Charles and Francesca had left for the city in late September. Besides, she didn't know if the *maître* would want them to know what had happened. She finally talked it over with Samson and Demetrius, and the three of them decided to prevail upon the overseer to come and help get the master interested in the plantation again.

It was only when Karl Hoffman pressed him to make some important decisions concerning the crops that André was finally able to snap out of his depression and grief.

As he rode out to the sugar factory, he glanced over his shoulder at the house, and up at Gabrielle's bedroom window.

You've destroyed our child, and my love for you, but you won't destroy me! He'd worked too hard to build this place to allow grief and depression to take hold any longer. But he vowed to himself never to go near his wife again. Now, he would work even harder to build Royal Oaks into the greatest plantation in Louisiana, but he would do it for himself. After all, Royal Oaks was all he had.

* * *

Up in the bedroom, Gabrielle was recovering far quicker than the doctor had anticipated. At first, she was very weak; but as each day passed, she forced herself to eat and gain back her strength. When André was ready to return to New Orleans, she was determined to be strong enough to accompany him.

What upset her most was the realization that not once since her accident had André entered the bedchamber to inquire as to her well-being. Each time Millie came into her room, Gabrielle would ask about André. "Is the *maître* in the house?"

Millie would shake her head. "*Non, Maîtresse.*"

Gabrielle would ask if he had inquired about her.

Millie would shake her head and say, "*Non, Maîtresse.*"

To every question, the answer was the same. André's indifference greatly annoyed Gabrielle; but more than that, it frightened her. She was his wife, she had just suffered a miscarriage, and he was completely indifferent to her recovery. Gabrielle, of course, conveniently ignored the fact that, more than once, she had told him she didn't want the baby and hoped she'd lose it. What frightened her most was, as her husband, Andre had total control over her life. What was he now thinking? How would he treat her when next they met?

By the third week, Gabrielle's curiosity got the best of her. She decided that she must know what was going on with André. Gathering her courage and the strength to leave her bed, she had Millie arrange her hair in a becoming style. Then, putting on her prettiest nightgown and loveliest robe, she slowly made her way down to join André for dinner.

As she entered the dining room, André glanced up but said not one word to her. Gabrielle smiled at him sweetly and took a chair next to his as a servant brought the food to her. She motioned to have her glass filled with wine, and waited. Still, André said nothing. He continued eating as though she wasn't there.

"André, have you nothing to say to me?" She smiled demurely.

Once again, he glanced at her, finished his mouthful of food, took a sip of wine, and asked, "What would you have me say?"

"You could say you're happy to see me and that you're pleased I'm recovering so quickly." Gabrielle smiled at him and reached out to touch his hand.

André pulled his hand away and continued his meal. But between bites, he said, "I am pleased to see that you're recovering so quickly, but I am *not* pleased to see you."

He paused to sip his wine, and then continued, "However, since you are recovering so quickly, I shall have Millie pack your trunk."

"Pack my trunk? Why? Where are you sending me?" Gabrielle was really frightened now. Would he send her away in disgrace? *Mon Dieu!* What would her family and friends say? What would they think? She looked at him with a face filled with fear.

"I'm sending you back to New Orleans. Isn't that what you want, to go to New Orleans so you won't miss any of the social season?" The look of fear left her face and one of relief took its place. André watched her expression change.

With contempt he said, "Don't worry, Gabrielle, I wouldn't disgrace myself by having others know what a stupid, selfish, fool I have for a wife! You may go to New Orleans and stay with your parents. However, knowing how much you dislike children, I think it best if you not be around Charles and Francesca's child anymore than necessary."

"But, but I—I thought we were going to the city together in December, around Christmas," Gabrielle stammered.

"*I* am going to New Orleans around Christmas."

"Then you don't care if I go now?" she asked, not sure how to take this wonderful news.

André finished eating, pushed his chair back, stood, and picked up his wine glass and drained it. Then, putting the glass aside, he stared down at her coldly. "Gabrielle, you can go to the devil, for all I care." Turning on his heel, he strolled from the room.

Gabrielle sat still, listening as his footsteps faded down the hall. He wasn't sending her away in disgrace. He was letting her go to the city! Well, then, she would. She'd go and have fun. She deserved it after what she'd been through.

* * *

The week before Christmas, André arrived in New Orleans. He spent most of his days at the wharf with his factor. Once again, his profits were such that he was able to pay his debt to Monsieur Charlevoix and have enough to pay his other bills. He was also able to speak to a contractor about having a home built in the city and told the man exactly what he wanted in his home.

Like all homes in *la Vieux Carré*, there would be a large courtyard in the center, and the house would be built around it.

The house would sit on *Rue St. Philip*. "I would like a large mahogany door with a fan-shaped window above to open onto a large foyer," he said. "I think a curved, hanging staircase leading to the second floor will look beautiful."

The architect agreed. "*Oui*, Monsieur de Javon."

André continued. "All rooms must be large and airy with high ceilings and tall windows and doors. The second floor will have six large bedrooms. Each will have a dressing room and French doors opening onto the *galerie*, which will overlook the courtyard. I want the *galerie* made of wrought iron and richly ornamental. In the back will be the carriage house, stables, and separate buildings for the kitchen and servant quarters."

Once the plans were drawn up, André signed the contract for the building of his home to begin at once.

There was much excitement in the city when André arrived. Word had reached New Orleans that a steamboat by that same name was making its way down the Mississippi, with the city of New Orleans its final destination.

"A steamboat? *Mon Dieu*, what type of boat might that be?"

"I have no idea. I have never heard of such a thing!"

"*Sacre bleu*. They say the thing can travel up to ten miles an hour! Can you imagine going that fast? How dangerous that must be!"

Conversations such as this concerning the steamboat filled the air. One heard about it on the streets, in the coffeehouses, at the theater, and at *soirées*, and, of course around the dining room table in every home.

* * *

From the day the steamboat set sail from Pittsburgh, slowly making its way down the Ohio river, people lined the banks of the river to watch this strange contraption that belched black smoke from its stacks and made strange noises.

There was a great deal of doubt as to its ability to travel through the rapids and then down the falls where the Ohio flowed into the Mississippi. But, much to everyone's surprise, the boat managed both the rapids and the falls and remained intact.

As it reached each town or village, word was sent ahead that the steamboat was coming. Many were frightened by the sight of it, especially the Indians, who would stand on the riverbanks watching for it. But its appearance, with smoke pouring forth, the noise of the engine, and the paddle wheels churning up the waters, would send them scurrying into the woods, where they would hide and watch from trees and bushes as it moved on.

The excitement of Christmas and New Year's were somewhat overshadowed by the excitement of the coming of the NEW ORLEANS.

André caught the mood and decided to remain in the city until the boat arrived. When he woke on the morning of January 10, 1812, he could feel the excitement in the air.

The steamboat would reach the city that very day! He hurried and dressed, ignoring Gabrielle, who still lay abed sleeping. He'd had little to say to her since his arrival. He ignored her as much as possible, but not enough for others to notice.

Going down to the dining room, he joined his father in-law and mother in-law for breakfast.

"*Bonjour*, André," his father-in-law said. "Are you ready to meet the NEW ORLEANS when it arrives today?"

"*Bonjour, Pappa, Maman.*" André nodded to both. "*Oui*, I'm looking forward to seeing this strange boat and how it operates. I'm also anxious to meet this Monsieur Roosevelt who is bringing the boat here. I would like to speak to him and learn more about the steamboat." His eyes sparkled, showing an excitement that had been lacking for months.

The *Place d'Armes* was alive with the bustle of people hurrying across the square to the levee beyond. There were fashionable ladies and gentlemen, military men in bright uniforms, and slaves who had been allowed to come out and share in the excitement. Indians in their tribal dress and farmers up from the delta were also waiting to see this marvel.

Mountain men from Kentucky and Tennessee who steered the keelboats, flatboats, and barges down river mingled about. They, too, were eager to see this strange boat that might jeopardize their livelihood.

At the town hall, a delegation of the Constitutional Congress had been meeting just that day. They had drawn up a document for presentation to the Congress of the United States asking for admission to statehood. They, too, hurried out, greeting friends as they headed for the levee.

Standing on the dock, André caught the excitement along with everyone else.

Tension ran through the crowd as people strained to see or hear the first sign of the approaching steamboat. In the river, many ships lay at anchor, their crews lining the decks, watching for the strange boat. Farther up the river, keelboats and flatboats were moored, with their crews drinking and calling to each other.

"Here she comes!" A shout rang out. The crowd grew strangely quiet as all eyes turned toward the bend in the river.

Then, suddenly, there it was! The tall stacks with smoke pouring from them, the paddle wheels stirring up the muddy waters of the Mississippi, and the loud roar of the engine.

"*Sacre bleu*, what a sight!" someone in the crowd yelled.

And many voices agreed.

All grew quiet as the steamboat docked and lowered its gangplank. Governor Claiborne, in full ceremonial dress, alighted from his carriage, Robert Livingston beside him. The two hurried to greet Nicholas Roosevelt, the gentleman who had successfully brought the steamboat to New Orleans.

Chapter 29

January was a month filled with parties and balls to honor Nicholas Roosevelt and his young wife, Lydia, who had accompanied her husband on the journey.

André, along with Jean-Claude Charlevoix, found himself in their company at many of these events.

Monsieur Roosevelt went to great lengths to explain the importance of the steamboat. He was anxious to sell subscriptions to the Ohio Steamboat Navigation Company that had been formed by Robert Fulton and Robert Livingston.

Later that evening, after listening to Roosevelt, Monsieur Charlevoix turned to André. "This may be a venture worth looking into. This steamboat could be the wave of the future and may well be worth investing in."

André agreed and they discussed it at greater length the next day over a cup of *café au lait*.

"I think I'll go north and look into this steamboat business," Jean-Claude said. "I'd consider it an honor, André, if you would accompany me."

André had been thinking the same thing. Until the appearance of this new means of transportation, the only way to travel down the rivers was by keelboat or flatboat, neither of which was comfortable or convenient.

André, who like his mentor, had no resentment against the Americans, had already cultivated the friendships of many of the important ones living in New Orleans.

When they started arriving in New Orleans back in 1803, the Americans found they were unwanted and unwelcome by the Créoles. But the land was rich and much of it unsettled, and New Orleans was fast becoming an international port so the Americans continued to migrate to the city.

Because of the cold reception from the Créoles, they settled in an area across the canal (which became Canal Street). Thus, the canal became a divider between the American city known as *Faubourg Ste. Marie* and the Créole city known as *la Vieux Carré*.

André crossed to the American section many times to meet and talk with the Americans and found them to be exactly as Monsieur Charlevoix said, hard-working and astute businessmen. But André had yet to venture beyond New Orleans and its surrounding countryside.

As he became acquainted with more Americans, he became eager to travel north to see what the rest of this vast country had to offer. Now, that opportunity presented itself, and André was eager to take advantage of it.

Together, he and Monsieur Charlevoix met with Nicholas Roosevelt and explained their desire to travel back up the rivers with him.

"What a splendid idea," Monsieur Roosevelt exclaimed. "My wife and I will be heading north by mid-February. Would you be able to leave by then?"

Both André and Jean-Claude assured him they could. This suited André just fine, as it would give him time to put his house in order, so to speak. Filled with excitement, he rode to Charles' home.

Charles greeted him warmly and ushered him into his library.

"Well, it's obvious you have something to tell me, André. So come on, out with it before you burst." Charles was chuckling as he poured his friend a glass of claret.

"You're right, Charles. Monsieur Charlevoix and I are going to accompany the Roosevelts back up the rivers to Pennsylvania!

"Just think, Charles, I'll get to see much of this country, and hopefully I'll learn something more about steamboats."

Charles found it all very interesting; but more than that, he was pleased to see André excited about something. He'd seen his friend tired and unhappy too much lately.

"I think you're brave to want to invest in this strange boat, André. But I have the utmost confidence in both your judgment and that of Monsieur Charlevoix."

"Charles, I have a big favor to ask of you. Would you keep an eye on Royal Oaks for me? I know Monsieur Hoffman is an excellent overseer and Samson a trusted foreman; still it doesn't hurt to have someone else keeping an eye on things."

"Of course, André, I'll be happy to stop by now and then just to see how things are going." Charles looked over at his friend and smiled, "Go on this trip, André. It will do you good."

Next, André went to speak to his father-in-law, who thought he was crazy to want to go north and be with the strange American *Yanquies*.

"André, are you certain you are doing the right thing?" Monsieur Ste. Claire asked with a worried look. "I mean, going north and trying to deal with those people? You might live to regret it. You certainly don't want to pour money into such a strange-looking boat. How do you know it will be a success and that you'll get your money back?"

Shaking his head, he continued, "*Non*, I feel I must advise against this. I feel it is much too risky, and I urge you to rethink this plan."

But André had already made up his mind. He knew all too well how his father-in-law felt about the Americans. He didn't argue with the older man; he simply let him have his say.

Monsieur Ste. Claire, seeing that he couldn't change André's mind, did agree to oversee the building of his son-in-law's townhouse while he was away.

The last person he had to confront about the trip was his wife, and Gabrielle was less than happy when she was informed he would be leaving for Pennsylvania in a few weeks. She became even more upset when she learned he would be gone for six months or longer.

Gabrielle's attempts to win back her husband's love had failed miserably; not that she had put forth much effort. It was not in her nature to pursue anything that didn't come easily. When she didn't see immediate results, she became frustrated and irritable, only making matters worse. Even André's lovemaking stopped, and this frightened her. So once again, the brandy became her solace.

"Six months or more!" she shrieked when André informed her of how long he would away. "What am I supposed to do all that time? It's the height of the social season. There are parties and Mardi-Gras balls we've been invited to. Do you expect me to miss all the fun just because you and Monsieur Charlevoix are running off to the north on some stupid venture?"

She glowered at André as he turned to speak to her. "This is not a stupid venture, Gabrielle," he answered angrily. "Farming, at best, is a risky business; you're at the mercy of the weather. One bad season could wipe out my entire crop of cotton and sugar cane. This steamboat business could be very lucrative."

Here, he paused and paced the floor for a moment. Then, turning to face her, his expression glacial, he continued, "You want to give parties and wear beautiful clothes and jewelry. Well, all of that takes money!"

Gabrielle was not impressed. "Well, my *pappa* says it's a stupid venture. *Pappa* says you will more than likely lose everything before you're through. He says he can't imagine how you could possibly want to go north and deal with those crazy Americans!"

André had turned to the mirror on his dresser to brush his hair. His hand stopped in midair as he glared back at her through the glass. "With all due respect to your *pappa*, he is *not* much of a businessman. Certainly, not like Monsieur Charlevoix, whose judgment I trust emphatically!" With that, he slammed out of the room.

A day later, André left for the plantation. He was happy to be back at Royal Oaks. That was where he was most at peace. After speaking to his overseer, André gathered his slaves together and told them all that was happening. In closing, he promised to write and let them know how he was on the trip. "Monsieur Hoffman will read all of my letters to you," he assured them.

* * *

The day of departure dawned gray and overcast, but it didn't dampen the spirits of the people who crowded the wharf and lined the levee for miles to watch the little steamboat NEW ORLEANS start its journey up the Mississippi.

Once again, the governor and the military turned out in full regalia. Once again, the *crème de la crème* of New Orleans society gathered to wish the boat and its passengers a *bon voyage*.

The Créoles, with their love for gambling, were already placing bets as to whether or not the steamboat would have the power to buck the current and travel back up the river. Many a fortune would be made or lost on the outcome.

Standing on the deck with Jean-Claude and the Roosevelts, André felt his pulse quicken. Not since he'd sailed from Europe had he felt such excitement. He smiled and waved to his family and friends as they stood together on the wharf.

He had seen Julie standing with Madame Gauthier and her family, but he'd not been able to speak to her. There was too much noise. And, much to his disgust, Gabrielle had maintained a firm grip on his arm and clung to him like a vine until he boarded the vessel.

Now, as the boat slowly pulled away from land and started up the river, André remained on deck until Julie and everyone else became small dots in the distance.

Only then, did he turn his attention to the steamboat and the people aboard. Besides the Roosevelts, their children, and their nanny, there was the pilot, Andrew Jack, plus the helmsman, the engineer, a cook, and a few other men whose job it was to clean the boat and feed wood into the engine.

The boat consisted of a galley, where a wood-burning stove for cooking stood, and a large cabin that was divided in two. The smaller part was for the ladies and children, the larger portion for the gentlemen. This area had berths lining the walls, each berth having a small curtain to afford privacy for the men.

In the center was a long table where everyone, passengers and crew alike, ate their meals. Several comfortable chairs were grouped around the cabin. These accommodations seemed quite lavish in comparison to the flatboats and keelboats.

The trip was slow but enjoyable. The Roosevelts were a delightful couple, and André was struck by the obvious love and devotion between the two.

Each day, the little boat slowly but valiantly fought the strong current; and as it moved up the river, people lined the banks to shout and cheer and ogle this marvelous new invention. The trip seemed a great success until they reached Natchez, then it soon became apparent, the NEW ORLEANS could go no further.

The pilot came up to Monsieur Roosevelt as he stood on deck with André and Jean-Claude. "Mr. Roosevelt, looks like we ain't goin' no farther."

"What's wrong, Captain Jack?" Roosevelt asked.

"It's the boat, Mr. Roosevelt. She's sitting so low in the water, no amount of stoking her furnace is gonna coax her poor engine to fight the current."

With much disappointment, the party of travelers was forced to continue their journey by land.

Several coaches were hired to carry not only the passengers but also their baggage. The NEW ORLEANS, however, was not laid to rest. Instead, she spent her remaining days traveling between Natchez and the city of New Orleans, carrying cotton and other cargo between the two cities.

The trip by coach was pleasant in spite of the disappointment. As they traveled north, André watched the scenery change. He saw great mountains thick with forest looming in the distance, their peaks layered with snow. Much of the countryside was also covered with snow, and often one of the coaches would get stuck.

When that happened, the men would get out and put their shoulders to the wheels and strain and push until the carriage was freed. There would be laughing and joking and an occasional snowball fight before they continued on the journey.

The Roosevelt's little girl found this great fun. "Oh, please," she would beg. "Please, let's build a snowman before we go any further." And laughing, the men would do her bidding.

At times, André felt like a child again, he was having so much fun; something he had almost forgotten how to do lately.

He was amazed at all he saw. There were heavily timbered forests and along the way they met Indians, some friendly, some not so friendly, but none caused them any real danger.

The inns they stopped at were always pleasant. Some were small and cramped, others large and comfortable. But all were clean, warm, and friendly and the innkeepers were happy to have such esteemed guests staying at their establishments.

André sampled different and assorted foods and heard strange-sounding accents as they traveled through several southern states: Mississippi, Tennessee, and Virginia. And in every state, the accent was different. But the people were the same, warm and friendly, especially when they learned who the travelers were.

With each day and mile, André found this country more beautiful than he could have imagined. "It is so vast!" he remarked to his fellow travelers. "There is still so much land that has yet to be developed."

Pennsylvania, with its rolling hills and farms, was a beautiful sight to behold. And the Philadelphia of the early eighteen hundreds was a splendid city.

Monsieur Charlevoix turned to André and said, "It was here in Philadelphia that the Declaration of Independence was signed. And, the Pennsylvania State House is the finest public building in the country."

André was duly impressed.

The streets of the city were well laid and paved with cobblestone. They were also broader and straighter than those of New York and other major cities in the north.

André and Monsieur Charlevoix checked into the best hotel, with promises to keep in touch with Nicholas Roosevelt and his wife.

Next Jean-Claude introduced André to his friends, and they were invited to dinners and other social events.

In meetings and discussions with some of the gentlemen, André and Monsieur Charlevoix learned that steamboat builders were springing up all along the Ohio River. However, many of them, knowing nothing about boat building, soon were out of business.

"You should be very careful whom you invest with, where steamboats are concerned," advised a gentleman named Preston.

"Why is that?" André asked.

He and Jean-Claude were guests of a man named Mr. Browning. They had just finished dinner when the subject of steamboats came up.

"Because," Mr. Preston answered, "Robert Fulton, the man credited with developing the steamboat, and his partner, Robert Livingston, have secured a monopoly on the rights to the lower Mississippi from the Territory of Orleans."

"But how is that possible?" André asked again.

"Livingston heads the syndicate that owns the New Orleans."

"But how can they hold the rights to the lower Mississippi?" André insisted.

"Mr. Livingston has a great deal of influence," answered their host. "At one time, he was the United States Minister to France, and he had much to do with the Louisiana Purchase. He also administered the oath of office to George Washington when he became President."

Shaking his head, André said, "I still don't understand how that gives him the right to control the Mississippi River." Taking a sip of wine, he looked around the table at the other gentlemen. "I thought this was a free country with the rivers belonging to everyone."

Mr. Browning nodded. "Mr. de Javon, that's how it is in this part of the country. Livingston and his cohorts tried unsuccessfully to secure the same type of monopoly on the Ohio and other northern rivers.

"However, they were met with great resistance and hostility. Our feeling here in the north is that our rivers must remain free. We fought too hard to gain that freedom to have our right to travel when and where we please controlled by a small handful of power-hungry men."

He paused, took a sip of wine, and then continued, "Livingston had more luck in Louisiana for the reasons I've already mentioned. The man is highly respected and has a great many influential friends in Louisiana politics."

André and Monsieur Charlevoix looked at each other, the same thoughts running through their minds. When they returned to the hotel, they stopped at the lounge for a glass of port before retiring.

"Well," Jean-Claude said, "I don't know about you, André; but I don't think we should even consider the Livingston Company. It wouldn't be a wise move. The possibility of becoming involved in an expensive litigation, which will surely happen sometime in the future, could prove to be a threat to our pocketbooks. It could also hold back steamboat travel for years."

André was disappointed and wondered what their next move should be. "I still think it's a good investment. Not with Livingston and Company, but the idea of being a part of a steamboat company."

"I couldn't agree more," Jean-Claude said. "Steamboats are the future. I'm sure of that. And there are many rivers here in the north where the boats can travel freely. One could still make a handsome profit if one had the boats. So, my young friend, we shall set out this week to find the right company to join. With all the boat companies springing up in this area, I'm certain if we inquire properly and listen carefully, we'll find the right person to do business with."

The two men traveled about Pennsylvania to towns along the Ohio River, talking to many boat builders and in doing so, they heard about a young man named Henry Miller Shreve.

In a few days, they met with Henry Shreve, and after much discussion, the three became partners in the Shreve boatbuilding enterprise. They discussed the monopoly that Livingston had on the Mississippi.

And when André showed a concern, Henry Shreve said, "Once our steamboat is built, I will personally sail it down the Mississippi to New Orleans, and I'll break that monopoly if it takes the rest of my life."

With the agreement signed, there was one last piece of business to take care of. Jean-Claude had a friend in Philadelphia who was an attorney. The man was hired to keep an eye on the business and look after André and Jean-Claude's interests from that end.

"We will be coming north often." Monsieur Charlevoix informed the attorney, "We'll have another meeting as soon as we return. Meanwhile, you must keep each of us abreast of what is going on by letter until that time."

Now, with youthful enthusiasm, André could hardly wait to return to New Orleans and share this good news with Charles and the rest of his family.

While André and Monsieur Charlevoix were in Philadelphia, they also learned that on April 30 of that year, Louisiana was admitted into the Union as the eighteenth state. There was much jubilation as their friends hosted several parties to honor them and to welcome the two gentlemen from New Orleans as citizens of the United States.

Chapter 30

W hile André was busy in the north, Gabrielle was busy having fun in New Orleans. She accepted every invitation that came her way. At first, her parents or her sister and brother-in-law accompanied her to these events. But Francesca was expecting her second child, and it wasn't long before her condition became obvious, thereby putting an end to her public appearances.

Her parents were not always able to attend every affair either, as Madame Ste. Claire was not in good health. There was quite a scene the first time Gabrielle decided to attend a Mardi Gras Ball by herself.

"But, *chérie*, you simply cannot go alone!" her mother cried, when Gabrielle made her intentions known. "Such a thing is not done; what will people say? What will they think? Such a thing is unheard of!"

When her father returned home later, he too put his foot down and told Gabrielle in no uncertain terms, "I will not allow a daughter of mine to attend any social function un-chaperoned."

But Gabrielle, being reckless and headstrong, did exactly as she pleased. "I will too go!" she screamed. "Why should I sit home and miss all the fun simply because André decided to run off to the north on that stupid venture!"

Stamping her foot and forcing tears to her eyes, she cried, "It's not fair for you to expect me to miss all the fun either. I've been stuck out in the country for such a long time, and now I finally have a chance to enjoy myself, and you won't let me."

"Then your *pappa* must go with you," Madame Ste. Claire said.

"*Oui*, if your *maman* is feeling better, I shall escort you to a few parties," her father said.

"*Non!*" Gabrielle screamed. "I am not a child. I do not need anyone to escort me. I shall go by myself."

She burst into tears, sending up such a wail, that finally her parents, in sheer desperation and with much apprehension, gave in.

It was at a Mardi Gras Ball that Gabrielle first met him. She had heard about him before that night. His name was Gaston Bochet, and he had recently arrived in New Orleans.

* * *

It seemed Gaston was a bit wild. His escapades in Paris had about driven his family to distraction. He had a weakness for drinking, gambling, and women. He ran up large gambling debts, carried on with many a young lady (not all of them single), and outraged many a father and husband. He fought several duels and had the scars to prove it. His drinking and carousing though the streets of Paris distressed his family greatly.

After many attempts to slow him down (none of which worked) and after much discussion, he was shipped off to New Orleans for a cooling-off period. He was twenty-two at the time, and the hope was that this might help him mature.

There was a close family friend living in New Orleans, Monsieur Henri Duval and his wife, Madeline. Letters were exchanged and finally Gaston arrived in the city.

Although the Duvals were more than happy ot have Gaston reside with them during his visit, the young man chose to have a place of his own and was able to rent a house on *Rue Dauphine.*

Gaston had a quick wit, a ready smile, and the ability to make every woman he met feel he was madly in love with her.

The French Revolution had not harmed his family. They managed to retain not only their heads but much of their wealth so his pockets were well padded when he reached the shores of America.

It was shortly after André left for the north that Gaston arrived in New Orleans. And with his wit and charm, he was the most sought-after guest by the Créoles.

* * *

The night of the *Bals Masques*, Madame Ste. Claire was in bed with a dreadful cold. Gabrielle informed her parents that she was again going alone. There was the usual scene, her father insisting it was not proper for his daughter to go unchaperoned, her mother crying about what would happen to her daughter's reputation, and Gabrielle demanding her right as a married woman to do as she pleased.

She took great care in selecting a beautiful ball gown of white slipper satin trimmed with gold lace and jewels. On her feet, she wore white satin slippers also trimmed in gold; and with her hair piled high and a white-and-gold mask to hide the upper part of her face, she sat off for an evening of dancing, flirting, and drinking.

The moment she entered the ballroom, Gaston noticed her. He was standing with another gentleman; and as he watched Gabrielle being greeted by the hostess, he turned to his companion.

"I wonder who that enchanting creature is?"

The other man followed Gaston's gaze. "That is Madame Gabrielle de Javon. She is married to a very successful and very ambitious planter, Monsieur André de Javon."

Gaston lifted an eyebrow. "How do you know her when her face is partially covered?"

The other shrugged. "Everyone knows Gabrielle when she arrives."

Gaston waited for the husband to follow his wife into the room; and when he didn't appear, once again, he turned to his friend. "And where is her very ambitious husband tonight?"

"He left just recently. He's riding that new steamboat up the Mississippi. He and his friend Monsieur Charlevoix are going to look into the steamboat business. He will be gone for quite sometime from what I understand."

The gentleman smiled. "That's another way one knows it is Gabrielle. She is the only young woman we know who attends these affairs unchaperoned."

This information intrigued Gaston, a beautiful woman; a beautiful, wealthy, married woman alone and without her husband. This could prove very interesting.

It wasn't long before Gaston was standing by Gabrielle's side, arranging an introduction. As he bent and kissed her hand, Gaston looked up at her with such an intense gaze, Gabrielle became flustered and felt her face grow warm.

"*Enchanté,* Madame." Gaston continued to hold her hand and stare at her, and Gabrielle didn't know what to do. Then he smiled and asked her to dance.

She gave him her loveliest smile in return "I should be delighted to dance with you, Monsieur," and melted into his arms.

As the evening progressed, Gaston stayed close by her side, paying her a great deal of attention, getting her a cup of punch but more often a glass of wine.

He had learned early on that married women were the safest, far safer than the single ones. Flirt with an unmarried girl of seventeen for so for very long, and you could find yourself expected to marry her. Flirt with a married woman, and the worst you would have to deal with would be an outraged husband, and he had handled a few of them in the past.

Gabrielle, when she first saw Gaston, was disappointed. He was of average height and build, and with the mask on, she was unable to determine how handsome he might be. He had dark, laughing eyes dark wavy hair straight, even teeth; and a sensuous mouth. But it was not until midnight, when everyone unmasked that she was able to see that, although he was not handsome in the truest sense, he was most attractive.

Gaston, in turn, was more than pleased to see what a beauty Madame de Javon was. "I can't imagine any man in his right mind going off and leaving a beautiful wife such as you. And to be gone for such a long time," he whispered in her ear as he held her in his arms while they danced.

Gabrielle's lips formed a pout. "Oh, Monsieur, my husband is very ambitious. All he thinks about is his plantation and making more money." She affected a wistful sigh and glanced up at Gaston through her lashes. "Sometimes I wonder if he loves me at all."

"Well, Madame, I can tell you, if I were your husband I should never leave your side." Once again, he whispered in her ear, sending chills down her spine and making her heart skip a beat.

Throughout the evening, Gaston paid court to Gabrielle. ignoring the other more available young ladies, he fed her vanity with compliments and sympathized with her plight of being the unappreciated wife of an ambitious man.

Gabrielle, in turn, lapped it up. Here was a man who appreciated her, who understood her need to be adored, who made her feel like the most desirable woman alive.

As the evening came to an end, Gabrielle found herself reluctant to say *bonne nuit* to this delightful gentleman.

When he took his leave, Gaston kissed her hand and whispered, *"Au revoir, ma belle Gabrielle, au plaisir."*

Riding back to her parents' home and all night as she lay in bed, Gabrielle relived the entire evening. She was infatuated with Gaston. He had paid her all the attention, to the chagrin of the other girls. But he had held out no promises, he only said he would see her again…but when and where and how soon?

Oh, she hoped he would be at the next party she attended. But he was not and when she arrived at that function, she spent the entire evening waiting and watching for him. Where was he? Why did he not send her a message telling her he wouldn't be there?

The fact that Gaston hadn't told her he would made no difference. The undue attention he paid her that first night convinced her that he owed it to her to be there or give her a reason why.

* * *

Gaston purposely made himself scarce. He sensed at once that Gabrielle was very possessive. Better to let her worry and wonder a little. On nights when he chose not to attend a party or such, he found his amusement elsewhere. His love for gambling was such that he would wager on anything, and he spent money with total abandonment.

About Gabrielle, there were two things Gaston was acutely aware of. She had a jealous nature and she drank too much. Being somewhat of a scoundrel, Gaston felt he could use these flaws in her character to his advantage if the need arose. She was wealthy, her husband had money; and Gaston felt if his luck were to run out and he needed money because of his gambling debts, Gabrielle could be a good source of income.

* * *

When finally she saw Gaston again, Gabrielle became angry. He arrived at the party before her and as she entered, she quickly spotted him across the room. Several girls surrounded him, all laughing and mooning over him.

For a brief moment, his eyes met hers, then without so much as a nod of his head, Gaston turned his attention back to the other girls.

For the first part of the evening, he continued to ignore Gabrielle until she could stand it no longer. Finally, she saw him standing alone near the French doors. His arms were folded across his chest, and his ankles were crossed as he lounged against the wall watching the other guests.

Their eyes met but again he made no acknowledgment. Quickly, Gabrielle made her way through the crowd to where he stood. But, as she drew near, Gaston suddenly turned and strolled out to the courtyard.

Angry and determined to make him accountable for his behavior, Gabrielle hurried after him.

Although there was a full moon, it took several minutes for her eyes to adjust from the bright lights of the ballroom to the pale light of the moon. Gabrielle looked around and finally saw him standing near a giant tree that shaded much of the yard. He was smoking a cheroot and seemed totally unaware of her presence.

"Gaston!" she hissed as she drew near. "Where have you been these past few nights, and what is the meaning of this rude behavior?"

Slowly, Gaston turned around and allowed his eyes to travel from her face to her feet and back to her face, pausing for a long moment at her bosom.

Taking a deep draw on his cheroot, he blew the smoke in the air and answered in a cold voice. "Since when must I report to you on my comings and goings? And as for rude behavior, who are you to come storming out here making such demands on me in the first place? I own you no explanation."

His remark took Gabrielle back, and she lashed out at him. "How dare you speak to me in such a manner! Just who do you think you are? Talking to me like that?"

But it did no good. Gaston was not impressed. "I will speak to you anyway I please." He looked at her with disgust. "Just who do you think *you* are talking to? I am not one of your *slaves!*"

Gabrielle became even more upset with him. But no matter how angry she got, it had no effect on Gaston; and in the end, it was she who apologized. "Oh, Gaston please forgive me for the way I've behaved. It's just that I thought you cared for me. I've been so lonesome without my husband, and you made me feel special." She lifted her beautiful eyes to his and the next thing she knew she was in his arms, allowing him to kiss her and to even fondle her.

Gaston wore a sardonic smile when, later, he led her back into the ballroom. He had her just where he wanted her.

Now, they were constantly in each other's company when they attended the same event. Gabrielle's conceit thrived on the fact that, with all the eligible young ladies around, it was she Gaston gave his attention to.

* * *

After while, there were some whispers and gossip about this obvious attraction between them. Even Gabrielle's parents and her sister heard rumors about her and Gaston. But any mention of what they heard sent the headstrong young woman into a fit of rage where she accused others of being jealous because a nice man from the Continent was being pleasant to her.

"After all," she cried, "André has gone off and left me alone. Why shouldn't other gentlemen pay me compliments and treat me nicely?"

Her parents tried to reason with her, "We have no objections to your enjoying yourself," her father said, trying to calm her. "And it is true, André is away and you are too young to be left sitting home. But you must not do anything to endanger *la nom de la famille.*" *Scandale* was their greatest fear. Monsieur Ste. Claire ended up giving his daughter an indulgent smile.

* * *

It was now April and nearing the end of the season. Those with plantations were making plans to return to the country. Each hostess now outdid herself, hoping to have the most successful *soirée* before the season ended.

Gaston was beginning to tire of Gabrielle. Her constant demands to know where he was, and what he was doing when he was not with her, were beginning to bore and annoy him. He was happy the season was coming to a close.

He knew she would be going to the country, and that suited him just fine. He wanted to get away from such a harpy.

Good lord, no wonder her husband went north. To have such a miserable creature around would make one want to strangle her!

But, until the season did end, he would continue to amuse himself with her. He also amused himself by thinking and planning how he could best take advantage of her. She was such a fool, such a conceited fool.

It was one of the last parties, and once again, Gabrielle was alone. And once again, Gaston gave her his undivided attention. It would be fun tonight and very interesting to see just how far he could go with Madame de Javon.

They danced together all evening and as the night progressed, it became apparent to Gaston that Gabrielle was drinking too much.

Slipping out to the courtyard, she allowed him to kiss and fondle her, only to push him away, acting shocked. "Really, Gaston, you must not do such a thing. What will people think?"

Gaston gave her a cool look. "Are you really concerned over what people might think, Gabrielle? You attend these social events unchaperoned. You allow me to give you far too much attention, and now you want me to believe you care about what others might think?"

"Well, of course I do," she insisted. But when she saw the cold look on his face, she tried a different tactic. Looking at him through veiled eyes, she sighed, "Don't be angry with me, Gaston. I'll be leaving for the country soon, and I shall miss you so much."

Not getting the response she expected, she tried again. "Will you miss me, Gaston? Would you risk *scandale* to come out to Royal Oaks to visit me?"

"Will you be alone at Royal Oaks?" Gaston asked coolly. "I mean, will your parents be with you?"

Gabrielle smiled. "Not if I don't want them. I could convince them to stay with my sister and brother-in-law."

"Then, perhaps, I will come out for a visit," Gaston said as he swept her into his arms and kissed and caressed her, letting his hands roam freely over her body.

For a long moment, Gabrielle allowed him this freedom then, once again, she pushed him away. "Really, Gaston, you take too many liberties."

Once they were back in the ballroom, she immediately ordered another glass of champagne. In fact, she had several glasses.

After a dance when the music stopped, he steered her back to the courtyard. "Gaby, *chérie*, I think I should take you home. You're drinking too much, and you will make a fool of yourself and disgrace your family if you continue."

Gabrielle gave him a mocking look. "Really, Gaston, you're beginning to sound just like my husband. I'm not drinking too much; I'm just having fun." She hiccupped and giggled. "Besides I've never made a fool of myself or disgraced my family yet."

"Well, there is always a first time."

Firmly, Gaston took her arm and led her to a bench in the yard. Pushing her down gently, and leaning over her, he kissed her lips. "Stay here, don't move. I'll go and explain to our hostess that you have a dreadful headache and asked me to escort you home."

Gabrielle stayed on the bench. She felt light-headed, and when she closed her eyes, she felt the courtyard spinning.

Suddenly, Gaston returned, took her arm, and forced her to stand. "Come, I have a carriage waiting."

Stumbling and giggling, Gabrielle entered the carriage and promptly passed out. Gaston looked at her with a mixture of amusement and disgust. *Well, this should be very interesting.*

Chapter 31

Slowly, Gabrielle opened her eyes. She was lying on a bed, but nothing in the room looked familiar. She heard a soft chuckle and turned her head toward the sound. Gaston was lounging in a chair, one leg thrown over the arm, watching her as he sipped a glass of wine.

He grinned at her as he heard her ask in a feeble voice, "Where am I?"

"You're in my bed."

"*Your* bed?" Gabrielle's eyes flew open, and she jerked herself up only to sink back on the pillows with a moan. Once again, the world was spinning and her head felt like lead. "Gaston, you said you would take me home!" she wailed.

Gaston set his wine glass down on the table next to his chair and ambled lazily over to the bed to sit on the edge. One lone candle was lit, and with a strange smile on his face, he leaned down and kissed her. "I did say I would take you home; I just didn't say which home I would take you to."

He had removed his coat and now proceeded to remove his shirt.

"*Ma chérie*, Gabrielle," he continued, "you passed out the moment you entered the carriage. Would you have me take you to your parents' home in your condition? What do you think *pappa* and *maman* would say if I knocked on their door with you passed out in my arms? What choice did I have but to bring you here until you woke up?"

206

Gabrielle felt sheepish. "Of course, you are right, *cher* Gaston." Her parents would be furious if they knew. Why, they might even write to André! And they certainly would never allow her to go anywhere by herself again. She was very grateful to Gaston and tried to sit up and tell him so; but the room wouldn't stand still, and her head felt awful.

Gaston leaned down and whispered, "No need to give me verbal thanks, Gabrielle, you know the kind of thanks I want."

His demanding lips came down on hers. Next, they slid down to her neck, and he felt her pulse quicken as he kissed her throat. She made no attempt to stop him. This was what she enjoyed when André courted her, the kisses, the soft romantic words. It was only after they married, and she found there was more to lovemaking than kisses and romantic words, that she had become cold and unresponsive. As time went on, the more she resisted André, the colder he became, until finally after the accident, he moved into a separate bedchamber.

Now, here in Gaston's bedchamber with the brandy and wine relaxing her, she found she enjoyed his overtures. It had been so long since she'd been held and kissed and caressed and told how desirable she was.

His kisses became more passionate as his hands slid over her body. She felt his lips on the satin fabric of her bodice over her breasts, and they seemed to burn through the fabric onto her flesh. She continued to submit to his lovemaking; but when he started removing her clothes, she halfheartedly tried to stop him to no avail. She had allowed him to go too far to stop him now.

"*Non*, Gabrielle, you've teased me long enough. For too many nights, you've held out promises. Tonight, there will be no games, tonight you will give what you have so often promised."

When it was over, she lay next to him in the semi-darkened room shaken and frightened. She never intended for this to happen! She only hoped to enjoy a flirtation with him. She always felt she was in full control of the situation. Not only was she frightened, but she had sobered up somewhat, and now she was furious!

"How dare you do such a thing to me!" she cried, clutching the bed sheet around her naked body. "How could you?"

It did no good to rail against Gaston; he only laughed and then turned sarcastic. "Gabrielle, spare me your indignation. You're not an innocent young girl. As a married woman, you certainly know the facts of life. How long did you think you could play your stupid game before you would have to pay?"

Gabrielle was so angry she could find no words to answer him. She started to cry but found no comfort or sympathy Gaston simply got up, started to dress, and told her to do likewise.

"Spear me your tears and your outrage. I am not impressed. Just get your clothes on. I'm taking you home."

"But, but you made love to me," she sobbed. "You do love me, don't you? Tell me you do, *please!*" Hesitantly, she reached out a hand as she looked up at him.

Gaston stopped dressing and stared at her for a long moment. "Love you? Is that what you asked?"

"*Oui-*" she nodded between sobs. "You must love me after what just happened."

Gaston threw back his head and howled with laughter. Suddenly, he stopped and, with a look of utter contempt, said, "*Non,* Gabrielle, I certainly do not love you; in fact, the truth is I am *bored* to death with you."

"Bored with me!" Gabrielle screamed as she jumped from the bed and hurled her body at him trying to claw his face with her nails. "How dare you say you're bored with me!" She was screaming and crying and almost out of her mind with rage.

Gaston caught her by the wrist and yanked her to him. His expression was one of disgust. "Listen to me, you little fool. You wanted to play this game. Kissing me, letting me touch you, leading me on! Well, I got fed up, so tonight, things went my way for a change. But now I'm bored; so shut up and get dressed!" He flung her from him, and Gabrielle fell back on the bed, crying, angry, and humiliated.

* * *

It was still dark when Gaston deposited Gabrielle at her parents' home. She crept up the stairs to her room hoping no one would hear her. The next morning at breakfast, she told her parents she wished to return to Royal Oaks at once. She looked awful. Her face was ashen, her eyes swollen and bloodshot from a night of crying and worrying, and there were dark circles under her eyes. What if she became *enceinte*! Who would she turn to? The more she thought of it, the more upset she became.

André was not due back for months. Since he'd left, she had

received but one letter from him. It was cold and business like and he gave no indication of how long he would be gone. Before leaving, he'd said he'd be away at least six months or longer, and he'd said nothing different in his letter.

The thought sent her into a frenzy. If she became *enceinte* because of Gaston, there would be no way to hide it until André returned! In fact, she would be about ready to deliver! If she tried to lose it as she did the last time, the doctor would surely know and perhaps tell her parents. Oh, what to do, what to do?

I'll go back to Royal Oaks, she said to herself as she got up that morning. *I can't stay here and risk running into Gaston every time I turn around. Oh, what will I do?*

Her parents couldn't understand her urgency in wanting to return to the plantation so soon. "But, *chérie,* why must you go now?" her father asked. "You've never enjoyed the country before. You usually put off returning to Royal Oaks as long as possible."

"Well, I've changed my mind. I'm tired of all the parties with the same old people all the time. I need a rest, and the country air will do me good." Gabrielle was adamant.

* * *

A week later, Gabrielle and her mother left the city. Her father would remain in the city to see about the completion of André's home. Demetrius drove the carriage, and Millie sat on the seat beside him while Gabrielle and her mother rode inside. Demetrius and Millie had fallen in love and now they spent much of the trip whispering to each other about their hopes for the future.

Madame Ste. Claire studied Gabrielle at close range. It was easy to see her daughter was tense and nervous; but when she asked if there was a problem, Gabrielle almost snapped her head off.

"*Maman,* you've asked me the same question at least a dozen times! How often must I tell you; there is nothing wrong!"

Gabrielle turned her head away and stared out at the scenery. She must do something to keep her mind busy. She couldn't stand the way her mother kept watching her. "I know what I'll do," she said half aloud.

"What, *chérie?* What did you say?"

"Nothing, *Maman,* I was just thinking out loud."

Yes, that's what she'd do; give a party like the one she gave last summer. She would have plenty of time to plan it. It would take her a while just to get the house ready, and by then, most of the families would have moved back to the country. Hers would be the first party of the summer; and with *Pappa* and *Maman* staying with her, it would be perfectly respectable.

Once at Royal Oaks, she went about planning her party. The servants polished the furniture, floors, woodwork, and silver until everything gleamed. Hundreds of new candles were made for the chandeliers that were washed until their prisms glowed and sparkled, catching the light and sending back bright colors.

Slaves were sent out to hunt wild game, and fish the river and streams. Once again, fresh vegetables were picked from the garden. Chickens were killed, and eggs were gathered, as were fruits, nuts, and fresh flowers.

Gabrielle kept everyone working at a fever pitch; and when something didn't suit her, it had to be done over again.

Just watching her wore her mother out; and the poor lady tried to stay out of her daughter's way as much as possible.

Pappa drove out the week of the party and said the townhouse was finished and André would be pleased with the results.

At breakfast one morning, her father said, "By the way, Gabrielle, have you heard from André lately? Does he say how much longer he will be gone?"

"*Non, Pappa*. He doesn't seem to have time to write to me. He's too busy with his stupid steamboat business to bother with me." Gabrielle didn't want her parents to know she had received only one letter from André since he left. They would wonder why, and she didn't dare tell them the problems they were having.

Francesca and Charles returned to Oak Grove, but Francesca was too far along to attend any parties. Her baby was due in August.

The night of the party, Gabrielle's parents were dressed and downstairs awaiting the arrival of the guests. Gabrielle was still in her bedchamber. When she had awakened that morning, she'd felt a slight queasiness in her stomach. When Millie brought her breakfast tray, the first whiff of food made her nauseous and fear gripped her. Was that how it started the last time? She couldn't remember. But as the morning passed, so did the feeling. She told herself it was just nerves, the heat, and the excitement of planning the party.

Throughout the day, she had gone about checking on everything. But when she went to the kitchen, once again her stomach churned. The kitchen was incredibly hot, even though the doors and windows were wide open. The hearths blazed, large black kettles bubbled, and the aroma of food filled the vast room.

Several women slaves were bustling about, their clothes damp from the heat and their bodies giving off the scent of perspiration. All of this combined to make Gabrielle's stomach rebel. Her knees turned to jelly and her face went pasty white. She grabbed the edge of the table and leaned against it heavily. The servants saw her condition and were concerned. One of them helped her outside.

"*Merci*, Eliza, I'll be all right now, it must have been the heat in the kitchen that upset me."

Gabrielle slowly made her way back to the house. By the time she reached the gallery, the feeling started to pass. She was glad her parents were unaware of what had happened. They would surely be concerned, and her mother would want to call off the party.

Now, as she finished her toilette and Millie fussed with her hair, a wave of nausea washed over her again.

Millie stopped and gave her a long look. "*Maîtresse* not feeling well?"

"*Non*, Millie, I'm feeling fine. It's just this heat. Oh, how I wish it would cool off a bit."

She was right about the heat. It had been an extremely hot and humid day; and now even as the sun went down, the heat had not abated one bit. There was not even a whisper of a breeze. Well, there was nothing to be done. In a very short while, she would have a house full of guests, and she must be there to greet them. Gabrielle heard some of her guests arriving by the time she felt up to leaving her room. She checked herself carefully in the mirror and, being pleased with her reflection, headed for the stairs.

She was descending as a new group entered. Suddenly, she found herself looking into the face of Gaston! He was standing at the foot of the stairs looking up at her with a sardonic grin on his face. As their eyes met, he gave her a sweeping bow. Just then, Madeleine Duval rushed up to her.

"Oh Gaby, *chérie*, how beautiful you look. And the house! Well, it is just too beautiful for words! We were so excited when we received your invitation; the first party of the summer.

"And look whom we brought with us. Gaston has never been to a plantation party. We just couldn't have him returning to France without having been to Royal Oaks. Everyone knows yours is the most beautiful plantation in the whole area!"

This rapid gush of words left Gabrielle no recourse but to smile and nod graciously. Coolly, she extended her hand to her guest.

As Gaston bowed and kissed her hand, he glanced up and gave her a wicked wink. She certainly hoped no one else saw him do such a thing. Her heart was in her throat. She had not considered the possibility that the Duvals would bring Gaston with them. She had secretly hoped he'd already sailed for France.

During the early part of the evening, she was kept busy greeting her guests thus, she was able to avoid Gaston. But as the evening progressed and the music started, she found herself dancing with him.

Gaston looked down at her with a smile and whispered, "Gabrielle, *chérie*, I've missed you these past few weeks. How well I remember our last evening together. Do you think that later when the other guests have left, we might steal up to your bedroom and pick up where we left off that last night in New Orleans?"

Gabrielle glared at him. "You are despicable!" she hissed between clenched teeth. "How dare you come to my house after what happened!"

"But, Gaby, I had no choice. The Duvals insisted I accompany them. You heard what Madeleine said. Besides, she thinks we're still friends." He gave her an innocent smile. "Of course, if you insist I leave, I'll go and tell them you have ordered me from your home." He paused and pretended to search the room for his friends. "Oh, there they are, excuse me, Gabrielle. I'll go and tell them you want me to leave. Oh, by the way, if they ask why, what should I say?"

Gabrielle panicked and grabbed his arm. "You'll do no such thing! And you will say nothing!"

"Well, Gaby, make up your mind, do I stay or do I leave?"

"I cannot abide you, but you may stay!" Her blue eyes grew darker with the anger she was feeling, and she gave him a look of such hate, Gaston pulled back.

"Now, that's no way to make a guest feel welcome. I think you had better be nice to me, Gaby, or I may decide to leave, and then the Duvals and your other guests will surely want to know why, and believe me I wouldn't hesitate to tell them." Although his mouth smiled, his eyes were cold and threatening.

Panic filled Gabrielle's throat so she couldn't speak but she tried to smile at Gaston when she noticed several other people watching them. Between clenched teeth, she said, "You may stay, just stay away from me!"

"But, Gaby, *chérie*, you are my hostess; I want to be close to you. I want to show you how much I enjoy your hospitality."

Gabrielle didn't know what to do so she tried as best as she could to ignore him.

The evening was a huge success for the guests, but a complete disaster for Gabrielle. At the late night supper, Gaston directed all of his conversation toward her. He stayed by her side the entire evening whispering suggestive remarks in her ear every chance he got. "Gabrielle," he said, when he found her standing alone for a second, "that gown is very becoming on you." His eyes slid down to her bosom, which was quite exposed. "It shows off two of your best features."

"Will you go away and leave me alone!"

"Not a chance," he said as he swept her into a waltz. "This is too much fun, and I am enjoying myself immensely."

He danced with her every chance he could, and refilled her wine glass frequently.

Throughout it all Gabrielle managed to remain sober, to smile and play the gracious hostess. Inwardly, she wished she'd never given this party and wanted nothing more than for it to end.

As he was leaving, Gaston, whispered in her ear once again. "Do let me know when your parents leave. I'll be most happy to come back and keep you from being too lonesome."

Chapter 32

Within a week of her party, the dreaded morning sickness struck. Gabrielle wondered why it was called morning sickness, since for her it seemed to last all day from the moment she lifted her head from the pillow until she laid it down at night.

She was frantically trying to decide what to do. Her main fear was that her mother would figure out what was wrong with her. She knew her parents would find her condition impossible to accept.

Pappa would probably challenge Gaston to a duel and then throw her out, that is, if he didn't get killed in the duel. Oh, *Mon Dieu,* what a terrible disgrace it would be.

And the slaves, they, too, would know before long. Even now, Millie looked at her with suspicion. And Delilah, oh, wouldn't she like to know what had happened! Delilah hated her but no more than she hated Delilah.

In her second week of morning sickness, Gabrielle's parents were leaving for Oak Grove. They were adamant that she accompany them, but Gabrielle was just as determined to remain at Royal Oaks. Finally, after an ugly scene, her parents left.

Now, with them gone, Gabrielle tried to think of a way out of her predicament. She had often heard that the slaves knew of ways to take care of this problem, but she had managed to alienate every slave on the plantation; and there was not one she could trust.

Besides, she didn't know if what she'd heard was true. And she certainly couldn't ask for help only to find out that the information was false. What if one of them were to tell André when he returned?

After spending a whole day and night trying to find a solution to her problem and finding none, she decided to write to Gaston. Surely, when he knew, he would want to help her, to take care of her. She sat at her writing desk and composed several letters, none of which pleased her. Finally, in desperation, she scribbled a short note asking him to please come to Royal Oaks at once.

She waited a week in a feverish state wondering if he had received the note and why he hadn't responded.

She had dispatched one of the stable boys with the message giving him strict instructions on how to find Monsieur Bochet's house. When the boy returned, he assured her that he'd gone to the right house and had given the note to *Michie* Bochet himself.

"Well, what did he say when you gave it to him?" she demanded.

"*Michie* Bochet, he say, '*Je vous remercie beaucoup.*'"

"And what else? What else did he say?"

The boy shook his head. "Nothin' else; he just smile and close da dooah."

In her frustration, Gabrielle drew back her hand to slap him but stopped in midair. Delilah was passing the room. It would not do for André to learn that while he was away, she had struck one of his precious slaves. Instead, she screamed at the boy, "Get out of my sight this minute!"

The poor child turned and ran like his life was at stake. Delilah stood for a long moment staring at the mistress of the house; then on silent feet, she moved on.

It was when Gabrielle had given up all hope, and least expected to see him, that Gaston arrived. She was sitting in her bedchamber nursing a goblet of brandy when she heard one of the yard boys yelling, "Company comin!'"

Gabrielle rushed to her window and saw Gaston cantering up the drive. Her first impulse was to rush downstairs and demand to know what had taken him so long. But she instinctively knew that would be the wrong way to approach him. Instead, she waited in her bedchamber until Millie came to announce him.

Gaston was standing by the hearth with his back to the door. When he heard her footstep, he turned around.

Gabrielle gave him her most fetching smile and held her hands out to him as she crossed the room.

"Gaston, how very happy I am to see you."

"Bonjour, Gabrielle." He took her hand and kissed it.

"Oh, Gaston, do sit down. I will ring for some refreshments." She waved him to a chair while she called a servant to bring brandy.

"Gabrielle, just what is it you want of me? You didn't send me that note just to offer me brandy."

"Why, Gaston, how cruel of you," she said with a pout. "I asked you to come for a visit because I found I missed you. After all, we did have some lovely evenings together at the *soirées* and such in the city."

Gaston raised an eyebrow, and smiled. *"Oui,* we did indeed. And I especially remember our last night at my house. But, Gabrielle, may I remind you that at your party you told me I was despicable and you wanted nothing more to do with me. Why this sudden change of heart?"

Just then, Demetrius entered with a tray. Gabrielle dismissed him and poured the brandy herself, and handed a goblet to Gaston. She lowered her eyes, then looked up at him through her lashes and said in demure voice, "Oh, Gaston, I wasn't myself that night. It was so hot, and I had worked so hard on my party. Please forget whatever I said." She paused for a sip of brandy, then said, "Tell me, Gaston, how soon will you be returning to France?"

Gaston shrugged. "I don't know...I haven't given it much thought. I suppose I'll leave when I become bored with New Orleans. Why do you ask?"

Gabrielle leaned toward him. "Gaston, I've always wanted to go to France, to see Paris and all the places I've heard about."

"Well, if you want to go so badly, why don't you get your husband to take you? Surely with all his money, he can afford it."

Gabrielle looked downcast and then said with a sigh, "André would never leave his precious plantation or New Orleans unless it was on business and was profitable. If I wait for him to take me, I'll never go."

"Gabrielle, are you telling me you would like to run off to France with me while your husband is in the north?"

Gaston took a healthy gulp of brandy. "What would your family say, your friends and most of all your husband?"

Gabrielle made a sad little face. "André probably wouldn't even notice I was gone. He pays so little attention to me as it is. And my parents are all excited about the birth of their new grandchild. That's all they think or talk about. As for my friends, well, I don't care about any of them anyway."

"But why this sudden interest in France? And why this sudden interest in me? Gabrielle, there is something you're not telling me. I can't believe you are willing to throw away all that you have here just to spend a short time with me in France. I know you too well—there is more to this than you are telling me."

Once again, Gabrielle pouted and started to protest, but Gaston held up his hand and stopped her. "Please Gaby, don't play games with me. I'm not some naïve boy you can twist around your finger. You will tell me what this is about and you'll tell me the truth, or I'll leave this minute." As he spoke, Gaston started to stand up and reach for his hat.

Suddenly, Gabrielle burst into tears. "All right, I'll tell you," she sobbed. "I'm going to have a *bébé*, your *bébé*, and I don't know what to do!" Her body shook with her sobs, and she half expected Gaston to gather her in his arms and calm her fears with words of love.

Instead, he sat down very slowly and stared at her for a long moment. "You're what?" he asked in surprise.

"You heard me. I'm going to have your *bébé*. André has been gone since February and is not due back for a while yet. In fact, I have no idea when he will return. Meanwhile, I'm *enceinte*, and I don't know what to do!" Her words ended in a wail.

"So you want me to take you back to France with me? And just what do you propose to do once you get there?"

"I don't know," she said between sobs. "Maybe...maybe we could get married?"

"Get married? Did I hear you correctly?" Gaston threw back his head and laughed until his eyes watered. "Oh, Gabrielle, you are too much. May I point out to you, dear lady, that you are already married? Besides, I'm not ready to marry just yet and when I am ready, it will certainly not be a woman who already has a husband." He started laughing again.

Gabrielle lost what little composure she had. She leapt from her chair and stood before him, her fists clenched, her face filled with rage. "Did you hear what I said? I am *ENCEINTE,* and it is your child! My husband has been gone for months. It may be months before he returns. In another month, I will no longer be able to hide my condition. You must help me! This is your child!"

Gaston looked at her calmly and said, "Gabrielle, I am truly sorry about your condition, but I have no interest in or desire to marry you. There is only one way I would even consider taking you to France with me."

Hope sprang into Gabrielle's eyes. "What is that?" she asked eagerly.

"Well, if you could give me twenty thousand dollars, I might be persuaded to let you travel with me."

"Twenty thousand dollars! Are you insane? Where would I ever get that kind of money?" Gabrielle shrieked.

"Well, you're always telling me how wealthy your husband is, so I thought perhaps you might be able to find it somewhere."

"There is no way in the world I could find that kind of money; and even if I could, I certainly wouldn't give it to you!" She looked at him with hate and rage.

"Very well. I understand there are ways to take care of your kind of problem; I suggest you look into it." Gaston stood up. "Now, if you will excuse me, I must return to New Orleans. I have an engagement later this evening."

Gaston bowed and headed for the door. "*Bonsoir,* Gabrielle, thank you for the brandy."

In shock, Gabrielle stood listening to the flying hoofs as Gaston galloped away. She ran out to the *galerie.*

"I hate you, do you hear me? I hate you," she screamed at his departing figure. She turned and fled to her bedchamber. Like a wild woman, she ripped the room apart and drank until she passed out.

Two days later, Charles rode over with the news that André would be home in less than a week.

Chapter 33

With their business completed far sooner than they expected, André and Monsieur Charlevoix were able to cut short their trip and return to New Orleans.

André was in high spirits, filled with stories of the steamboat company he and Monsieur Charlevoix had become partners in, and excited about the steamboat Henry Shreve and his partner Daniel French were building.

He stayed in New Orleans checking on his new home and making arrangements for the furnishing of it, visiting his American lawyer in *Faubourg Ste. Marie*, and putting him in touch with the lawyer in Pennsylvania.

While in New Orleans, André was invited to several small *soirées* and dinner parties. One such party was given by Monsieur and Madame Duval. They, like everyone else, were excited and eager to hear about his adventures in the north.

During dinner, Madeleine Duval turned to him. "André, we're so happy you're back safe and sound. We missed you terribly, but we managed to keep Gabrielle happy and busy."

Gaston, who had been introduced to André at the start of the evening, smiled at this remark.

Madeleine continued in her unctuous manner. "Your darling Gaby gave the first party of the summer at Royal Oaks. What a splendid affair it was. Jules and I took Gaston to it. As I told Gabrielle, Gaston had never been to Royal Oaks and we simply couldn't let him return to France without seeing one of the most beautiful plantations around."

Gaston smiled and lifted his wine glass to André. "Madeleine is correct, Monsieur de Javon, your plantation is truly beautiful."

"*Merci beaucoup*, Monsieur."

"I might add that your wife is also beautiful," Gaston continued. "You're a lucky man, Monsieur de Javon. I wonder how you could go off and leave such a beautiful wife for such a long period of time."

"*Merci,* again, Monsieur. I do not make it a habit of leaving my wife or my plantation for very long; but there are some opportunities one cannot afford to pass up. Sometimes one must take advantage of an opportunity when it presents itself. Not to do so would be foolish."

"*Oui.*" Gaston nodded with a sardonic smile. "I know exactly what you mean, and couldn't agree with you more."

There was something disquieting about the man, and André found he didn't care for Gaston at all.

Madeleine broke in, "Gaston tells us he has decided to return to France in the next week or so." She turned to him, "You're a naughty boy, Gaston. We had hoped you would stay longer."

Gaston smiled. "Ah, *oui*, Madeleine, but if I stay much longer, the waters could become rough. I prefer sailing on smooth waters." Everyone thought he was speaking about the ocean crossing.

Once again, André found his remark disquieting; but when the conversation turned to the war that was being fought in the north against the British, he quickly forgot about Gaston.

"It seems in June of this year, America declared war on England," he said in answer to a question from a gentleman.

"War?" Madeline cried. "Oh, dear me. Will we be fighting the British in another war? And just when everything has been going so well."

"But, André, why is America fighting with the British now?" Jules Duval asked.

New Orleans was so isolated from the rest of the country that its citizens were sometimes unaware of what was taking place elsewhere in their country.

"Well, the British have gained control of the seas, since they defeated Napoleon. And they've taken to seizing American ships on the pretext of looking for British sailors who might have deserted. Of course, they never find any; so they seize the crew and force them to serve on the British ships under the worst conditions. The American Government can no longer tolerate this so America has declared war."

After more conversation, the general consensus was that the war was the problem of the American *Yanquies* of the north. And since most Créoles still didn't think of themselves as Americans, they felt no need to concern themselves with the matter and so the conversation shifted to more pleasant topics.

* * *

When André arrived at Royal Oaks a few days later, the call went up even as he was coming down the river road. *"Maître comin'!"*

The yard boy who had been on the lookout for him ran up the avenue and out to the big bell that hung near the pasture gate. The bell that called them in the morning and home in the evening and to Mass on Sunday was now calling to tell them the *maître* was home. They came from every corner of the plantation. From the fields of cotton and sugar cane, from the factory, kitchen, and stables, men, women, and children threw down their work and hurried to welcome André.

He shook as many hands as possible and thanked them for their loyalty and for the excellent job they had done in his absence. "And tomorrow," he announced, smiling broadly, "will be a holiday."

Even Gabrielle seemed genuinely happy to have him home. She flew from the house and down the stairs to fling herself into his arms. "Oh, André, darling, you're back. Oh, darling, I've missed you so." She kissed him and clung to him and told him how much she loved him.

André was quite taken aback by this reception. When last they were together, things had been dreadful. Now she was sweeter and more loving than she'd been in ages.

"Darling, is there anything I can get for you, or do for you?" she asked the next morning when they were having breakfast.

"Non, Gabrielle," André replied, smiling at her. "I'm fine. I'm just so happy to be home."

"And I'm happy to have you home, my dearest," Gabrielle replied as she returned his smile.

For the next few days, she fussed over him, catering to his every need, kissing him and telling him how much she loved him. André wondered about this change in her and had his guard up. He simply didn't feel the same about her anymore. However, they were married, so better to enjoy it while it lasted.

Gabrielle even joined in the holiday the next day. She stayed by André's side as he took the time to speak to each family and play with the children.

For the first time since long before her miscarriage, she welcomed André into her bed. And for the first time in a long while, André went. He'd been celibate far too long.

Their lovemaking also took a new turn. Gabrielle was more passionate and responsive than she had ever been. And although André found it a pleasant surprise, still she had done so much damage to their marriage already, he found himself holding back.

Lovemaking for him became a form of relief, nothing more. And try as he may, he couldn't change those feelings. Too much had happened. Gabrielle had killed much of his love, and he doubted if he would ever feel differently.

In her selfish way, Gabrielle didn't seem to notice. She continued to act loving and interested in all André said and did. The drinking stopped, and even the servants were amazed at the change in their mistress. She was sweet, thoughtful, and soft-spoken.

Together, she and André went to Oak Grove where they spent a few days with Charles, Francesca, and both sets of parents. "Do tell us all about your trip," Francesca said once they had greeted André and Gabrielle. "What is it like in the north?"

"And tell us all about the steamboat," Madame du Fray added.

"*Oui*, André, tell us everything," exclaimed Monsieur Ste. Claire

André spent much of that day answering all of their questions and telling them about his adventures in the north.

Not only was everyone delighted to see him, but they were pleased to see the change in Gabrielle. She was nicer than she had been in ages, and she and André seemed at peace with each other. She drank little and seemed sweet to her little nephews.

When they returned to Royal Oaks, André felt that, finally, he could relax. Perhaps being away for such a length of time had helped. He smiled and whistled as he went about the plantation.

The change in Gabrielle lasted a little over a month. As a leopard can't change its spots, so Gabrielle couldn't change her nature.

"I'm sick of hearing about that stupid steamboat!" she muttered as she brooded over her condition. "I'm sick of acting interested in what goes on with those stupid servants and this plantation! And I'm really sick of playing the loving wife who welcomes André into my bed with open arms every night!"

She was still having occasional bouts with morning sickness, although they were diminishing, and she certainly didn't feel in the mood for lovemaking. Her figure was changing and she could see and feel it happening. These feelings coupled with the fear that André would wonder why she was getting so big so quickly put more stress on her that added to the problem. And before he knew what happened, André had the old Gabrielle back.

* * *

It was one day while he was riding out in the fields that Samson told André the good news.

"*Maître*, my Delilah gonna have ah *bébé* in January, she." The black man's face was filled with pride.

André was delighted. "Congratulations, Samson. I'm so very happy for you. I'm certain you will have a fine, healthy *bébé*." He shook Samson's hand. "I would like you to join me tonight at the plantation office. We'll enjoy a glass of my best brandy."

Later that evening as the two men sat with their goblets, André said, "Congratulations again, Samson. You're a lucky man to have a wife like Delilah, and I'm lucky to have the two of you for my friends." He went on to assure Samson that Delilah's duties would be lightened considerably. "I assure you she will not have to lift anything heavier than a dust cloth. We have more than enough servants to do the heavy work."

When next André saw Delilah, he told her that her work would be lessened during her condition and made it clear to the other servants that they were to help her as much as possible, telling them if they were with child, the same consideration would be shown to each of them.

If André had expected Gabrielle to be pleased over the news of Delilah's coming child, he was sadly disappointed.

"Well, if she thinks that being *enceinte* will allow her to shirk her duties, she is badly mistaken," was her reply.

When André explained how Delilah was to be treated during this time, Gabrielle only glared at him.

As the weeks passed, the morning sickness disappeared, as did Gabrielle's waistline. It soon became apparent to all who saw her that she was expecting a child.

For André, there were mixed emotions. He wanted the child and was happy at the prospect of becoming a father but he found no joy at the thought of Gabrielle's becoming a mother. His concern was in what kind of mother she would be.

In trying to handle the anger, fear, and frustration she felt over her condition, Gabrielle once again sought relief the only way she knew, through the bottle of brandy she always found in the lower shelf of the highboy in the dining room.

In no time, she reverted to her old ways. The days were filled with her acting like a demented fishwife one minute, because of her condition, and a whining spoiled brat the next, then becoming sweet and loving, begging André's forgiveness.

"It's only because I feel so miserable that I sometimes lose control," she would whine. "Oh, darling, please forgive me."

And because he wanted to understand how she felt, André would try to forgive her. But the peace never lasted long.

To prevent a similar accident as had befallen her before, André sent strict instructions to the stables that under no circumstance was Madame to be allowed to ride her horse.

* * *

In spite of her condition, André found himself reluctant to spend time with Gabrielle. Instead, he gravitated to *Château Charlevoix*. He enjoyed Jean-Claude's company. The *Château* was peaceful and serene. And, Julie, oh how he enjoyed being with her.

Except for the night of the slave uprising, he had seen little of Julie. Gabrielle was so jealous it would have been difficult. She made it clear from the first she would not tolerate having Julie around, and Julie herself chose not to be around.

André had been busy with the building of his new home, and many other things had taken up his time. Not until his return from the north was he able to spend any time with Julie, and it happened by sheer accident.

Chapter 34

I t was a lovely warm day. André had spent most of the morning riding about Royal Oaks with his overseer and Samson. He returned to the house for the noon meal, but it was miserable because of Gabrielle's foul mood.

As soon as he finished eating, André escaped her temper and went for a ride. He was tired, discouraged, and depressed over his marriage. Turning his horse toward *Château Charlevoix*, he soon came to the glade where he and Julie had spent her twelfth birthday.

As he drew near, he thought he heard someone laughing. Yes, someone was laughing, and it was Julie. He'd know her laugh anywhere. It was melodious and infectious, and made him smile.

Slowly, André turned his horse toward the sound. Julie was sitting on the grass; and the reason for her laughter was two small squirrels that were chattering at her and each other as they chased one another around a nearby pecan tree.

André sat quietly watching the scene. It was such a lovely sight, Julie dressed in a gown of soft pink, her rich, dark curls tied with a wide ribbon of the same color. She was speaking softly to the small furry creatures. The squirrels were peeking through the leaves of the tree, answering her back.

André smiled again. All the pent-up anger seemed to flow out of his body at the sight of this beautiful picture.

Suddenly, Julie stopped. It was as though she sensed someone was watching her. For just a second, a look of fear crossed her face. Then she caught sight of Andre's horse.

André urged the animal forward and made his presence known.

"*Bonjour*, Julie," he said as he dismounted.

The little squirrels, frightened by his voice and the scent of the horse, scampered further up the tree and continued their chatter.

"Oh, André, I'm so happy to see you. But I'm afraid you and your horse have upset my little friends." Julie laughed and smiled up at him. "Just hear how they're scolding you." Then she patted the grass. "Come join me, André. You look tired."

André sat down, drew one knee up against his chest, and draped an arm across it. He studied Julie for a long moment. She grew more beautiful with each year. "Julie, it's so good to see you. We've missed you at Royal Oaks. Everyone asks about you."

"I've missed you and Royal Oaks also," Julie answered in a wistful voice. "Tell me, how is everyone; Samson, Delilah, Suzy and the others?"

She asked about so many and remembered their names. She was delighted to learn Samson and Delilah would soon be parents and sad to hear that Joe, one of the stable boys, had been ill with a cold.

"He's getting better now, and I know he'll be happy to learn you asked about him," André assured her.

Julie asked about the crops and the factory and all kinds of questions concerning the plantation; and André told her everything that had happened lately. It was so good to talk to her again, to find she hadn't lost interest in Royal Oaks.

He told her all the news. The one thing he didn't speak of was Gabrielle. And Julie asked no questions concerning her, and for that, he was grateful. It was peaceful and pleasant here in the glade with someone whose company he truly enjoyed.

"André, you look as if you've had a lot of worries. But with everything going so well, what would you have to worry about?" Julie studied his face for an answer, but there was none.

André merely shrugged and looked away.

In a soft voice, she said, "Here, why don't you lie down and put your head in my lap and close your eyes."

With a smile, André did as he was told and felt her cool, slender fingers gently caress his forehead and temples. She started to hum a pretty little tune. Her voice was soft and sweet, and it had a therapeutic effect on him.

After a few minutes, André opened his eyes. "Tell me, Mademoiselle Charlevoix, what would your *pappa* say if he knew you were here alone in this glade, unchaperoned, and with a married man no less?"

Julie laughed softly, "He would probably want to fight a duel, that is, until he found out who the married man was."

André arched an eyebrow. "Oh, you don't think he would find me worth fighting a duel with? I'm not bad with a saber, or a pistol for that matter."

"*Non*, silly. What I mean is he wouldn't worry if he knew the man was you." Julie looked down at him with eyes filled with love. "André, *Pappa* trusts you and knows you would never do anything to harm me. He's very fond of you. I think he thinks of you almost as a son, and he greatly admires you."

They both fell silent. Julie continued to stroke his forehead and sing softly. It had been ages since André felt so relaxed and at peace. So many feelings were conjured up within him as he lay there. They were good feelings, feelings of love and trust and happiness.

This beautiful young girl could bring such peace and tranquility to him just by her presence. It was hard to believe she was almost fifteen. Soon she would be sixteen and making her debut. Then there would be many young men competing for her hand, and this realization came as a shock. André had no idea how long he had slept, but he woke to find Julie tickling his nose and ears with a blade of grass.

"Wake up, sleepyhead," she said softly. "It's getting late, and I must get home before 'Toinette has the entire place out searching for me. You know what a worrywart she is."

André opened his eyes to find the sun had shifted, and dark clouds were forming in the distance. He sat up and stretched for a moment, then jumped to his feet. Looking around, he realized he hadn't seen Julie's horse. "Where's *Minuit*?" he asked.

"I started out for a short walk, but I just kept walking and ended up here" Julie smiled at him. "That's why I must hurry, it will take me a while to get home, and it looks like rain."

"Well, you certainly won't walk home," André replied, reaching out his hand to her.

As Julie stood up, she stumbled and fell against him.

"Oh dear, my legs have fallen asleep; they won't support me." Her hands went up to his shoulders to give herself more support, and her body went limp against his. Her face was lifted to his, and, suddenly, André had the strongest urge to kiss her. As quickly as the thought crossed his mind, the shock hit him. Julie was only fourteen; he was a man of twenty-five, a married man at that, soon to be a father. Roughly, he pulled her arms from his shoulders and in a gruff voice said, "Here, let's get the blood circulating again."

Slipping his arm around her waist, André made her walk about for a few moments. There was a look of hurt in Julie's eyes when he'd spoken to her, and he realized he was taking his anger at himself out on her. More gently, now that she was steady on her feet, he said, "I can't let you walk. It looks as if a storm is brewing. I'll take you home."

"You do love me, you do," Julie whispered softly. "You love me but think of me as a child, and you're a married man." Reaching up, she gently touched his face with her fingertips, and the touch sent a jolt through André.

"Yes, I love you," he admitted, a mixture of pain and love clearly written on his face. "I've loved you almost from the moment I first saw you." He looked at her intently. "I love you, but you're so young, and I am married, and there's nothing to be done about it."

"Oh, André, my dearest André," Julie's breath was warm on his chest where his shirt was partly opened. Once again, her face was tilted to his. Then she lowered it to his chest and he heard her sob. "Oh André, I love you so. I can't live without you."

It took every bit of strength André possessed to keep control of his emotions. "Julie, dearest, I can't let this happen. You're so young, and I love you too much to ever hurt you."

Once again, Julie lifted her eyes to his and they were so filled with love they overwhelmed him.

Gently, he held her away from him. Softly, he said, "Julie, dear heart, I love you, but I can't let you ruin your life. You're a beautiful young girl. When you're older, you'll find the right man, get married, and forget all about this."

Shaking her head, Julie gazed up at him. "I'll never forget. I'll never marry anyone else. I couldn't."

They stood there for a long moment...neither spoke. Then André picked her up and put her on his horse. "I'm taking you home, little one; home where you can think more clearly."

The thoughts racing through his head were all a jumble. Holding

Julie next to his heart, André caught the faint scent of her perfume. Her soft thick hair brushed against his face as the breeze touched it. He loved her so much. How could he not love her? She was sweet, kind, gentle, funny and beautiful. Someday, in the not too distant future, she would marry. He wondered who the lucky man would be.

As they reached the *Château,* rain began to fall. Both Monsieur Charlevoix and Julie insisted André stay for dinner, and he found it impossible to refuse.

The sky was filled with dark angry clouds as they sat down to eat. And by the end of the meal, rain was pouring from the heavens and lashing at the windows. Thunder rolled across the land, and the sky was illuminated with jagged streaks of lighting. The storm became so violent that Jean-Claude insisted André stay the night.

"There is no way you can possibly ride home in this weather. I insist that you stay."

"*Merci,* Monsieur. I should hate to try and make it home in this storm." André had to admit to himself it would be a pleasure not to have to return home to Gabrielle, especially in such weather.

The evening passed with André still feeling guilt for what had happened in the glade. Julie was so innocent; her father was his friend. He felt he'd betrayed the man's trust, and determined such a thing would never happen again.

Later, the servant named Beau, showed him to a guest room. As he crossed the threshold, André realized it was the same room he'd slept in the first time he'd visited the *Château.*

Later still, when he was in bed, Beau returned to see if he needed anything. André assured him he didn't.

With a deep sigh, André closed his eyes and fell into the first peaceful sleep he'd had in a long time.

* * *

The next morning, André woke to find the storm had finally ended. After bathing, shaving, and dressing, he went down to the dining room where Monsieur Charlevoix had just sat down.

"*Bonjour*, André, I hope you slept well in spite of the storm." Jean-Claude was in his usual good humor.

Smiling, André returned the greeting. "*Oui*, I slept soundly, thank you. It seemed strange to be back in the bedchamber I used the first time

I came here. So much has happened since then."

"*Oui*, André, your life certainly has taken many turns in these past three years. Turns I hope have all been for the better."

Monsieur Charlevoix studied André's face for a long moment.

"Well," he said quickly, "Julie will be down shortly."

Just then Julie appeared, fresh and lovely. Wearing a gown of lavender-sprigged muslin, her hair falling loose around her shoulders, she was the loveliest creature Andre had ever seen.

She gave her father a kiss and smiled warmly at André. "I hope you slept well, André," she said as she took her seat.

"*Oui*, Julie, I slept like a *bébé*. Even the storm didn't disturb me." Once again, she gave him a warm smile. André knew she was trying to ease the tension and guilt he felt, and for that he was grateful.

Breakfast passed with easy chatter between the three, and André found himself reluctant to leave. When the meal was over and he had enjoyed one last cup of coffee, he said good-bye after promising to return soon.

On the ride back to Royal Oaks, his thoughts kept returning to *Château Charlevoix*. It was such a happy, peaceful home. There were only two people in the family, yet the house seemed full, and he realized the feeling came from the warmth and love that filled the place.

There were only two people living in his home at Royal Oaks, yet the house seemed vast, cold, and empty. No laughter rang through the rooms and halls as it did at the *Château*. His home would never be filled with warmth and love as long as Gabrielle was there. And she would be there until death.

* * *

When André entered the avenue of Royal Oaks, he was filled with dread of having to face and deal with his wife, dread of having to listen to her voice as she hurled accusations at him and vented her anger on him.

He wasn't wrong. Gabrielle met him at the top of the stairs leading to the second floor. "And where have you been all night, my darling husband?" Her eyes were bloodshot, her voice strident, her hair a mess, and she reeked of brandy.

André moved past her, but she reached out and grabbed his arm. "I demand to know where you've been! Do you think you can stay away all night and then come waltzing in without an explanation? If you do, you're very much mistaken!"

André disengaged his arm from her grasp, and gave her a look of total disgust. "I owe you no explanation as to where I go and what I do, but I will tell you. I spent the night at *Château Charlevoix*. I couldn't leave in the storm, so Monsieur Charlevoix invited me to spend the night."

"You were with that girl?" Gabrielle shrieked. "How dare you!" She grabbed his arm again. "How dare you go off and stay the night at that girl's house!"

In a rage, André jerked his arm from her grasp. "Oh, shut up! You're a fool, Gabrielle. And every time you open your mouth, you sound like a bigger fool. Julie is a sweet child, and her father is my friend. Any crazy thoughts you may have concerning my relationship with Julie are just that *crazy*!"

Once again, Gabrielle tried to grab his arm. "I won't have it! Do you hear me? I won't have it!" she screamed.

André whirled around. White with rage, his eyes scorched her, and such a look of hatred filled his face that Gabrielle recoiled.

"GET OUT OF MY SIGHT!" he roared. He lifted his hand as though to strike her, then slowly lowered it. *Non*, he wouldn't hit her. He wanted to, but he'd never in his life struck a woman. But oh, how he hated her! This crazy woman who had turned his life into a living hell! "Get out of my sight before I strike you. Get out of my sight and stay out! You disgust me!"

Turning, André entered his bedchamber, slamming the door in Gabrielle's face. He stood for a long moment listening to her, then crossed to the window and, pulling back the curtain, stared out at his land. His face was white and drawn, his fists clenched and unclenched, and his jaw was clamped so tight it made his head hurt. He could hear Gabrielle screaming on the other side of the door. Her fists pounded it, she rattled the doorknob; he could hear her panting with rage, and screaming at the top of her lungs.

"OPEN THIS DOOR, ANDRÉ! DO YOU HEAR ME, OPEN THIS DOOR!"

André stood like a statue; his heart pounding, his head splitting, and his stomach in a knot. Putting his hands over his ears, he tried to blot out the sound of her. He wished he could blot her completely out of his life. Was this what the future would be? Was this his life for as long as they both lived?

The pounding continued for several minutes. André had all he could do from opening the door and hitting her. Then, finally, it stopped.

Chapter 35

André continued going to *Château Charlevoix*. He knew he shouldn't, but it was so peaceful there. He and Monsieur would spend time talking or playing chess and often Julie would play the pianoforte or the harp while they concentrated on their game.

He stopped going to the glade so often yet it was the only other place where he could find peace and quiet. And one day when he got there, Julie was waiting for him.

She was sitting quietly, and at first André didn't see her. He dismounted, tethered his horse to a tree limb, and dropped down on the grass. For a long moment, he just sat staring off into space.

It was then that Julie finally spoke, *"Bonjour,* André."

At the sound of her voice, André turned with a startled look. "Julie, I didn't see you." There was a long pause, and then he cleared his throat. "So, what brings you out here today?"

"I was hoping to see you, André." She got up and slowly walked toward him. "I was hoping we could just talk. You know, like we used to."

"Well, of course, *chère coeur,* of course we can talk." Smiling at her he asked, "What would you like to talk about, little one?"

Julie sat down next to him, smoothed her skirt, and said in a sad little voice, "We'll be leaving soon for the city. I have to finish my last year at the convent."

Turning his head, André looked away as he picked a glade of grass and stuck it between his teeth. He felt a wrench in his heart at the thought of Julie being in the city while he was still here in the country. In a soft voice, he asked, "And after you finish school, what will you do?"

"Then I'll spend my time with *Pappa* both here and in New Orleans." Julie smiled and added, "And I'll prepare for my debut when I am sixteen."

André turned back to her with a smile. "Then you'll be courted by every eligible bachelor for miles around, and soon you'll be married." He paused and added in a wistful voice, "I wonder who the lucky man will be."

Julie shook her head. "There will be no 'lucky' man. You know, André, there are many girls in New Orleans who are married at fourteen and to men much older than themselves." She glanced at him out of the corner of her eye as she spoke.

André knew this was true. These were usually marriages *de convenience*, where two families of great wealth joined their fortunes together.

"I also understand that Monsieur Roosevelt fell in love with his wife when she was only twelve and he was already in his twenties," Julie added.

André knew this to be a fact also. Nicholas Roosevelt himself told the story of his courtship and marriage to his young wife when she was all of fifteen and André had seen firsthand how happy and devoted the couple were.

"It can happen, André. Young girls can fall in love when they are still considered children." Julie turned and looked at him with loved-filled eyes that caught at his heart.

"But Nicholas Roosevelt was single when he and his wife met. And when she grew up, they were able to marry," he answered with candor.

"And we can't," Julie added. "But I love you, André. I'll always love you. The thought of not spending my life with you is so terrible I can't even think of it."

"Julie, *chérie*, this has got to stop. Dear heart, you simply can't throw your entire life away on me. I'm married. You have a right to a life of your own, with a husband and children and all that goes with it." His eyes searched her face. He couldn't bear to see her hurt, wishing for something that could not be.

"But I don't want any of that," Julie insisted as tears filled her eyes. "I only want you."

André took her hands in his, and looked at her intently. "Julie, listen to me, and listen carefully I love you, I've always loved you. But I'm a married man about to become a father. You're still very much a child. You've got to get over this obsession you have for me. You have the rest of your life to live, and I won't have you pining away over me."

Julie said nothing. She knew he was right, but it didn't change things. They sat and talked for another hour, and finally André told her it was time to head for home.

Hoping to lighten her mood, he smiled at her. "I tell you what let's do; let's have a picnic before you leave for the city. Would you like that?"

"Oh, *oui*, André." Julie's face brightened at the thought. "I'll bring the food this time."

* * *

The day before Julie was to leave for the convent, they had their picnic. André rode out to the fields at daybreak but returned to the house to freshen up before riding to the glade.

He didn't see Gabrielle, but she heard him as he strolled down the hall to his bedchamber. She watched him from her window as he rode away toward *Château Charlevoix* a short while later.

She was filled with rage that she couldn't ride after him and see just what it was that he did at *Château Charlevoix*!

But she couldn't get anyone to saddle her horse and was too frightened of the animal to ever try and saddle it herself. She checked the clock to see what time André left and would watch to see what time he returned. Meanwhile, she would ease her frustration with a little brandy.

* * *

With the picnic over and Julie back at school, André continued going to *Château Charlevoix* to visit Jean-Claude until such time as he too would leave for the city.

Gabrielle became more enraged when she thought of how much time André spent at the *Château*.

"It's that girl!" she shouted at him one day. "I know it's that girl! I saw the look on her face the day she learned we were to be married. That little bit," she had started to say *bitch* but thought better of it, "baggage has had her eye on you ever since you arrived here."

"You will leave Julie's name out of this. She's a sweet young girl who is a dear friend to me. I go to *Château Charlevoix* because I enjoy the company of Monsieur Charlevoix; and the atmosphere there is peaceful and happy, unlike at this house! So just shut up, Gabrielle, and get out of my sight!"

* * *

Returning from the fields one day, André was shocked to see Delilah staggering across the yard weighed down by a heavy carpet that lay across her shoulders. As he neared her, he could see that beneath her dark skin, Delilah's face was ashen and beads of perspiration stood out on her brow and dripped into her eyes.

"Delilah, what are you doing? You have no business carrying such a heavy load in your condition." The black woman stopped.

"Madame de Javon ordered me to beat dis heah rug 'till it be free of dust."

André dismounted and lifted the carpet from her shoulders.

"Madame de Javon had no business putting this task on you." He placed the carpet on the ground and took Delilah by the shoulders. "Now, I want you to go to your cabin and lie down for the rest of the day. I'll come by later this evening to see how you're doing."

Delilah nodded, thanked him, and slowly started for her cabin.

"Gabrielle!" she heard his angry voice as he entered the house. She was sitting in her bedchamber drinking. Now, as she heard his footsteps mounting the stairs, she rushed to hide the brandy bottle in her dressing room.

"Gabrielle!" André burst into her room to find her sitting calmly in her chair. His large frame seemed to fill the room as he glowered at her. "What possessed you to make Delilah carry that heavy carpet outdoors? Good lord, woman, don't you know she will have her child soon?" Andre's eyes were blazing, his fists were clenched, and it was all he could do to control his temper.

Gabrielle, trying to act as if she hadn't been drinking, looked up at him calmly. "That carpet needed a good beating; it was full of dust.

Delilah has done little lately to earn her keep."

André raked her with his eyes. "I'll be the judge of that. You, too, are *enceinte*. How would you like to carry that rug across the yard on your shoulders in your condition?"

"Why, I shouldn't like it at all, and I certainly wouldn't do it. But then, I don't have to concern myself with such matters. After all, I am the mistress of this house, and I'm going to have the heir to Royal Oaks." Gabrielle gave him a nasty smirk.

"That child is just as important to Samson and Delilah as our child is to me—and no less precious." André's voice shook with rage. "I will not let you do anything to endanger my child—and the same applies to Delilah and her child."

Gabrielle had had just enough to drink to make her careless.

"Your child! That's all I've heard since you realized my condition. You won't let me go to the city. I can't ride my horse. You've kept me here at Royal Oaks and watched me like a hawk, and I'm sick of it! I'm a prisoner and all because of this child!" She leapt from her chair and was now pacing the floor throwing her usual temper tantrum. "I don't want this *brat* anymore than I wanted the last one! I'm sick of being cooped up here when all of my friends are in New Orleans! I'm sick of being *enceinte*! I hate you, I hate this *brat,* and I hope I lose it!"

André watched in shock as she screamed and paced about the room. Suddenly, he reached out and grabbed her wrist. "By heaven, Gabrielle, you'll do nothing to harm this child! *My* child—since you seem to want nothing to do with it. It is *my* child you are carrying, and as God is my witness, nothing had better happen to this one!"

"*Your child!*" she spat. "*Your child*! Ha, that's all *you* know." Suddenly, she stopped, aware of what she had said, and a look of fear crossed her face.

André saw the look, held her wrist tighter, and jerked her to him. "What do you mean, that's all I know? If not my child, then whose child is it?"

"André, you're hurting my wrist!"

"Who's child are you carrying, Gabrielle?" André shook her so hard her head flopped back and forth like a rag doll. "Tell me, Gabrielle! If not my child, then whose child?"

"Gaston's child!" Gabrielle screamed. "Gaston Bochet's child. Gaston cared for me. He gave me a great deal of attention! He didn't ignore me and treat me with indifference like you do."

She saw the look of pain and shock on André's face, and it gave her a perverse feeling of pleasure to know she was hurting him. In her alcoholic mind, it was just what he deserved.

In a dazed voice, she heard him say, "Gaston's child? You're carrying Gaston Bochet's child?"

Gabrielle's eyes were bright from the brandy and her voice had a rough rasp to it. "*Oui,* I am carrying Gaston Bochet's child, and his child will be heir to Royal Oaks. And there is *nothing* you can do about it." She sneered at him. "What will you do? What can you do? Disgrace my family, my sister and your brother-in-law who also happens to be your best friend? How do you think my parents and Charles' parents will feel if you brand their grandchild a bastard?" She had an ugly sneer on her face.

"*Non*, André, the price is too high even for you. This child will be yours in the eyes of the world, and you will just have to learn to live with that fact."

André knew he'd never hated anyone as much as he hated this crazy woman who was his wife.

"But since you want this child so badly," she continued, "I will do my best to give it to you." She paused and took a deep breath. "But you will always know you are not the real father. Ha!" She threw back her head and started to laugh.

A strange animal sound issued from André's throat as he drew back his hand and hit Gabrielle across her face with such force that she screamed and stumbled back, falling into her chair. Blood dripped from her mouth where she bit her lip, but he didn't care. He turned and rushed from the room, down the stairs, and out of the house to the stables where he mounted his horse. She was still screaming, and the sound followed him as he rode away.

Chapter 36

André had never before struck a woman, but Gabrielle had driven him to it! The wonder was he hadn't done it before. He knew he had to get away from her before he did her some real harm.

He had no idea where he was going, and he didn't care. He thought of Gaston sitting at the table that night at the Duval's. Did Gaston know at the time that Gabrielle carried his child? He would seek out Gaston and kill him. So many thoughts were racing through his mind at such a rate that none of them made sense.

He was unaware of where he was heading until he found himself at the steps of *Château Charlevoix*.

André left his horse with a stable boy and mounted the stairs to the *galerie* of the house. 'Toinette appeared at the front door, and when she saw his face, she hurried to invite him in and called one of the yard boys, "Go find *Michie* Jean-Claude, and hurry."

André's face was drained of all color, and he had a wild, wounded look in his eyes. Gently, 'Toinette steered him into the parlor. "Heah, *Michie* de Javon, you rest yo'self. *Michie* Jean-Claude, he be heah soon, *oui*." She helped him to a chair and went to get some wine. Returning with the liquid, she poured a glass and handed it to him. "You drink dis wine, *Michie* de Javon. It help calm yo' nerves."

André took the goblet in shaking hands and took a sip. 'Toinette stood quietly watching him.

Finally, he looked up at her. *"Merci,* 'Toinette, *merci* I'm better now."

'Toinette smiled and patted his hand. "Everythin' gonna be all right, *Michie* André, you see. *Michie* Jean-Claude, he be heah soon. You jes' sit heah and rest, you."

'Toinette left the room and a short while later Jean-Claude arrived. After speaking to 'Toinette, he hurried into the parlor. He, too, was shocked by André's appearance. It was obvious the man had suffered a terrible shock. Gently, Jean-Claude put his hand on André's shoulder. "What ails you, dear friend?" he asked in a soft voice.

For the next hour, André poured his heart out to the older man. He had never before spoken to a soul about his marriage and his life with Gabrielle. He had covered for her, protected her, tried never to let her family or anyone else know how much she drank and what life was really like with her. He'd played the role of loving, devoted husband. "I couldn't believe it at first, when she told me the child isn't mine!" he said in a rage. "She flaunted the fact that she had had an affair with this Gaston Bochet!

"And her jealousy is unbelievable. She is jealous of everything and everyone. If I speak to anyone, there she is to yank me away. She is possessive to the point of smothering."

He jumped up and paced about the room, then stopped and looked over at the older man. "I tell you, Monsieur, sometime I think I'll go crazy living with her. The emotional upheavals are more than anyone should have to tolerate. I never know what to expect. I never know how she will act or what will happen from one minute to the next. Life with Gabrielle has become absolutely intolerable. Sometimes, I feel as if I would do anything to end it, never to have to lay eyes on her again."

André went on to tell his friend about the loss of their first child. "She didn't want our *bébé,* and said so. I swear she took that horse out on purpose to try to lose it, and she succeeded. Now she is going to have a child, and it isn't mine!"

When, finally, André stopped speaking, he looked at the older man in complete despair. Dropping down into a chair, he put his head in his hands. "On, *Mon Dieu,* Monsieur, what am I to do?"

Jean-Claude had sat quietly and patiently while André unburdened his heart. He was thoughtful for a moment, then said, "André, it is a terrible thing you've had to live with, and it's a terrible thing she has done to you. But as terrible as it sounds, she is right about one thing. If you say anything about this, the people you will hurt the most are the people you care the most about her family."

André nodded, as Jean-Claude continued, "Oh, you could divorce her and, under the circumstances, no one would blame you. It would certainly be justifiable. But the disgrace to her family would be difficult to say the least not that others would blame them, or you for that matter. But you know better than most that her mother has a weak heart, and, I fear the shock might kill her."

André agreed. "*Oui*, I know. I certainly don't want to harm her family in any way if I can help it. I care very much for them, especially my mother-in-law. She is a very sweet person."

Jean-Claude was thoughtful and then said, "André, you are in a very difficult situation. You are right to be concerned about her mother. Celeste Ste. Claire is a shy, gentle person, and she has had much to contend with, with her husband's gambling and losing her family's plantation."

When he saw the look of surprise on André's face, he said, "*Oui*, it was her family's plantation before she married Frédéric Ste. Claire. Her father gave it to them right before he died.

Celeste was born and raised there and she loved the place. But Frédéric loved to gamble more. And when he lost her lovely plantation, Celeste suffered a near fatal heart attack, and she has never been the same. Frédéric also has a love of liquor, but he manages to keep it under control, except when he gambles."

Jean-Claude continued, "He was quite a hell-raiser in his youth, and it continued long after his marriage; oh, not that he doesn't love his wife. I don't mean to imply that. But his weakness for gambling and drink has caused them some serious problems. I fear Gabrielle has taken after him as far as her love of alcohol is concerned. So you can see why it would be a terrible thing for her family if you were to divorce her and proclaim to the world the kind of wife she has been."

Monsieur Charlevoix took a sip of wine and added, "André, I wouldn't blame you if you did file for divorce from a woman who has caused you such pain and misery. But I would advise you to give it a great deal of thought before making any decision. There will be repercussions if you choose to take such measures; and, like it or not, you'll have to live with the consequences."

André looked up with eyes filled with guilt. "It's really my own fault, Monsieur. I married Gabrielle knowing I wasn't truly in love with her." He took a sip of wine and continued speaking.

"Oh, I told myself I loved her. But even when we were engaged, there were problems. We fought all the time. She would make me so angry, I could hardly stand her." He paused for a second, staring off into space. "I knew we were making a mistake, but I let her dowry get in the way. It was quite a bit of money, and I knew it would be a great help to me in getting what I wanted."

Another sip of wine, and he continued, "More than once, I thought I should try and find a way to break off our engagement. But I needed her dowry and I was afraid if I broke it off, I'd alienate Charles and his family and many of the people I'd met through them, including you. I needed all of you to help me achieve my goals."

He paused again and gave Jean-Claude a look filled with shame. "I've used you, all of you, and I used Gabrielle most of all in order to realize my own selfish desires. My greed took over." Softly he said, "I have no one but myself to blame for what has happened." He looked at the older man. "Now that you know, can you ever respect me again? Can you ever forgive me, Monsieur?"

Monsieur Charlevoix smiled gently. "There's nothing to forgive, André. Perhaps you did allow Gabrielle's dowry to blind you to some truths, but once you took your marriage vows, you honored them. You've been true to your vows, and you've been a good husband to Gabrielle. You've stood by her and tried to protect her. No man could have done more.

"And as far as respect, I have a great deal of respect for you, as does everyone who knows you. And I know that if they were aware of this tragic story, and how well you've handled it, they would respect you even more."

He reached over and patted André's hand. "Don't beat yourself up over what has happened. Gabrielle is sick in her mind and you can't blame yourself for that. I've watched how you've cared for her, and I know you've done your best."

Together, they sat in the parlor discussing the problem, and later they had dinner. As they finished the meal, Jean-Claude said, "Stay here tonight. Try to get a good night's sleep, and perhaps tomorrow you'll be able to make a clearer decision." He placed his hand on André's shoulder as together they left the room. "André, I want you to know that, whatever you decide to do, I will stand by you and I will always be your friend."

* * *

There was a gentle tapping at the door. Sleepily, André called out "*entrée*." A young servant girl hurried in carrying a small tray on which sat a pot of steaming, fresh coffee and a plate with a warm, fresh *brioche*. A single rose in a slender silver vase was also on the tray. The girl placed the tray on the bedside table and proceeded to open the drapes to let the sunshine in.

"*Michie* Charlevoix say you is to have *petit dejeuner* now, and when you is ready you is to come down an' join *Michie* fo' *grand dejeuner*." She gave André a broad smile as she placed the tray on the bed next to him and left the room.

André was far hungrier than he'd realized. He'd only picked at his food the night before when he shared dinner with Jean-Claude. Now, as he relaxed in bed, he ate every morsel of *brioche* and drank every drop of coffee. Slowly, he removed the rose from its vase, and toying with it, his thoughts went to Julie.

There was pain at the thought of her married to someone else, someday, and sorrow and anger knowing he would not be the lucky man. There would come a time when their age difference wouldn't matter. But, for now, it did matter. And, he *was* married there was no changing the fact.

Oh, Julie, if only I could have married you.

The thought of Gabrielle was like a sharp knife to André's heart. All the ugly memories of the previous day came rushing back. Monsieur Charlevoix was right, of course. He must think of the end results if he left her. His next thought was of his mother-in-law. She was sweet, gentle, and soft-spoken. He never heard her raise her voice to her daughters or her servants. That Gabrielle could be her child was hard to believe, considering how different the two women were.

The night before, he had prayed fervently asking for guidance in making the right decision. Now, as he lay in bed toying with the rose, he knew in his heart that he couldn't bring disgrace and pain such as he had experienced to the rest of her family.

He also thought of Charles and Francesca. Charles was his best friend, the brother he never had, and he had grown to love Francesca like the sister he'd lost so long ago.

André knew how happy Charles and Francesca were in their marriage. They were now the only family he had. *Non*, he would not hurt these two people and the others who were so dear to him.

He married Gabrielle for better or worse in the sight of God. Somehow, someway, he would get through this. With a heavy heart, he bathed, dressed, and went down to join his host for breakfast.

"I hope you feel better, André," Monsieur Charlevoix said, smiling as Andre entered the dining room.

"Oui, merci," André smiled in return. He went on to explain that he'd thought and prayed all night and had decided to say nothing to anyone. "I can't hurt her family. I shall stay married to Gabrielle and try to make the best of it."

* * *

When André reached Royal Oaks later that day, he ordered Gabrielle's trunks packed. He informed Millie that she and her mistress would leave for New Orleans as early as possible the next morning. Then he slowly mounted the stairs and went to Gabrielle's room where he found her sitting in her chair brooding.

With a look of disgust, he said, "You will stay with your parents until your child is born."

Gabrielle had been drinking and it showed. *"My* child? I think you mean *our* child," she sneered.

André's face settled into hard lines, his eyes were as cold as steel, and once again he had the strongest urge to slap her. It took all of his strength to resist the temptation.

"Do not goad me, Madame. If I keep silent about your behavior, it is through no love for you. Rather it is out of love and concern for your family. But I warn you, Gabrielle, I have little, if any, patience where you are concerned. If you continue to push me, you will live to regret it." Without another word, he turned and left the room, and Gabrielle didn't see him again.

The next morning, she was on her way to New Orleans, and André breathed a sigh of relief. For a while, he would have peace.

Chapter *37*

When finally André returned to the city, he went directly to his new home. It was beautifully furnished, and he felt a sense of pride in how it looked. He brought some of his servants with him, and settled down to enjoy the place.

But his peace was short-lived, as one day he was shocked to see Gabrielle entering the parlor. "What the devil are you doing here?" he demanded as she sailed into the room.

"Why, André darling," she answered, smiling at him as she removed her gloves and bonnet. "I've come to live in our lovely new house. What did you think I was doing?" Turning to Millie, she said, "Have the boys put my trunk in the master bedroom."

André's fists clenched and his face blanched white. "I don't want you here. And you certainly will not be staying in the master bedroom!"

Gabrielle lowered herself into a chair and, brushing the wrinkles out of her skirt, gave him a sweet smile. "Well, here I am, and here I shall stay, whether you like it or not."

Cocking her head to one side, she continued, "After all, *cher* André, we *are* married. And in my condition, where should I be but at my husband's side? What would people think or say if I weren't here?"

"I don't give a damn what people think or say," André answered, "I don't want you here!"

"Well, I'm staying, so you may as well get used to the idea,"

Gabrielle shot back. And nothing he said would change her mind. André tried as best he could to ignore her and pretty well succeeded, until one day, as he entered the house, he heard her crying and carrying on in the parlor.

Gabrielle was sitting on the sofa holding a bunch of cards and wailing at the top of her lungs.

"Oh, for heaven's sake, Gabrielle, what the devil is the matter with you now? And what do you have in your hand?"

"Invitations!" she cried. "Invitations to balls, and parties, and *soirées,* and I can't go to any of them."

"Well, you knew that before you came to the city, so stop your belly aching." André was in no mood to put up with her nonsense and refused to show her any sympathy. Instead, he found escape in another part of the house.

Because of her condition, Gabrielle could go nowhere except the theater where she was forced to sit behind the *loges grilles*. This fact alone put her in a black mood from the very start and after listening to her whine and complain several times, André finally lost his temper.

"If you dislike sitting behind the *loges grilles* so much, why do you even go to the *théâtre*? Why not just stay home and be miserable by yourself instead of inflicting your bad humor on every one else!"

Gabrielle glared at him and started to cry even harder. "You're a beast! You don't care how unhappy I am. You don't care how miserable I am in my condition." She went on and on until, once again, André lost control.

"*Shut up*, Gabrielle! This time you can't blame your condition on me, and if I have to listen to you any longer, I swear you won't be going anywhere. I'm sick to death of listening to you. In fact, I'm *sick to death of you!*"

The look André flung her way was filled with such outright hatred that it frightened Gabrielle. She realized she'd pushed him as far as she dared, and for a short while, she held her tongue. But she continually demanded he take her to the theater, and grudgingly he did.

André would seat her behind the *loges grilles*, then go and sit with friends during the performance, ignoring Gabrielle completely and not bothering to return until the curtain rang down on the last act.

Gabrielle would be infuriated. From where she sat, her vision was somewhat limited. She could see the stage, but the *loges grilles* hampered her ability to see all over the theater. Sometimes, she could hear a young lady's voice saying, "Ah, Monsieur de Javon, how kind you are." She could hear the words, but she couldn't see the speaker, nor could she see André; and this fact alone drove her wild.

Finally, André could stand her no longer and sent her back to her parents' home. His reason was that he was so busy taking care of his many enterprises that he felt she was better off with her family.

The only thing that truly made André's stay in New Orleans pleasant was his visits to Monsieur Charlevoix's home.

His Christmas visit was delightful, as he, Monsieur Charlevoix, and Julie enjoyed exchanging gifts and then sitting down to a delicious dinner.

André gave Monsieur Charlevoix a beautiful pearl stickpin; and to Julie, he gave a lovely gold locket.

"Oh, André, it's beautiful," Julie exclaimed as she asked him to fasten it around her neck. Once it was in place, she stood and looked in a mirror that hung on the wall. Turning to André, she smiled and said, "I shall treasure this locket as long as I live." Then she said, "I have a gift for you also."

When André opened the box she handed him, he found a beautiful scarf. "I made it especially for you," Julie said. "I thought you might want to wear it when you're riding around Royal Oaks on a cold winter morning."

André smiled. "How thoughtful of you, little one. It is just what I've needed on more than one of those winter mornings. You may be certain I shall make good use of it."

Every time André left Jean-Claude's home, he dreaded having to see Gabrielle at her parents' home. All he thought of was getting back to his plantation.

* * *

Finally, in January, André was happy to escape to Royal Oaks. The year 1812 had been good to him. He had reaped an excellent profit from his fields of sugar cane and cotton, and there was still more land to be developed. He'd bought more livestock, and with each year, the plantation was becoming more self-sufficient.

In many ways, a planter's success seemed to depend on luck. Luck: if the weather continued to cooperate. Luck: if prices held steady. André heard of planters on large plantations doing very well for several years;

then because of an early frost, a flood, or a drastic change in climate, their crops failed and they saw all of their hard work lost. A large drop in prices could also have an adverse effect on a planter's income. Knowing this, André determined to find other ways to safeguard his income.

He felt positive about the steamboat company. He had recently received a letter from Henry Shreve telling him that Daniel French had completed building the boat, and in the near future, Shreve himself would sail it down the Mississippi to New Orleans.

Julie rode over to Royal Oaks frequently, once she was assured it would cause no problem.

André delighted in showing her around the house. She had never seen it before and went from room to room extolling the beauty of the place. Everyone was pleased to see her again, and she was met with broad smiles.

One day, as they rode side by side over the plantation, she asked, "When will Delilah have her *bébé*?"

André was rather startled by the question. Most young ladies would never broach such a delicate subject to a man. But Julie was so open and honest with him about everything that he realized she thought nothing of asking.

"Her *bébé* is due this month."

"Do you think me unladylike for asking such a question? I would never ask it of anyone but you." Julie lowered her head and glanced at him out of the corner of her eye.

André laughed. "*Non*, Julie, I certainly don't think you're any less a lady for asking. In fact, that's what I love most about you; you're yourself, there's no pretense with you."

They rode in silence for a while; and when next he looked over at her, André saw a puzzled expression on Julie's face. "What are you thinking about?"

"Oh," she answered with a sigh. "I have wondered and wondered about it, but I still can't figure it out."

"Well, now you're talking in riddles. What is it you can't figure out?"

"I can't figure out how the *bébé* gets in there. I think I might have figured out how it gets out, but how it gets in there in the first place has me completely baffled." Julie looked over at him as though expecting him to give her an answer. But André didn't; he simply looked straight ahead.

There was a long pause, and finally she said, "I'm certain you know, but I don't imagine you'll tell me, will you?"

"*Non*, I don't imagine I will."

It took all of his strength to smother a roar of laughter. Julie looked so confused, and she was so adorable. But André knew he wouldn't touch this with a ten-foot pole.

Chapter 38

Shortly before Julie had to return to the Convent, Delilah gave birth to a healthy eight-pound baby boy.

Julie was thrilled with the news; and not long after the baby's birth, she and André rode together to the cabin to see the infant. What a beautiful baby he was! His small, round head was covered with a soft down of baby hair; his eyes were big and black and fringed with long, thick lashes.

Julie asked Delilah if she might hold him, and the mother happily relinquished him to the *petite* mademoiselle. André was standing next to her and offered his finger to the baby; and a tiny, dimpled hand grabbed it and wouldn't let go.

"He's going to be a mighty strong boy," a delighted André said with a chuckle. "Just see how he holds on to my finger."

"Oh, Delilah, he is so sweet and beautiful." Julie studied the baby. "Look, he has lovely dimples when he moves his little mouth. What are you going to name him?"

Samson, who was standing close by, beaming as any proud father would, threw out his chest and answered, "Delilah and me, we be thinkin' of da Bible stories to find ah name, and we remember Fathah Dominique tellin' 'bout ah man named Tobias. We likes dat name,—so we's gonna name him Tobias."

Shortly thereafter, André arranged for Father Dominique to visit

Royal Oaks and baptize the child. He invited several friends and declared the day a holiday. Little Tobias took it all in stride and slept through most of the ceremony. Tobias seemed such a heavy, formal name for a baby that it was shortened to Toby; and that was how he was known throughout his childhood.

* * *

On another cold damp day in mid-February, André received word that Gabrielle had been delivered of a son that morning. He knew, for the sake of appearances, that he must return to the city at once. The thought gave him no pleasure, and he wondered in his heart if he could show any feelings over the birth of this child.

Upon reaching New Orleans, he went directly to his house where he bathed and put on fresh clothes before going to the home of his in-laws.

When he reached the house, his father-in-law met him in the parlor. "André, congratulations, you have a son. Scrawny little thing to be sure; but with time, hopefully he will fill out. I'm so glad you're here, because Doctor la Poyntz wants to speak to you. He and Madame Ste. Claire are up in Gabrielle's room right now."

Just as he spoke, they heard the doctor coming down the stairs. When he entered the room, Monsieur Ste. Claire offered both him and André a glass of sherry to toast the new arrival. After a few pleasantries, Doctor la Poyntz asked André if he could have a word with him in private. Monsieur Ste. Claire excused himself; and when they were alone, the doctor turned to André with concern.

"André, I must tell you, this child was born full term. I can't pretend he was premature. He was conceived while you were away. He is small but had he been born three months early, he would never have lived."

When André remained silent, the doctor continued. "I say this because I don't know how you wish to handle this. People are not stupid it is not hard to count the months. No one in the family has said anything or asked any questions yet. And although I doubt they will, there is always the chance they might." He saw the look of pain and anger on André's face.

Finally, André spoke. "I know the *bébé* is full term, Doctor la Poyntz. You know these Créoles better than I. Do you think there will be talk or questions?"

Doctor la Poyntz shrugged. "André, as you know, this family is highly respected among their own. The Créoles are fanatics when it comes to avoiding *scandale* and preserving the family name. If there are questions, they will never be asked or addressed in any way, unless you make it obvious that you are upset."

"But will I be considered a fool; a blind fool who hasn't got enough sense to know what happened?" André asked, anger flaring in his eyes.

"Oh, I imagine some may think that but the majority will think you are a proud man who is considerate enough not to want to cause pain and disgrace to her family. But only you can make that decision."

André nodded. "*Oui*, Monsieur Charlevoix has told me as much."

He then related how it was that Monsieur Charlevoix knew. "I think of my mother-in-law and her poor health, her bad heart, and I think also of the child, the innocent child. It is not the child's fault, and the knowledge could make his life miserable."

The doctor agreed. "*Oui*, a *scandale* like this could kill Madame Ste. Claire. Even if she herself knows, and I am sure she does, she will never admit it. The thought is too shocking. And, of course, the brand of illegitimacy on her grandchild would scar the child for life."

The doctor sipped his sherry and continued, "I must also tell you that Gabrielle had a long and difficult delivery. And because of what happened last year with the miscarriage, I doubt she will have more children."

This information neither pleased nor distressed André. He knew Gabrielle would never have another child, at least not by him. He would never go near her in that way again.

A short time later, they shook hands, the doctor left, and André went up the stairs to his wife's bedchamber. As he entered the room, his mother-in-law hurried to him.

"Here is your son, André." She handed the infant to him.

André took the baby in his arms as Madame Ste. Claire continued, "He's a mite thin and looks not too healthy but hopefully he'll fatten up with time. Now I'll leave you two alone." She gave her daughter a light kiss on the forehead and left the room.

"What do you think of our son?" Gabrielle's voice was weak.

André placed the baby in the cradle and went to stand beside the bed. Gabrielle's face was chalk white and dark circles lay beneath her eyes. Her hair was a tangled mess, and she looked frail and helpless, but André could find no pity or real concern in his heart.

"He is *your* child, he is not *our* child. However, I cannot make an innocent *bébé* suffer for the stupidity of its mother. Therefore, I shall care for him as though he were my own. I'll try to love him, not for your sake, but for his and the sake of your family. But I warn you, Gabrielle, do not push me. If you do, I will turn you out. And if that happens, I will keep the child and raise him myself."

He continued, "Only four people know I am not this child's father. Let's keep it that way."

"Four people?" A look of shock filled her face. "What four people? Whom have you told?"

"Think, Gabrielle that is, if you are capable of rational thought. Two of those people are you and me, the third is the doctor."

"And the fourth person? Who is the fourth person?"

"Never mind who that person is. My confidence will never be broken by that person."

Gabrielle tried to sit up only to fall back against the pillows. "It's that girl; that's whom you told! That stupid girl!"

"If you are speaking of Julie, you are a bigger fool than even I thought. For heaven's sake, Gabrielle, Julie is an innocent child. Do you think for one moment I would tell her such a thing? I have nothing more to say to you."

He started to leave the room, but Gabrielle stopped him. "What should we name him?" she asked, looking calmer.

"You may name him anything you wish. You will also stay here with your parents until such time as they return to the country for the summer." Once again, he started to leave.

"And what will you be doing all that time?"

"I will be attending to business. In the summer, I will bring you and the child back to Royal Oaks; and when you return, there will be definite changes I will expect from you."

"Such as?"

"Such as no more drinking. This child will not grow up seeing its mother drunk and out of control. You will not mistreat the servants. This child must learn to respect my people and treat them with kindness and consideration. Think about it, Gabrielle, and decide if you will live by my rules. Otherwise, you will not return to Royal Oaks at all." Without another word, he was gone.

Chapter *39*

While in the city, André immersed himself in business transactions. He bought three large vacant lots on *Rue Tchoupitoulas*. Some thought him crazy to do so.

"*Tchoupitoulas* is the most dangerous street in the city," his father-in-law had said. "You know, much of it is lined with brothels, flophouses, gambling dens, and taverns."

André nodded, "*Oui*, I know, but there are no warehouses in the city, and those lots came cheap."

"Those crazy mountain men from Kentucky and Tennessee, and the sailors from all the ships in the harbor, are always down there on *Tchoupitoulas* where there were fights and frequent murders."

"I'm aware of all that, *Pappa*," André answered. "But *Tchoupitoulas* is near the waterfront."

"Warehouses? Why the devil would you want warehouses?"

"I shall build three warehouses. One warehouse will be for furniture. Most people here in New Orleans order much of their furniture from Europe and around the world. For a fee, I will allow them to store their furniture until such time as they need it. The other two warehouses will be for storing cotton, sugar, molasses, and other products waiting for shipment."

Monsieur Ste. Claire shook his head and continued to tell André how foolish he was. André listened, but said no more.

Riding about the city, he also realized that, with the increasing influx of people migrating to the area, the city would have to expand. So he bought several large pieces of land on the outskirts of town.

This, too, made Monsieur Ste. Claire shake his head. "André, you are throwing your money away foolishly. Why on earth would you spend money on land that is wild and completely undeveloped?"

"It won't be that way forever, *Pappa*. I shall wait; and when the time is right, I shall sell off each plot at a good profit."

André liked his father-in-law; but sometimes, the man tried his patience. He was much like his daughter or rather, she was much like her father. Neither could appreciate André's desire to be financially secure.

In the spring, Henry Shreve, true to his word, arrived in New Orleans on the little steamboat Daniel French had built. It made the trip safely and without incident to New Orleans but lacked the energy to return up the Mississippi, the current being too strong for its engine to handle. Seizing another opportunity, André offered to buy the engine. Once again, his father-in-law had a fit when he found out.

"You bought the steamboat engine! Why?" Monsieur Ste. Claire's eyes grew wide. "Why on earth would you buy a steamboat engine? This is *too* ridiculous!"

"It is not ridiculous, *Pappa*. I've had the engine taken to Royal Oaks. I shall use it to pump and drain the water that accumulates at the back of my land. That water prevents good drainage. You will see. The result of this procedure will give me drainage that is more complete. I'll be able to extend my fields farther back." Once again, André was right and once again, his father-in-law shook his head in amazement.

Shreve spent several weeks visiting both André and Jean-Claude. "Daniel is even now building a bigger and better boat," he informed his partners. "And when she is ready, I will sail her from Pittsburgh to Louisville transporting cargo. I will also bring her to New Orleans sometime in the future; so until then, I shall stay in the North."

Although André could not convince his father-in-law that his business ventures were sound, Monsieur Charlevoix was greatly impressed. "André, you constantly amaze me. You certainly have an excellent head for business. You may well become the wealthiest man in the State of Louisiana." He smiled warmly at his young friend. "That was ingenious, taking that little engine to Royal Oaks. And I have no doubt your warehouses will pay off also."

255

The older man was right. No sooner were the warehouses built than they were each filled to capacity, and André was able to see a healthy profit.

Since his fields were expanded, he was able to plant more crops, which also netted him a nice revenue.

* * *

Now, with summer drawing near, André returned to Royal Oaks, and in a short while, Gabrielle and her child followed. Motherhood had done nothing to improve his wife's disposition.

Frédéric, who was named after his grandfather, was a thin, fussy baby who's crying drove his mother to distraction. She fluctuated between being overly attentive to screaming at him when he cried and ignoring him completely.

André watched this behavior and worried about what effect it would have on the child.

"Gabrielle!" As André entered the house, he heard her yelling at the baby. "Gabrielle! What do you think you're doing?"

Gabrielle swung around in anger. "The brat won't shut up! All he does is cry, and I'm sick of listening!"

They had a terrible fight, and the next thing André knew, Gabrielle grabbed Frédéric up in her arms and began kissing and hugging him, calling him her little darling. This change in behavior only frightened Frédéric and made him cry even more.

Besides being thin and fussy, Frédéric was always sick with a cold and a runny nose, or an ear infection. Doctor la Poyntz made many trips to Royal Oaks; and more than once, there was concern as to how long the child might live.

"I'm very concerned," the doctor said after one such visit. "Gabrielle is a healthy young woman. She should have given birth to a healthy *bébé*." He paused and shook his head. "That poor child is so thin and sickly."

André said nothing. Since no one but he knew of Gabrielle's terrible drinking problem, no one could associate that with the baby's poor health.

He tried to be a loving and patient father to the baby, especially after Gabrielle would scream and scold the child, but poor little Frédéric was not an easy baby to love. He was nervous and frightened when around his mother, much preferring Millie and Delilah, which only made things worse.

* * *

Julie completed her education and now spent her days tending her father's home and riding across the land with him. At fifteen, she knew almost every facet of running the huge plantation.

She loved nothing better than when André would stop by, stay for dinner, then linger after the meal to discuss Royal Oaks with her father.

"How are your crops doing, Andre?" she asked one evening. "*Pappa* told me about the steamboat engine that is now working on the back of your property. *Pappa* was very impressed."

André smiled. "Between you and your *pappa*, I feel quite confident in whatever I do. You have both shown such faith in me over these past few years."

Neither Jean-Claude nor André minded when Julie joined in the conversation and put forth her own ideas on many subjects.

After spending time with Julie and her father, André was always reluctant to return home to Gabrielle.

Gabrielle's physical and mental condition continued to deteriorate right before André's eyes, and she filled him with loathing. This was not the beautiful girl he married. Now, she looked more like an old hag. Her hair was seldom combed, her face was usually flushed and bloated, and her clothes were wrinkled and often soiled.

Another one who was deeply concerned about the situation at Royal Oaks was Charles. But since he had no idea what was wrong with his sister-in-law, the subject was never brought up.

At the start of summer, Gabrielle insisted on resuming her entertaining, but after a while, even that stopped.

Soon the rumors started. "Gabrielle de Javon does not seem quite right in her mind." No one said anything to André directly, but the rumors and whispers continued and grew.

Several of André's close friends were worried about him. He had developed lines of strain in his face, and his eyes no longer held the sparkle everyone admired. Now they held a look of anger, pain, or sadness.

There was the usual reprieve from his wife when Gabrielle and Frédéric left for the city. The two would stay with her parents until such time as André arrived for the Christmas season.

For the next few months, André's life was full and busy; but before he knew it, the holidays were upon him. And once again, he returned to New Orleans.

* * *

Gabrielle and Frédéric were now living in the new townhouse on *Rue St. Philip*. André forced himself to play the role of devoted husband and loving father when family and friends were present.

Christmas was spent quietly with family, but Gabrielle was no better. If anything, she seemed to be getting worse. She not only screamed at Frédéric, she screamed at her two little nephews; and many times, André found himself apologizing to Charles and Francesca for her behavior.

"André, Gaby seems to be getting worse," Charles said one day as they sat in the parlor of his home, each relaxing with a glass of wine. "What do you plan to do about it?"

André stared into his glass reflectively, saying nothing for a long moment. Then he sighed and looked at Charles with pain-filled eyes. "I really don't know what to do about her. I know her condition has worsened, but what can I do?" He turned his head away and stared out of the window.

Charles took a sip of wine and sighed. "You know, as much as Francesca loves her sister, we simply cannot have her around our children. She upsets them too much; and of course, she upsets Francesca also." Charles paused for a second. André said nothing. "Our poor mother-in-law is another she greatly upsets. We've discussed it at length and decided that until the boys are older and can understand, they can no longer be around Gaby." He looked at André with apprehension. "I hope you understand."

"Of course, I understand." André smiled, but still his eyes held the look of pain. "She frightens and upsets Frédéric also. That poor child is a nervous wreck after an hour with her."

"Have you spoken to Doctor la Poyntz about her condition?"

André nodded. "*Oui*, I've spoken to him. However, the good doctor has no more answers than I. He has no good suggestions either except one, and he hesitated to even say it." André paused for a moment and then said in a soft voice, "He said I could place her in an asylum."

He shook his head at the thought of this suggestion. "But, Charles, I can't do that. I've heard what is said about those places; the way the patients are treated. As much as she has made my life a living hell, I can't do that to her."

Charles gave him a sympathetic look. "I know, André, I couldn't do it to Francesca if she were the one who was ill."

The two men sat for a while longer talking of other things; then André took his leave. Riding back to his own home, his mind was filled with the problem of his wife. Not only was her life in total turbulence, but so was his.

* * *

The year 1814 dawned with the war against Britain still raging in the North. Both André and Jean-Claude received letters from Henry Shreve informing them the new steamboat was almost completed. Although there might be problems sailing the boat safely through the northern waters because of the war, Shreve didn't seem worried. He certainly intended to sail if at all possible.

The New Year also saw a happy event taking place: A young lady was eagerly preparing to make her debut. Julie was now sixteen, and it was time to present her to society.

Jean-Claude ordered a most exquisite white gown from Paris. Cards were sent out to all the important Créole and American families. Monsieur Jean-Claude Charlevoix would have the pleasure of presenting his daughter, Mademoiselle Julie Marie Charlevoix, to the society of New Orleans on the first Saturday in the month of February at the *Théâtre St. Philippe*.

On the night of Julie's debut, Charles and Francesca invited André and Gabrielle to join them at the theater.

Gabrielle was having one of her better days; but at first, she was reluctant to go. She looked at André with disgust, "Why would I want to go and watch that girl's debut? It would bore me silly."

André felt relief upon hearing this. "Fine, don't go. You can stay here with Frédéric and the servants." His attitude of indifference infuriated Gabrielle.

"Oh, you'd like that, wouldn't you? You'd love to leave me here so you could go and make eyes at that girl. Well, I will not sit home while you run off to the *théatre* to flirt with that creature and every other female there." She threw him a venomous glare. "Besides," she added, "now that I think of it, I would like to see how unsuccessful her debut will be. I'm sure it could never compare to mine."

In the hope of turning others' attention from Julie, Gabrielle chose a gown with a decidedly low neckline. It exposed far more of her breast than was considered proper. She also applied a little too much makeup, something she'd started to do as her drinking became worse.

When André saw the way she was dressed and made up, he gave her a look of disgust. "Where do you think you are going in that?"

Gabrielle tossed her head and gave him a look of defiance. "Why, I'm going to the *théâtre* to see that girl's stupid debut, of course. But I hardly think she will be noticed once I arrive."

"You look like a trollop, and you are *not* going anywhere dressed like that." André's face was white with the rage he felt just looking at her. "*You* may not care about your reputation but as long as you are married to me, you will dress and conduct yourself, at least in public, like a lady. Now, get upstairs and change that rag, take off that paint, and put on something decent!"

Gabrielle started to hurl angry words at him, but André stopped her. There was cold fury in his face and voice. "I will give you exactly two seconds to get out of this room and do as you are told, or so help me God, you will regret it!"

In a rage, Gabrielle turned and rushed from the room. When Charles and Francesca arrived, André explained that Gabrielle was not quite ready, so the three of them settled down to wait for her. When Gabrielle finally reappeared, she was dressed in a gown far more suitable to the occasion, and her face was devoid of paint. But she was furious with André and spent the entire evening shooting looks of pure hate at him.

The theater was starting to fill as the two couples arrived. Taking their places in the box, they could see that Monsieur Charlevoix's box was overflowing with flowers. The flowers had been sent by young men hoping to impress the beautiful young girl making her debut.

Francesca commented that neither she nor Gabrielle had nearly as many flowers when they each made their debuts. That comment did not sit well with Gabrielle, and she was about to make a tart remark when, just then, a murmur rose throughout the theater.

"She's coming. Oh, how beautiful she looks!"

The carriage had drawn up before the theater, and Joshua jumped down to assist Jean-Claude and Julie as they alighted.

When they entered the lobby, many of her friends pressed around Julie exclaiming over her beautiful gown and how exquisite she looked. She was indeed a vision of beauty.

André stepped out of the box and was standing where he could see Julie quite clearly as she and her father made their way to their box. Her gown was of white slipper satin, the bodice sprinkled with tiny seed pearls and diamonds.

It hugged her slender body in the front, showing off her white shoulders and firm young breasts, and fell into soft folds in the back with a slight train.

Her dark, thick hair was arranged in a cornet of curls, with tendril curls framing her face. White satin ribbons and tiny flowers were interwoven in her hair. She wore long white gloves and carried a bouquet of delicate pink tea roses and baby's breath from which streamed white satin ribbons. A beautiful fan of white satin and lace completed her outfit.

André, watching Julie as she made her way to the box, knew that he had never seen anyone so exquisite. Her beautiful eyes sparkled and danced, and the color in her cheeks was heightened by the excitement of the occasion.

He felt such a surge of love for her that it almost took his breath away. He returned to his box and watched with interest as the scene was played out before him.

Créole girls did not make their debuts, as did the American girls. Instead, the young girl was brought to the theater by her parents where gentlemen called on her before and during the intermission of the play.

Julie had no sooner taken her place in the box, when several young men crowded in after her. Each acknowledged her father and then turned their full attention to her. They bowed to her, kissed her hand, and made light conversation. Julie was gracious to each of them and politely acknowledged the nods of approval from the many dowagers who watched with interest from their seats. Word spread quickly through the theater that this young beauty would most definitely be the belle of the season.

With so much attention from so many, Julie didn't have a chance to look for André when she first arrived. Then the house lights dimmed and the play began, making it impossible to find him. During intermission, when the candles were lit, Julie searched the boxes for André. She quickly spotted Charles, Francesca, and Gabrielle, but there was no Andre! Her heart fell. Where was he? Then, suddenly, he was standing before her, and she was sure her heart would stop beating all together from joy and excitement. He looked so handsome in his evening clothes.

Now, with André standing over her, smiling at her, it was as though the entire theater and all the people in it suddenly disappeared. There were only two people in the world herself and the man she loved.

"Oh, André," she said in a breathless whisper, "you did come. I'm so happy to see you." Her eyes were shining with love, and she didn't care who knew it. She loved him, and he was here for the most important night of her young life; and that was all that mattered.

André flashed his handsome smile and with his eyes never leaving her face, he took her hand and kissed it. "Julie, how beautiful you look. Of course, I'm here. I would never miss such an important and special night as this." He then bid her father good evening and lingered in the box making conversation with them until the lights dimmed for the next act.

When André returned to his box, Julie found it almost impossible to concentrate on the rest of the play. He had come to her debut! Having him here, kissing her hand and telling her how beautiful she looked, made her evening complete.

Later that evening in their parlor, Gabrielle went into her usual tirade. "How dare you make a spectacle of yourself and a fool of me in front of the entire *théâtre*! Fawning over that girl as if you were still a bachelor!"

André tried to hold his temper. "Julie and her father are two of my dearest friends. As for you looking like a fool, well, you do a very good job of that without any help from me!"

Gabrielle started to say more, but with a loss of patience, André turned on her. "Get out of my sight before I slap you!"

Shortly thereafter, André returned to Royal Oaks. It was heaven being away from Gabrielle for a while.

Chapter 40

At the start of summer, Gabrielle and Frédéric returned to Royal Oaks. André was not at all happy to see them but he kept so busy he was able to avoid his wife much of the time.

He maintained a separate bedchamber from Gabrielle in the country as well as the city so he could avoid her as much as possible.

He did, however, try to spend time with Frédéric, who was now one year old. André could see the insecurity already growing in the child. Like his mother, Frédéric was given to temper tantrums. André tried to counteract Gabrielle's inconsistency with the child; but since he spent little time with Frédéric, his efforts were not too successful.

The summer was extremely hot and humid. The sun beat down relentlessly, and the humidity made the days almost unbearable. The rains came but brought no relief, only making the ground steam and the humidity more pronounced. Tempers were short, clothes stuck to the body, and energy was easily spent.

Gabrielle's behavior continued to grow worse, and André wondered if her mind was completely gone. Even her family didn't come to visit anymore. It was too unpleasant.

One day as André rode in from the fields, he saw a horseman coming up the avenue of oaks and knew at once it was Charles. With a whoop and a laugh, André urged his horse into a gallop and in a few minutes pulled alongside of his brother-in-law.

"Charles, how good of you to come by. To what do I owe this pleasant surprise?"

"I was over visiting with Monsieur Charlevoix, and I decided I'd come by and visit you also," Charles answered.

"Well, you will stay for dinner and spend the night, I hope. I could use a little diversion, maybe a game of cards or chess? Francesca won't worry if you're not back tonight, will she?"

"*Non,* Francesca won't worry .I told her I would be stopping by. And *oui* to both of your offers. I'll stay the night and I'll be happy to play cards or chess after dinner."

They had reached the house, and each handed the reins of his horse to the stable boy. As they mounted the stairs, André put his hand on the other's shoulder.

"Charles, I can't tell you how happy I am to see you. I've been so busy lately, and we've had no company for quite a while."

Entering the house, they crossed to the main parlor. As they entered the room, they heard a strange moan. André looked over to where the sound came from and stopped in his tracks.

There, slumped over in a chair, sat Gabrielle. She held a glass that was tilted to the side, and amber-colored brandy dripped onto the rich, plush carpet.

"Oh, dear lord," André murmured under his breath. Quickly, he crossed to where she sat and shook her roughly. "Gabrielle, what the devil are you doing down here in this condition!"

As André shook her, Gabrielle's head flopped around on her neck. She tried to answer, but only succeed in mumbling something incoherent.

André shook her again. "Gabrielle!" His voice was filled with rage, and he shook her even harder. "For heaven's sake, woman, wake up!"

Gabrielle opened her eyes and tried to focus them. "Oh, issss you, André." She started to get up from the chair only to fall back again. "Dear, loving André, my devoted hus..ss..ban." Suddenly, she became aware of Charles, and once again, she tried to stand. But when she did, she hiccupped. That sent her into a fit of giggles.

"Oh, Charles..ss," she slurred as she held her hand out to be kissed. "Sss...sweet, dashing Cha..rles..ss. Have you come to visit with my dear, loving hus.ss..ban?"

Gabrielle managed to lift herself from the chair but was so unsteady that she reached out and grabbed Charles' arm to keep from falling.

"Do you know what a dear, loving hus..ss..ban I have, Charles?" Her body swayed as she continued holding on to Charles' sleeve.

"Well," she slurred as she pointed her finger at Charles. "Let me tell you. He is..s..s a dear, loving, husband; the only problem is he isn't dear and loving to me! He is dear and loving to that miserable *brat*, Julie Marie Charlevoix! Ye...ss that's who he loves." She ended with a hiccup. "He hates me! Do you hear me, Charles? He hates me! He wiss..hes..ss I were dead!"

"Gabrielle, that's enough!" André roared. Reaching out, he grabbed her arm and swung her around to face him. "You're a disgrace coming down here in this condition! Go to your room this instant!"

Although she was very unstable, Gabrielle pulled her arm from André's grip, and stamping her foot, she screamed, "I WILL NOT GO TO MY ROOM! You can't order me around like one of your darkies. I'm the mistre.s..s of this place..s..s and I will do as I please!" She stumbled around, flinging her arms out and almost falling.

She continued to carry on until, finally, André swung her up in his arms, and with her kicking and screaming, he carried her to her room where he dumped her on her bed and left her in the care of Millie.

"Stay in this room!" he roared, his face livid with the fury that coursed through his body. "Don't you dare show your face downstairs again tonight, or so help me you'll live to regret it!"

Meanwhile, down in the parlor, Charles couldn't seem to move. He was shocked to see Gabrielle in such a state. Never before in his life had he seen a lady drunk, and this was his sister-in-law!

When André returned to the parlor, he was followed by one of the maids who proceeded to mop up the brandy. "Come, let us go to the library," he said softly.

Once they entered the library, André turned to Charles. "I can't tell you how sorry I am that you were privy to that terrible scene. I had hoped that no one in her family would ever see Gaby in such a state."

"Oh, André, I had no idea things were that bad." Charles' face was filled with sympathy for his brother-in-law. "Please, don't feel embarrassed. You had no idea Gabrielle would be in the parlor when we entered, and maybe it's just as well someone else in the family knows." He paused and then asked, "How long has she been like this? How long has this been going on?"

André stared out of the window. "Too long," he answered in a tired voice. "I really don't know when it actually started. It seemed to happen so gradually. We always had problems. Gabrielle was so possessive, so demanding, and so unhappy in the little cabin. I think it started way back then; but for a long time, she seemed able to control it. Now she has no control, and I don't know what to do with her." There was bleak despair on his face.

There was no answer to his problem; and after a few minutes, André insisted they put the incident out of their minds.

"I don't want your visit to be bogged down with my problems," he said with a bright smile that was somewhat forced. "Let's have a drink before dinner and you can tell me some funny story you've heard lately. And after dinner, we'll have a game of cards."

It was a pleasant evening and for the first time in a long time, Andre was able to relax.

The next morning when Charles took his leave, he laid a hand on André's arm. "Remember, André, you don't have to carry this burden alone anymore. If you need someone to talk to, you can come to me. And I assure you I will tell no one without your permission. Not even Francesca or her parents. I will keep your secret."

André gave him a grateful smile. "Thanks for understanding. I appreciate it." So saying, he bid Charles good-bye.

There was another terrible scene that night. The evening was as hot and miserable as the day. The sun's going down made little difference in the temperature.

It was dinnertime; André had entered the dining room and began eating. A little later, Gabrielle stumbled in. When she saw that he had already been served, she was furious. "I am mistress of this house, and as such, you should have waited for me before you started eating!"

"I told you I didn't want to see you," André replied, not bothering to look up. "I certainly didn't expect to see you after that disgusting display yesterday. Besides, I have things to do. I can't sit around waiting for you to decide to show up."

"Oh, you have things to do," Gabrielle mimicked his voice.

Turning to Demetrius, she ordered her glass filled with wine. She drank it down quickly and ordered another. Neither Demetrius nor Delilah moved. "Well, don't just stand there, you idiots! You heard what I said! Fill my glass!"

"*Non*, they will not fill your glass. One glass of wine is enough."

André excused the servants and continued to eat.

"What do you mean one glass of wine is enough? I need something to quench my thirst with my meal."

"You have not touched your meal. And I mean exactly what I said: One glass of wine is enough!"

"Oh, it is, is it? Well, we'll see about that!" Gabrielle jumped up and went to the highboy. Opening the lower door where the wines, brandies, and whiskeys were kept, she found the shelves empty. Whirling around, she demanded. "Where are they?"

"If you are speaking about the wines and such, they have been removed and are now under lock and key," André answered coldly, as he continued eating. "After the way you behaved yesterday, I thought it best. Thank God, it was only Charles who saw you."

Gabrielle looked around wildly, stamped her foot and pounded the table with her fist as she screamed. "Where have you hidden them? I have as much right to them as you!"

"You have no right to drink yourself into a stupor and put on such a disgraceful scene as yesterday. You pick fights with your family and insult any guests we may have visiting.

"Also you have no right to be in such a state around Frédéric. That poor child is a nervous wreck because of your behavior. I should have put those bottles away long before now. It might have saved us all a lot of heartache."

Gabrielle refused to remain in the dining room, and she did not eat her meal. Instead, she turned and ran up to her bedchamber where she tore the room apart, then threw herself across her bed in a fit of rage. André could hear her screaming all the way downstairs.

Later that evening when he went to his bedchamber to retire, André was shocked to find Gabrielle standing in the middle of the room.

"What the devil are you doing here?" he demanded with blistering contempt.

Slowly, Gabrielle walked toward him, and when she reached him, she put her arms around his neck. "Oh, André, darling, I'm so sorry, please forgive me." She fluttered her lashes. "Make love to me, André. It's been so long since you've made love to me." She tried to look seductive but only succeeded in looking ridiculous.

Backing away, she turned around slowly and unsteadily. "See, André, Millie brushed all the tangles out of my hair, and I've put on my prettiest nightgown. Don't you think I look pretty? Don't you want to make love to me?"

Her hair that had once been so lovely lay lank on her shoulders. Her body was so emaciated it was repugnant. Her face that had once been so beautiful was bloated, and her eyes were swollen and dead looking. Everything about her repulsed André; he could smell the brandy. It seemed to ooze from every pour of her body, and her breath reeked of it. The smell turned his stomach.

His eyes were cold as marble. "It's over, Gabrielle. I have no love for you. I want nothing more to do with you than is necessary for the sake of your family and Frédéric." Firmly, he took her arm and steered her to the door.

Gabrielle tried to fight him. She tried to stay in the room. "Oh, please, André, darling, please don't put me out. Don't do this to me! I'm your wife! Don't do this to me!"

"Good night, Gabrielle!" Shoving her from the room, André closed and locked the door.

Gabrielle stood still for a moment; then her body began to shake as she screamed, "I hate you! I hate you! I'll kill you! I'll kill myself! I need my brandy! You can't do this to me"

She pounded on the door until her fists were raw. Sinking to the floor, she whimpered like a sick animal. "André, please, I need my brandy…please, André." There was no sound from the other side, and finally she crept off to her room.

Chapter 41

André hoped that with locking the liquor away, the problem would go away and, with time, Gabrielle would get better. He had no understanding or knowledge of how serious her addiction was.

Gabrielle nearly went out of her mind. She needed the brandy. Her body couldn't tolerate not having it. Her nerves screamed for it, she got the shakes, her stomach was in knots, and she couldn't eat or sleep. She went from shaking to sweating, then getting the dry heaves. She would scream and plead and demand that André give her a bottle of brandy; but André, still not understanding her dependence, only turned a deaf ear.

In desperation, she came up with a solution of her own. She took to driving over to Oak Grove as often as possible, carrying with her several large crystal decanters.

She knew where Charles kept his supply of liquor; and each time before she left, she would sneak to where the bottles were kept and fill her decanters. And when she could, she would sneak a half-empty bottle of whatever was available home with her.

She hid the decanters and bottles in her dressing room; and since Andre never entered her rooms, he had no idea she was keeping herself well supplied.

Now, when she appeared for dinner; which was not all that often, she would calmly drink the one glass of wine allowed her, then pick at her food and leave the table as soon as possible.

André didn't notice any great improvement in her appearance or behavior, but he thought she wasn't drinking as much as before. He assumed it would take time before she showed improvement and somehow they managed to get through the summer.

The first of September was drawing near, and again Gabrielle was preparing to leave for the city. Her mood was not uplifted as it had been in the past. There was a strange nervousness about her, and she spent her days in her rooms brooding and muttering to herself.

* * *

It was afternoon. André had been exceptionally busy all morning. The day was hot and humid, and he was tired. After lunch, he wanted nothing more than to bathe, put on fresh clothes, and escape from Gabrielle and find some peace and quiet.

He would ride out to the glade and rest. He never could rest or relax with Gabrielle in the house. He could hardly wait for her to leave for the city.

Heading for the glade, André wondered if perhaps Julie would be there. He hoped she would—he needed someone to talk to and laugh with. He knew Julie and her father would be leaving for the city soon, and oh, how he would miss their company.

As André mounted his horse, Gabrielle watched from her window. She was aware that he always rode off toward *Château Charlevoix* in the afternoon, sometimes not returning until the next day. Well, today, she would follow him and find out just what he did.

As soon as he'd left, Gabrielle ordered her horse saddled. Still unsure of her ability to handle the animal, she started out at a walk. André was some distance from her, and she could see him drawing farther away at each step. Finally, in desperation, she urged the horse to a trot.

She had a difficult time staying in the saddle and took her eyes from André for a moment, only to look up and find him gone. He'd been there a second ago. It was as if he'd disappeared into thin air. But where did he go? Gabrielle urged her horse on faster and found herself bouncing all over the saddle. She rode for a while at a fast clip, but she was being jarred so badly she finally slowed the horse to a walk.

She'd ridden a distance when she thought she heard voices. They were speaking in normal tones, and she knew the voices belonged to André and that stupid girl! Following the sound, Gabrielle suddenly found herself in the spot where André and Julie met.

André was stretched out and Julie was sitting next to him. When Gabrielle suddenly appeared, they both looked up in surprise.

"So!" A nasty sneer distorted Gabrielle's face. "I see you both look surprised and shocked to see me, as well you should! Sneaking around behind my back meeting here! How long did you think you could get away with this before someone found you?" She turned her attention on André. "How dare you carry on like this with this creature! I should tell my *pappa* how you've been behaving. He would kill you in a duel if he knew.

And *YOU*!" She now turned her rage on Julie. "You cheap little piece of baggage. You've had your eye on my husband ever since you've known him. Well, when I get through with you, no one in proper society will ever have anything to do with you!"

Gabrielle was circling her horse around the two of them, shouting and waving her riding crop. The horse was nervous; and André, fearing she would spook the animal and cause one of them to get hurt, jumped to his feet and grabbed the reins.

He tried to calm Gabrielle, because it was obvious she'd been drinking. She, in turn, tried to lash out at him with her riding crop but unable to reach him, she turned back to Julie who had also jumped to her feet.

"Everyone says how beautiful you are!" Gabrielle spat the words out. "Well, we'll see how beautiful you are with a few slashes across that face!"

Julie couldn't move; she was in a state of shock as she watched Gabrielle. While she spoke, Gabrielle lashed out and tried to hit Julie.

Julie put her hands up to ward off the blows and the riding crop slashed her palms instead, drawing blood as the leather cut her flesh.

André, seeing the blood appear on Julie's hands, let go of the reins. The horse, suddenly finding itself free, bolted for the fields and headed back to the stable. Gabrielle, clinging to its neck, managed to keep her seat as the horse covered the distance at a gallop.

"Julie, let me see your hands." André drew her down on the grass and examined them. "Oh, dearest, I'm so sorry such a terrible thing happened to you."

"André, please it wasn't your fault. I'm not hurt that badly." Julie tried to reassure him, but her face was white as death and she was visibly shaken.

Dipping his handkerchief in the stream, André gently bathed the palms of each hand until the bleeding stopped. He then helped Julie to her feet. But when she rose, she stepped on the hem of her gown, lost her balance, and fell against him.

As she looked up, André suddenly kissed her. Holding her slim, young body in his arms, he kissed her with all the pent-up desire within him. Her lips were soft and sweet, and he felt a timid response. One hand went up to cradle her head and his fingers were entwined in her thick hair as he kissed her deeply. It was as though he couldn't get enough of her.

Then, just as suddenly, he stopped and looked at her for a long moment. "Oh, Julie, forgive me. I'm a married man and had no right to do such a thing. I love you so much I would never do anything to hurt you. Can you ever forgive me?" His voice was soft and pleading as he continued to hold her in his arms. His eyes searched her face and pleaded for forgiveness.

Julie kept staring at him. She had never before been kissed like that, and something strange had stirred within her. A feeling she'd never had before; and because it was strange and new, and overwhelming, it frightened her. She wanted to tell André that she loved him, that she could forgive him anything, but she couldn't find her voice. She could only stare at him.

Gently, André said, "Come, I'll take you home. Your hands are in no condition to handle *Minuit's* reins. Besides, I must tell your father what happened and offer my apologies."

Lifting her into the saddle, André took the reins of *Minuit* in one hand, swung himself into the saddle behind Julie, and slowly made his way to *Château Charlevoix*.

During the ride, neither of them spoke. André realized how much he loved Julie. For so long, he'd loved her as a sweet little girl. Now, he knew he loved her as a sweet young woman, and it filled him with pain.

Here, nestled in his arms, was his heart's desire, but he could never have her. He was married, married to a crazy woman. He lifted his eyes to heaven. *Oh, Mon Dieu, what am I to do? I love Julie so much, but everything is changed. I don't dare be alone with her. My desire for her is too great. I can't hurt her. I would never do anything to harm her. Oh, please, Mon Dieu, help me.*

André felt a sick panic fill his heart. Julie had looked at him in such a strange way. What was she thinking? What was she feeling? He longed to say something but was unsure. He longed to ask her if she hated him. Was she disgusted by him?

Oh, Julie, my precious one, don't hate me for loving you as I do, he silently prayed.

Julie nestled against André's chest, feeling his arms holding her close, wanted to tell him how much she still loved him but she was afraid to speak. He was married, married to that crazy woman, Gabrielle. They had a child; there was nothing anyone could do about it. It was a fact that wouldn't change. André told her he loved her many times. But this time, it was different. There had been such a look in his eyes. A look she'd never seen before.

When he kissed her, she felt so strange, so weak. Her knees turned to rubber, and her heart almost fell out of her chest, it beat so hard. His lips had been soft but demanding, and she wasn't sure what to do. Would he think her awful for letting him kiss her like that? Was he disgusted with her? What was he thinking, what was he feeling? On, how she longed to say something, but fear kept her quite.

When they reached *Château Charlevoix,* 'Toinette took Julie to her bedchamber to tend her cuts. Julie was unusually quiet. 'Toinette bathed her hands again, then applied a thick home made salve, and finally bandaged both hands. She watched Julie all the while she worked. But still the young girl said nothing.

'Toinette attributed Julie's silence to the fact that she was probably in shock from the attack by that crazy Madame de Javon.

All the slaves at *Château Charlevoix* knew about Gabrielle. Whenever slaves from the plantations came together for a holiday or special occasion, one of their favorite pastimes was swapping stories about their masters' family. The slaves at Royal Oaks loved André but hated Gabrielle; so whenever they told stories, it was never to hurt André. Instead, it was because they felt sorry for him being married to such a terrible woman.

As 'Toinette was leaving the room, she heard Julie say, "Toinette, please tell my father I will not be down for dinner."

Meanwhile, down in the main parlor, André was telling Monsieur Charlevoix what had happened with Gabrielle. It was obvious to the

273

older man that André was very upset and shaken by the incident.

"André, you can't blame yourself for your wife's behavior. It's obvious Gabrielle is very ill, and I know you feel somewhat responsible for what happened with her. It must be a terrible burden for you. As for my Julie, well, 'Toinette has wonderful remedies for everything; and I'm sure that, with her tender care, Julie will be as good as new in no time."

He invited André to stay and join him for dinner, but André insisted he must get home. So after being reassured by 'Toinette that Julie was resting and in no pain, he left.

* * *

Riding back to Royal Oaks, André felt shame. He was a coward! He had told Monsieur Charlevoix everything that had happened before and up to the time Gabrielle attacked Julie; but he'd said nothing about what happened after. He'd broken Jean-Claude's trust. And the man had always trusted him.

He'd hurt Julie, he'd seen it in her eyes. He'd ruined their friendship. He could no longer have her at Royal Oaks when Gabrielle was in New Orleans.

He could never meet her in the glade to talk and laugh and enjoy her company. He must keep his distance, and he would have to stay away from *Château Charlevoix*. How could he accept Jean-Claude's hospitality knowing he'd broken the man's trust?

* * *

In her room, Julie lay on her bed staring at the satin canopy and thinking of André. Closing her eyes, she could feel his arms around her, her body pressed against his muscular frame. She could smell the mixture of the fragrance he wore and the tobacco from the pipe he sometimes smoked. There was a wonderful masculine scent about him that she loved.

Now, it came rushing back to her. With her eyes closed, Julie could feel his lips pressed against hers; and once again, the strange feeling washed over her. She remembered his eyes and the look in them; an intense look, a look that seemed to burn right through her.

Julie, raised within the strict Créole culture and the strict moral code of her day, was as innocent as a child of three. She knew nothing of a man's love for a woman, the desires of the heart and body.

The only love she knew and understood was the love she received as a child. She had no idea what stirred the strange feelings within her, and there was no one to ask.

Had her mother been alive or had she an older sister, she might have asked some discreet questions, and perhaps she would have gained some insight into her feelings. But there was no one to talk to, no one to ask questions of.

Why did love have to hurt so? Why was love so painful? At first, her love for André made her happy but now, it only caused her terrible pain. Tears sprang to her eyes. *Oh, André, why didn't you wait for me to grow up*? Turning her face to her pillow, Julie wept bitter tears.

* * *

When finally André headed home, he wondered what he would find when he got there. What he found was a wife completely out of control and his home in shambles.

Gabrielle had been on a rampage since her return. She had stormed through the parlor throwing any object light enough to lift. Broken vases lay all over the floor, and a beautiful gilt-edged mirror was shattered. Even a small chair had been hurled across the room and broken, as was a small table.

The dining room was also a disaster, with broken dishes, shattered glassware, and silver scattered all about. She had terrorized the servants until all but Millie and Delilah had fled the house.

The sight of Gabrielle's destruction on the main floor so enraged André that he took the stairs two at a time. He looked into her bedchamber to find that room had also been destroyed. Millie crouched in a corner, holding a screaming, hysterical Frédéric in her arms, while she too cried and shook. Delilah was busy picking up the broken china and shattered glass so no one would be cut.

"Where is she?" André demanded.

Delilah motioned down the hall, and André could hear Gabrielle muttering as he approached his bedchamber.

When he reached the room, he stopped in horror. Gabrielle had his armoire open and was pulling out each item of clothing, ripping and cutting them to pieces with a large pair of scissors. There was quite a pile of what had once been his wardrobe.

As André stood in the doorway, Gabrielle looked up and suddenly hurled the scissors at his head. He ducked and heard the shears fly across the floor into the hall. Now Gabrielle grabbed another piece of clothing and started ripping it apart with her bare hands.

André crossed the room and grabbed her. She tried to fight him off, attempting to scratch his face and claw his eyes with her fingernails. Her own face was distorted and looked hideous. She was growling like some crazed animal.

"Gabrielle, what in God's name are you doing? Have you lost your mind? Have you gone crazy? What are you trying to do, destroy this house?" André tried as best he could to control her.

"*OUI, OUI*, I HATE THIS HOUSE! Do you hear me? I HATE THIS HOUSE. But most of all, I HATE YOU!" She was screaming and fighting. Her strength was unbelievable and her appearance frightening. Her hair was flying, her eyes were wild; she bared her teeth and tried to bite him. Strange animal-like sounds issued from her throat.

Looking at her, André knew she was truly insane. And her madness seemed to give her added strength. It took several minutes before he was able to get her under control. He knew there was no way she would listen; and finally, in desperation, he shook her and finally slapped her hard across the face.

Her screaming stopped she gave him a dazed look and suddenly went limp; she had passed out. André carried her back to her bedroom and laid her on the bed. Looking around, he realized the extent of damage she had done.

Quietly, he took Frédéric from Millie. "Millie, go and fetch the other servants to come and help Delilah clean up this room.

"I think Madame de Javon will sleep for a while, but we must get this mess cleared up before she wakes."

Millie ran off to get the others and André took Frédéric to the child's room. It took quite a while before he had Frédéric quieted down enough to sleep. When finally he left the boy, André went back to his own room to view what was left of his clothes.

Gabrielle had managed to destroy better than half of his wardrobe. He would have to go to New Orleans and order new clothes as soon as possible.

Next, he went down to the main floor to view the damage there more closely. He couldn't believe one person could wreck such havoc in such a short period of time.

The servants worked feverishly, but quietly, to clean up the bedchamber before their mistress awoke. When they had Gabrielle's room cleaned and back to some semblance of order, they returned to the main floor where they set about cleaning up the broken glass and china, trying to put the parlor and dining room back in order.

André sat in the parlor and silently watched them work. He felt as if he'd just lived through the worse nightmare of his entire life. His home was a wreck; there was so much that would have to be replaced. His clothes were destroyed. And his marriage, his marriage was a complete disaster. How long he sat there, he didn't know. But later, Delilah came and told him dinner was ready. The dining room had been straightened as much as possible. The broken glass and china had been removed. The silver had been collected, washed, and put away.

André had little appetite and only picked at his food. When he had eaten what he could, he left the house and went to the plantation office. He would try to get his mind off of what had been the worse day he could imagine. He'd work on his books and write in his diary; anything to keep his mind occupied. Tomorrow, he would try and decide what he should do about his wife, his sick, crazy wife. Something had to be done. But what?

André lost track of time. Then, suddenly, he was aware of a strange, red glow reflected on the office window and he heard the dreaded word "FIRE!"

"Fire! *Maître*, there be fire at da big house!" It was Samson calling André as he ran across the yard. Then he heard the overseer calling to him and the door of the office burst open.

"Monsieur de Javon, your house is on fire!" He turned and ran toward the house.

André leapt from behind the desk and rushed outside to find flames curling out from Gabrielle's bedroom window. As he raced toward the house, he yelled orders for the men to get buckets of water and form a human chain.

He saw Millie rush from the house carrying Frédéric, who was half-asleep and crying. More servants came rushing out behind her.

"Where are Delilah and Madame de Javon?" André shouted to anyone who could hear him.

Demetrius ran up to him. "*Maître*, Delilah, she be in da house. She tryin' to git da *maîtresse* to leave. Da smoke, it be bad! I go back and help."

The black man turned and ran back into the house with André and the overseer close on his heels.

The smoke was indeed bad. The entire upper floor was now engulfed in flames. André and the other men took the stairs two at a time.

Delilah was at the top of the stairs trying to beat back the flames with a small carpet. She was coughing and sneezing. Her eyes were swollen and tearing so badly she could hardly see.

"Where is Madame de Javon?" André shouted, as the smoke made him choke.

Delilah had difficulty speaking, the smoke was so thick and her throat was so dry. She pointed to Gabrielle's room.

"She *non* come out! Oh, Lawd, *Maître*, Ah tries to git her to come out, but she fight me bad, and she say *non*!"

André tried several times to reach Gabrielle, but the flames and the heat made it impossible; and finally all four had to flee the house. As they rushed outdoors, someone screamed, "Madame de Javon, it be her!"

André looked up to see Gabrielle falling from what had been her bedchamber. Her robe was on fire, and a hideous, piercing scream issued from her mouth as her body was hurled to the ground.

Delilah rushed to Gabrielle and started beating the flames out with the carpet. André rushed to her also, but there was no sign of life. Her body was badly burnt, as was her once beautiful face.

There was nothing to be done. Gently, André lifted the body of his dead wife and carried her to the nearest *garçonnière*. As he walked away, the entire upper floor collapsed and the flames shot up higher in the sky.

The slaves formed a human chain, each passing buckets of water to those who frantically tried to contain the fire. But they were no match for the inferno. André could only say a silent prayer and thank God there was not the slightest hint of a breeze. If the sparks didn't fly too far, perhaps he would lose only one building. Every time sparks flew, someone tried to douse them with water. André called some of the younger boys. "Take the horses and the other animals farther back near the swamp. We can't afford to lose any livestock and, least of all, the horses."

The fear of sparks setting a tree on fire also loomed. The giant oak trees, their branches dripping with Spanish moss, and the pecan trees that stood perilously close to the house had to be soaked with water continually.

André and his slaves worked the entire night and most of the next day. The men held the line with buckets passed from one to the other. The women and the bigger children each had a sack or some type of heavy cloth soaked with water, and they beat back the smaller flames that continually sprang up all around.

It was late the next day when the fire was finally contained. All that was left of André's beautiful home was a mass of smoldering ruins. André sent the slaves back to their cabins. All needed a much-deserved rest.

Some suffered from smoke inhalation and required care, and others suffered from minor burns. André saw to all of their needs before he could even begin to think about himself.

Someone took a horse and went to the city for Doctor la Poyntz. Later, as André stood alone at what had once been his home, he thought of Gabrielle's terrible death. Sinking to his knees, he began to cry.

He hadn't cried since he was a small boy and had been sent away from his parents, and his little sister died. Now, he felt that same devastating grief. He cried over the loss of his wife, his child, his home, and all of his dreams. His broad shoulders shook with the terrible sobs that racked his body.

How long he knelt there he never knew, but he became aware of someone standing next to him.

Jean-Claude Charlevoix had rushed over as soon as he'd heard through the grapevine that there was a fire at Royal Oaks. He'd brought most of his slaves with him; but in the confusion, André had been unaware of his friend's presence.

André felt a gentle hand on his shoulder and heard a soft voice say, "Come dear friend. Come and rest. I will take care of everything for you."

JULIE
1814-1817

Chapter 42

Gabrielle was buried in the family tomb at the Saint Louis Cemetery after a Mass held at the Saint Louis Cathedral.

The cathedral was packed with friends and relatives of the family and when the Mass and burial were over, many approached André and his family to offer their condolences.

"Dear Monsieur de Javon, how tragic to lose your wife and your home," one lady said. "But how merciful God was to spare your child."

André wondered if any of them knew Frédéric was not his son but the bastard child of Gabrielle and Gaston Bochet. He said nothing. He would not bring more pain and grief on her family.

Frédéric had no other parent now. His mother was dead, his father had sailed to France long before his birth, and André was the only parent the child would ever know.

* * *

When André first settled in Louisiana, he had been encouraged by Charles, Monsieur du Fray, and Monsieur Charlevoix to join the Louisiana Militia. His first involvement in the Militia came with the slave uprising in 1811. Now, it seemed the Militia might be needed again.

Several things had happened recently that would have a profound effect on the citizens of Louisiana and on the country as a whole.

In August, André learned, along with the other citizens of the city, that the British had burnt the nation's capital. Now, he heard of another incident that had taken place in early September.

Governor Claiborne, determined to put an end to Jean Lafitte's enterprise, had requested that the Secretary of the Navy order an attack on *Grande Terre* and wipe out Lafitte's stronghold.

However, a few days before the attack was to take place, a British ship sailed into Barataria Bay.

Lafitte, sitting on his gallery, watched as the ship came into view. When it entered the bay, it fired a shot at one of the sloops belonging to Lafitte. The shot aroused the population; and about two hundred of Lafitte's men rushed to the waters edge to see what was going on. Lafitte also hurried to the shore to watch as a small boat bearing the flag of Britain and a flag of truce row toward him.

When the boat reached land, two officers stepped ashore and introduced themselves. "I should like to speak to Mr. Jean Lafitte," said one. "Could someone please direct me to him?"

"I am Jean Lafitte," said the tall handsome, elegantly dressed man who stood before them.

The Baratarians were in an ugly mood at the invasion of the British on their soil.

"Hold them prisoners," one man shouted.

"Put them in irons," shouted another.

"Throw them in the dungeon," screamed another.

The men were in a murderous mood. But Lafitte calmed them by saying, "The British have come under a flag of truce, and I would at least hear what they have to say." He then turned to the British officers. "I would like you to come to my home where we can discuss the nature of your business."

"They are spies; nothing but spying dogs! We should hold them prisoners and take them to New Orleans," cried the men.

Lafitte stood and glared at the crowd, then said in a stern voice, "I shall talk to them first and find out what has brought them here. You men stand guard. Make sure no others try to come ashore."

That said, he turned and led the two officers to his home.

It didn't take long for Lafitte to learn the reason for the visit. He was handed a document that showed the British were ready to encourage the Creek Indian Nation to rise up against the city. They also hoped to incite a slave uprising.

When Lafitte was finished reading, one of the officers said, "Mr. Lafitte, the British government is ready to offer you thirty thousand dollars in gold and the rank of Captain in the British Navy if you and your men will join us in the attack on New Orleans."

Lafitte waited a long moment before speaking, then said, "You saw how angry my men were toward you. You will have to give me time to speak to them. I must see if I can persuade them to accept your offer." Lafitte then invited the two officers to join him in dinner and later to spend the night as his guests.

When the two men returned to their ship the next morning, they still had no idea if Lafitte would accept their offer or not.

As soon as the two left, Lafitte drafted a letter to Governor Claiborne telling him of the British offer to him and their plan to capture New Orleans.

When Governor Claiborne received the letter, he called a meeting with the legislature and other high-ranking officers: Commodore Daniel Patterson of the United States Navy Colonel George Ross, commanding officer of the 44th Untied States infantry; and Major General Jacques de Villers, commander of the Louisiana Militia.

Also, in attendance were Jean-Claude Charlevoix, Monsieur du Fray, and Monsieur St. Claire, all of whom held the rank of Colonel in the Militia.

Once the Governor read the letter, he had only two questions.

"Do you gentlemen think the man is telling the truth? And would it be proper for the Governor of Louisiana to have any dealings with the pirate, Jean Lafitte?"

There was much discussion; but, in the end, the majority felt that Lafitte was lying. Only four, Major General de Villers, and Colonels du Fray, St. Claire, and Charlevoix came to Lafitte's defense to no avail.

Before the assembly left, Claiborne said, "As you gentlemen know, I sent a letter to the Secretary of the Navy to destroy Lafitte's stronghold. Even now a ship, the Carolina, is nearing the designated spot."

Within three days of the Governor's statement, the ship reached *Grande Terre*. Lafitte had already started to move his arms and ammunition to a farther island where they would be safe in case of a British attack. He was not at *Grande Terre* when the attack took place.

The Carolina succeeded in sacking *Grande Terre*, but they took few prisoners. Only Dominique You and eighty others were captured and taken to the *calaboose*.

When word reached Lafitte that his home had been destroyed, along with much of the village, instead of seeking revenge, he immediately made his way to New Orleans where he met personally with the Governor and tried to convince Claiborne that he had been telling the truth.

"I cannot imagine why you chose to attack *Grande Terre*," he said in an icy voice. "But all of that aside, you must realize the danger the British pose."

After listening to him, the Governor said, "I appreciate your offer, Mister Lafitte. However, the Army and Navy are dead set against help from you or your men. Also, as you well know, public opinion has turned against you in some areas." He looked at Lafitte for a long moment and said, "However I'll turn the matter over to General Andrew Jackson. He is in Mobile at the present, so I'll send him your offer. He will be in New Orleans shortly."

Lafitte bowed and started to leave, only to stop and remind the Governor, "My men and I are the only ones who really know the maze of waterways through the swamps and bayous. We could be very helpful in the event of a British attack, which now seems imminent."

It wasn't long before an answer came from the General, and the answer was a resounding, "NO! I'll have no hellish pirates joining forces with my men!"

A lesser man might have been discouraged with this news, but not Lafitte, who knew better than most the situation facing the city. He felt certain that once Jackson was made aware of the danger, his offer would be accepted.

Chapter 43

André learned much of this from Monsieur Charlevoix when he reached the city. He knew he would be called should the Militia have need of him. But, until then, he went about putting his life back in order. He tried not to think of the past four years with Gabrielle. Much of it seemed like a terrible nightmare, and emotionally he was drained. If he could keep busy, fill his mind with other things, he would be better off.

He spent much time with his tailor getting fitted for an entire new wardrobe. Frédéric also needed a complete wardrobe, as every stitch of the child's clothing had been lost in the fire.

What to do with Frédéric became his next problem; and Andre voiced his concern to Charles and Francesca. "I don't know how I can keep him with me until I get my life back to some semblance of order," he said one evening when he was visiting them.

"Charles and I have discussed your problem and we are more than willing to keep him with us until you feel able to care for him yourself."

There was deep relief in André's face as he smiled.

"*Merci*, Francesca, that is very kind of you. I appreciate your offer and will be happy to accept. I'll bring Frédéric over first thing in the morning. I'll also bring Millie with him. Frédéric likes Millie, and she will be a great help to you both."

Next, André met with the architect. "I want this home larger and even more beautiful than the first," he said when he and the architect poured over the plans.

He also got busy ordering all that would be needed to furnish his new home. It was a tremendous output of money; and André could only thank God he had the foresight to make wise investments, and his crops had been successful also.

When finally, in October, he returned to Royal Oaks, the pile of ruins that had once been his home was being carted away by some of the slaves.

"We had to wait until this mess stopped smoldering," the overseer said.

André nodded. "I understand." He wandered through the ruins. There was not one trace of the beautiful things that had once graced his home. As he shuffled through the ugly mess, his foot suddenly unearthed something that looked familiar. Clearing away the rubble, he saw the cover of his Bible. It was the one his mother had given him when he was sent away from her. He'd held on to it all these years and read from it every morning.

Standing amid the ruins, he let the book fall open to the Book of Job, one of his favorites. He stood for a long time reading. When he was finished, he closed his eyes and said a silent prayer, thanking God for His many blessings in spite of all that had happened. Then, tucking the Bible in his pocket, he mounted his horse and headed for the sugar factory, which was going full blast.

One *garçonnière* had been badly damaged, its roof partly burnt and the side nearest to the main house burnt. But it could easily be repaired at no great cost.

A large pecan tree that stood near the house had also been damaged; and it was to be chopped down for fear of its falling at a later date. André mourned the loss of the beautiful tree, as it had afforded a nice shade to that portion of the house.

"*Michie* André, where you gonna stay while you heah Royal Oaks?" Delilah asked when she saw him.

"I'll move into the *garçonnière* that hasn't been damaged. It is small, but it has all the comforts of the big house."

In a short while, André returned to New Orleans. He'd received a letter from Henry Shreve telling him that the new steamboat was finished and ready to sail down the river to the city.

Our steamboat is named the ENTERPRISE, Shreve wrote. *It is much larger than our first boat. I am looking forward to seeing both you and Monsieur Charlevoix in the near future. I have sent a similar letter to Monsieur informing him of my plans.*

André spent time with his in-laws and Frédéric. The child was almost two years old, small for his age, and still nervous and sickly. "How is Frédéric doing?" he asked, when the little boy had been put to bed.

Charles and Francesca looked at each other for a moment then Charles said, "We would be less than honest if we didn't say that Frédéric is a trial. He is given to terrible tamper tantrums and spends a lot of time in tears."

"Nothing we do seems to please him," Francesca added. "But we try to be patient with him. I'm certain the fire and all he went through has something to do with his behavior."

"I'm sorry he is causing you so much trouble," André said. "But the truth is that he was like that long before the fire. I'll take him back with me if you prefer. I wouldn't blame you if you agree."

"*Non*, André, that is not necessary," Francesca assured him. "You have enough to deal with right now. We will keep him and gladly until you are better able to care for him."

Frédéric did seem like such an unhappy little boy that André's heart went out to him. "I shall try to spend more time with him while I'm here in the city. I'll take him for a carriage ride tomorrow, and buy him a toy and a treat."

And André did just as he had said, although, it didn't seem to make much difference. It appeared that nothing anyone did pleased Frédéric. And this caused André to remember how difficult Gabrielle had always been. He wondered if he would have to deal with this problem while raising her son.

When he was alone at night, his thoughts always turned to Julie. He loved her and wondered if she ever thought of him, and if she did, what her thoughts were. Thinking of her caused him such pain that he tried to put her completely out of his mind, with little success.

No sooner had André begun to get a semblance of order back into his life than something else happened that totally disrupted it again.

The British were getting ready to attack New Orleans.

* * *

New Orleans was in a great state of unrest, and André could feel the tension all around him when he was in the city. Many were aware of the British plan, and a feeling of panic had seized the citizens. Governor Claiborne was in constant communication with General Andrew Jackson, who was at present in Mobile, Alabama. The general had recently won a hard-fought battle against the hostile Creek Indians on the Florida front. Now, he was in Mobile to keep the British from attacking that part of the country.

Frustrated and ill, his body reduced to skin and bone and wracked with dysentery, General Jackson was dismayed. He had written Washington in August requesting more troops and supplies. But, just then, the British burnt the nation's capital, and the government officials all fled the city. Jackson received no answer to his request.

The British not only burnt Washington but also raided the Chesapeake, sent ships to the West Indies to collect black troops, and also established a beachhead at Pensacola.

Now, the General received a dispatch from Governor Claiborne informing him of the British offer to Lafitte, and telling him that the city was in peril.

This news only served to throw Jackson into a fit of more frustration. There were problems from all directions. Everyone needed his help, but he didn't have enough men to help anyone much.

Finally, on December the third, General Jackson arrived in New Orleans. All the dignitaries of the city, along with a large crowd of the citizens, greeted him.

The General was taken to a building and led out to the second floor *galerie* so he could address the people. As the crowd stood in the street, a light rain began to fall. The rain did nothing to dampen the spirits of the people nor did it drive them away. It did, however, give them all a good laugh as they heard the Mayor of the city said, *"Mon_ Général*, the sun is never shining more brightly than when you are among us."

The sun was nowhere in sight, and even "Old Hickory," as Jackson was called, had a twinkle in his eye and his stern face creased with a smile.

When word of the General's arrival reached the citizens, André like most of the men of New Orleans, donned the brand new uniform he'd received from his tailor. He held the rank of Major, as did Charles.

Now, as the General stood on the *galerie,* the troops who would help defend the city paraded before him. And what a colorful sight they were.

Clad in gorgeous uniforms, many of them copied from units of Emperor Napoleon's army, they dazzled the eye.

Plumes of emerald green, bright yellow, royal blue, and scarlet waved in the breeze. In uniforms covered in brilliant gold braid and flashes of brass mounted on saber tacks, the New Orleans elite of the Battalion marched pass the reviewing stand. There were the Carabibiers d'Orleans, the Francs, the Dragon a'Pied, the Chasseurs, and the Louisiana Blues.

The crowd cheered, women and girls waved their handkerchiefs and blew kisses, and the few men who were not a part of the marchers tipped their hats, clapped, and whistled.

Julie had come with Madame Gauthier and her daughters, and she stood with the rest of the crowd to watch her father and André march by. She felt such a burst of pride when she saw how handsome both men looked in their uniforms.

It was a good show but when it was over and General Jackson met with those in command, he was terribly upset to learn how ill prepared the city was to defend itself. The forces immediately available consisted of fewer than one thousand United States Regulars and about two thousand Louisiana Militia. The British were reported to have at least ten thousand seasoned veterans.

"How many ships have we to defend ourselves?" Jackson asked.

"There are only two naval vessels in this military district," answered Commandant John Hendly. "There's the USS CAROLINA, a small converted merchantman with fourteen guns, and then there is the USS LOUSIANA, a vessel rigged and armed with sixteen twenty-four-pound guns."

Jackson glared at the officers assembled and paced the room, his thick brows drawn together in a scowl. "How the devil am I supposed to defend this city with such an armada? I've sent word to Major General William Carroll's Brigade of Tennessee Volunteers and also to Major General Thomas's Kentucky Militia to come and help us. But I've had no word from either of them. God only knows where they are right now."

Once again, Jackson was reminded of how important Jean Lafitte and his men would be in any fight against the British, and once again, he refused to consider such a move.

Chapter 44

"There is only one man who can convince *Général* Jackson to use Jean Lafitte and his men in our fight against the British," said Monsieur Charlevoix as he and André sat in the older man's parlor. "And that is Jean Lafitte himself."

"But how can he do it? From what you tell me, the *Général* refuses to even consider talking to the man."

"Lafitte is here in the city today. He is keeping a low profile until tonight when he plans to slip out and go see Jackson."

"Do you think he will have any success in seeing the *Général*?" André asked.

"If I know Jean Lafitte, he will not only speak to Jackson, he will convince the man that his help is needed. *Général* Jackson is a stubborn man. But once Lafitte explains to him how necessary he and his men will be, I don't see how the *Général* can refuse. God help us if he does."

* * *

Later that evening while General Jackson was resting, there was a knock on the door. A young sentry entered and saluted. "Excuse me, General Jackson, sir, but there is a man outside who demands to see you at once."

Jackson's long, lean body was stretched out on a sofa, his eyes closed; but at the sound of the young man's voice, the General opened his eyes and turned his head slowly.

"Who is this man who demands to see me at once?"

"I have no idea, sir. He refuses to give his name. But he insists that the very defense of the city depends on your willingness to speak to him."

Jackson slowly started to rise from the sofa. "Well then, tell him to come in."

The General was standing by his desk as the sentry opened the door to admit the stranger.

A tall, well-dressed man wearing an expensive cloak entered. Jackson saw the man's boots were made of the finest leather, his clothes well cut, and he carried himself with an air of authority.

The man stepped farther into the room, bowed, and said, "*Bonjour*, Monsieur *Général* Jackson, I am Jean Lafitte."

Jackson continued to stare at his visitor. So this was Jean Lafitte, the famous pirate whom he'd heard so much about. But the man was not at all what the General expected. Not waiting for Jackson to speak, Lafitte continued, "Monsieur *Général*, before you throw me out, I wish you would listen to what I have to say."

The General gestured for Lafitte to take a chair, while he himself sat in one behind his desk. "Very well, Mr. Lafitte. Now that you are here, I suppose I could at least listen to what you have to say."

It didn't take Lafitte long to convince Jackson to take him up on his offer to help fight the British.

"No one else knows the waterways of the swamps and bayous like my men and I. You could be at a great disadvantage if you didn't make use of our knowledge."

Jackson listened intently to all Lafitte said, never taking his eyes from his visitor's face. Finally, he said, "Mr. Lafitte, you certainly seem sincere. But, tell me, why are you willing to do this for the United States? After all, you are considered an outlaw; there is a price on your head. Why your own brother has been in jail, and as you say, the Americans attacked and destroyed your headquarters and your ships at *Grande Terre*. So why are you now offering yourself and your men for this fight?"

Lafitte leaned back and seemed to relax a bit. "Monsieur *Général*, I love my adopted country. I hate the British. Too many lives were lost just a few years ago in the fight for independence to let the British come back now and try to reclaim this country." He paused; but when Jackson said nothing, he continued. "I also lived through the French Revolution and the Reign of Terror. So, believe me, I appreciate what this country stands for. And I speak for my men also. I can assure you there is not a one of them who would not lay down his life for the Untied States."

Jackson called for some wine. When the sentry returned with the beverage, Lafitte continued. "Now if you will accept my offer, there is only one thing I ask in return."

"And that is?"

"I ask that all charges against myself and my men be dropped, that a full pardon be granted to each of us, and that each of us be granted full American citizenship."

Once that was agreed upon, Lafitte spent the next two hours apprising the General of how best to handle the fight that lay ahead.

General Jackson was quite impressed with Lafitte's knowledge of warfare and realized that he had made an excellent bargain with the man. He was also impressed with the amount of weaponry Lafitte had at his disposal.

At about that same time, Henry Shreve sailed into the port of New Orleans on the steamboat, the ENTERPRISE. General Jackson immediately commandeered the boat for military duty. But even before the General made his move, Edward Livingston, on behalf of his brother Robert and Robert Fulton, attached the ENTERPRISE. Shreve posted bail at once so that the steamboat couldn't be held, then turned her over to Jackson. The General had guns mounted on her decks and ordered the steamboat to patrol the river on lookout for the British ships. Jackson then departed, leaving Henry Shreve in command.

Later, Jackson rode his giant of a horse out to Fort St. Charles where he had ordered all the units to meet. He sat on the great mount and watched his troops march by on their way to where the British were camped. And what a strange army he had! As he watched, he shook his head.

There were the French-speaking Créoles, the English-speaking Americans, the Germans from the coast, the Irish from the Irish Channel, and the strange mountain men of Kentucky and Tennessee. Marching also were the "free men of color" and the men of color under the command of Major D'Aquin, and a few stray Choctaw Indians also in their full war regalia under the command of Pierre Jugeat, who was himself the son of a Créole father and a half-breed Choctaw mother.

The sun-bronzed Acadians from the bayous and backcountry came next and the small handful of regular military men who were the only seasoned fighters.

Some of the marchers wore clothes too fine for fighting, others wore uniforms far too fancy for war. Still others wore rags, and some wore the uniform of the United States Army.

The young Créole aristocrats were excellent at dueling; but one had to wonder what they were doing here. There were the rough mountain men who knew how to fight and brawl and kill, and who could pick a bird out of a tree with one shot and not disturb a single leaf, but who had no knowledge of organized warfare. And, of course, there were the Indians who carried their tomahawks and arrows. However, few had rifles. How would they fare in this battle?

As diverse as Jackson's troops were, they all marched with great pride. For the first time, they were all united, all Americans, and all had one purpose in mind To defend their beautiful city and countryside, and defeat the British!

Lafitte and his men were also a part of this strange group. The buccaneers felt even greater pride because all charges against them had been dropped, each had been given a full pardon, and all were now citizens of the United States.

The Americans fought in any way they could hiding behind trees and bushes and suddenly jumping out and striking, only to disappear in the night, then striking out again from another area.

The British found this battle unlike any they had ever encountered. They fought in the European custom of the day marching forward in formation, beating drums, and carrying flags, their brilliant red coats easy targets.

December twenty-eighth found the enemy in full attack. General Jackson rode his horse among the men, slapping them on the back and giving them words of encouragement, all the while dodging bullets and barking commands. Suddenly, a man rode up to inform the General that the State Legislature was ready to give up and surrender the city to the enemy.

"The Governor wants to know what to do about it?"

Jackson sat silent for a moment. "I doubt that the city is ready to surrender to the British," he replied.

"But, General, the Governor wants to know what to do in the event the legislature tries to surrender," the man insisted.

Jackson was tired, sick, and exasperated, and finally yelled, "I still can't believe those people want to surrender the city to the British. However, if they should persist with such an outrageous idea, then BLOW THEM ALL UP!"

It was an exhausting fight, one that many thought could not be won. But, much to the surprise of everyone, especially the British, the Americans were successful.

Jean Lafitte had a great deal to do with their success; and the steamboat the ENTERPRISE made short order of the British fleet and returned to the city in triumph.

Chapter **45**

The Americans were wild with the flush of victory. They had beaten the mighty British who had ten times the men, ships, and ammunition.

When word reached New Orleans, the city also went wild with jubilation. The women and children set about decorating the *galeries* of their homes that overlooked the street. They hung flags and tied ribbons with beautiful flowers to the lacy railings. Then they eagerly awaited the return of their men.

As soon as she heard, Madame Gauthier rushed to tell her daughters and Julie. "Ah, *ma chères*, I have wonderful news. Armand and Emile are alive, and the British have been beaten! We won, we won the battle!"

When the news penetrated Julie's mind, she let out a squeal. Then laughing, singing, and dancing, she grabbed Marie-Annette's hands, and together they danced around the room. Marie-Annette's little sister, Adele, joined in and Madame Gauthier also as they danced in a circle.

They were upstairs. But Julie dropped Marie-Annette's hand, grabbed Madame's hand, and started down the stairs. The servants who had heard the news came running, and Julie had them all join in the chain. Together, white and black, mistress and servants weaved their way throughout the house still laughing and singing until Madame Gauthier finally collapsed on the sofa in the parlor, now completely out of breath. Julie and her friends fell in a heap on the floor, laughing and gasping for breath.

The next day, a great victory parade was planned for the returning heroes.

The morning of the parade was filled with excitement at Madame Gauthier's house, as all four prepared for the event. Julie could hardly eat breakfast she was so excited.

When they reached the *Place d'Armes*, everyone breathed a sigh of relief that the rain had stopped. And although the day was cold and brisk, the sun, as if it too was sharing in the fun and festivities, shone brightly.

The committee to welcome the General and his army had built an *Arc de Triomphe* in the middle of the *Place d'Armes*. On either side of the arch stood eighteen pillars, nine on each side. Each pillar represented a different State and in front of each pillar stood a small girl dressed in white, carrying a basket of flowers.

The doors of the Saint Louis Cathedral had been thrown open and Father Dubourg would say a special mass later in the day.

The excitement and noise died down as the crowd waited for the first sound of the approaching horses and men. Then, slowly, the sound of horses' hoofs and men marching could be heard in the distance. And a soft murmur ran through the crowd.

"Listen, I hear them coming."

Then the murmur grew louder. "*Oui*, I hear them also."

"I can see them—yes, here they come!"

"Look, there is *Général* Jackson. Does he not look proud and oh so grand?"

The band struck up a lively tune, and the crowd grew louder as people cheered, clapped, and whistled.

General Jackson, riding his great horse, led the parade and he certainly did look proud and grand. His bone-thin body sat ramrod in the saddle, he held his head high, and there was the slightest hint of a smile on his stern face.

Directly behind the General at the head of the parade rode Jean and Pierre Lafitte. Next came Major General de Villere and his Louisiana Militia. And amongst the Militia rode André, Monsieur Charlevoix, and other members of the Créole society.

Julie, along with everyone else, stood and watched as the men passed in review. Tears stung her eyes when at last she saw her father and

André, both so handsome and so proud as they passed her. Her heart swelled with pride and gratitude that the two most important men in her life were home safe and sound.

* * *

Two nights later, the city held a victory ball. It was the biggest ball New Orleans had ever seen. Everyone who was anyone was invited. The ladies whose families belonged to the French Exchange spent hours working their magic. On the ground floor where the dinner would be served, long dining tables were beautifully decorated. Clusters of jewel ornaments and a crystal bowl filled with flowers native to the State sat on each table. The magnificent, brilliant crystal chandeliers with their thousands of candles gleamed down on the guests.

The *crème de la crème* of New Orleans society were all gathered together that night. General Jackson was all decked out in a magnificent dress uniform. Jean and Pierre Lafitte, along with Dominique You, were also in attendance. The three men looked dashing in their evening clothes and looking at them, it was difficult to believe that they were pirates.

Many people had already arrived as Julie entered the building on her father's arm. The two could see General Jackson standing on one side of the room surrounded by admirers.

"We must pay our respects to the *Général*," Monsieur Charlevoix said, as slowly he and Julie made their way to where Jackson was standing, pausing to greet friends along the way.

When finally they reached him, Julie found herself being introduced to one of the most polished gentlemen she had ever met.

As everyone else, she had heard stories of Jackson's short patience and quick temper, of his tendency for swearing at the top of his lungs when frustrated. She'd heard how he drove himself and his men to utter exhaustion and demanded more than most. Her father had also told her that the General was highly respected and loved by the men he commanded, because he never asked more of them than he did of himself. Now, she only saw a charming, soft-spoken gentleman.

General Jackson bowed to Julie, took her hand, kissed it, smiled, and said, "I am honored to meet such a beautiful young lady. And I might add that I was mighty proud to have your father serve with me during the battle. He was an excellent soldier."

Julie's heart swelled with pride upon hearing this. She returned the General's smile and said, "*Merci, Général*, you are most kind." After a few more words with Jackson, she and her father moved on so others might have the same privilege of speaking to the man.

Just then, Julie spotted André and Charles. They were standing with some other men, and Julie realized that Charles' family was not with him. Gabrielle's death had been too recent. Francesca, her parents, and in-laws could not be at the ball however, it was decided that Charles and André should attend out of respect for General Jackson.

Julie looked exquisite. She was dressed in a gown of silvery blue lampas, the bodice encrusted with tiny diamonds. She was the most beautiful girl in the room. The gown showed off her slender figure, and the diamonds around her neck and in her hair enhanced her beauty.

At the same moment that Julie saw André, he saw her. Their eyes locked and neither could look away. But before they had a chance to greet each other, dinner was announced; and Julie and her father were ushered to a table near the General's. She lost sight of André in the maze of people who were also being directed to their places.

The meal was delicious, and many toasts were made. When finally the dinner ended, everyone adjourned to the upper floor that had been transformed into a replica of a Parisian ballroom.

André watched as young Armand Gauthier asked Julie to dance. The music had started and several couples were already on the dance floor. Julie accepted, and André could only stand and watch Armand whirl her around.

Monsieur Charlevoix, seeing Charles and André, walked over to them. After greeting both men, he said, "Well, André, I imagine you are happy to have this war over. Now you can continue getting your life back to normal."

André smiled. "*Oui*, Monsieur Charlevoix." He found it difficult to concentrate on what was being said. His thoughts and his eyes were on Julie. He knew that tonight he could not ask her to dance. A man whose wife had recently died would not only make himself look bad but would also insult a lady should he do such a thing.

When the music stopped, Armand led Julie to where her father and the others stood.

Charles bowed and kissed her hand. "Julie, you are indeed the most beautiful young lady present."

When André smiled at her, Julie saw the look of love and tenderness in his eyes. Then he became stiff and formal. It would not do to let his true feelings show at the moment. He was supposed to be in mourning for his wife.

André saw the hurt and pain in her eyes and on her face with his change of attitude. He wanted more than anything to tell her how he truly felt and why he was acting this way, but knew he couldn't.

He had only seen Julie a few times since the day in the glade when Gabrielle attacked her; and each time, he'd been cool and withdrawn toward her. Not being certain how she felt since that day, he was apt to withhold his true feelings. He wanted so much to tell her how much he loved her, that he had never meant to hurt her but the opportunity never presented itself.

Giving André an icy look, Julie decided to act as if she didn't care one bit if he chose to treat her in such a manner. She would flirt and dance with every available gentleman who asked her.

Jean Lafitte was strolling about the huge ballroom, stopping to speak to the people who rushed up to him with praise for his help in winning the war. When finally he reached the three men and Julie, he stopped to speak to them. He had visited *Château Charlevoix* in the past but had seldom seen Julie. Now, as the buccaneer was introduced to her, there was a look of admiration and appreciation in his eyes when he bowed and kissed her hand.

"*Enchanté*, Mademoiselle Charlevoix. *Comment allez-vous?*"

"*Tres bien, merci*, Monsieur Lafitte," Julie said, giving the tall, handsome man her most brilliant smile.

Once again, the music began, and Lafitte turned to Julie. "Mademoiselle, may I have the pleasure of dancing with you?"

With a quick glance at André, Julie gave Lafitte another dazzling smile. "I would be delighted to dance with you, Monsieur Lafitte."

When Lafitte swept her into his arms, he said softly, "I have traveled over much of the world before coming to New Orleans. And I have seen many beautiful sights, but never have I seen any thing as exquisite as you, *ma chère*."

Julie looked up at him through her long lashes and said, "I have heard that you are a buccaneer, perhaps even a pirate but I had no idea you were also a poet, Monsieur Lafitte."

"Your beauty would inspire even the most inept man to poetry, Mademoiselle." Jean Lafitte's eyes swept over Julie's face with such intensity, it made her heart skip a beat.

Out of the corner of her eye, Julie saw André watching her. And he didn't look all too happy.

André wasn't the least bit happy. He watched as Lafitte bent his head to say something to Julie, and felt envy when the man threw back his head and laughed at whatever she had said in return. And, knowing Julie's quick wit and funny sense of humor, it was probably something clever and amusing.

As the evening wore on, André grew quieter. He was filled with frustration. He knew he could do nothing; but oh how he longed to hold Julie in his arms and dance her around the room.

Suddenly, Charles came up and put a hand on André's shoulder. "I think it's time I left—how about you?"

André looked over at his friend. "I'm not quite ready to leave. I think I'll stay a little longer. After all, I really have nothing to go home to."

Charles nodded. "I understand. I'll see you later this week."

The ball lasted until the wee hours of the morning. André knew he should have left when Charles did, but he couldn't. Instead, he found a quiet corner where he had an excellent view of the room. Here, he could watch Julie.

* * *

The city went back to normal. Henry Shreve left for the north. He was still unable to break the monopoly but assured André and Jean-Claude that he would never give up. "I'll break that monopoly if it takes the rest of my life!" he said as he boarded the steamboat. He also told the two that he was dissolving his partnership with Daniel French. "I'll be relocating to Virginia. I'll let you know how you may reach me as soon as I get settled."

* * *

By the end of April, André returned to Royal Oaks and one day Monsieur Charlevoix came to call. André was delighted to see him and invited the older gentleman to join him for dinner.

When the meal was over and the two were relaxing with a glass of wine, Monsieur Charlevoix said, "I shall be leaving for Virginia in a week. I am going to a friend's plantation to look at some horses." He took a sip of wine and added, "I shall also visit Monsieur Shreve. I want to see his plans for the new steamboat he wrote us about. And while I am gone, Julie will be staying with Madame Gauthier and her family."

That last remark caused André's heart to tighten. The thought of Julie always made him feel pain. He loved her so much. Clearing his throat, he said, "Speaking of Julie, now that she has made her debut and is the belle of New Orleans, I imagine you will have a lot of men asking for her hand in marriage."

Monsieur Charlevoix chuckled. "André, several men have already asked for her hand."

"And what did you say?"

"I told each of them to ask Julie. If she said, '*Oui*,' they would have my blessing."

The pain in André's heart increased. "What did she say? Did she accept any of the offers?"

"*Non*, she did not. André, Julie will not marry someone she does not love."

"Do you think she would accept a proposal from me? I've been married, and I have a child, and I am much older than she."

"Of course, she will. André, Julie has been in love with you most of her life. I know this not by anything she ever said, but by the way she always looked at you." He paused, and added, "besides, I know my daughter well. When your year of mourning is over, if you don't ask her, not only will Julie be heart-broken, but I too will be terribly disappointed."

"But does she still love me?" André asked. "Lately, she has become so cool and distant toward me when we meet."

Monsieur Charlevoix smiled. "Strange, she says the same thing about you. How cool and withdrawn you have become toward her. She thinks you might not love her anymore."

"But, Monsieur, I *do* love her with all of my heart. My life without Julie would be unbearable."

"Then I suggest you tell her so. There is nothing so tragic as a foolish misunderstanding that drives apart two people who are deeply in love."

André felt as if a huge weight had been lifted from his shoulders. "*Merci*, Monsieur, you have no idea how much I appreciate your telling me this."

From that moment on, André felt like a new man. Julie still loved him and she would marry him when he asked her. The only problem was he would have to wait until the period of mourning was over; and this thought threw him into a black mood. To have to mourn for a wife he had stopped loving long ago, who had turned his life into a living hell. But, if that is what he had to do in order to win Julie's hand, then he would. The end results would be worth it.

Chapter 46

In mid July, a case of yellow fever broke out in the city. It had been an unusually rainy fall and spring, and the gutters and streets were filled with water.

When the rains stopped, there was no place for the water to go so it sat in the gutters and turned stagnant. There was a slimy green scum on the surface, made worse by garbage, human waste, and dead animals that also collected.

This caused some concern and complaints from a few doctors and citizens who were worried about the health of the city. However, nothing was done to alleviate the problem.

Early in July, the temperature had zoomed upward along with the humidity, and the mosquitoes came out by the thousands, hovering over the stagnant waters and attacking the humans who inhabited the city.

Since yellow fever was a common occurrence during the summer months, those who could, escaped to the country. Every year, there were at least a half dozen cases, but the Créoles felt they were immune to the fever. Only the Americans and newcomers fell under the scourge of *"Bronze Jean."* It had been quite a while since there had been a serious outbreak so no one paid much attention to the problem.

The first to come down with the fever this year was a sailor whose ship had just dropped anchor in port. The sailor was staying at a cheap flophouse on *Rue Tchoupitoulas*; and when he died, someone threw his body in the river. No report was made to the authorities.

Two days later, three more sailors died from the fever. Still, no notice was taken. Slowly, at first, word got out that several people down by the levee had caught the fever and died. Still, nothing was done.

The Créoles didn't like to admit that yellow fever was a threat. It was bad for business and would drive people away. Then someone on *Rue St. Philip* died. The fever was moving into the better part of the city. Now, people were becoming frightened.

"*Mon Dieu*, it's *Bronze Jean;* he's come to kill us!"

More deaths occurred, and real panic set in.

Out at Royal Oaks, it was one week before word reached André that *Bronze Jean* had, indeed, attacked the city in earnest. And the death toll was rising.

When André heard the news, his first thought was of Julie. She was still in the city with Madame Gauthier! She could be struck with the fever!

He called his overseer, Samson, and his house servants. "The fever has hit the city. The death toll is rising, and I must go and fetch Mademoiselle Julie and Madame Gauthier and her family." He turned to Delilah. "I want you to get my *garçonnière* ready. I'll put Madame Gauthier, her daughters, and Mademoiselle Julie there. Then I want you to get the other *garconnière* ready for Madame's sons. They'll stay with me."

To his overseer and foreman, André said, "I trust you two to carry on while I'm gone, just as you have in the past."

Demetrius was willing to drive him to the city but André said, "I'll take the carriage myself. No sense in exposing you. I certainly wouldn't want any of you to catch the fever."

Reaching New Orleans, André found the city in a state of panic. People, using any means to escape, clogged the streets. Some were walking, others riding on anything available. No one knew how to combat the dreaded disease; but it was believed that if cannons were fired, they would clear the air. It was also believed that setting barrels of tar on fire helped.

As André rode through the streets, he thought it looked more like the British were attacking. Cannons boomed throughout the city and the noise was deafening. Barrels of tar blazed on every street corner, and the smoke and smell made one's eyes and nose water and burn.

'Toinette answered the door when André reached Madame Gauthier's home. "Oh, 'Toinette, thank God, you're here and well. I've come to take you, Julie, Madame Gauthier, and her family back to Royal Oaks."

'Toinette looked down and sadly shook her head.

"*Mon Dieu*, 'Toinette what's wrong? Don't tell me Julie has come down with the fever, or died!" André's eyes and voice were filled with panic.

"Oh, *Michie* de Javon, thank heaven you come. Mam'selle Julie, she be well. But Madame Gauthier's *petite* daughter, Adele, she die three days ago. Now Madame, her two sons, and Mam'selle Marie-Annette, they all got da fever."

'Toinette dabbed at her eyes before continuing. "Mam'selle Julie, she be carin' fo' them. *Michie* de Javon, my *petite maîtresse* be wore out, she need rest. Ah fear she catch da fever too."

"Where is Julie now?"

"She be in da back parlor. Ah made her lie down and rest. She too tired fo' her own good."

"And Madame's servants' are any of them ill with the fever? Are there any to care for Madame and her family?"

'Toinette wiped her eyes again. "Da servants, they all be well. Madame's maid, Pauline, she been helpin' Mam'selle Julie and me to care fo' da others."

André paced the floor and thought for a moment. "Toinette, I want you to send Pauline to me; then I want you to go and pack Julie's trunk. I can't let her stay here and fall ill. I'm taking you both to Royal Oaks. Now hurry."

When Pauline entered the parlor, André inquired as to her mistress's condition.

"She be very sick, *Michie* de Javon she don't know no one. She be out of her head with high fever, *oui.*"

When André heard this and also learned that her sons and daughter were no better, he knew it was imperative to get Julie out as quickly as possible.

Pauline nodded when he explained this to her and assured him she and the other servants could care for the family.

'Toinette appeared at the head of the stairs, dragging the heavy trunk behind her. Between the two of them, she and André carried the trunk to the carriage and strapped it to the back of the vehicle. Then he ordered her to go and pack her own things, and wait in the carriage while he went to fetch Julie.

He found her lying on a small sofa in the back parlor. The shutters and drapes were drawn and the room was hot and stuffy. André pulled back the drapes and opened the shutters to let in a little light and fresh air.

Kneeling on one knee next to the sofa, he saw that Julie was asleep. He looked at her for a long moment, then softly said her name. "Julie, *chère coeur*, it's me, André. Wake up I've come to take you to Royal Oaks."

Julie's eyes fluttered as she came out of a deep, exhausted sleep. At first, she looked confused; but then recognizing André's face in the dim light, she gave him a weak, tired smile.

"Oh, André, I'm so glad to see you, and I'm so happy you're here. Madame Gauthier and the others are very ill and I've been trying to care for them. And, André, Adele died the other day. I tried to save her, but I couldn't."

Tears streamed down her face and all the exhaustion and fears of the past few days suddenly overpowered her as her body shook with deep sobs.

André picked her up in his arms, sat on the sofa, and held her. Clinging to him, Julie cried heartbreaking tears. He stroked her hair and gently kissed her forehead as he said in a soft voice, "Hush, dear heart. Don't cry; you'll tire yourself out more. I know you did everything in your power to save Adele. 'Toinette told me how you've cared for everyone. But, Julie, dearest, if you stay here, you, too, will catch the fever.

"'Toinette is waiting in the carriage. We're going to Royal Oaks where you can rest and get your strength back."

"But what about Madame Gauthier and the others?" Julie cried. "I can't just leave them to die! André, who will care for them if I leave?"

"Pauline and the other servants will care for them, and the doctor will be stopping by soon. Julie, I won't let you stay. Madame Gauthier wouldn't want you to. You're too exhausted and much more likely to catch the fever if you don't get some rest." Without another word, André rose from the sofa and, still holding Julie, left the house.

Julie gave a low moan and buried her head in André's broad chest, as the bright sunlight sent a stabbing pain through her head and eyes. The cannons booming made her head and ears hurt, and the thick smoke and odor of burning tar left her feeling nauseous.

Gently, André put her in the carriage next to 'Toinette. Once he had her comfortable, he headed out of the city.

As the carriage rolled across the countryside, Julie felt a slight chill overtake her. 'Toinette watched with anxious eyes. These were the same symptoms that caused Madame Gauthier and her family to fall ill.

By the time they reached Royal Oaks, Julie was feverish, and both André and 'Toinette were deeply concerned; but she assured them there was nothing to worry about.

"I'm sure it's only because I'm so tired and I've not eaten much these past few days. If I lie down for a while, I'll be fine." While Julie rested, 'Toinette unpacked her trunk and André went to order a light meal for her when she woke. Then he sat in the parlor, read his Bible, prayed, and waited to make sure she was indeed all right.

Two hours later when she appeared, Julie looked rested and seemed to have her strength back.

Rising from his chair, André hurried to her side. "How are you feeling, little one?" he asked anxiously, slipping his arm around her waist and walking with her to the dining room.

"I feel much better, André." Julie looked up at him with a reassuring smile. "My goodness, you mustn't look so anxious. It was only because I was so tired that I felt a little ill. The rest helped me greatly."

When they finished eating, Julie suggested they take a stroll around the garden. "I've been cooped up at Madame Gauthier's house for so long, I'm sure the fresh air will do me good."

André took her hand in his, smiled down at her, and headed for the front door. But as they reached the parlor, Julie turned deathly pale and almost fainted. Fear gripped André's heart as he picked her up and carried her to her bedchamber, all the while calling for 'Toinette.

Within a short time, Julie's body was burning up with fever. Her eyes were bloodshot, and she thrashed about the bed, tossing her head and flailing her arms. 'Toinette rushed to get a basin of cold water and a couple of cloths.

"*Michie*, we gotta cool my little *maîtresse* fever down, befo' she get worse." 'Toinette handed André a cloth.

André nodded and, together, they sponged Julie's face, arms, and legs--anything to cool her body and lower the fever. Her lips became dry and cracked, and she moaned and whimpered for water.

As the evening progressed, so did the fever. Julie became delirious and struck out at both André and 'Toinette. She moaned and cried again and again for water, and her body jerked as she went into convulsions. André was terrified.

"I've never seen anyone struck with yellow fever before," he confessed to 'Toinette. "I feel so angry and frustrated because I don't know what to do! 'Toinette, what else can we do to help her?"

"Ain't nothin' mo' we can do, *Michie*. 'Cept maybe call da doctor."

"*Non!*" André was adamant. "I won't call a doctor. I've heard about the kind of treatments they give a person with yellow fever. And from what I've heard, many patients die from the cure rather than the fever. *Non*, you and I will have to help her."

Together, he and 'Toinette kept watch at Julie's bedside sponging her body, giving her tiny sips of water, and trying to keep her as comfortable as possible, until finally she seemed a little better.

Long into the second night, the white man and the black woman sat beside the bed of the young girl they both loved. One lone candle burned on the bedside table; and when finally Julie seemed to calm down and fall into a some what restless sleep, André and 'Toinette relaxed their vigil and each dozed off.

André had no idea how long he slept, but suddenly he was awakened by the sound of Julie struggling for breath. The candle had burned out so he reached into the bedside table and found a new one. When he had it lit, he was shocked to see Julie's face. It was dark, and the veins in her neck stood out and looked like they would burst. Blood began to ooze from her lips, nose, gums, and eyes; and once again, her temperature shot up. Her body was jerking with convulsions, and now a thick, black substance issued from her mouth.

'Toinette, who had also awakened, looked at André with terror-filled eyes. "It be da black vomit, *Michie* de Javon! It be da last stages of da fever! She sho' will die." Tears began to stream down the woman's face. "*Bronze Jean* will take my little *maîtresse*. Oh, Lawd, help us!"

"Hush, 'Toinette!" André's face was fearsome as he spoke in a low but harsh voice. "She will *not* die, do you hear me? Julie will not die! I won't let her die! Now, stop that carrying on and help me."

Although she cried and prayed, 'Toinette continued to wash the blood and black vomit from Julie's nose, mouth and eyes, while André sponged her body.

The rest of the night was a nightmare of sponging Julie's body and cleaning the blood and nasty vomit from her face and hair. They

310

watched the fever recede, only to have it shoot back up higher than before. And they prayed that somehow Julie would live through this terrible night.

As dawn broke, André and 'Toinette thought they saw some improvement. The fever had subsided somewhat, and Julie seemed to be resting.

André turned to the servant and, placing his hands on her shoulders, gave her a gentle smile. "'Toinette, I'm sorry I was harsh with you earlier. We're both so tired from the stress and strain that I overreacted. I want you to go to a cabin I have ready for you and rest. I can't have you falling ill also. Julie will need you when she gets better."

'Toinette wanted to argue. She wanted to stay with her little mistress, but André was firm. "It won't do for us both to fall ill, and you've been nursing sick people for quite a while now. I'll take good care of Julie and will call you if I need you."

'Toinette had no choice but to leave; she knew he was right. She was no longer young, she was exhausted and needed rest; and her little mistress did seem to be better.

Just about the time André's hopes began to rise, the fever returned. He couldn't believe how desperately ill Julie was.

He knew her body had to be sponged there was no other way to keep the fever under control. As carefully and gently as a mother would, he removed her nightgown and sponged her until he brought the fever down. When, once again, the fever was reduced, he put a clean, fresh nightgown on her, and then decided to change the bedding. It was something he'd never done before, and he found it quite a job, especially since he kept Julie in the bed while he changed it. More than once, she almost fell out when André tried to put the fresh sheet on the mattress. He would have to rush around to the side she was on and catch her before she fell.

In spite of his fears, he found himself grinning at what she herself would say if she knew what was happening.

When finally he had all back to normal, his patient lying between clean sheets, with a fresh pillowcase under her head, Andre felt quite proud of himself.

"You see, my darling, you see what I can do when I put my mind to it. I've learned how to change a bed! And don't you worry, little one," he whispered as he gently caressed Julie's face. "I love you, and I'll take care of you and get you well, I promise."

André left orders that no one was to enter the *garçonnière*. Delilah would bring a tray of food and leave it on the *galerie*. André couldn't think of eating much. More than once, Delilah took mostly untouched food back to the kitchen.

The other servants were filled with fear. They had no idea what was happening in the *garçonnière*. What if the *maître* fell ill? What if he died? At night, they gathered to pray and practice their voodoo spells, hoping to ward off any danger to André.

It was well into the fifth day before André could finally relax and know that somehow Julie had survived the yellow fever. In that five-day period, he wept, prayed, and cried out to God to spare her life. Several times when he felt her slipping away, he talked to her between clenched teeth ordering her to fight for her life. "Julie, Julie, don't you dare die! I love you, Julie; I couldn't bare life without you. Now that I'm free, I want to marry you. Julie, don't die, *please!*"

He would hold her hand and kiss it, stroke her forehead, and smooth the curls back from her face, his eyes filled with the fear of losing her.

Then, finally, the crisis passed. Julie's temperature went down and stayed down for more than twenty-four hours. Her body relaxed and for the first time in days, Julie slept a deep, undisturbed sleep.

André was thoroughly drained. He hadn't slept much and had eaten little since his return to Royal Oaks. Now, suddenly, hunger and exhaustion overcame him. He ordered food to be brought to the bedchamber where he could eat while keeping an eye on Julie.

"But you, *Michie*, you need rest, too," 'Toinette insisted when he refused to leave the bedroom.

"Now, 'Toinette, don't you worry about me. I'll place a mattress on the floor near Julie's bed. I can sleep there and be near her if she needs me." He gave 'Toinette his winning smile. "*Chère*, 'Toinette, without you to work with me, Julie might not be alive. I certainly don't want you falling ill. Julie will need you when she grows stronger, so no arguments. Go and eat and rest, and I'll come and tell you how she's doing later."

When finally Julie had the strength to speak, she was so weak André had to put his ear to her lips to hear what she said and even then he wasn't sure he'd heard correctly. But when he finally realized he had heard right, he laughed so hard he almost cried. In her weak little voice, Julie whispered, "Next time you decide to change my bed, please put me in a chair while you do it. I came so close to falling out, I was a nervous wreck."

Gathering her in his arms, André hugged and kissed her and rocking back and forth, he laughed until his sides ached. "Oh, Julie, there is no one in the world like you."

* * *

Meanwhile, back in New Orleans, the yellow fever continued to strike the inhabitants. Within three hours after André left with Julie and 'Toinette, Emile Gauthier passed away. And later that night, Madame Gauthier also died. Armand and Marie-Annette hung between life and death for a few more days before they slowly began to recover.

Chapter 47

The rest of the month of July was hot and humid, and there was little relief from the heat. The workmen were busy constructing André's new home, and the plantation hummed with activity.

Julie's recovery was painfully slow, and it tore at Andre's heart to see how thin she was. The violent illness and raging fevers had racked her body and left her so weak she could hardly move.

Until he was sure the fever was really broken, and Julie was completely out of danger, André slept every night on a mattress by her bed. Although he slept, he was always alert to her slightest movement. If she moaned or became restless, he was on his feet, with a candle lit, leaning over her to gently touch her forehead and check her breathing. Her forehead remained cool, and she would quiet down at his touch. When he was sure her breathing was normal, he would blow out the candle and return to his mattress.

Each day, he ordered fresh soup made and would sit on the side of the bed and feed Julie the clear, rich broth. At first, she was too weak to lift her head from the pillow; so André would cradle her in his arms and feed her like one feeds an infant.

Julie's face was pale and gaunt, and there were black circles beneath her eyes; but at the sight of André, her eyes would light up, and she would give him a weak smile.

Once she was rested, 'Toinette took over much of her care but at first, all Julie did was sleep.

André finally broke down and sent a note asking the doctor to come out and check on her. When he arrived, Doctor la Poyntz assured André that rest was the best medicine.

"Her body has been through a great trauma and needs all the sleep and rest possible," he said after examining her.

André worried that the workmen would disturb her. He wanted them to stop until she was stronger; but Julie assured him the noise didn't bother her at all.

"I like knowing that when I am well enough to leave this room, I shall see your beautiful home rising like the Phoenix from the ashes."

Her voice was still so weak he had to lean close to hear what she said and as he did so, he let his lips brush softly against hers.

While Julie slept and struggled to regain her health, André returned to the business of running Royal Oaks. Although he was gone at daybreak, he always returned to share the midday meal with her. He ordered mild dishes that were easy for her to digest. It was a while before Julie could feed herself without getting too tired to hold the fork but when that fatigue happened, André was always there to take over.

Finally, one day when they had finished eating, Julie said, "André, would you please help me to the parlor? I should like to see how your house is progressing. I'm so tired of being in this room all the time."

André helped her with her robe and slippers and would have lifted her from the bed, but Julie stopped him. "You don't have to carry me. I'm sure I can walk downstairs."

"Julie, dearest, you've been so ill. I don't want you to overextend yourself." André's look of concern made Julie smile, but she insisted she was strong enough.

Slowly, she eased herself into a standing position, but she was shaking so, André became alarmed. "Julie, you're just too weak; let me carry you."

Shaking her head and leaning against him, Julie took several steps. "See," she said brightly, smiling up at him, "see how well I'm doing." But as they reached the top of the stairs, her face turned chalk white and her legs gave out. She would have fallen had not André scooped her up in his arms.

"Oh, André, I'm so sorry. I really thought I was strong enough to walk." Her face was filled with such distress, that Andre chuckled.

Gently kissing her forehead, he said, "Don't worry about it, *chérie.*

315

Each day, we'll walk a little until you're strong again. Besides, you're as light as a feather."

'Toinette opened the front door and André carried Julie out to the *galerie* where she could get a better look at the building that was going on. As he stood there holding her, André explained where each room would be.

Julie turned sparkling eyes to him. "Oh, it will be the most beautiful house of all. I can hardly wait until it's completed."

Together, they watched the men working for several minutes, but André could see she was beginning to tire. Stepping back into the parlor, he sat down in a large chair near the window, with Julie curled up on his lap as they continued to watch the men work.

Julie snuggled in his arms. "André, I want to thank you for taking 'Toinette and me away from New Orleans and bringing us here. You've been so good to us, especially me. You've taken such good care of me."

André put his finger under her chin and tilted her face up to his. "Julie, don't you know how much I love you? I've loved you since the first day you appeared riding that giant of a horse, Thunder. But you were such a little girl; a child of eleven, and I was a grown man. I loved the beautiful little girl then, and now I love the beautiful young woman." He bent his head and brushed his lips against hers.

He felt her arms go around his neck and her lips respond to his. At first, the kiss was soft and gentle, but then, desire rushed up, and he kissed her; not like he'd kissed the child of yesteryear, but with the desire a man has for the woman he loves.

When their lips parted, André took her face in his hands and gazed at her for a long moment. "Julie, I love you so. I want to marry you and spent the rest of my life with you. I never knew I could love anyone as I love you. When you were ill and I thought you might die, I couldn't stand the thought of losing you. Now that I have you back, I will never let you go. Will you marry me, my darling?"

Julie looked up at him, tears glistening on her long lashes.

André saw the tears, and searching her face, asked in a soft voice, "What's wrong, my love? What's the matter?"

Julie shook her head and turned away, and he heard her whisper, "Oh, André, I'm so happy. I've loved you for such a long time. And I've always wanted to be with you; but I never thought it would happen."

She laid her head on his chest. "My dearest, I've loved you since the

first moment I set eyes on you, long before I rode Thunder over here."
Suddenly she giggled softly.

"What's so funny, young lady?"

"Remember the first time we met? You and Charles were on your way to meet with my father, and I was on my way to the Convent."

André nodded.

"Well," she continued. "after you rode off, I told 'Toinette that when I grew up, I was going to marry you."

"You did? What did 'Toinette say?"

She looked shocked and said, "*Michie* de Javon he grown man. You jes' little girl, you only eleven years old.' But *I* said, I wouldn't be eleven forever, and when I grew up I *would* marry you."

"Mmmmm, pretty sure of yourself, weren't you?" André asked with a wicked gleam in his eye.

Then, Julie turned serious. "In answer to your question, my love, *oui*, I will marry you. I wouldn't ever want to be married to anyone but you. And I will do my best to make sure you never regret asking me."

André's eyes caressed her face and drank in her loveliness. He marveled that anyone could be so lovely in spite of the terrible illness. Even *Bronze Jean* could not dim Julie's exquisite beauty. His eyes lingered on her sweet mouth and, once again, he lowered his head and sought her lips. In a slow, almost reverent, manner he kissed her gently. "Kiss me back, my sweet," he murmured against her lips, and felt a burst of joy when Julie responded.

They sat in the chair talking, planning their future, and speaking of their love. André would stop talking, kiss Julie again, and know that he would never get enough of her.

* * *

Their love worked magic within them. There was a bounce to André's step that had been missing for a long time. Gone were the lines of stress and strain that had creased his handsome face these past few years. Gone, too, was the sad melancholy look that had haunted his eyes. Now, his eyes sparkled and danced. And when he smiled, which he did all the time, he was the handsomest man around.

He was always whistling or humming, and his laughter could be heard all over the plantation. His happiness was contagious, and the house servants and field hands seemed to laugh, sing, and whistle more than they had in years.

"It be good to see *Maître* so happy," one kitchen maid said to another, as they both smiled and waved at André when he rode past the kitchen one morning. He returned the smile and wave, and they heard him whistle as he headed out to the sugar factory.

Love worked its magic on Julie also. Her appetite improved, the dark circles under her eyes disappeared, and there was color in her cheeks. Her beautiful eyes radiated her love for André, and she was rapidly regaining her strength.

A letter arrived from Monsieur Charlevoix, and André hurried to share it with Julie. Her father wrote from the town of Wheeling, Virginia (West Virginia had not been formed yet) where he had met with Henry Shreve. Jean-Claude went on to say he'd sent a letter to Julie at Madame Gauthier's home informing her he would be home within the next three weeks.

When André finished reading the letter, Julie looked up with a shocked expression. "Oh, André, first I was so ill, and lately I've been so happy I completely forgot about Madame Gauthier and her family! How cruel of me, especially since she lost little Adele. André, I must go to New Orleans and see how the rest of them are doing."

"You'll do no such thing. You're still much too weak to make such a journey in this heat. But, I promise I'll ride to the city and check on them. I understand there have been no new outbreaks of the fever for the past three weeks."

When Julie continued to look upset, he added, "I promise I'll leave for New Orleans within the next three days."

Two days later, riding in from the fields, André saw a horse and rider approaching. He knew at a glance it was Charles and happily rode out to meet him.

When Julie had fallen ill with the fever, André sent word to Oak Grove that they should stay away until she was recovered, and Charles had followed his wishes. Recently, his servants had told him that Julie was now well.

"Charles, how good to see you," André said with a happy smile as he pulled up beside his friend.

"*Bonjour*, André, my servants heard though their grapevine that Julie had recovered from the fever; so I thought I'd ride over and see how you are doing. We've all been worried about you."

"I'm glad you're here, Charles. Julie is resting at the *garçonnière*, and I know she'll be delighted to see you. Poor little thing has seen no one but 'Toinette and me since I brought her here so you'll be a welcomed sight."

As they rode together, André told Charles about his first experience with Julie's illness.

"Yellow fever is a terrible disease. Watching her suffer through it was the worst thing I could ever imagine. Several times, I was sure she would die, but she's a fighter. I only hope that someday soon a cure is found."

Julie was sitting in a chair in the parlor, and her face lit up when André and Charles walked in. *"Bonjour*, Charles, what a nice surprise,"* she said as he bent to kiss her hand.

"Julie, how lovely you look. Seeing you now, it's hard to believe you so recently suffered from the fever and came so close to death." Charles smiled as he appraised her.

"I owe my life to André and 'Toinette; they took such good care of me," Julie replied as she smiled up at André.

Charles was invited to join them for lunch. When they had finished the meal and returned to the parlor, Julie said, "André received a letter from my father just the other day. *Pappa* will be home very soon."

"Does he know of your illness?"

André shook his head. *"Non*, I didn't write him about it. Julie fell ill so suddenly, and I knew writing Jean-Claude would only cause him a great deal of worry. I'll send him a letter from New Orleans this week; then he can see for himself how well she is doing when he returns."

Julie explained that her father had written her a letter and sent it to Madame Gauthier's home, but she'd already left. "André is going to New Orleans tomorrow to see how Madame Gauthier and her family are doing. They all caught the fever." Her face grew sad and her eyes filled with tears as she told him about Madame Gauthier's daughter, Adele, dying.

The room grew quiet, and the only sound was Julie's sobbing over the loss of her little friend. André took her in his arms and sat holding her. "Julie, darling, you did everything possible to save Adele. I know how much it grieves you; but I hate to see you get so upset. It will tire you out."

In an effort to lighten the mood, he turned to Charles. "Julie and I have some wonderful news, and you will be the first to know. May I tell him, Julie?" She nodded her head and André continued. "Julie has

319

agreed to marry me. Isn't that wonderful?"

"Indeed, it is. I can't think of two people more suited to each other. I'm very happy for you both."

Drying her tears, Julie turned to André. "When *Pappa* comes home, you'll have to ask him for my hand."

Andre gave her a knowing grin. "I already have."

"You did? When?"

"Right before he left for Virginia."

"And what did he say?"

"He said if you said *oui*, he would say *oui* also."

"Pretty sure of yourself, weren't you?" Julie's eyes were twinkling.

Andre threw back his head and laughed. "*Touché*, Mademoiselle.

Later, when Charles was ready to leave, he asked André to walk outside with him.

When they were out of Julie's hearing, he turned to his friend. "I didn't want to say anything in front of Julie for fear of upsetting her more. But you should know that both Madame Gauthier and her son, Emile, died from the fever."

"Madame Gauthier is dead and Emile too? How do you know this, Charles?"

"Frédéric was ill last week, and Doctor la Poyntz came out to see him. He was telling us about the outbreak of the fever, and that's when he told us about their deaths."

"What about Marie-Annette and Armand? Did he say anything about them?"

"*Oui*, he said they'd both been very ill, but they are now recovering." Charles looked over at André. "How will you tell Julie? This news will upset her terribly. She was very close to Madame Gauthier. Madame was like a second mother to her, and I know it will greatly upset her father. Madame Gauthier was his wife's best friend."

"You're right, Julie will be very upset when I tell her, and I must tell her. I promised her I'd go to New Orleans tomorrow, and I will. So I think I'll wait until I return before saying anything. I must first see how Marie-Annette and her brother are and do whatever I can for them."

André then asked about Frédéric and Francesca and the rest of the family, and Charles assured him that everyone was fine. "Frédéric is doing much better now. He wasn't very ill, but he seems to live with a cold."

Andre thanked Charles again for his willingness to care for the child and insisted on paying the doctor bill.

"Do not worry, André. You concentrate on all that is going on here. *Au revoir, mon ami.*"

* * *

Early the next morning before the sun was very high, André headed for New Orleans, wondering how things would be when he got there.

It had been almost a month since he'd gone to fetch Julie. Now, it was the end of August, and he knew the heat would make the city as hot as an oven. It would be suffocating, the stench from the gutters would be overpowering, and the mosquitoes would be vicious.

When he reached the city, it was every bit as hot as he had anticipated, and the stench was as bad as he had remembered. At least the cannons were no longer booming and the barrels of burning tar had been removed. The city was abloom with flowers, and the streets were swarming with people. A newcomer would have found it difficult to believe that just the month before, New Orleans had been gripped in a panic over yellow fever.

Pauline answered the door when André reached the Gauthier residence. "*Bonjour* Pauline."

"*Bonjour, Michie* de Javon."

"Pauline, I'm so very saddened over the loss of your mistress and her son, Emile, and her daughter, Adele."

Pauline lowered her head and nodded.

André continued. "I've come to pay my respects to Monsieur Armand and Mademoiselle Marie-Annette, offer my condolences, and see if I can be of any help to them."

The servant led him into the parlor and bid him sit down while she went to call *Michie* Armand. It was several minutes before Armand Gauthier appeared in the doorway. He was a short man standing about five feet six inches, a plain young man with small, dark eyes, a round nose, and a diminutive full-lipped mouth. The dark brown hair that covered his head was fine and straight; and already, he showed signs of balding.

André was shocked to see how thin Armand was and as he stood to greet the younger man, his height made Armand appear even smaller. After their greeting, André said, "I would have come sooner; but the day I took Julie to Royal Oaks, she, too, came down with the fever and...."

"What happened to Julie?" Marie-Annette stood in the doorway leaning on Pauline's arm.

Both men rose, André greeted the young woman and extended his condolences to both at the loss of their mother and siblings.

He helped Marie-Annette to a chair and continued. He told them how ill Julie had been. "She came so close to death. Even now, she is terribly weak."

"Marie-Annette and I were fortunate. Neither of us had the fever as bad as the others. I suppose that's why we're still here," Armand said in a tired voice.

"It was only when Charles stopped for a short visit that I learned of the deaths of your family members; so of course I came at once. I also received a letter from Julie's father recently. He will be returning soon."

He paused for a moment, then continued. "Monsieur Charlevoix mentioned that he sent a letter to Julie; but it must have arrived after I took her to Royal Oaks. I just wrote him a letter telling him of your loss and Julie's illness, and assuring him that she is much better and that she is staying at Royal Oaks until his return. Has his letter to her arrived?"

"*Oui*, it came while Armand and I were ill. Pauline put it on my dresser, and it's still there. I'll have her fetch it."

"How is Julie doing? Is she in good spirits?" Marie-Annette asked.

Andre was tempted to tell them about his forthcoming marriage to Julie but remembered that she had asked him not to tell anyone else except Charles.

"It isn't that I don't want people to know but I do think we should wait until we can tell my father. I think it would be very sad and show a lack of respect if he were to come back and find that everyone else knew about our plans before he did."

Andre assured them that Julie was in fine spirits and was regaining her strength.

Marie-Annette said in a sad voice, "It will be so empty without the rest of our family here in the house." There was along pause. Then she smiled at André. "Speaking of homes, Monsieur de Javon, how is your plantation house coming along?"

"It's almost finished, Mademoiselle. I hope to move in by October."

"Oh, how wonderful! I'm sure it will be beautiful." Marie-Annette gave André her nicest smile.

The young girl looked much like her brother. Short in stature and with a tendency to plumpness, although she too had lost much weight because of the illness. Her hair, like Armand's, was dark in color, fine in texture, and straight. Today, she wore it in a small bun at the back of her neck, and with her plain features, she appeared older than her seventeen years.

"I imagine you'll be giving a fine ball soon after you move in," she went on, "to let everyone see how beautiful it is."

"I really hadn't thought about that," André answered. "But perhaps I will."

"What a shame Armand and I won't be able to attend. We'll be in mourning for the next year."

"Then I'll have to invite you both to an intimate little dinner sometime soon," André replied, smiling at her.

Marie-Annette blushed furiously. André had no idea the girl was in love with him and now assumed that he was interested in her.

Chapter *48*

André spent two days in New Orleans. He went down to *Rue Tchoupitoulas* to check on his warehouses and was pleased to find them filled to capacity.

He stopped at *Rue Toulouse* to speak with his banker and cotton broker and then went on to see his factor.

And it was then that he saw Marie. She was walking toward him as he left his factor's office.

When their eyes met, André saw the blood leave Marie's face. At first, he didn't recognize her and wondered at the change in her expression. Then he looked more closely and realized who she was.

He had only seen her once. At the time, she was sixteen and wearing a beautiful gown, her hair done in a lovely style, and she was in a ballroom surrounding. Now, he saw her wearing a plain cotton frock, with a white apron, and her hair wrapped in a *tignon*. The only jewelry she wore was a pair of gold loop earrings.

"André" Her voice was a soft and sweet as he remembered.

André smiled. "Marie, how nice to see you, *comment allez-vous*?"

"*Tres bien, merci*, André." Marie paused, then said, "I heard about your tragic loss: your plantation burning to the ground and your wife's death. I'm very sorry."

"*Merci*, Marie. It was indeed a tragedy."

There was a long silence. André cleared his throat.

"Tell me, are you still going to the Quadroon balls?"

"*Non,* André, I haven't been to a ball in years."

"Then you found a proctor?"

"*Non,* I have no proctor. I still live with *ma mère.*"

Marie looked at André for a long moment. "I only wanted to be the *placée* to one man, and that man was you."

She waited, but when André said nothing, she added, "I would still be your *placée,* if you wished."

"Marie, I am going to be married in the near future. And I am deeply in love with the young woman I am marrying. As much as I appreciate the offer, I could never have another woman in my life."

Marie nodded. "Of course. It was never meant to be."

After a few more remarks, the two bid each other *au revoir.*

Crossing to the American side to confer with his lawyer, André thought about Marie. She was still lovely, and he wished for her sake she could find someone else but that was not his problem. So after a few minutes, he put her out of his thoughts.

* * *

When André reached Royal Oaks, he gathered Julie in his arms and, kissing her, murmured, "I missed you so much. These past two days seemed more like two months." Then, hungrily, he kissed her again.

Julie's eyes glowed as she told him how much she'd missed him also. With her arms around his neck, she clung to him for a long moment. "Now tell me about Madame Gauthier and her family. Are they recovering from the fever? Tell me everything."

However, before answering her question, André drew her father's letter from his pocket and handed it to her. "Wouldn't you like to read his letter first?"

As Julie took the letter and started to sit, André gently led her to the big chair and drew her down on his lap. "Sit with me, little one. I have something to tell you when you're through reading your letter."

After she'd read the communication aloud, Julie once again inquired about Madame Gauthier and her family. It pained him to tell her about the deaths of the mother and her son; and after he spoke, he held and comforted her as she wept.

It was several days before Julie could shake the deep depression she felt. André could only love and comfort her as she told him of the many

325

acts of kindness Claudine Gauthier had shown her over the years.

One evening after dinner, Julie turned to him and asked, "Do you have a chess set?"

André nodded, *"Oui*, why do you ask?"

"Well, I thought we might have a game before I retire."

André sent Demetrius to his *garçonnière* for the set. Once the chessmen were set up, he smiled at her and said, "I've known you most of your life, and I never knew you could play chess. Why didn't you ever tell me this?"

With a teasing glint in her eye, Julie answered, "You never asked. Besides, I had to keep a *little* mystery about myself. That way, I'd be more interesting."

André laughed. "Oh, Julie, my sweet, you were *always* interesting. From the moment I saw you on my land, you had me interested. I remember the funny stories you would tell me about your time at the convent."

André was surprised at how well Julie played; and although he won, she gave him a run for his money. "Well," he said when the game was over, "you certainly play well. Who taught you?"

"My father taught me, silly. Whom do you think he played chess with before you came along?"

* * *

When Monsieur Charlevoix returned, he was delighted with the news of their plan to marry. And when André formally asked for his daughter's hand, he was more than overjoyed to say yes. "I've always wished for a son like you, André. And now my wish will be granted."

Later that evening when Jean-Claude bid André good-bye, he took Julie back to *Château Charlevoix*, and André realized how terribly empty life would be without her.

He rode over to the *Château* every chance he got, and Julie would have Joshua drive her to Royal Oaks as often as possible. After spending the past two months together, the separation now seemed almost impossible to bear.

They discussed their wedding plans with Julie's father and explained that they wished to be married before Christmas.

"*Pappa*, I know the proper way for us to do things is to be engaged for a year. But André and I have known each other for six years, and we love each other and don't want to be apart any longer than necessary." Julie gave her father a pleading look.

"Julie, I'm not concerned with what people will think about an early wedding, I'm concerned with your happiness and that of André. If you two wish to be married before Christmas, then you shall. I'll give you the finest, most beautiful wedding New Orleans has ever seen. Then we'll see if tongues wag."

Jean-Claude was planning to return to the city with Julie but before he did, Julie asked André if they could have another picnic.

"Of course, sweetheart, I'll have Delilah fix us an especially delicious lunch," André answered.

The day was lovely. The sun was warm, without being too hot. The sky was an azure blue, and Andre felt the day had been ordered just for them. They spread the cloth and André served. They ate slowly, enjoying the food Delilah had prepared; and André was happy to see Julie's appetite had increased a little more.

"Would you care for another biscuit?" Julie asked as she held out the plate to him.

Smiling, André shook his head.

"You don't seem to be very hungry, Monsieur de Javon. Could it be that you're in love?"

André leaned toward her and in a soft voice, asked. "Love? Tell me, little one, what do you know of love?"

Julie too leaned forward until their foreheads were touching. "Oh, I know a great deal about love, because you see, Monsieur, I am very much in love," she whispered as she melted against him.

Cradling her in his arms, André kissed her with a hunger he tried to control, then pressed her down upon the grass. "Oh, my sweet," he whispered, as he leaned over her. "How will I ever wait until December to make you mine? I want you with me now and forever." His voice was husky with desire and his body ached for wanting her, as once again his lips sought her. His arms tightened around her as his kiss deepened. His lips moved on hers, shaping her lips to his, kissing her long and lingering with an aching tenderness.

Julie clung to him, returning his kiss with a passion that surprised him. She pressed against him until André could feel every curve of her body.

His hands ached to caress her sweet body, to feel her response to his lovemaking, but with the last vestige of control he possessed, he tore his lips from her and suddenly sat up.

Julie wore a look of startled surprise and puzzlement as André gazed at her and said in a soft voice. "My darling, unless you want to drive me completely insane, I'm afraid this is something we cannot do, at least not until we are married."

* * *

In early October, father and daughter moved back to the city; and in November André followed.

Chapter 49

It was too late to order Julie's wedding gown from Paris so Monsieur Charlevoix hired the best seamstress in New Orleans to make the gown. There was much to do in preparation for the wedding; and Jean-Claude had everyone working around the clock.

Julie and André were married at the Saint Louis Cathedral. The Cathedral was ablaze with thousands of candles and decorated with holly, garlands, and ribbons.

It was also packed with the *crème de la crème of* Créole families of the city and the Americans who were friends of both Monsieur Charlevoix and André. The day was cold, but sunny, and everyone was in a festive mood.

That day, when Julie first appeared in her wedding gown, her father could only stare at her. He watched as slowly she descended the stairs into the foyer, and knew that never in his life had he seen his daughter looking more beautiful.

The gown, made of creamy white satin and lace, had a sweetheart neckline. The bodice was encrusted with seed pearls and tiny diamonds. The sleeves, which were puffed at the shoulder and tightly fitted to the wrist, were also encrusted with seed pearls and diamonds and ended in points at the back of her hands.

The gown had the high empress waistline that was all the fashion, then fell in soft lines to the floor. The hem of the gown was scalloped in the same pearl-and-diamond-encrusted lace, as was the train that seemed to go on forever.

Julie's hair fell in soft waves and curls down her back and on her head, she wore a diamond tiara that held her long, flowing veil that was edged with the same design as the hem of her gown. When she reached the bottom of the stairs, Julie paused, then stepped down to the floor, and slowly turned around so her father could see her from all angles. Smiling up at him, she asked in a soft voice "Will I do? Do you think André will find me pretty?"

Jean-Claude saw the twinkle in her eyes, and chuckling, he nodded. "Julie, when André sees you, he might very well faint from the impact. You are, without a doubt, the most beautiful bride I have ever seen, and that includes your mother."

The church was already filled to overflowing when André arrived. And while he waited for the appearance of Julie and her father, he was a figure of nervous energy.

The organist struck the first chord, and the procession began. The Swiss Guards in their colorful uniforms were the first down the aisle. The rest of the procession was like all Créole weddings.

Finally, it was Julie's turn and with eyes brimming with love, she turned to her father. *"Pappa, this is the happiest day of my life."*

Jean-Claude looked down at her and gave her a quick kiss on her forehead. He patted her hand, smiled, and said, "That is what counts, *ma chérie."*

André had carried a picture in his mind of how Julie would look at this moment; but nothing he had imagined could prepare him for the exquisite vision that was walking toward him. Love for her and pride in her made him almost burst with joy at the sight of her. No bride *had* ever, *could* ever look as beautiful as she did.

Julie held her head high and walked with the grace of a ballet dancer. She seemed to float down the aisle. As André watched, she lifted her eyes to his and kept them on him until she was standing beside him.

Everyone watched as André stepped forward to claim his bride. He looked exceptionally handsome in a suit of dark blue velvet. And when he took her hand and smiled down at her, every woman in the Cathedral felt their heartbeat quicken. This was so obviously a love match.

André thought his heart would burst with joy when the priest pronounced them man and wife. He'd never known such happiness; and looking down at his beautiful young bride, he knew that he would, indeed, love and cherish her all the days of his life.

A lavish reception was held at Monsieur Charlevoix's large home. The guests crowded in, filling every room and spilling out into the courtyard, which had been tented for the occasion.

Tables laden with food fit for a king lined the side of the large dining room. There was champagne, wine, brandy, and punch, and much dancing. At the appropriate time, Julie and André cut the huge wedding cake the servants had spent hours baking.

As the evening progressed, 'Toinette appeared and took her young mistress upstairs to a bedroom that had been turned into a bridal suite. She helped Julie out of her wedding gown and suggested she take a warm bath.

"Da bath will relax you too much excitement all day."

Julie agreed and sank into the tub of hot water. 'Toinette poured perfume into the water and gently rubbed Julie's back with a soft cloth. Once Julie was dry, 'Toinette brought out the exquisite negligee and nightgown made especially for this night.

Both were made of white silk that shimmered in the candlelight. The gown had beautiful smocking across the bodice, with tiny sleeves and a scooped neck. Both sleeves and neckline were trimmed with delicate lace. It gathered under the bust and fell in soft flowing lines to the floor. The negligee, too, was smocked and trimmed in lace. It had long sleeves and a silk ribbon tied at the neck. After Julie was dressed, 'Toinette brushed her hair until it shone and fell in soft waves and curls around her shoulders.

As 'Toinette looked at her mistress in the mirror, she saw a look of apprehension on her face.

Taking a deep breath, Julie said, "'Toinette, what will happen when André comes up to the bedroom? I don't know how I know, but I know something happens between married people."

Julie had never put such a question to her maid before, and she couldn't believe she was doing it now; but some instinct told her there was more to marriage than met the eye.

"*Ma petite Maîtresse*, you not to worry. *Michie* André, he love you so, he crazy wid love fo' you. And you," she said as she gazed at the young girl she'd raised from birth, "you be da same 'bout him. But you be so innocent, jus' an innocent child and children especially be 'fraid of da unknown. But young *Maître*, he be gentle and patient wid you, and soon things will be beautiful fo' both of you, you see."

Meanwhile, André waited in the library. Suddenly, Monsieur Charlevoix appeared. Pouring them each a glass of wine, he sat opposite André and spoke in a soft voice, "André, I don't need to tell you how innocent Julie is. Our young Créole brides know nothing about the marriage bed until they are in it. And without a mother, Julie is more innocent than most. A lot of these young, hot-blooded Créole bucks are used to indulging their every whim; and so they don't hesitate to indulge themselves on their wedding night, no matter what the consequences.

"And, sometimes, the consequences cause great unhappiness, because their bride is frightened and unprepared. Although she submits, she is usually left unfilled and will forever consider the marriage bed a duty, and an unpleasant duty at that."

He paused and waited, but André said nothing. So he continued, "I know how much you love my daughter. I know how much you desire her, because I felt the same about her mother. But I took time with my young bride and waited until she was comfortable, relaxed, and ready. It didn't happen the first night but when our marriage was consummated, it was a beautiful experience for both of us, and remained so until her death."

Having said this, Jean-Claude raised his glass. "May your marriage be all you wish for, André."

André was left with his thoughts. He, too, knew how innocent and unprepared Julie was for the act of love, and he remembered how frightened Gabrielle had been on their wedding night.

He also remembered how he'd forced himself on her, and now wondered if that had helped contribute to their many problems. The pain she experienced had frightened and upset her. As a result, she never enjoyed lovemaking, at least not with him.

Well, he was older and wiser now and would not make the same mistake again. He'd follow his father-in-law's advice.

'Toinette appeared in the doorway, "*Michie* de Javon, *ma petite maîtresse* be waitin' fo' you." As André rose and started for the stairs, 'Toinette laid a hand on his arm. "*Maître*, be very gentle and patient. My little *maîtresse*, she love you so; but dis all be new to her and she *avoir peur*."

André gave the servant a gentle smile. "Do not worry, 'Toinette, I adore your *petite maîtresse*. Rest assured, I shall be the essence of gentleness and patience."

When he stepped into the bedchamber, Julie was standing by the window. A fire burned in the grate, and one lone candle was lit. The drapes were partly closed, and the blue velvet fabric with the moon shining through the lace curtains, made a lovely backdrop for her beauty.

André caught his breath; and for a long moment, he simply stood looking at her. Then crossing to her, he took her in his arms and kissed her, "Oh, my darling, I love you more than life itself," he murmured as once again his lips sought hers.

"André...I....I don't know what to do!" Julie looked so perplexed, so sweet and innocent and childlike that a soft laugh escaped André's lips.

Kissing her again, he murmured, "Don't worry my sweet, I do, and I shall teach you."

As André kissed her, he removed her negligee and let it drift to the floor. His lips traveled down Julie's throat and he felt her pulse quicken at the touch.

Julie's arms went around his neck, her body pressed close to his, and André felt her knees buckle under her as her body went completely limp against him.

With a soft moan, André swooped her up in his arms. His heart was hammering as he carried her to the bed and gently laid her down. He pressed her onto the pillows and leaned over her.

"Oh, Lord, how I want you," he whispered. He kissed her forehead, her eyes, her cheeks, and throat, and tried to remember what his father-in-law had said about waiting until she was relaxed and ready. But his longing, his desire was so overwhelming that he wondered if he could keep control of his emotions.

Holding Julie in his arms, André kissed her with the passion he had been holding back for ages. When the kiss ended, he took her face between his hands and with adoring eyes caressed it, then covered it with feather-like kisses that became more demanding as his lips met hers.

Holding her in his arms, he murmured, "Julie, my dearest, don't be frightened of me. I want to make love to you; but the first time I do, you will have some pain." He stopped and watched her face in the candlelight.

Julie said nothing, but her eyes never left his face.

"I want you to know this, my sweet, because I don't want it to frighten you, and you must know it is a one-time thing. After that, there will be only pleasure. I'll be as gentle as possible, and I'll stop if you tell me to."

Caught up in a whirlpool of desire such as he had never known, André felt himself trembling. He wanted her so badly, every fiber of his body ached just looking at her. But he wanted her to want him as much; and much to his joy, Julie's desire was as great as his own.

His lips captured hers, and he murmured words of love as his lips slid down her throat. He kissed and caressed her, and found her returning his kisses with the same urgency. They were lost in a world of wonderful sensations.

André felt Julie's fingers reach up and become entwined in the hair at the back of his neck. Then suddenly her body jerked with the shock, and André heard a gasp and a muffled cry. He held her tighter, wishing he could absorb the pain for her.

"I'm sorry I hurt you, darling," he whispered as he gently kissed her.

"Did...did I hurt you?" Julie asked. And in the candlelight, he saw a look of distress on her face.

Stifling a chuckle, André shook his head and smiled. *"Non, chérie,* you certainly did not hurt me. In fact, you made me feel wonderful."

André waited before he continued making love to her; and he loved her with such exquisite tenderness, Julie's response was complete.

The soft rosy glow of morning was peeking through the curtains and drapes as Julie stirred and opened her eyes to find André with his head resting on his arm, looking at her.

She gave him a sleepy, sensuous, smile, put her arms around his neck, and drew his lips to hers. As their lips parted, she whispered, "What are you thinking?"

Propping himself up on his elbows, André took her face between his hands and studied it closely. "I'm thinking," he said in a soft, husky voice as he gently kissed her lips, "that you are the most beautiful woman in the world."

Softly, he kissed the tip of her nose. "I'm thinking how much I love that little nose of yours, the way it crinkles up just a little when you laugh."

Gently, he kissed her eyes and whispered, "I'm thinking how beautiful your eyes are and how I love the way they look at me." His lips traveled to her forehead. "I'm thinking of your lovely mind, and how fortunate I am to have such an intelligent woman for my wife."

His lips slid down to her throat; and as he kissed her, he murmured, "I'm thinking that I love every inch of you, from the top of your beautiful head to the tip of your lovely toes. And I'm thinking of how you filled my night with ecstasy." His eyes continued to caress her face.

Julie drew his lips down to hers and whispered, "Love me again, my dearest."

As was the Créole custom, the newlyweds spent five days and nights together in the bridal suite and had no desire to see or speak to anyone. In that time, André taught Julie that there should never be any feelings of embarrassment between them. He marveled at her passionate nature and was overwhelmed when she matched his passion with her own.

She gave herself to him in willing abandonment and was as eager to please him as he was to please her. The five days and nights were sheer heaven for both of them, and when finally they left for André's townhouse, they were as comfortable with each other as any two people could possibly be.

* * *

Now that they were established in André's home, Julie spent the next two weeks preparing for the holidays.

One evening during dinner, she asked André if they could invite their families to their home for Christmas day.

"I'd like to invite the du Frays and the Ste. Claires. I always think of them as your family, and of course my father and Frédéric."

She paused, then said, "And, I'd like to invite Marie-Annette and Armand Gauthier."

"Julie, my sweet, you may invite whomever you wish. I think it is a wonderful idea." André was eagerly looking forward to Christmas. It had been a long time since he'd enjoyed that most sacred holiday. Putting his arms around Julie's waist, he nuzzled her neck. "But let's not encourage our guests to stay too long. I want you all to myself."

For the Créoles, Christmas day was not the day for celebration or gift giving that was reserved for New Year's Day. Christmas was a day to go to Mass and spend quietly with family and friends rejoicing in the birth of the Christ Child.

Julie and 'Toinette spent hours with the cooks, planning the Christmas dinner. Everything must be just right. It was on one such day that Marie-Annette came to call.

"I'm so happy to see you," Julie exclaimed as she entered the parlor. After embracing her friend, she ordered *cafe au lait* and chocolate cake.

"Julie, I've come to tell you that Armand and I will not be here for your Christmas dinner." Marie-Annette had tears in her eyes as she spoke. "I begged him to change his mind, but he insists we go to our aunt's house.

"I would rather be here with you and your family. My aunt is very critical and never lets me forget that I'm not pretty like my cousin Danielle."

She gave Julie a wistful smile. "But Armand is still smarting over your marriage to André. He feels an injustice was done him. He is even angrier because André refused to fight a duel with him."

When Julie looked shocked at this last remark, Marie-Annette said, "Oh, *oui*, when Armand learned about your wedding, he went to André and challenged him to a duel. He told André you were supposed to marry him."

Julie looked shocked. "But that is not true. I never said I would marry Armand."

Marie-Annette gave a little sob. "I know that. Oh, Julie, I don't want this to ruin our friendship."

Julie put her arms around her friend. "It will never hurt our friendship. You've been my best friend all these years. Do you think, for one moment, that would change because of Armand's stubbornness?"

She hugged Marie-Annette tightly. "I had no idea Armand challenged André to a duel. And I'm certainly glad André refused. How terrible it would have been if one of them had been killed. Here now, dry your tears, and let's have another cup of *cafe au lait*." Julie smiled at her friend. "We'll get together again after Christmas."

When Marie-Annette left, Julie went back to the business of planning her Christmas dinner. But the thought of Armand being so foolish as to challenge André to a duel bothered her. She could only thank God that André refused.

After Christmas Mass, everyone gathered at André and Julie's house. André was filled with pride; his home looked beautiful and so did his bride.

Throughout the house, the rooms were filled with vases and bowls of holly. Julie had fashioned a wreath of holly, ribbons, and bows and had hung it on the front door.

On the gleaming white tablecloth, she'd placed a great clustering bouquet of holly in a crystal bowl. From the bowl, she had red and green streamers leading to each lady's plate, with a tiny sprig of holly at the head of each place setting.

André knew the days and hours Julie had spent planning for this occasion and felt especially happy when everyone praised her for the excellent job she'd done. The meal was every bit as impressive as the decorations.

The three little boys, Charles and Francesca's sons and Frédéric, ate in the *petit* dining room, and André insisted the doors between the rooms remain open so he could listen to the children's voices as they chatted.

It was a joyous time with much laughter, and André watched as Julie got everyone involved in the conversation.

When the meal was over, all gathered in the parlor. Julie went to the pianoforte and started playing Christmas carols. At first, only her sweet, clear voice was heard. But in no time at all, she had everyone else singing along with her.

When, finally, the evening ended and the last guest had departed, André took her in his arms. "Julie, you constantly amazed me when you were a child, and you amaze me even more now that you're grown. Tonight was the most beautiful Christmas I've ever known. Everything was perfect, especially you."

He bent and kissed her; then together they went up to their bedchamber where their night was filled with delicious lovemaking.

Chapter 50

They had been married a month when one morning, André woke up and looked over at Julie who was still asleep. Propping his head on his arm, he lay watching her. After a while, he took a strand of her hair and lightly passed the curl across her nose. In her sleep, Julie wrinkled her nose, but didn't wake up. He did the same thing again. This time, her hand came up and brushed against her nose, but still she slept. With a devilish grin, he drew the curl across her eyelids and down the side of her face, but still she slept. Finally, he leaned over and whispered in her ear, "Julie Marie de Javon, wake up. Let's go out and play."

Slowly, Julie came awake. Her eyes were sleepy, and there was a soft smile on her face. "André, did you say something to me?"

"*Oui*, I said wake up. Let's go out and play."

Putting her arms around his neck, she slowly drew his lips down to hers. "What would you like to play, Monsieur de Javon?"

He grinned at her. "On second thought, I think I'd rather stay here for a while."

Julie gave a deep sigh and whispered, "I love you so much. I love everything about you."

André brought his lips to hers and kissed her endlessly with long, deep kisses. Julie responded with a hunger he had not thought possible. To love and be loved in return like Julie loved him was the most wonderful experience he could imagine. After the long years with Gabrielle's cold unresponsiveness, he couldn't believe this was really happening.

It was two hours before they left their bedchamber.

Later that evening when they were in the parlor, André sat watching Julie, a pastime he thoroughly enjoyed. "Sweetheart, there are two things I must talk to you about."

Julie was working on some needlepoint, but she stopped and looked up at him. "What is it, my love?"

"The first thing we need to talk about is Royal Oaks. I would like to go there for a while this month."

Julie's face broke into a smile. "Oh, André, I want to go, too. Do you realize I haven't seen the house completely finished, furnished and decorated?"

"You wouldn't mind leaving New Orleans with all the parties, balls, and such?"

"André, the parties and balls are fine, but I'd much rather be at Royal Oaks with you."

André looked over at her with a grateful smile. "No wonder I'm so in love with you. I want you with me but I was afraid you'd be disappointed about leaving the city at the height of the social season."

Julie put down her needlepoint and, crossing to where he sat, curled up in his lap. She took his face in her hands and looked at him very seriously. "André, you're the most important person in my world; and wherever you are, that's where I want to be. I wouldn't have any fun at an old party without you." She drew his head down and kissed him, then sat back and asked, "Now, what is the other matter you want to talk about?"

"Frédéric. I never intended to leave him with Charles and Francesca for so long, but I had no choice. First, there was the fire and Gabrielle's death; and before I could rebuild the house, there was the war with the British; and then...."

Julie laid a finger on his lips. "My darling, you don't have to explain. I know all you've gone through. I certainly understand why you left Frédéric with Charles and Francesca."

"They've been wonderful about caring for him. But he's my responsibility," André said. "I'd planned to ask you if you would mind if we took him to Royal Oaks with us this month. I mentioned it to Charles and Francesca." He paused and looked at her for a moment.

"André, I wouldn't mind if your little boy came with us."

"Thank you, sweetheart." There was a look of relief on André's face. "I was sure you wouldn't mind. But Francesca suggested that perhaps it would be better if we waited. She's very fond of you and thinks you'll be a wonderful mother to Frédéric. But she thought you're so young to take on such a responsibility, and that maybe we should wait until we return to the city.

"If we take him now, he might get lonesome and miss his cousins and be upset and cry a lot. And that wouldn't be a good start for any of us. He's a difficult child as it is."

Julie nodded in agreement. "I'm sure Francesca is right. After all, Frédéric hardly knows me. When we return next month, we can bring him here to spend a few nights and see how he does. And, gradually, we can keep him longer and longer until he is used to being with us."

"That's exactly what Francesca said. Julie, for one so young, you certainly have a good head on your shoulders."

"Oh, I'm not so young. I'm an old married lady of one month, six hours, and twenty-two minutes."

André pushed a curl back from her forehead. "One month? Has it only been one month, my dearest? You've become such a part of me I can hardly remember life without you." He held her close and felt more peace and contentment than he thought possible.

* * *

The drive to Royal Oaks was the most pleasant André could remember. The day was sunny and the air was crisp. As the carriage swayed gently down the road, Julie kept up a constant chatter about the scenery, the fresh country air, and about seeing old friends again.

Demetrius drove the carriage with 'Toinette beside him. Demetrius was quiet because his thoughts were on Millie. He and Millie were in love and hoped to marry when André returned from the north in 1812; but Gabrielle had put the fear of God in Millie.

Now Demetrius hoped to convince Millie their worries and her fears were over. They should speak to the *maître* about getting married. But Millie was living at the home of Charles and Francesca in order to care for Frédéric; so he would have to wait a while longer.

As the carriage turned onto the avenue of oaks, Julie suddenly fell silent. She had watched the house being built. But, now, seeing it in all of its opulent splendor took her breath away. It was twice as large as the original structure.

Once it was completed, Andre had a garden planted; and the beautiful flowers and plants surrounding the majestic home only added to its grandeur. Watching her face, he leaned down and whispered, "How do you like your new home, Madame de Javon?"

"Oh, André, it's absolutely the most beautiful home I've ever seen, and it's so big! I never realized how big it was."

A little black boy had climbed into an oak tree to watch for the carriage and ran to ring the bell to tell everyone that the master was coming. Now, as the carriage drew up before the house, Julie and André saw all the servants waiting to greet them. The sea of black faces smiling and waving and calling out welcome brought a lump to Julie's throat. It had been a while since she'd seen many of them, and still they remembered her!

Delilah and Samson, carrying Toby, came forward to welcome their new mistress.

"Samson, Delilah," Julie said as she greeted them warmly. "I'm so happy to see you again. And Toby; is this Toby?"

When the proud parents smiled and nodded, Julie exclaimed, "But he's grown so much! What a handsome little boy he is."

Toby gave her a bashful smile and held out his arms to her. Julie took him and held him for a moment, telling him she remembered when he had been a tiny baby.

There were over two hundred slaves at Royal Oaks, and she insisted on greeting and saying a few words to each of them. André stood by her side as men, women, and children came by single file to shake her hand and then his. The overseer also greeted them. And when all had filed by, André informed them they could have a party that night.

When he and Julie reached the massive front door, he picked her up and carried her over the threshold. As he stepped into the foyer, Julie gasped. It was as large as a ballroom with an immense crystal chandelier hanging from the ceiling. The floor was mirror smooth and the double staircases that curved so gracefully to the second floor were the widest she'd ever seen. Her eyes were filled with wonderment as André kissed her and then put her down.

"Do you like it, *chérie*?"

"Like it? Oh, André, I *love* it! But it's so big!"

He was delighted and threw back his head and laughed. "This is only the entrance. Wait until I show you the rest of it!"

"Oh, but before you do, there's something I *must* do."

With a giggle, Julie took a few running steps and slid across the huge floor. When she came to a stop, she turned around and, taking the running steps again, slid back across the floor right into André's arms.

Laughing and shaking her head, she said, "Oh, my darling, I know that was not a very dignified thing for the lady of the house to do. But this floor is so big and so smooth I just had to try it. I promise to be much more dignified from now on."

André joined in her laughter; then brushing his lips against hers, he smiled a delicious, lazy smile. "My lady, this is your house and you may slide across the floor anytime you please. Besides," he said, kissing the tip of her nose, "I don't want any old, stuffy, dignified lady. I want my fun-loving lady. In fact, you may want to try the banisters sometime. Seems to me that was once your mode of transportation to the chapel at the convent. And, they look as if they would be great fun to slide down."

"Don't tempt me or put any ideas in my head, Monsieur." Then with her eyes sparkling, Julie grabbed his hand. "Come, my love, and show me the rest of our beautiful home."

Although she had been consulted on every aspect of the furnishing and decorating of the house, Julie had been much too weak after the attack of yellow fever to really have a hand in any of it.

The house was not completely finished before she and her father returned to New Orleans. Then she was busy with the preparations for her wedding. Now, as André led her from room to room, Julie could only gasp at the splendor that met her eyes.

The rooms on the ground floor had doorknobs and keyhole guards made of sterling silver with tiny detailed roses engraved on their surfaces. The ceilings of the first floor reached sixteen feet in height, and each room had tall windows and French doors that kept them light and airy.

The ballroom was forty feet square, and the dining room could seat twenty-five easily and forty, if necessary. The *punka* that hung over the dining room table was the largest Julie had ever seen; and when it was pulled by a thick, silver cord, it gave off a delightful breeze that would keep the dinner guests cool and comfortable in the warmest weather.

The furniture was so beautiful that one could only marvel at the overall effect of each room. Julie's favorite colors were blue, white, and gold so André had the rooms done in those colors, using different shades, hues, and fabrics.

The furniture was from France, the marble fireplaces from Italy, the carpets from Holland, and the rugs from Persia. The huge chandeliers were more dazzling than the ones that had graced his first home. Everything was more magnificent than before. Andre had spared no expense.

Paintings by artists from Europe graced the walls of the main floor, and exquisite objects d'art were found throughout.

Besides the main parlor, dining room, and ballroom, there was the *petit* dining room and the *petit* salon, music room, and a library whose walls were lined with books from floor to ceiling.

"Have you read all these books?" Julie asked as she stood in the middle of the room and looked up at the shelves.

"Not all of them; but sometime during my life I'd like to be able to say I've read them all." André took her hand. "Come, there is still much more to see."

He led her to the music room where she found the golden harp that once belonged to her mother, also her rosewood pianoforte. "Your father sent these over for you. He says now he'll have an excuse to come visit often and listen to you play."

"*Cher Pappa* as if he would ever need an excuse to come and visit." Julie let her fingers run lightly across the keys. But, once again, André said, "Come, young lady, we're not through yet." Laughing, he led her down the hall.

He showed her the huge pantry where the servants could polish the silver and set the dishes up for serving the food.

André took her up the front staircase to the second floor where she found eight bedchambers, each with twelve-foot ceilings, each large and each with a dressing room attached.

The doorknobs of these rooms were made of imported porcelain with tiny hand-painted roses on each. Every bedroom held an elaborate four-poster bed with a canopy that reached to the ceiling. The canopy of each bed was made of satin, and each room was decorated in a different color scheme. The floors were covered with thick, plush carpets; and each dressing room held a slipper-shaped tub on wheels.

The fireplaces in the bedchambers were of marble and as elegant as those in the rooms below. Besides the bedrooms, there was a playroom for the children they both hoped to have. Beyond the playroom was a room that later would serve as the children's schoolroom. There was also a small apartment for the future tutor who would be hired to instruct the children.

"Why, Monsieur de Javon, I do believe you've thought of everything," Julie said with a smile.

André nuzzled her ear. "I wanted this house to be so perfect that you would never object to spending time out here in the country, away from the social whirl."

Julie put her arms around his neck and kissed him lightly. "André, I love being out here in the country. You know that. But more than anything, I love being wherever you are."

They spent the rest of the day inspecting the gardens that were a delight to the eye. Walks bordered with the many flowers that grew in the area wandered through the grounds. There were rosebushes, wild azaleas, asters, ground orchids, white and lavender crepe myrtle, green and gold acacia, night-blooming jasmine, dogwood, and redbud.

The large magnolia trees gave off their heavy fragrance and iron benches, tables, and chairs had been placed in certain areas of the garden so one could sit and enjoy the scene. A little gazebo, painted white and filled with blue cushions on which to sit, completed the garden. The grounds looked like a beautiful park, and it had just the effect André wanted.

* * *

They spent the month of January and most of February at Royal Oaks, and it was the happiest time André had ever known on his land.

Monsieur Charlevoix sent Julie's horse *Minuit* over, and they often went on picnics in the glade, which brought back memories of the times they'd gone there in years past.

On Julie's eighteenth birthday, André gave a small party and invited her father and a few guests from neighboring plantations.

He'd planned it, and with the help of the servants, had worked on it for days. Right before they went down to greet their guests, Andre handed Julie a velvet box, "Happy birthday, sweetheart. I have a gift for you, my love. I hope you like it."

As Julie opened the box, her eyes grew wide in amazement. "Oh, André," she said breathlessly. "They're beautiful. I've never seen such diamonds."

"Here, let me help you with the necklace." André stood behind her and fastened it around her neck. "Now, put the earrings on and let us see how they look."

Julie was standing before the mirror, and after fastening the earrings to her lobes, she stood looking at herself.

André put his arms around her waist and kissed the nape of her neck. "Those diamonds are beautiful, but they can't compare with the beauty of my wife."

Julie turned in his arms. "My love, you're so good to me. I don't know if I deserve to be spoiled like this."

"Nothing in the world would give me greater pleasure than to lavish you with gifts and spoil you—although I doubt I *could* spoil you. It's not in your nature to be spoiled." André pulled her even closer as his lips sought hers.

Julie felt her heartbeat quicken, but, suddenly, André released her. Looking at her seriously, but with a twinkle in his eyes, he murmured, "Let's go down and greet our guests, before I forget all about them and have my way with you."

Giving him a seductive smile, Julie whispered, "When the party is over, and everyone has left, you may have your way with me for as long as you like."

André pulled back from her, grinning. "Why wait? Why don't I just go to the head of the stairs, whistle down, and tell them the party is over and to go home?" He wiggled his eyebrows and gave Julie a wicked wink.

Julie shook her head and laughed. "André, you're terrible! Can't you just see the expression on their faces? *Non,* my darling, I'm afraid this was your idea. You invited these people. So, now you'll have to be a gracious host and behave yourself until our guests leave. But I promise, if you're a good boy, I'll make it up to you." Giving him a quick kiss, she took his hand and, together, they headed downstairs.

The party was a great success. Everyone admired the beautiful home, and all admired the beautiful young lady for whom the party was given. André felt such pride in Julie. She was a vision in a gown of periwinkle blue chiffon sprinkled with glittering silver flecks. Not only was she a joy to behold, she was a charming hostess, making their guests feel comfortable by including everyone in the conversations. More than one guest came up to André to extol his wife's beauty and warmth. And when she danced with another gentleman, André felt no jealously, only pride in how graceful she moved and how all eyes were on her until the music stopped. They stood together on the *galerie* and watched as their last guests rode away. Julie stood in front of him; and with his arms around her and his lips near her right ear, André whispered, "Well, my darling, if I remember correctly, you made me a promise a while ago. Something about if I was a good boy and a gracious host, which of course I was... So now do I get my way?"

Looking up at him in the moonlight, Julie felt irresistible love and desire. She laughed softly at the expression on his face. Smiling at him, she nodded, "You certainly do get your way." She turned to go indoors, when suddenly André swung her up in his arms. With a wicked little chuckle, he whispered, "I can cover more ground faster than you can sweetheart; my legs are longer."

Chapter *51*

André considered himself the most fortunate and happiest man alive. His marriage was all he'd ever dreamed of. He and Julie were so close. He often found himself watching her, but not like he'd watched Gabrielle. He loved to watch her as she entertained guests, to see the way others responded to her charm and wit.

He loved to hear her sweet laugh, so melodious and infectious. There was no way he could hear Julie laugh and not smile or laugh himself. The house rang with her laughter and her songs.

She loved to sing, and he often caught her humming or singing to herself as she went about the place. The servants adored her. He'd never seen his people as happy as they were now.

Both house servants and field hands knew they had a mistress who truly cared about them, their families, and their welfare. Whenever a slave was ill or hurt, it was Julie who was there to make certain they were properly cared for.

One day, as André returned from the fields, he saw Doctor la Poyntz's carriage in front of the house. Wondering at the reason for the doctor's visit, he hurried in to find Julie and the doctor in the parlor. They were deep in conversation; but both looked up at the sound of his footsteps.

"What's going on here?" André bent and gave Julie a light kiss. "Are you ill, my love?"

Julie smiled. *"Non*, I'm fine. I sent a note to Doctor la Poyntz asking him to come out for a visit, because I wanted him to help me understand what I can do and how I can help our people when they fall ill. Of course, if they are very ill, naturally we would send for Doctor la Poyntz; but for minor problems, I would like to know how I can help them."

André raised an eyebrow and looked at the doctor. "Isn't that just like her? Not content with all she does around here, now she wants to take care of everyone else."

Julie gave him a quick look and was relieved to see the teasing glint in his eyes.

Doctor la Poyntz spent the day giving Julie written instructions on some of the medicines he carried in his black bag. When, finally, he left for the city, Julie had her own little black bag filled with small bottles of medicines, creams, and cures that would help with minor illnesses.

One evening, after a particularly enjoyable day of riding about Royal Oaks together, enjoying a delicious dinner, and later a game of cards where Julie soundly trounced him, André looked at her with a wicked gleam in his eyes.

"I never should have taught you how to play that game, young lady. That's the thanks I get for being so nice. You beat me!"

His look of martyrdom was such that Julie burst out laughing.

"I'm sorry. I can't help it if I'm so smart and catch on so quickly." Her eyes were twinkling. "It's all that education I received at the Convent."

André drew himself up in his chair and, scowling at her, said in a funny voice, "Ah declare, Mam'selle Julie, wad da sistahs gonna' say iffen day finds out you is gamblin'?" His imitation of 'Toinette sent Julie into gales of laughter until she was rocking back and forth and tears were running down her cheeks.

"Oh, if 'Toinette could hear you now, she would probably agree with you wholeheartedly. We mustn't let her know. She would be very disappointed if she thought you were corrupting me so soon after our marriage. She thinks you are a very nice man, you know."

The time Julie and André spent at Royal Oaks was an extended honeymoon. They were alone and they cherished every moment together. Both knew that when they returned to the city, they would have to bring Frédéric into their lives; and although he never spoke about it, the truth of the matter was that André was dreading it. He wanted Julie all to himself for as long as possible. He didn't want an ill-tempered, sickly little boy clouding their relationship. Had Frédéric been their child, his and Julie's, André knew he would have felt differently.

Poor little Frédéric was the only fly in the ointment, so to speak; and it bothered André that he felt this way. He wished he could love the child like his own. But Frédéric was not his own, and he reminded André all too much of Gabrielle.

* * *

When André and Julie returned to New Orleans in February, they gradually brought the little boy into their home and their lives. It wasn't an easy task. The child was demanding and given to temper tantrums, much like his mother before him.

Frédéric turned three in February, and the hope was that, being so young, he would adjust without too much trouble. Julie did her best to make him feel loved and welcome, but it was difficult; and André often marveled at her patience.

It's not right, he thought, *Julie is just eighteen. She shouldn't have to worry about raising someone else's child before she has one of her own.*

But he couldn't voice his feelings to Julie. She would wonder what type of man she'd married, not to want his own son living with them. Like everyone else, Julie thought Frédéric was his, and André wasn't ready to tell her differently.

Spring arrived and, with it, a letter from Henry Shreve telling André he was ready to sail the new steamboat, the WASHINGTON, to New Orleans and would arrive in June.

They put off returning to the country. André was eager to see this new boat that he had invested in. There was much excitement in the city at the arrival of the boat that was so different from any seen in the past.

Shreve had mounted the boilers and machinery on the main deck rather than in the hull as had been done previously. Because the hull was shallow rather than deep, the boat seemed to ride on top of the water instead of in it. Shreve had also added a second deck for passengers.

When it was first built, people laughed at the sight of it. "Is the man crazy?" many asked.

"Does he really think such a strange-looking thing will be a success?" asked another.

They stopped laughing when the WASHINGTON was the first steamboat to successfully sail upstream as well as downstream. Because of its high-pressure engine and the way it was built, it made the trip in record time.

The trip downstream, however, was not without incident.

Julie came into the parlor, one day, to find her father reading a letter to André; and the look on both of their faces told her something was very wrong. "What's the matter? You both look so solemn."

"I just received a letter from Henry Shreve," answered her father. "The new steamboat ran aground in Georgia, and a boiler blew."

"Oh, how awful! Was anyone hurt?"

"*Oui,* several passengers and crew were scalded, and a few others were killed," André answered.

"Unfortunately, that's a risk everyone who travels by steamboat has to be willing to take," Monsieur Charlevoix said. "I'm afraid there may be more such accidents in the future."

Letters were sent back and forth between the three men, and the WASHINGTON was laid up for a while for repairs. After burying the dead, Shreve continued the trip and arrived in New Orleans on June 4, 1816.

Once again, the city turned out to greet him. André, Julie, her father, and Frédéric were on hand to see their new investment. Their joy in seeing this new boat was short-lived, because as soon as the WASHINGTON arrived, it was promptly seized and impounded by the Ohio Steamboat Navigation Company.

"I won't stand for this!" Henry Shreve said when he told André and Monsieur Charlevoix what had happened. "We must obtain a court order immediately. We will make Robert Fulton and Livingston liable for any damages our company might suffer as a result of our not being able to make use of our steamboat."

Much to their shock, Fulton and Livingston found public opinion turning against them. Henry Shreve was still very much a hero in the eyes of the citizens, because of his role in the Battle of New Orleans. The city of Shreveport would be named for him.

People were also impressed with the fact that this new boat was not only able to carry cargo but also passengers, and in such a style of luxury previously unknown. Now many wanted the privilege of traveling on it.

"I should like to take you, your wife, and Mr. Charlevoix on a tour of the boat before anyone else goes aboard," Shreve said one night when they all dined at André's home.

"Oh, I'd love to tour the boat!" Julie said, her eyes shining.

The next day, the three went aboard, with Shreve showing them around. They were duly impressed with what they saw. The public rooms were beautifully appointed with carved woodwork, soft carpets, comfortable chairs, and sofas. Cut-glass windows, stunning window coverings, and lovely mirrors were also part of the decor. The food served was as deliciously cooked as any in good restaurant. Now, passengers could travel in real luxury.

Although the monopoly was not broken, a few days later, Henry Shreve was ready to return north. The Fulton Company was forced to relent and allow the WASHINGTON to leave New Orleans. The fight for the river rights would go on for two more years.

Chapter 52

Julie and André spent a quiet and peaceful summer at Royal Oaks. That is, as quiet and peaceful as possible, considering they still had to contend with Frédéric.

The happiest part of the day was when they left him with Millie and went off by themselves to roam the plantation.

However, they always had to return to the house and to Frédéric. They both felt a sense of relief when he was finally put to bed in the evening and they could once again be alone.

Over a period of time, the child began to put a strain on their relationship. Julie would tell Frédéric to do something; the little boy would stamp his foot, double his small fists, and shout *NON*!, and then turn and run away from her.

At first, she tried handling the problem herself but when Frédéric's behavior did not improve, she finally spoke to André. "Sometimes, I just don't know what to do with him. He's only a baby, really but he can be so obstinate and impossible to handle that he tries my patience."

The first time Julie told him of the problem, André got a hard, cold look on his face. "He's just like his mother!" he muttered under his breath.

Now, whenever she spoke to him about a problem with Frédéric, Julie would see the hard look settle on André's face, and he would march off to find the child and give him a good spanking.

Julie always tried to talk André out of it. "Frédéric is still so young; he's having a difficult time adjusting. He really isn't all that bad."

She felt guilty for having complained. She shouldn't have bothered André with the problem. She was sure she could handle Frédéric after all he was only a baby. But her pleas fell on deaf ears.

André would glare at her, and she could see the tension in his face. "He needs to be disciplined, Julie. He can't be allowed to get away with this type of behavior! I think I know better how to handle this than you!"

They would argue every time André disciplined Frédéric. Julie felt upset when she heard the child crying at the top of his lungs. She knew André wasn't spanking him hard, but one would think Frédéric was being killed to listen to him.

After one such outburst, Julie tried to speak to André about the problem. "Why do you treat Frédéric so coldly? You have so little patience with him. Sometimes, it seems as if you don't like your own son."

She paused, and again she saw the hard, cold look cross André's face. But she had finally gotten up her courage to ask and was determined to get an answer, if possible.

Taking a deep breath, she continued, "Do you know that in the entire time we've been married, I have never once heard you tell the child that you love him." It was obvious André was uncomfortable. "Do you love him, André?"

André's eyes scalded her as he lashed out, "Of course, I love him! What a ridiculous question! How can you think such a thing? Or ask such a thing? I would prefer not to discuss Frédéric any more, if you don't mind!"

And without another word, he stormed from the room, leaving Julie to wonder how it would be when they had a child of their own.

Something was wrong; something was very wrong, and it frightened her. If only she could get André to tell her what it was. She had made him angry, and that was not her intention. *Oh André,* she thought, as she stood alone in the parlor after he left. *Please don't let this problem come between us. Please, share with me the problem you seem to have with Frédéric.*

André headed out to the sugar factory. He felt angry and miserable. Gabrielle had come between him and Julie in the past with her terrible jealously. Now, it seemed she was coming between them again, because of her child!

He had hurt the one person he loved more than anyone in the world. He knew he had acted abominably toward Julie. She was a sweet, kind, loving person herself. So naturally, she would be concerned about his attitude toward, and treatment of, Frédéric. He should be grateful she was the way she was, instead of lashing out at her. God knows he'd had to deal with a hateful wife for too many years when he was married to Gabrielle!

André vowed to try harder to show affection to Frédéric and made up his mind to do whatever was necessary to make things right with Julie.

Neither could stay angry with the other for long. So when he returned to the house later that day, he sought Julie out. His arms felt like steel bands as he held her to him.

"I'm sorry I was ugly and angry earlier," he murmured "I love you so much, Julie, and I don't want us to be at odds with each other. Will you forgive me?"

His face showed repentance; and although his eyes were filled with love, there seemed to be a hint of torment in their depths.

Julie gave him a gentle smile as she slid her arms around his neck. Standing on tiptoes, she gave him a long and loving kiss. "Of course, I forgive you sweetheart. I didn't mean to upset you with my questions. But, André, darling, I wish you could tell me what the problem is between you and Frédéric."

"Let's not talk about Frédéric right now," André murmured in her ear. "We'll discuss him later, all right?"

Not wanting to have another fight, Julie agreed to let the subject rest for a while. They each put their anger and hurt feelings aside and once again life was blissful, but the problem remained.

Julie was tormented with both André's behavior toward Frédéric and her own feelings toward her husband when he acted that way. It was a problem she didn't know how to handle and since it caused such trouble between them whenever she brought the subject up, she stopped speaking of it all together. But it didn't go away; instead, it hung over them like a dark cloud.

The summer became extremely hot and uncomfortable, and Julie found her riding habits too warm and uncomfortable. They weighed her down, and when she and André rode out in the hot sun, they left her weak from the heat. One day, she hit upon an idea that would solve her problem and make riding about the plantation more bearable.

While in New Orleans, she had bought quite a bit of fabric for the seamstresses to make clothes for the slaves who were in need of them. Now, as she thought about the fabric, she decided to pay a visit to the sewing room. She waited until a morning when Andre had ridden out to the fields. Once he was gone, she hurried to the room.

As always, she was greeted with bright smiles and a warm *bonjour*. She explained to the women what she needed, "Do you think you can make the clothes I want?" she asked.

"*Oui, Maîtresse*," the head seamstress assured her. "We make dem now, and day be ready real soon, *oui*."

A few days later, Julie hurried back to the sewing room to collect her new riding apparel. She was delighted with the results, and now hurried to hide her treasures in the back of her armoire. She didn't want André to see her new clothes just yet.

Later that day when he returned to share lunch with her and Frédéric, André asked her if she would like to ride out to the sugar factory with him.

"I'd love to my darling," she answered, her eyes twinkling. "But I will have to meet you there. I promised Frédéric a story before he takes his nap. And, of course, I must change clothes."

André nodded. "Very well, but don't be too long." He bent and gave her a long kiss before leaving.

Once the story was read and Julie could turn Frédéric over to Millie, she picked up her skirts and ran to her bedchamber, where she quickly changed into her new riding outfit.

Pulling her hair up, she plunked a wide-brimmed hat on her head. Just as she stepped out of the bedchamber, she ran smack into 'Toinette.

The old woman gave her young mistress a startled look; and when she saw what the lady of the house was wearing, her look changed to one of distress.

"Oh, Mam'selle Julie, what you doin' dressed like dat! Now you is da lady of a big, fine house. What da sistahs gonna say iffen day eveh finds out!"

Julie couldn't help herself and burst out laughing. "Oh, 'Toinette, are you still worrying about what the sisters at the convent are going to say?" She laughed again and shook her head. "I hardly think the sisters would be interested in what I'm wearing now that I'm all grown up and, as you say, 'the lady of the house.' Don't worry so, dear 'Toinette.

Besides, these clothes will be far more comfortable in this heat."

Giving 'Toinette a quick hug and still laughing, Julie skipped down the stairs and dashed outdoors to find *Minuit* saddled and waiting for her.

'Toinette watched as Julie rushed from the house and then continued down the hall shaking her head and muttering to herself.

"It ain't fittin', it jes' ain't fittin'! Ridin' 'round like po' white trash! What dose sistahs gonna think iffen day eveh finds out!"

When she reached the sugar factory, Julie found that André had just left and was headed for the cotton fields. Quickly, she followed him; and when finally she caught up with him, André almost didn't recognize her.

Dressed in a pair of boys' breeches, a shirt, long stockings, and a pair of boys' shoes, with her hair pulled up on top of her head and the hat pulled down over her face, she brought back memories of the first time he saw her on a horse.

After his initial surprise, André threw back his head and laughed. "You look very much like you did that day I found you hiding amongst the trees, watching my slaves and me build our cabins," he said when he finally stopped laughing.

"I thought these clothes would bring back memories," Julie giggled. "I just couldn't stand those hot, old riding habits another day. This is ever so much more comfortable, although 'Toinette had a fit when she saw me, and is even now worrying and fretting about what the good sisters at the convent will say if they find out."

This last remark sent them both into peals of laughter and the rest of the day was spent riding about laughing and remembering the times when Julie was a child and they had spent whole days together.

* * *

A happy event took place at Royal Oaks that summer, Millie and Demetrius were married. Julie had a lovely white wedding gown made for Millie and the ceremony was held on the *galerie* of the main house.

André invited his former in-laws, Julie's father, and the white families from neighboring plantations, along with their slaves. A reception and party was held out by the slave cabins; and later the white folks returned to the house to continue their party.

André gave the bride away. And for a wedding gift, a new cabin had been built for the newlyweds, and they were given a week off from work.

Chapter 53

Summer ended, and although Julie would have been perfectly content to remain in the country for the winter, André felt they should return to the city. He wanted to check on his various business ventures and confer with his factor and cotton broker.

Winter in the city was filled with parties and balls. In December of 1816, William Charles Cole Claiborne left the office of governor. He had held the position from the time Louisiana was a territory in 1803, until long after it became a state in 1812. Now, he was constitutionally ineligible to continue in office. Because of his great popularity, he was promptly elected to the United States Senate and would be leaving the city soon to take office in the nation's capital.

There were many social activities held in his honor; and André and Julie were a part of each function. It was a round of parties and balls that seemed endless.

There was another reason for such celebration. Although Claiborne was very popular and everyone was saddened to see him leave, for the first time in the history of the state, a Créole had been elected to succeed him.

Major General Jacques Philippe de Villere would be the new Governor; and the Créoles were delighted to have one of their own in control of their destiny.

Jacques Philippe de Villere was a remarkable man who would lead his fellow Créoles and Americans to great prosperity. During his four years in office, the need for more warehouses would increase, and André was one of the first to add more down on *Rue Tchoupitoulas*.

The port was filled with ships and steamboats and André and Monsieur Charlevoix's steamboats were among them. Real estate rose in value and the city limits expanded.

Once more, André was in the forefront. Having bought much real estate earlier, he was now ready to buy more. New laws were created for the welfare of the city and the people.

André couldn't believe how his good fortune continued. It seemed every time he turned around, he was making more money. He was supremely happy in his marriage; and even though he and Julie had their problems, especially where Frédéric was concerned, Julie was everything, and more than, he had hoped for in a wife. As their first wedding anniversary drew near, André thought perhaps Julie would like to do something special.

"Julie, would you like to have a party to celebrate our first year of marriage?"

Julie shook her head. *"Non*, my love, the only party I want is a party for two; just you and me."

The truth of the matter was that she was not feeling at all well. There were already too many parties to attend in honor of both the retiring and the incoming Governors. She was quite worn out. For the past week, she had been having attacks of nausea off and on during the day, especially in the morning when she first woke up. She had no married sisters to ask about this, and no mother to counsel her and, because she didn't know what was wrong, she hid the problem from André so as not to worry him.

One morning as they sat down to breakfast, the nausea hit her so hard she had to leave the table. Without warning, she jumped up and rushed from the room. André had noticed she didn't look well when they sat down, and he immediately ran after her. She was leaning against the wall in the hall, holding her napkin to her mouth. When she looked up at him, André saw how pale she was.

Seeing the concern on his face, Julie smiled weakly. "André, darling, don't look so frightened...I'm sure it's nothing to worry about. My stomach is just a little upset. Perhaps, if I lie down for a while, I'll feel better."

Leaning on him, Julie started to walk toward the stairs; but she felt so ill and faint she almost fell. André, filled with concern, picked her up and carried her to their bedchamber. He then ordered one of the servants to fetch the doctor.

When Doctor la Poyntz finished examining Julie, he found André waiting anxiously in the hall. "How is she doctor? Is it serious? Will she be all right?"

The doctor smiled and shook his head, "André, for heaven's sake' calm down. I understand your concern, but Julie's fine. I'm happy to tell you that your wife is *enceinte*."

"Julie's going to have a *bébé*?"

"*Oui*, she should have it sometime in July. Meanwhile, make sure she eats well and gets plenty of rest."

After the doctor left, André hurried into the bedroom. He was beaming from ear to ear.

Julie was lying in bed, still looking pale and wan.

"André, did the doctor tell you? I'm going to have a *bébé*." Picking up her hand and kissing it, his eyes filled with love and joy, André softly murmured, "*Oui*, sweetheart, he told me, and I couldn't be happier."

"André, I hope it's a boy and he looks just like you."

Brushing a lock of hair from her forehead, he gently kissed her. "My love, I hope it's a girl who will be as beautiful and as sweet as her mother. But as long as it's our child, I'll take whatever the good Lord sends us and be supremely happy."

Julie's pregnancy was not easy. The nausea continued to plague her throughout the remaining months, often leaving her weak and feeling faint, although the good doctor assured her that, with most of his patients, it ended after the third month.

She had little energy, and that was unusual for her. Her feeling of tiredness drove her to distraction. She tried to remain patient with Frédéric but his constant demands and temper tantrums, coupled with the way she felt, often made her impatient with him and wore her out. Sometimes, it was all she could do to keep from giving him a good slap. Many times, she heard herself raising her voice to him. After such an outburst, she would feel bad.

By the first of May, Julie was more than ready to return to Royal Oaks. "André, could we please go back to the country soon?" she asked one evening at dinner.

André was more than willing to oblige. "Of course, sweetheart; we'll leave the first of next week."

* * *

"André, I'm so happy to be home," Julie said as they lay in bed their first night at the plantation. "I love New Orleans; but this is where I'm happiest, especially now that I'm *enceinte*."

André reached out and drew her to him. "I'm happiest here also, and I'm always happy when I'm with you."

It was true, they both enjoyed the city but their hearts were always at Royal Oaks.

Julie especially had a freedom in the country that she couldn't have in the city. Here, she could sit on the *galerie* during the day or go for a stroll in the vast gardens. She could walk to the kitchen and talk to the cooks, or stroll out to the slave quarters and visit with the younger children during the day and with their parents in the evening.

In the city, she had been mostly confined to the house. It was unthinkable for a pregnant woman of her station to walk about the public streets. She would be limited to the house and the courtyard.

In the city, when she rode in the carriage, she had to cover herself from the waist down with a light blanket, no matter how warm the weather. And going out in the carriage in New Orleans was less than pleasant.

The spring rains arrived in March, and the streets were mostly mud and filth that made a carriage ride miserable. The wheels sank to their axles in the muck.

When finally the rains stopped, steam rose from the ground as the sun beat down baking the mud and turning the streets into hard, deep ruts that made the carriage bump and sway and jar her bones unmercifully.

Frédéric also seemed to do better at the plantation. He could run and play to his heart's content and make as much noise as he liked. There was enough room so that when Julie was tired of being around him, she could leave him in the care of Millie and go off by herself and rest.

The summer was exceedingly hot, and Julie was extremely uncomfortable. She hadn't gained much weight, but for one who was always slender, the extra weight made the heat seem worse and sapped her strength

She woke one morning in July to a strange pain. André had long ago left for the fields. Julie called 'Toinette to prepare her bath. It was already eleven o'clock. André would be back in an hour to eat lunch with Frédéric and her.

As she started down the stairs to watch for him, the pain hit her again. It had been a while since she'd felt the first pain, so she gave it no thought. Stepping out on the *galerie*, she saw André in the distance.

When he reached the house, he dismounted, gave the reins to a young stable boy, bounded up the stairs, and swept her into his arms. "Did you sleep well, my beautiful darling?"

Julie hadn't slept well at all. But she wouldn't worry him. So she assured him she had. "I don't know how you can say I look beautiful when I'm so fat and I have this huge stomach."

"I like your huge stomach," he answered, smiling and patting it gently. "There is someone in there I am most anxious to meet." He studied her for a moment and added, "Besides, your face hasn't changed; it's still as beautiful as ever, maybe even more so because you are *enceinte*."

Slipping his arm around her waist, André walked with Julie to the dining room. Millie and Frédéric were already in the room.

"*Bonjour*, Frédéric, have you been having fun playing?" Andre asked as he tousled the child's hair.

"*Non, Pappa,* I'm hot and I don't want to play." The little boy looked angry. "Why does it have to be so hot? I don't like it. Make it stop, *Pappa*."

André spent the next few minutes trying to explain the change of climate in terms a small boy could understand.

Julie was glad he was distracted, because another pain passed over her; this one stronger than the first two. She knew she had grimaced when it hit and she knew if André had seen her expression, it would have upset him. And she didn't feel it was anything to worry him about.

When the meal ended, André patted Frédéric on the head and told him he would see him later. Then he turned to his wife.

"Julie, my love, I must go back out and check some fences that need repair. I shouldn't be gone long, then we'll spend the rest of the day together."

Julie walked out to the *galerie* with him but before he left, André studied her face for a long time. "Are you sure you are feeling all right, dearest?"

"*Oui*, André, I feel fine. Why do you ask?"

"Suddenly, you look so pale. You have no color in your face. I worry about you, especially now that the *bébé* is due."

361

"André, you are a terrible worrywart. If I look pale, it's no doubt because of this heat and the extra weight I'm carrying. There is nothing for you to worry about. Now go and see to the fences. I'll be fine, I promise."

He gave her a long, searching look, bent and kissed her, then ran down the stairs and swung himself into the saddle.

Another pain hit Julie as she watched him ride away. It was even stronger than the others. Still, she refused to pay any attention to it. She crossed the *galerie* and sat in a rocking chair that had been made especially for her. With her hands resting lightly on the chair arms, she leaned her head back, closed her eyes, took a deep breath, and gently rocked.

The air was filled with the fragrance of flowers, and it filled her with delight. Oh, how she loved being in the country. It was so pleasant and peaceful. She loved the sounds of the plantation. If she listened carefully, she could hear, off in the distance, the field hands talking and singing as they worked. Closer to home, she could here the soft murmur of the cooks working in the kitchen. She heard the chickens rooting around the yard, the lowing of a cow, and the whinny of a horse in the meadow. Royal Oaks was alive with activity, but the sounds of the plantation were not loud and harsh as they were in the city.

The kitchen maids were laughing and joking now, and it made Julie smile to hear them. She was so contented she started to hum a little tune when suddenly another pain hit. She gripped the chair arms until the skin on her hands drew taut, and her knuckles turned white. The smile left her face, and the song she was humming turned into a gasp and a moan.

When the pain finally passed, she found herself weak and shaken. Was the *bébé* about to come? Until this moment, she had not really thought about how it would feel to give birth. There was no one to tell her what to expect. Now, as another sharp pain jarred her body, Julie became frightened. Frightened of this sudden horrible pain that left her weak and shaking until she had no energy to walk. Before she had yellow fever, she had never had a sick day in her life, except for a mild cold or two. She was not used to feeling bad and right now, she felt *terrible*!

Tears filled her eyes. She wanted André, she wanted her mother. *Oh, maman, why aren't you here? I need you to tell me what to expect. I need you to help me. Oh, Cher Seigneur, I am so frightened. Please*

Dieu, don't let the pain get any worse.

Slowly, Julie rose from the chair. She felt so weak that her knees were like rubber, and her heart was racing with fear. She reached the huge foyer when another pain hit. There was no one around, and the pain was so sharp it took her breath away. She sank to the floor crying and gasping for breath.

Several moments later, 'Toinette came to check on her and found Julie lying on the floor. She quickly called for help. Both Demetrius and Delilah came running.

Demetrius picked Julie up and turned to Delilah. "Send fo' da *Maître*. Then order a hoss ready fo' me to ride fo' da doctor." To Julie, he said, "Shhh, *petite Maîtresse*, don't you worry none. Demetrius take you upstairs. 'Toinette stay wid you 'til *Maître* come. You gonna be all right, *oui*."

It took a while for the stable boy to find André but before he could get a complete sentence out, André was on his horse and headed back to the house. Demetrius had already left for New Orleans by the time André raced up the stairs to the bedchamber.

'Toinette had Julie out of her dress and into her nightgown and had made her as comfortable as possible.

André bent over her. "Julie, dearest, I'm sorry I wasn't here. I never should have left you."

Julie tried to smile, but, just then, another wave of pain washed over her. She grabbed his hand, and André was amazed at the strength of her grip. She whispered and moaned, "André, the pain is so bad."

"I know, my darling, I know." But he didn't know. How could he possibly know? He felt like a fool for saying it. He tried to think of something to say that would make sense, but words failed him. All he could do was stand there and let her grip his hand as each new pain arrived.

'Toinette left the room and returned with a bowl of cool water and a cloth. "Ah sponge her down, help keep her cool in dis heat."

"'Toinette, I'll sponge her; you go and watch for the doctor. I'm certain he will need your help when he arrives."

André took the basin from the servant, put the bowl on the nightstand, and sat on the edge of the bed. For the next few hours, he sponged Julie's face, arms, and body. Sweat covered her as each new pain attacked. And with each pain, her body jerked and she moaned and cried out.

André had never seen a woman in labor before and felt so helpless that it about drove him crazy. Watching Julie like this brought back the nightmare of her bout with yellow fever. All the fear came rushing back.

"Oh, please, *Cher Dieu*," he prayed in a low voice, "she survived that terrible attack of yellow fever please don't let me lose her through childbirth."

Chapter 54

"Where is that doctor? Why doesn't he get here?" André muttered as he wrung out the cloth and once again sponged Julie's face and smoothed her hair from her forehead.

When finally the doctor arrived, 'Toinette brought him to the bedchamber, left, and returned carrying a couple of bed sheets.

André stood by helplessly and watched as 'Toinette tied the sheets to each bedpost at the foot of the bed, then knotted them together in the middle. The doctor put the sheets in Julie's hands. "Julie, Julie, listen to me. Hold on to these sheets and pull on them when you have a pain. Do you understand?"

André could see Julie struggling through the haze of pain as the doctor spoke to her. Her hands closed around the sheets and as another pain arrived, she pulled on them with all of her might.

The doctor looked up at the young man. "Now, André, I think you should go downstairs and have a glass of wine and relax. It will be a while before this little one arrives. There's nothing you can do here."

Doctor la Poyntz removed his coat and started rolling up his sleeves as he spoke. "Oh, and André, I had one of your boys ride over to *Château Charlevoix* to tell you father-in-law. He should be here soon to keep you company. Now, go along with you. I'll take good care of your wife."

André did as he was told. He wanted to stay by Julie's side; but the doctor said *non*. "You will just be in the way."

André went down to the parlor and when Monsieur Charlevoix arrived, he found his son-in-law pacing the floor like a caged lion. Demetrius brought wine, and Jean-Claude tried to engage André in conversation.

As the hours ticked by, André became more and more nervous. Finally, he insisted on waiting in the upper hall that was so large there were sofas and chairs scattered around on which to sit.

Now he was closer to Julie and could hear some of what was going on. After a couple of hours, the doctor stepped out of the bedchamber.

André leapt to his feet. "How is Julie? Has the *bébé* arrived?"

"*Non*, André, the *bébé* has not arrived. I just stepped out for a moment." His face was covered with perspiration, and he took out his handkerchief and mopped his brow. He looked at André for a long moment.

Doctor la Poyntz searched his brain. How to tell this young man the truth? There was a serious problem, but the doctor was almost afraid to mention it. André had already lost one child and his first wife.

The baby was turned so that its shoulder was blocking the birth channel. The doctor realized that to save both Julie's and the baby's life he would have to try to turn it so its little head would be in the right position to emerge. But would he be able to do it? That was the question.

"It will be a while yet, André." He would wait. He would wait and see if maybe the baby would turn on its own. He would not say anything unless it was absolutely necessary.

"Will she be all right?" André asked, his face filled with fear. "Is her life in any danger?"

Doctor la Poyntz laid a hand on André's arm. "Only God knows that for certain. However, she's trying to cooperate with me and is doing as I tell her."

The doctor stood up, and it was easy to see how tired he was. As he returned to the bedroom, he assured André he would keep him posted on Julie's progress.

André resumed his pacing. He could hear Julie moaning and crying, and each sound she made pierced his heart. If only there were something he could do for her! But there was nothing he could do and the feeling of helplessness filled him with despair.

He stopped pacing and suddenly sat down next to his father-in-law who was as anxious and worried as he.

"*Pappa*, how did you get through this three times with your wife? I don't think I could stand to go through this again."

His father-in-law shook his head. "André, I think we men have the easy part. Think of what the woman has to go through."

"That's what I mean, *Pappa*. I can't stand to think of what Julie is going through. I just don't know if I can ever watch her go through this again."

"Well, André, if you make love often, sooner or later you make *bébés* unless of course you plan to remain celibate for the rest of your marriage."

At this last remark, André gave his father-in-law such a strange look the older man could not help but give a soft chuckle.

"That's what I thought. But there are ways of preventing it. If you have never heard of them, I will tell you later."

Staring off into space, André said, "It doesn't seem right for Julie to go through such pain, when together we had such pleasure." He got up and paced the floor for the next few minutes as his father-in-law watched.

Then Monsieur Charlevoix spoke "André, childbirth is the most dangerous thing a woman can go through. There are many men in New Orleans who have lost more than one wife while begetting children.

"With all the other things that can kill people here in Louisiana; the climate, the fevers and such, still, the greatest toll on a woman's life is childbirth. I tell you this because it is a reality we men must come to accept. Not an easy thought, but one that is fact."

Jean-Claude's face was filled with the same fear and concern as his son-in-law. "Hopefully, with God's grace, Julie will be fine. Don't worry, André, Doctor la Poyntz is an excellent doctor and has delivered many babies." He tried to sound reassuring. The night wore on, and the doctor came out of the bedchamber several times to tell André and Monsieur Charlevoix that the baby had not yet arrived.

It was morning when André and his father-in-law heard a series of screams. André stopped pacing as he heard the screams coming from behind the bedroom door. They seemed far worse and more intense than anything he'd ever heard in his life.

He could stand it no longer. Flinging open the door, he rushed into the room to see the doctor's hand and part of his arm covered with blood. He saw his wife screaming and twisting and thrashing as her body endured the pain. He saw the wild half-crazed look of pain on her face, and then he saw the miracle of miracles. He saw the tiny head slowly start to emerge from its mother's body.

Suddenly, the baby was out and when the doctor held it upside down by its feet, and slapped its little bottom, André heard the sound of its cry. He witnessed all of this while standing at the foot of the bed. He hadn't felt sick at the sight of blood or birth. He'd felt rage that Julie had to endure such unspeakable pain in order to give birth.

Doctor la Poyntz turned to André with a weary voice. "Well, young man, you have a son. He appears to be sound and healthy in spite of his difficult arrival, but Julie is another matter."

He went on to explain what caused the problem. "I had to reach in and turn his body. I'm sure it was very painful for Julie." He paused and mopped his brow. "This birth was far more difficult than I could have imagined. Julie's lost a great deal of blood, is worn out, and will need a long rest in order to regain her strength."

"Will she live? Will she be all right?" André whispered the question, almost afraid to hear the answer.

"I certainly hope so, André. But, first, I must stop the bleeding. Now go and look at your son, while I tend to your wife."

In a daze, André did as he was told. 'Toinette had finished cleaning the baby. She let André examine his tiny son then wrapped the infant in a blanket and handed him to his father.

"Michie Charlevoix, he like to see da *petit* one too," she said with a broad smile.

Still in a daze, André stepped out into the hall and handed the infant to the older man.

"How is Julie?" his father-in-law asked, anxiously searching André's face.

"Oh, *Pappa,* the pain she endured; what she went through was terrible!"

"I know, André, I know," Monsieur Charlevoix patted André's shoulder. "But praise God she's alive, and you have this beautiful, healthy little son." He looked down at the small bundle he held. When, finally, the doctor left Julie's bedchamber, he felt her life was somewhat out of danger.

Wiping his brow, he turned to André: "You must keep her very quiet. We don't want her hemorrhaging. That could prove fatal." He left strict instructions for what André should do if he had any fears. "I'll come at once if you need me."

So saying, he headed for the *garçonnière* that had been made ready for him. He would spend the day and night resting, and check on Julie before heading back to New Orleans.

Julie lay very still, and for a moment, André panicked. She was so still, he thought she was dead. He fell on his knees beside the bed and took her hand in his and pressed her hand to his lips.

"Oh, Julie, I love you so much. My dearest, precious, Julie, you are my heart of hearts, my very life. Thank God you're alive!" He closed his eyes. "Thank you, *Mon Dieu,* for my little son. But, mostly, thank you for sparing Julie."

He sat in a chair by the bed the entire night. He would wake the moment he heard Julie stir. Leaning over her, he would check her breathing, check to make sure she wasn't losing too much blood. Finally, when he was sure she was all right, he dozed off again.

It was late morning before she stirred. André woke up at once. Leaning over, he kissed her gently. "Julie, my dearest love, you've suffered so to give us a son."

Drawing the chair closer to the bed and picking up her hand, he kissed it and held it to his cheek as he brushed her damp hair from her face. His love for her was so great it brought tears to his eyes as he thought of all she had endured to bring their son into the world.

Her eyes fluttered and slowly opened. Then, in a voice so weak it was barely a whisper, she asked, "André, is it over? Do we have a *bébé?*"

"*Oui*, dearest, it's all over and we have a little boy."

"Is he perfect?"

"Of course, he's perfect, my darling."

"May I see him, please?"

'Toinette, who had just come into the room, unwrapped the blanket and laid the baby next to her. Slowly, Julie checked the tiny hands and feet to be sure there were ten little fingers and toes. It took all of her strength, and for a moment, André thought she might faint. But, slowly, she raised her eyes and looked at him. "He is a beautiful *bébé*, isn't he, André?"

"*Oui*, my love, he certainly is."

Her father had spent the night at Royal Oaks. Now, he entered the room and walked over to the bed. Bending down, he kissed his daughter and said, "Julie, *chérie*, you've made me so proud. I have a beautiful, healthy grandson. I am so happy to be a *grandpère.*" Julie was too weak and too tired to answer. She simply smiled, closed her eyes, and slept.

Chapter 55

They named him Jean-Paul after both their fathers. Julie found him a wonder. She would sit for long periods just watching her baby as he slept. It filled her with awe that this perfect tiny child had grown within her. She would stroke his perfectly shaped little head, which was covered with a soft down of light baby hair. She would caress his little hands and marvel at the fingernails so tiny, yet so perfectly formed. When he was awake, she would cradle him in her arms and sing and coo to him. She would talk to him, telling him of this beautiful place named Royal Oaks where he had been born. She told him how his father had carved it out of the wilderness with his own hands.

When André returned from the fields or the sugar factory, he would hurry to the bedchamber to join Julie in playing with, talking to, or just watching his tiny son. Like any proud father, he would tell Demetrius, Samson, Hoffman, or anyone who would listen, about the baby. He'd wanted a daughter. But once he set eyes on Jean-Paul, it was love at first sight.

It took several months for Julie to regain her strength. The long labor and difficult delivery had taken their toll. She longed to be out of bed, riding across Royal Oaks with André, doing the things she enjoyed; and so she concentrated on regaining her strength as quickly as possible.

Everyone was happy with Jean-Paul. Charles and Francesca, along with their two sons, Antoine and Reynard came with both sets of parents for a visit a few weeks after the baby's birth.

Julie was still weak and far from recovery; but André carried her downstairs and made her comfortable in a chair so she could visit with their guests.

"Here she is," he announced with a broad grin as he entered the parlor with Julie in his arms. "However, if she starts looking tired, I shall take her right back to bed so she can rest."

Julie was greeted with hugs and kisses; and everyone commented on how lovely she looked.

She did indeed look lovely in a robe of blue silk trimmed with delicate lace and ribbons. Her hair was tied back with a blue ribbon; and on her feet, she wore blue satin slippers. There was color in her face, and her eyes sparkled with the joy of being a new mother.

'Toinette followed, carrying Jean-Paul and the first person she handed the child to was Monsieur Charlevoix, who beamed like any proud *grandpère*.

"He certainly is a beautiful baby," Francesca said as Julie's father turned the baby over to her. She gently stroked his head that was covered with tiny light brown ringlets. "And he is going to have eyes as dark as your eyes, Julie."

The baby was handed around as first Madame du Fray and then Madame Ste. Claire each held and cooed over him. Even Charles took a turn holding and admiring him.

The little boys, Antoine and Reynard, were equally fascinated with this tiny creature and crowded around to inspect him. Everyone but Frédéric thought Jean-Paul wonderful.

While the adults visited, Frédéric and his cousins went out to play. After a while, Frédéric became angry when he couldn't have his way, and left his cousins to sneak back into the house. Quietly, he edged himself into the parlor and stood half hidden in a corner, and watched the fuss being made over this new addition. His little face was dark with anger. It wasn't fair the way everyone was carrying on! No one had paid much attention to him! For well over a year, Frédéric was the only child in André and Julie's lives. And before that, he'd been the baby at his aunt and uncle's home. Now there was another baby, and everyone fussed and carried on about this one, but ignored him! At four and a half, he didn't understand or know how to cope with the jealous feelings building within him.

Just then, his aunt Francesca looked over and saw him. "Why,

Frédéric, why are you hiding in the corner? Come here, *chérie.*"

Slowly, Frédéric crossed the room and stood beside her.

Francesca put her arm around the little boy's waist. "Did you come back inside to see your sweet *bébé* brother?"

The little boy shook his head. *"Non!* I don't like that *bébé.* I don't want him here. Send him away!"

Francesca smiled and gave him a hug. "Oh, Frédéric, you don't mean that. I know you love your *petit* brother. He's so sweet. Go and look at him and see how sweet he is."

Frédéric scowled and shook his head again. *"Non!* I don't like that *bébé.* He's bad!" With that, he turned and ran from the room.

There was a strained silence for a moment. Everyone had the same thought. Frédéric was obviously very jealous of the baby, and André and Julie would have their hands full helping him to adjust to Jean-Paul's arrival.

Frédéric's resentment and jealously toward his baby brother did not lessen; and it became more apparent to Julie over the next few months. Both she and André always tried to include him in any activity with the baby.

"You are his big brother," André said one day. "He will look up to you, and want to be like you. But you must treat him with love and kindness."

They encouraged him to play with Jean-Paul when the baby was awake and lying on a blanket on the floor. But Frédéric continued to view this newest member of the family as a threat.

"Non! I don't want to play with a *bébé!* I don't like him!"

Nothing André or Julie said; no amount of coaxing made a difference. Frédéric didn't like his baby brother and wouldn't have a thing to do with him.

André now had a new worry and decided to discuss it with his father-in-law one evening when Jean-Claude rode over for dinner.

Julie had retired to their bed to rest, and the two men sat in the *petit* salon.

Monsieur Charlevoix looked at his son-in-law for a long moment. "What's on your mind, André? I know something is bothering you. Would you like to tell me what it is?"

André smiled. "How well you know me, *Pappa.* I do have a problem, and I want to discuss it with you."

"Well, tell me what it is. And if I can, I will do my best to help you."

373

"It has to do with Frédéric." Concern was clearly written on Andre's face. "When he was born and I was married to Gabrielle, I had no idea that soon I'd be a widower. I had no idea someday I would marry Julie and have a son of my own."

He paused and stared off into space for a moment, then continued. "Well, to get to the point, *Pappa*, I have allowed everyone to believe that Frédéric is my flesh and blood, my first born, as such, my heir. If something were to happened to me, Frédéric would fall heir to Royal Oaks and everything else I own." He looked over at his father-in law with a distraught expression on his face.

Monsieur Charlevoix nodded. "*Oui*, I see what you mean. Now that you have a son of your own, you naturally want him to be your heir. That is only right. But, in order to do that, you will have to admit that Frédéric is not your son that he is, indeed, a bastard and, as such, is not entitled to anything."

André's handsome brow creased with worry and his face was sad. "*Oui*, and that's the problem. I will not only hurt an innocent child but his family as well, and his grandparents and his aunt and uncle. It's such a terrible stigma to put on the boy! But by the same token, I cannot allow Frédéric to inherit my estate and deny my own son what is rightfully his. Frédéric is still my son; so of course, he will be well taken care of. But he is not my heir."

He looked over at the older man. "You're so much wiser than I. What should I do, *Pappa*?"

Monsieur Charlevoix pressed his fingertips together, rested his chin on them and thought for a long moment. "Well, the first thing I think you should do is talk to your lawyer, your American lawyer, since it is the American law we live by.

"You must be honest with him and tell him the truth. Then have him help you write up a will that cannot be contested in a court of law." He saw the look of distress on André's face. "I know, André, it will not be easy, but it is the only way you can protect Jean-Paul.

"You don't have to say anything to anyone for a while. Of course, your lawyer is sworn to say nothing. What you tell him is strictly confidential. Then, when the time is right, you must tell Julie and Monsieur and Madame Ste. Claire, although I feel certain that all but Julie know the truth." He paused and added, "Of course, someday, you must also tell Frédéric. But I don't think you will have to do any of that this week; so don't look so distressed. Take first things first. Pray on it, the Lord will let you know when it is the right time to tell the others."

André sighed heavily. "*Pappa*, being married to Gabrielle was a living hell. Being married to Julie has been as close to heaven as I could imagine. Now, my heaven must be disturbed by this most unpleasant problem." He smiled wistfully. "But, then, God never promised us heaven on earth, did He?"

* * *

It was hurricane season, and André was ever on the alert for the first signs that a hurricane was brewing.

The hurricane hit with a force that was truly frightening, The wind uprooted trees, and several of the slave's cabins suffered damage. There was also some damage to the stables and the summer house where vegetables were stored.

Thunder crashed across the sky, shaking the earth and house. Jagged streaks of lighting illuminated the heavens; and the rain caused the river to rise to an alarming height.

André ordered the slaves up to the big house where he felt they would be safe. They crowded in and filled the back part of the house; and Julie was kept busy, at first, making certain no one had been hurt as they ran across the fields and yard to escape the fury of the storm.

Finally, when she had everyone calmed down, Julie went to the parlor. She held and cuddled Jean-Paul while she stood listening to the wind as it roared around the house. Frédéric followed her into the parlor, crying and even more upset because Julie held Jean-Paul instead of him.

"Please, Frédéric, please, stop crying so," she said almost absentmindedly. "Come, *cher*, we will sit in the big chair, and you can cuddle up to me. I won't let anything happen to you."

Julie reached down and took the child's hand and guided him to a large chair where she sat holding Jean-Paul. She tried to pull Frédéric up beside her, but the little boy resisted. He stood before her, his short legs apart and a scowl on his face.

"*Non*, I don't want to sit down next to that *bébé!*" he cried at the top of his lungs. "I hate that *bébé*, put him down!"

Suddenly, Julie became exasperated. She'd had just about all she could stand of Frédéric's behavior. She resented the fact that the child never called his little brother by his given name. It was always "that *bébé*."

Now, as she viewed the defiant little boy standing before her, she had the strongest desire to shake him and yell at him and tell him how she felt about the way he treated Jean-Paul.

Instead, with an edge to her voice and a look that was less than motherly, she said, "Frédéric, you have your choice You may sit here with Jean-Paul and me, or you can stand there until it's time to go to bed! I'm sick and tired of your behavior, and I shall certainly tell your *pappa* how you have acted!"

Frédéric was somewhat shocked by Julie's look and tone of voice. She was usually so patient with him; but something told him he had pushed her too far. So with a hiccup and a dry sob, he finally crawled up into the chair, all the while glaring at Jean-Paul.

The windows and shutters had been closed, making the house as dark as if it were night. And, indeed, outside it did look like night. Julie had the servants light the candles; and once she had Frédéric somewhat calmed, she tried to relax as though nothing were wrong. She felt that would be best for all three of them. She didn't want Jean-Paul to feel the tension in her body.

André could only wait for the worst of the hurricane to subside before going out to check on the havoc it had caused. He was shocked and dismayed when he saw what a mess the winds and rains had made of his well-ordered plantation. There were lost crops, and several buildings would need repair. Several slave cabins would need repair as well. He would need to do much planting to recoup his losses, and it would be weeks before everything was back to normal.

But, before he could do much of anything, another disaster struck.

Chapter 56

André spent the next two weeks checking the levee that kept the Mississippi from overtaking his land. Each planter was responsible for the levee that ran the length of his property; and both planter and city dweller lived in fear of a break in the bank. More than once the river had reclaimed the land and many a planter had seen his fortune wiped out when the river destroyed his crops.

These levees were very tall, and also broad. One could drive a carriage across the top. You could not see the river from the road. One had to go up to the *galerie* to see the boats passing by in the distance.

* * *

The hurricane finally blew over. But the wind and rain continued; not so violent, but still causing problems.

It was early one morning, while André was having breakfast, that he heard a banging on the front door then he heard the overseer's voice shouting over the wind and rain to Demetrius. "Tell him to come quickly! It is getting very bad!"

Demetrius appeared at the dining room door, his face filled with fear. "*Maître, Michie* Hoffman say come quick; da levee it done broke! Da river comin' through bad!"

André threw down his napkin and jumped to his feet. "The levee broke? But that's impossible. I've been checking it every day." He took a last gulp of coffee.

"Demetrius go and get my oldest work clothes ready. Delilah!" He shouted for the house servants, and gave them orders. Samson suddenly appeared, and André said, "Call the field hands and every man we might need, and get out to the south end as quickly as possible. Take the wagons and all the picks and shovels you need. I'll meet you there as soon as I change clothes."

"What's wrong, André? What has happened?" Julie appeared at the top of the stairs. She had been awakened by all the commotion.

"It's the levee at the south end," he answered. "It has given way under the current of the river. The hurricane must have weakened it. Monsieur Hoffman says the water has already crossed the road." André was running to the bedroom where Demetrius had laid out his clothes.

Julie followed him, a frightened look on her face. "What can I do to help?" she asked anxiously.

"You can send word to the women that if they see the water approaching, they are to come here to the big house and stay with you. I want no lives in danger because of the river."

As soon as he had changed, André headed down the stairs with Julie close on his heels. His horse was saddled and waiting for him.

As he reached the gallery, André stopped and took Julie in his arms. "Don't worry sweetheart. You just stay safe here in the house. If the water should rise, take the children and everyone else to the attic. I'll be back as soon as possible." Giving her a long kiss, he ran down the stairs.

Julie stood on the *galerie* and said a prayer that no one would be hurt or lost while trying to repair the damaged levee.

Many of the men were already there when André reached the south end of the plantation. The levee was, indeed, breaking away from the force of the river. The current was running at an alarming rate, and the water was gushing from the crack in the soil.

It was imperative that the levee be strengthened as quickly as possible; otherwise, the entire plantation could be lost. Fortunately, the rains had finally stopped, which made it easier to work. But the skies remained dark and foreboding, and they knew it was only a matter of time before the rain would pour down again.

Shovels and picks were handed out. André himself grabbed a shovel; and side by side with his overseer and his slaves, he worked to stop the break.

It was a near impossible job, but one that had to be done. The river had risen to an alarming height and André was fearful that some of the men would lose their footing and slip into the water.

"You men, stay away from the edge of the levee as much as possible! I do not want anyone swept away by the river. Even for those of you who can swim, you would be no match for the mighty Mississippi."

André worked side by side with the men; and as the day grew darker, he shouted, "Light some torches, so we can continue working."

Suddenly, Samson shouted over the roar of the river, "*Maître*, look!"

A string of wagons was coming down the road. André stopped long enough to look up. It was Monsieur Charlevoix.

Oh, thank God, he thought. *Pappa, you always seem to come to my rescue whenever I am in trouble.*

When, finally, Monsieur Charlevoix his men and wagons pulled up, the two greeted each other warmly. They wasted no time in talk but got right to work strengthening the levee.

It started to rain again, at first a light drizzle, but then a heavy downpour, making it impossible to keep the torches lit. The rain would drown the torches, and the men couldn't see what they were doing.

Finally, the rains stopped, and once again, the torches were lit; and the men worked on. All through the night and long into the next day, the white men and the black slaves worked side by side. Finally, the levee was repaired and the river was no longer gushing over the road. But André knew much damage had been done.

Andre got down on his knees, and everyone followed suit as he prayed and thanked God for sparing his land, for keeping the men safe from harm, and for giving him such a wonderful father-in-law.

Slowly, the weary men made their way to their homes. Julie, watching from the upstairs *galerie*, saw them as they came up the long avenue. She flew down the stairs, out of the house, and into André's arms as he dismounted from Rex.

"Oh, thank God you're safe," she cried, tears filling her eyes. "I was so worried, my darling."

André was covered with mud; his face, arms, clothes, and boots. But Julie was unaware of it as she kissed him and clung to him.

"Sweetheart, I'm sorry you worried but there was no way to send back word that all was well." He looked exhausted. "Your father came to the rescue, as always." He smiled down at her.

"I know," she said as she slipped her arm around his waist. "I sent word to him, and I saw him from the upper *galerie* as he went down the road. I'm so glad he was there to help you, my dearest."

As they entered the house, she said, "Demetrius has your bathwater ready. You must bathe and rest, and I'll send word to the kitchen to have a nice hot meal ready for you when you wake up."

A fire was burning in the grate in the bedchamber when André entered. There was an unusual chill in the air. Demetrius helped him off with his clothes; and when he sank into the hot water, he felt relaxed and sleepy.

It was late in the evening when, finally, André opened his eyes.

Julie was curled up in a big chair near the hearth. When he saw her, André smiled. "What are you doing sitting over there?"

"I didn't want to disturb you. You needed your rest."

"Well, I am quite rested now." He grinned at her and pulled the covers back. "Come here, you sweet thing."

Julie rose from the chair, crossed to the bed, slipped under the covers, and gave herself up to his wonderful lovemaking.

When their desire had been fulfilled, André smiled at her and, kissing her eyelids gently, said, "God must be very fond of me."

"I'm sure He is, but why do you say that?" Julie asked, a contented look on her face.

"Because He gave me you, because He gave me such a wonderful father-in-law, and gave me such a beautiful little son. I am a very blessed man."

An hour later, Julie rang for the food; and the two of them ate at a small table in front of the fire.

They spent the rest of the night in each other's arms.

André was up and gone the next morning before Julie was awake. He rode out to the south field to see what the damages were. They were terrible. The entire crop of sugar cane at that end was a total loss. It was all under water, and it would be days before the water receded. Mentally, he appraised his loss.

Between this damage and that caused by the hurricane, he knew he would feel it for a long time to come. Thank God the water had not traveled any farther and thank God he had been wise enough to make other investments otherwise, he could have been completely wiped out.

Julie was just waking as he entered the room. "Hello, sleepyhead," he said, smiling.

"Hello, my darling. Have you been out to the fields?"

"*Oui.*"

"How much was damaged? Is it very bad?"

"*Oui*, it's very bad but it could be a lot worse. We lost the entire crop in the south field but nothing else, thank heaven. We've already suffered enough damage with that blasted hurricane." He gave her a weary smile. "But don't worry, *chère coeur*, we will not suffer in any great measure.

"I have given the men some time off. It will be a few days before the water recedes and we can clean up the mess."

Julie listened to this with a serious look on her face. Now, she gave him a seductive smile as she said, "Would you think me a brazen hussy if I asked you to lock the bedroom door and stay here with me for a while?"

"Madame, are you making advances to me?"

Julie giggled and, pulling his head down, whispered softly, "*Oui*, I certainly am. Now, go and lock the door."

Andre had a wicked grin as he hastened to do her bidding.

Chapter 57

It was now November. The rains had stopped, and the days were more comfortable. The ruined crop of sugar cane had been cleared, and the field hands were readying the soil for the next planting.

Julie often sat out in the yard in the afternoon with Jean-Paul. The days were still warm but not humid and uncomfortable. It was here that André found her one day as he rode in from the fields.

Julie was sitting under a large magnolia tree. She had spread a blanket on the ground, and Jean-Paul was lying on his stomach kicking his little legs and watching with happy interest as Frédéric and Toby tumbled about on the grass near by. They made such a lovely picture that André stopped for a moment to gaze at the two most important people in his life.

Julie looked up and smiled at him. "Hello, my dearest, come and join me. It is so nice and pleasant here in the shade."

André scooped Jean-Paul up in his arms. Hugging and kissing the infant, he made the baby coo and smile with delight. After a few minutes, he placed Jean-Paul back on the blanket and crossed to where Julie sat.

Dropping down in the chair next to her, his legs stretched out and ankles crossed, André quietly watched as Demetrius appeared bearing a silver tray with a pitcher of lemonade. The black man greeted André with a smile, poured the lemonade, and after being assured that there was nothing more to do, returned to the house.

André took a sip of his lemonade then reaching over, he took Julie's hand, brought it to his lips, and kissed it.

"What was that for?" she asked with a gentle smile.

"That, my lovely, is because you are so sweet, and I love you. Also, I have something to ask you."

There was a teasing gleam in Julie's eyes. "Tell me, Monsieur, are you trying to soften me up and bribe me before you ask?"

André laughed. "*Oui*, you might say that."

"Well, what is you wish to ask me?"

"I was wondering if you wanted to return to New Orleans for what is left of the social season before Christmas." André waited, wondering what she would say. He was sure she would enjoy going to some parties. They had been out in the country for quite a while, and he worried that she might be getting bored. But, much to his delight, Julie shook her head. "I am perfectly content to remain here at Royal Oaks as long as you wish."

"Julie, I want you to know how much I appreciate your understanding." There was a look of relief on André's face.

Pulling Julie over onto his lap, André gave her a gentle kiss. "I would like to return to the city sometime soon. But, right now, I'm thinking of putting a sawmill on the plantation. I'll put it back near the swamp so I will have much to do in finding the right spot."

"Oh, André, a sawmill will be a wonderful addition to Royal Oaks. Think of how much easier it will be to cut the cypress trees, and perhaps you can rent the use of it to some of our neighbors."

André nodded. "That's exactly what I've been thinking also." He gazed at her for a long moment. "Julie, you are such a joy. You and I think so much alike. No wonder I'm so in love with you."

Once again, he kissed her lips; and they sat quietly watching the children playing and Jean-Paul kicking and cooing.

* * *

Julie was, indeed, content to remain in the country. She always kept busy with the house and the children. Often, they entertained their neighbors who lived nearby.

Sometimes, they had a dinner party with dancing afterwards. At other times, they played charades. And there were times when Julie played the harp or the pianoforte and got everyone singing. But whatever they did, the evenings were always fun; and they were always topped off with André and Julie wrapped in each other's arms in the privacy of their boudoir creating their own special magic.

Julie had always enjoyed the social season in the city; but now that she had Jean-Paul, she was just as content to stay at Royal Oaks.

One day, she was resting in the bedchamber. Jean-Paul was asleep in his cradle across the room. Julie leaned her head back and closed her eyes. She was dozing when, suddenly, she heard the baby let out a frightened cry.

Her eyes flew open, and she jumped up to see Frédéric shaking the cradle so hard he nearly turned it over. Rushing across the room, Julie shoved the child away and scooped the frightened baby up in her arms.

"Frédéric, what are you doing? You could have turned the cradle over and hurt your *bébé* brother seriously!" She sat on the bed holding and soothing Jean-Paul until he quieted down.

Meanwhile, Frédéric stood where she had pushed him, his small fists doubled, an angry scowl on his face.

When, finally, she had the baby quiet and she herself was calmer, Julie turned to the little boy. "Frédéric, why do you dislike Jean-Paul so?"

"I hate that *bébé*! I don't want him here! He's bad! All he does is cry!"

"But, Frédéric, all babies cry. When you were a baby, you cried. Besides, Jean-Paul only cries when he needs something. That's his way of telling us when something is wrong."

Frédéric continued to frown at her. "I wasn't like that *bébé!* I don't remember being like that! And I don't believe you!"

Julie held out her hand to the angry little boy. "Come, *cher*, come here and kiss your *bébé* brother and tell him you're sorry and that you love him."

"I'm not sorry! I won't kiss him, and I don't love him! I hate him!" Frédéric stamped his foot, glared at Julie, then ran from the room.

Julie remained where she was, holding and comforting her son. Her heart was beating rapidly. She was upset, frightened, and confused. What was wrong with Frédéric? Would he always be such a problem? And what should she do about it?

Whenever she tried to speak to André about the child's behavior, the cold, hard, look would fill his face; and the next thing she knew, the two of them would be having an argument or a fight. But now she had no choice. This new attack on Jean-Paul was too serious.

Later that evening when the children had been put to bed, she and André took a stroll in the garden. The night was warm and pleasant, and they sat in the little gazebo.

André had his arms around Julie, but her body was tense. She felt his lips brush the top of her head as he spoke in a soft, tender voice, "What's on your mind, sweetheart? I know something is bothering you. Would you like to tell me what it is?"

Julie lay back in his arms and sighed, "Oh, André, it's Frédéric; he hates Jean-Paul so." She then proceeded to tell him what had happened in the bedroom that day. "He could have turned the cradle over and injured Jean-Paul badly, and he wasn't the least bit sorry. He's only a child, not much more than a baby himself; yet sometimes he frightens me."

André wrapped his arms around her tighter. "Well, my love, I really don't think you have to be frightened of Frédéric, although I agree he certainly could have harmed Jean-Paul seriously." He stopped talking and looked at her for a long moment. "Julie, my sweet, I have something to tell you. I suppose I should have told you long before now. But I'm a coward, so I kept putting it off."

"You, a coward? Oh, André, don't be silly. You are the last person in the world who would be considered a coward." She reached up and gave him a light kiss.

"Nevertheless, I should have told you," André insisted. There was a long pause. Then looking at her with an expression of sadness, he said, "Julie, Frédéric is not my child." Julie gasped and her eyes grew wide. "Frédéric isn't your child?"

"*Non*, he is the illegitimate son of Gabrielle and some Frenchman who was visiting here in New Orleans the year your father and I were up north.

"I know this is a terrible shock, Julie. But I had my reasons for not saying anything at the time." He then told her everything concerning Frédéric, Gabrielle, and Gaston Bochet. As she listened quietly, Julie thought of the pain and heartache this must have caused André.

When he was through, André looked at her searchingly. "Can you ever forgive me for not being honest? You were so young and innocent; there was no way I could tell you."

"Oh, André, dearest, there is nothing to forgive. After all, you're not to blame for what Gabrielle did." Julie paused for a moment, and then said, "I often wondered why you always seemed so cool toward Frédéric. It worried me so when I thought of how you treated him. And I must confess I worried about how you would treat any child we had." She paused again. "And I wondered if you even loved Frédéric." She searched his face for an answer.

A pained expression crossed André's face as he tried to explain his feelings for the little boy "Julie, I've tried to love Frédéric honest I have. But, unfortunately, he's so much like his mother that I sometimes find it very difficult. He might even be much like his father. I don't know, since I only met the man once. And, of course, at the time, I had no idea Gabrielle was carrying his child.

"I know I shouldn't let my feelings about his mother and father affect the way I feel about Frédéric. But love him?" Sadly, he shook his head. *"Non*, Julie, I won't lie to you. There must always be truth between us. I do care for him, but I would be a liar if I said I loved him."

André paused for a long moment, then in a soft voice he continued, "Someday soon I will have to tell his grandparents and both Charles and Francesca the truth about Frédéric although I have a strong feeling they all know the truth."

Julie glanced up at him with a startled look. "They do? How?"

Brushing his lips against her temple, André smiled. "Julie, Gabrielle was at least three months *enceinte* when I returned from the North with your father. People aren't stupid; and it was no big problem to count the months before she delivered."

Nodding his head, he said, *"Oui*, I'm sure they know the truth; it's just that no one has ever spoken of it, and it must be spoken of sometime. They must understand that I cannot allow Frédéric to inherit my wealth. That belongs to Jean-Paul."

Julie sighed. "You will also have to tell Frédéric someday."

"Oui, and that will probably be the hardest task of all. I certainly don't look forward to telling the child that he is illegitimate. I can't tell you the nights I've lain awake struggling with the thought that someday I will have to tell him the truth." André's face was filled with sadness and pain.

Julie sighed again. "Poor, unhappy little Frédéric. What will we do about him? I feel so sorry for him But André, what are we to do about his anger toward Jean-Paul?"

They spent quite a while discussing how to handle this very unhappy little boy, how to keep him from hurting their son. André told Julie about his talk with her father and how he had already spoken to his attorney and had made out a will to protect Jean-Paul's inheritance.

"I will never abandon Frédéric, Julie. I may not love him, but I am fond of him; and I am the only father he has ever known. And although I will always be his father, I certainly will never allow him to harm any child of ours or to lay claim to what is not rightfully his.

"As soon as he is old enough, I shall see about placing him in a boarding school. Perhaps, the priests can straighten him out. Meanwhile, we will have to be very careful not to leave him alone with Jean-Paul."

Julie looked up at André, her beautiful eyes filled with love and understanding of what he must have gone through when he first learned that Frédéric was not his child. She loved and admired him even more when she thought of how he had stood by Gabrielle and let everyone think Frédéric was his.

Slowly, she put her hand up to his face and gently stroked his cheek. "Oh, my poor darling," she said softly, "how much pain you have gone through over these past years. How sad it must have made you to learn the truth about Frédéric."

André wore a sardonic smile as he chuckled and said, "It was more like rage and a desire to murder, rather than sadness."

Julie drew his lips down to hers. When the kiss ended, she whispered, "Well, all of that is over. We have each other, and we have Jean-Paul..."

"And we have Frédéric," André added, once again wearing a caustic expression. Then his expression changed as he looked at Julie for a long moment. Slowly, almost reverently, he kissed her. Molding her lips to his, tasting their sweetness, feeling the desire he always had for her rising up and overwhelming him. "Oh, Lord, how I love you," he whispered fiercely. "I love you so much." He buried his face in her hair, then let his lips slide to her throat. "I love you, I love you, I love you," he moaned as he kissed her again, this time, with an urgency that left them both shaken.

Together, they started back to the house. There was a full moon, and the heavens looked like a large swath of black velvet strewn with thousands of tiny diamonds. As they reached the *galerie*, André stopped and turned to look out over his land.

Julie stood in front of him and leaned her head back on his broad chest. André wrapped his arms around her shoulders, and Julie put her hands on his arms as, together, they gazed at the beautiful grounds surrounding them.

André felt such peace standing there with the love of his life. He had become the quintessence of the wealthy gentleman farmer. He'd worked hard to carve this beautiful plantation out of the wildness. Now, he had everything he'd ever wanted: a beautiful wife whom he loved above all others, a sweet baby son, a great deal of money, and a successful plantation.

He had, indeed, carved a world of his own out of this strange, wild land. A world where he knew he belonged.

There would be stormy times ahead, this he knew. Dealing with Frédéric would not be easy. Breaking the monopoly on the Mississippi so the steamboats could sail freely on the river would not be easy. No one knew what the future held. But no matter what lay ahead, André knew he could handle it, especially with Julie by his side. He looked down at her and whispered. "I am the luckiest man alive to have you for my wife, sweetheart. I love you more than life itself."

Julie tilted her head up and, giving him a seductive smile, said, "Would you like to show me how much you love me, my darling?"

"I most certainly would," he answered in a husky voice, his eyes caressing her face.

Taking him by the hand, Julie started for the front door. "Well, then, come on."

Suddenly, André scooped her up in his arms and kissed her long and passionately. With a wicked grin, he whispered, "Remember what I told you once before, sweetheart, I can cover more ground faster than you can. My legs are longer."

LA FIN

Breinigsville, PA USA
12 August 2010
243494BV00004B/2/A